CW01024009

Relight My Fire

Also by C. K. McDonnell

THE STRANGER TIMES
THIS CHARMING MAN
LOVE WILL TEAR US APART

Relight My Fire

The fourth *Stranger Times* novel

C. K. McDonnell

bantam

TRANSWORLD PUBLISHERS
Penguin Random House, One Embassy Gardens,
8 Viaduct Gardens, London SW11 7BW
www.penguin.co.uk

Transworld is part of the Penguin Random House group of companies
whose addresses can be found at global.penguinrandomhouse.com

First published in Great Britain in 2024 by Bantam
an imprint of Transworld Publishers

A CIP catalogue record for this book
is available from the British Library.

ISBN
9780857505354 (hb)
9780857505361 (tpb)

Typeset in 12/18pt Van Dijck MT Pro by Jouve (UK), Milton Keynes.
Printed and bound in Great Britain by Clays Ltd, Elcograf S.p.A.

The authorized representative in the EEA is Penguin Random House Ireland,
Morrison Chambers, 32 Nassau Street, Dublin D02 YH68.

Penguin Random House is committed to a sustainable future
for our business, our readers and our planet. This book is made
from Forest Stewardship Council® certified paper.

To Zombie Gary, for the friendship, the laughter
and, most of all, the zombies.
To Christopher Brookmyre, for being the originator
of the frustrated rockstar genre of fiction.
And to the dead, who I am reliably informed cannot sue.

AUTHOR'S NOTE

It has been brought to my attention that authors should probably start including a note at the beginning of their books indicating whether artificial intelligence was used in its writing. First off, I am inherently suspicious of such a thing as, while I have my doubts about whether AI can come up with a novel that is any good, it can definitely write a note telling you it didn't.

Second, I own a dog. Two, in fact, but one of them in particular is a high-maintenance, over-anxious, allergic-to-everything, financially crippling idiot. One day, I'll probably be able to buy a robot to walk the idiot, feed the idiot, groom the idiot, give the idiot all of his various medications. It'll even stand outside getting soaked while holding an umbrella over the idiot's head because he's terrified of the rain but is having one of his dodgy belly days. I can get a robot to do all that, and then I will have lost the greatest friend I have ever had.

Creativity isn't about imitating others to get it right, it's about getting it wrong in the right way. So, rest assured, I wrote every word of this bugger, and I even held an umbrella over its head while it worked out some issues in the rain. Seriously, I stood in a downpour for twenty minutes because Chapter 56 wasn't quite working. You're welcome. Let's see AI do that.

Now, if you'll excuse me, I have to walk the beloved idiot immediately because we live in Manchester and it is currently not raining.

Caimh (C. K.) McDonnell

DRAMATIS PERSONAE DRINKIPOSIUM

The Stranger Times staff

Vincent Banecroft – editor. Whiskey, occasionally rum/whatever is available.

Hannah Willis – assistant editor. Milky coffee or white wine.

Grace Yeboah – office manager. Builder's tea, three sugars.

Ox Chen – features writer, UFOs and conspiracy theories. Unpronounceable Russian energy drink banned in twenty-three countries.

Reginald 'Reggie' Fairfax the Third – features writer, paranormalism. Herbal tea/G & T.

Stella (no known last name) – trainee journalist. PRIME.

Manny* – printer/Rastafarian. Tea *au naturel* (like himself)/herbal cigarettes for his glaucoma.

Greater Manchester Police

DI Tom Sturgess – Detective inspector. Diet Coke.

DS Andrea Wilkerson – Detective sergeant. Glass of malbec, preferably large.

Other Parties

John Mór – pub landlord/Folk elder. Pint of London Pride.

Cogs – bard/man who can only tell the truth. What have you got?

Zeke – talking dog/not-really-a-dog. Whatever Cogs has.

Dr Veronica Carter – Founders' representative. Cosmopolitan.

Tamsin Baladin – millionaire entrepreneur/Founders recruit. Cucumber water.

Alan Baladin – millionaire entrepreneur/monstrous megalomaniac. Blood.

---

*Angel that cohabits Manny's body – guardian of the Church of Old Souls. No beverage preference available.

PROLOGUE

And with a gasp, she was awake.

The first thing she became aware of was the torpid thumping of her heartbeat reverberating through her body.

Shyanne blinked repeatedly, trying to bring the world into focus. It was a world she did not recognize. She was in a room with what seemed to be discoloured metal walls, and there was no other furniture except for the metal chair she was sitting on.

No. Not sitting on, strapped to.

She looked down at her hands. Metal clasps were securing her forearms to the arms of the chair. She tried to move her feet but something was holding them in place, too. And her chest – there was something across her chest. She drew her head back and looked down. There was a metal restraint there, too. Beneath it, she could see that she was wearing a green hospital gown.

Two cannulas were inserted into the top of her right arm; one tube was attached to a blue IV and the other to a green. They led off to something behind her she couldn't see.

Incongruous plinky-plonky music was being piped into the room from unseen speakers. It was the kind of stuff wellness spas played during massages in the mistaken belief it provided ambiance.

The cloying sound from the tinny speakers was joined by a female voice. 'Test thirty-one; 11.22 a.m. Subject has regained consciousness. Seems relatively alert.' The tone changed from clinical to irritated. 'Do you have to eat that in here?'

'What?' came a gruff male voice. 'I've not had me breakfast. I've got to do the clean-up after and—'

Shyanne tried to speak, but she couldn't. The noise coming from her throat was no more than a wheezy rasp.

'At least use a plate. You're leaving crumbs everywhere. You unhygienic toad.'

Shyanne gagged, worked her jaw and desperately tried to locate her voice. The slow drumbeat of her heart picked up pace ever so slightly as she did so.

She finally spoke, her voice croaky. 'Hello?'

'And do your flies up, you awful worthless lump of ineptitude.'

The response to this was an unintelligible grumble.

'I can hear you!' shouted Shyanne, finding volume at last.

The voices stopped, then the woman spoke in a sniping whisper. 'The mic is live? You blithering idiot!'

'Have you got it on mute?'

'Of course, I've—'

'Please talk to me,' pleaded Shyanne. 'What's going on?'

The voices stopped squabbling and after a moment, the female voice came through, louder now, speaking in a slow, measured tone. 'OK, Shyanne. You're all right. Relax. Everything is fine.'

'Where am I?'

'You are safe. There was an accident, but you are OK now.'

An image flashed into Shyanne's mind. She was looking down at a supermarket shopping trolley, trying to lean on the handle as it rolled away from her and she stumbled to the ground. 'I don't . . .'

'For the record,' said the voice, 'can you please tell me your full name?'

'I . . .' Shyanne scanned the room again. The tempo of the drumbeat kicked up another notch. 'Where am I?'

'You are in a hospital. Just relax and let me help you. Now, what is your full name?'

'Shyanne Jane Rivers,' she said, almost on autopilot. She looked down again. 'Wait, why am I strapped to this chair?'

'It's just a precaution,' answered the voice. 'Now, what are your parents' names?'

'Martin and Philomena Rivers' – she paused – 'only, Mum is dead.'

'Excellent. I mean – and are you married?'

'Yes, to Kieran. Oh God, where's Kieran? I need to speak to Kieran.'

'He's waiting outside.'

The tempo picked up once more. 'The kids? Someone needs to pick the kids up. Sarah's at ballet and Tom's at . . . his friend's house . . .' The friend? How could she not remember Tom's friend's name? 'I . . . I can't remember but Kieran will know. Tell him to get the kids.'

'Your children are with Kieran. Everything is fine. Try to remain calm.'

'I want to see them.'

'You will soon.'

'I . . .' Shyanne tugged at the restraints. 'Let me go. This . . . What kind of hospital is this?'

'You're fine. You became confused, Shyanne, and we just need to make sure you're OK, and then the restraints will be removed and you can see your—'

'Confused? What do you mean confused?' The tempo nudged up again, the drumbeat growing ever faster. Louder now too. 'How am I confused?'

'That's not important,' said the voice. 'The sooner you answer our questions, the sooner you can get out of here. Now, what is your date of birth?'

'The seventeenth of June, nineteen eighty-one. What hospital is this?'

'We're a private clinic. Where did you go to school?'

'St Martin's Primary and . . . Wait, why do you need to know that?'

'We're just testing your memory. Relax. These are just standard questions. Please, take a deep breath and calm yourself.'

Shyanne tried to comply with the instruction. It felt weird though, drawing breath in. Like something was very wrong. Like she hadn't been doing it until she'd been instructed to do so.

'Can you tell me the last place you went on holiday?'

'Mexico.'

She scanned the room again. There were no windows, and everything was metal. Why was everything metal?

'OK, Shyanne, did you have any pets when—'

'What's that smell?'

'I'm sorry?'

Shyanne tried to concentrate as the thumping of her heartbeat threatened to drown out her thoughts. 'It smells of petrol in here. Or something like petrol.'

'Just a moment.' Shyanne heard a soft click and then the voice spoke again. 'Interesting. Subject reports olfactory functionality, which is—'

'Why did you refer to me as the subject?'

'I . . .' The voice stopped and then could be heard hissing off-mic. 'The stupid mute button doesn't work. You had one job.'

'It was working yesterday,' whined the male voice.

'Sorry about that, Shyanne,' said the female voice again, back to sounding detached and reasonable. 'Nothing to worry about.'

'Let me out!' screamed Shyanne.

'You need to remain calm.'

'Stop telling me to stay calm. Let me out!' The drumbeat was frantic now, her pulse thundering in her ears.

'Shyanne, if you want to see your—'

'Let me out!' she yelled at the top of her lungs, while rocking back and forth, straining every sinew against the metal restraints. 'Let me out! OUT! OUT!'

'Just—'

Shyanne screamed again. No words this time. Just wild, visceral rage. Then she turned her head, wrapped her teeth around the tubes that were pumping God knows what into her right arm and wrenched them out.

The flesh of her left forearm was sliced open from where it had worked against the restraint and her entire arm was hanging at an unnatural angle. Like it was broken, but there was no pain. No blood. It meant she could pull it out. She tilted her back and roared. Freedom. Of a sort.

The female voice gave a resigned sigh. '11.24 a.m. – Test thirty-one terminated.'

Shyanne screeched primal fury at the soot-marked ceiling as the rhythm of her heart consumed her world, no longer individual beats but one continuous indistinguishable wall of sound.

She waved her freed left arm about, her hand dangling at a sickening angle as she screamed with everything she had.

Some small remaining part of her mind was dimly aware of a clicking noise somewhere behind her.

Then.

A pause of a couple of seconds.

And . . .

Ignition.

1

The thing about life is that it is fundamentally impossible.

Not that Wayne Grainger didn't believe in the whole theory-of-evolution thing, it was just that he had realized we'd all been looking at it from the wrong end. We were the result. The result could believe in itself because it was self-evident. Nobody thought about it from the other end of the equation. Imagine being that single-celled organism however many million, billions of years ago and somebody pulled you aside and said, 'All right, champ, I'm going to level with you; we need you to get your shit together and fast because you and your descendants are going to have to evolve into sponges or something, then fish, then those fish are going to have to decide that water is so last millennium, grow legs and go for a beach holiday. You'll then become mammals with nipples – nipples are, like, crazy important and pretty fun, and then you're going to need to become monkeys, and then, here's the hard bit, stop being monkeys, which is tough as it's clearly the most fun stop on the trip, but you've got places to be and things to avoid being eaten by because, oh yeah, did we mention all the way along everything else has evolved into other stuff designed to kill you in like a hundred different why-you-don't-go-outside-in-Australia kind of ways? One of those evolutionary bros will be a *T-Rex*, which will be the size of a triple-decker bus, which doesn't seem like a fair fight, does it? But don't worry, they'll all get wiped out in a mass-extinction event and, heads up, keep an eye out for those big-boss moments too, and run away from any large, rapidly approaching bright lights in the sky or massive sheets of ice heading your way. You don't want it too hot or too cold. You'll basically need to Goldilocks the shit out of this, and, assuming you avoid that part of the evolutionary assault course, you'll need to pick up the pace, because 'team you' needs to be evolving into Homo basic, who'll learn how to use simple tools – just like those lads in school who sat at the back of the bus and the teachers pretended not to be afraid of. Then, eventually, you're going to end up evolving into man, proper man, with Crocs, and orgasms, and iPhones and student debt, and one day you'll go to university to study film, while trying to continue evolving by telling people to call you Zack, but Daniel bloody Wallace from your old school will turn up and make sure everyone knows you're really a Wayne. So, the point is, little single-celled organism guy, that's the evolutionary slalom run you and the progeny have got ahead of you, and the question is, are you up for this?'

They'd have reasonably said, 'No, thanks, that sounds like a total nightmare. Entirely impossible.' And they would be right. From their perspective, life is so utterly unbelievably improbable as to be fundamentally impossible.

The thing is, once you realize life is fundamentally impossible, it is a wonderfully freeing thing. It being impossible means that the impossible is not impossible. *Ipso facto*, QED.

Jeez, whatever was in these tablets he'd scored from Deano was good. Really good. Wayne needed to write this stuff down. He'd meant to take one when they went out later, but he didn't like the idea of not knowing what was coming. He'd had an awful experience with vodka in sixth-form college and he really did not want to shit himself again. The social stink of that had not washed off. Daniel bloody Wallace had only kept schtum about it after Wayne had slipped him fifty quid, but it didn't feel like a long-term solution. He had been considering leaning into it and becoming a total party monster, but he wasn't sure he had the constitution for it.

Still, now he knew anything was possible.

Wayne had always secretly believed, deep down, that he could fly. The old him knew that was nonsense, the new him was more of a freethinker. Wayne couldn't fly, but maybe Zack could? Mankind had been stuck in the mud for quite some time now. A bit of evolution was required and maybe he was the man for the job.

Some small part of his brain was also aware that he was not the first person to take drugs and decide he could fly. So yes, he was going up to the top of a thirty-two-storey building, but he wasn't going to jump off it. He wasn't an idiot. Doing it up there just meant distractions would be kept to a minimum. It felt like he was meeting the sky halfway.

Deano had nabbed the security code for the roof when the window cleaners had been in a couple of weeks ago. The view from up there was absolutely mental. They'd gone up last Monday for a quick recce.

Wayne stopped at the top of the stairs, gathered himself and punched in the code. After a moment, the light turned green and the door buzzed open. This was a sign from the universe. It was behind him all the way on this one. He could feel it in his bones.

The sight of Manchester lit up and laid out before him wasn't any less breathtaking the second time around. Up this high, how could you not feel like a god?

With a gust of wind, the door slammed shut behind him. He looked at it. The first time they'd come up here, Deano had wedged the door open. Why had he done that? There was a code panel thing on this side too, wasn't there? He had a sudden sinking feeling that he might not have been paying total attention to everything Deano had told him. Along with Zack's strong, reassuring voice in his head, telling him he could fly, there was now another little, distinctly Wayne voice informing him he might be in the shit here. Maybe he should try to open the door now? See if he was in trouble in the unlikely event he couldn't fly?

No, screw that, no negative thoughts. Only forward.

Positivity.

He positioned himself in the centre of the rooftop and closed his eyes. The razor-edged autumn wind whipped at his skin and there was a taste of rain in the air. He didn't recall there being any wind when he'd trudged home from lectures an hour ago, but then again, he was one hundred and nine metres above the earth now. It was another world up here. A world of freedom. A world of flight. It's evolution, baby!

He just needed to think flighty thoughts. There was no point in jumping in the air. Jumping in the air was something somebody who was trying to fly would do. Wayne – no, Zack – already *knew* he could fly. He just needed to let it happen. His body would simply decide that gravity was more of a guideline than a hard and fast rule, and would act accordingly.

He stood there and centred himself. He didn't actually know what that meant, but he'd heard people say it and it sounded like something he should be doing. Last Friday, that Zara chick had been telling them all about how she was into Zen and all that. Wayne had tried to bluff that he was too, but he needed to get a book from the library and really nail that shit down. Zen dude and party animal were his two current life choices, but he was leaning towards the former. He was pretty sure that achieving spiritual enlightenment would be great for getting laid.

He slowed his breathing and listened to the wind. He had to become one with the magnificent, impossible universe.

Reinvent.

Evolve.

Fly.

As time ticked by, he was fighting to hold on to his positive state of mind, but the little voice, his inner Wayne, was back, pointing out to Zack that he probably should have put on something warmer than a retro Nirvana T-shirt if he was going to stand on a freezing-cold rooftop in October, in Manchester, like a twat. He tried to ignore Wayne, but the longer he stood there, trying to think flighty thoughts, the more his buzz was wearing off and the more Wayne-y he felt. His mind kept coming back to how the door had blown closed and how he didn't have his phone with him. Jesus, the code had better work on this side too, or he was going to be in all kinds of shit. They couldn't kick you out after just a couple of weeks, could they? That was assuming he didn't die of hypothermia first, of course. If he did, his mum was going to hit the roof.

The roof.

He was on the roof.

He needed to get down off the roof fast and not tell anyone about this and . . .

Wayne opened his eyes.

Only he wasn't Wayne any more.

Wayne had been standing on the roof, Zack was now hovering above it.

Wayne was earthbound, but Zack, Zack could fly.

He reckoned he was a good ten feet above the rooftop. He glanced down at his feet, dumbfounded that they were floating below him. He tentatively moved the left one. Nope, it wasn't in contact with anything.

HOLY SHIT!

Adrenalin surged through his body.

This was it.

This was IT!

He'd known it. He'd always known it. Impossible was just a word. He was Zack and he could bloody well fly! This'd show Johnny and his crappy guitar a thing or two. Best of luck dominating the next halls party now, closing your eyes when you sing 'Wonderwall' like a bellend. And Daniel bloody Wallace could jog on as well. Nobody would care that the flying guy had needed to phone his dad to pick him up and bring a spare pair of trousers because he'd defecated in his other pair while drunk.

This was going to get him laid. He'd been putting in the groundwork with Susan, but screw that. This was a game-changer. Her best mate, the unattainable Zen-filled Zara, was now definitely in his sights. Sod it. Why not both of them? Zack was nothing if not a convention-defying dude. The guy who directed the *Thor* movies had done something like that. He'd seen it on Insta. Two smoking-hot babes at the same time in, like, a relationship thing. Unattainable was just a word. Just like impossible. Words that did not apply to the Zack he now definitely was.

It says something of the workings of the teenaged male mind that a mere minute after achieving the dream of flight, Zack was almost entirely focused on sex. So focused, in fact, that he was oblivious to his surroundings. His environment was irrelevant now. He had mastered it. He had made gravity his bitch.

He turned his head, drinking in the view. The view he was now experiencing in a way that nobody in the history of the world had experienced before him.

He was a legend.

A god.

He was probably going to meet Beyoncé.

Christ, what do you say to Beyoncé? She was Beyoncé, after all, whereas all he could do was fly.

He was not paying any attention to the wind or to the fact that it had been steadily nudging him in a particular direction.

Eventually, the now teeny-tiny whisper that was all that remained of Wayne made itself heard, and he looked down.

He was now no longer hovering over the roof. He had drifted

and was about one hundred and twenty metres above Hulme Street.

His mind might now believe that he could fly, but apparently his bladder didn't share its confidence.

As a stream of rapidly cooling urine leaked down his leg, his belief dripped away with it.

The thing about making gravity your bitch is that the bitch can bite back.

2

As soon as the lecturer had wrapped up with his humorous 'enjoy your Thursday night, but not too much' bit, Stella had shoved her notebook in her bag, jammed her headphones on and headed for the door. She told herself her hurry was because she needed to get back to work, but that was only partly true. Hannah had been back as assistant editor of *The Stranger Times* for a couple of months now and while things were, well, not exactly running smoothly, they were certainly running more efficiently than they had done in all the time Stella had been there.

Hannah had managed to force a bit of forward planning into proceedings, which meant there was less of a panicked rush to get stuff done on a Thursday night for publication the following day. Vincent Banecroft still screamed, shouted, reprimanded, belittled and occasionally eviscerated his staff, but connoisseurs of his moods had noted a reduction in their intensity. It was like having a hurricane downgraded to a tropical storm – better, but still not kite-flying weather. He said all the same mean things, but they were delivered at a less ear-splitting volume. Maybe it was because of Hannah's organizational improvements or perhaps it was because of 'the other thing'.

Speaking of things, the whole uni thing had been Banecroft's idea. He'd been saying for a while that Stella was going to be sent on a training course. Then, what happened happened and a few weeks later she was suddenly a 'non-assessed' student at Manchester Metropolitan University studying for an undergraduate degree in Multimedia Journalism. Seemingly, Vincent Banecroft's guilt was a powerful motivator. From what she could glean from Hannah, through a combination of him cashing in whatever favours he was still owed on Fleet Street, some badgering, cajoling and outright blackmailing, plus enlisting some lady called Cathy who was, as Hannah put it, 'good with computers', Stella was now attending classes at Manchester's second most prestigious university. She wouldn't be taking exams or receiving any other form of official assessment but, as Banecroft seemed to believe, that was entirely irrelevant, as the only assessment that mattered was his.

Stella had also been informed that, should anyone ask, she had A levels in English, Maths and French. Not that it was her biggest concern, but why did they pick French? She didn't know a word of it. She was so freaked out by the prospect of someone trying to speak to her in the language, she'd downloaded an app and was trying to learn some words daily. So far, she had to hope that any chatty French people would primarily be interested in discussing where the library was, otherwise she was screwed.

As she exited through the revolving doors of the Business School, the cold autumnal air hit her like a slap to the face. From here, she could just point at the library, which made her newly learned French redundant. Having a lecture on a Thursday evening had been the cause of much moaning from her classmates, it being the big going-out night of the week. Lots of students were milling about in groups outside already, laughing, talking too loudly, enjoying life. It looked nice.

Pulling her hoodie around her, Stella was reminded yet again that she really needed to get some proper winter clothes because Manchester had proper winters. She turned on her music and the vocals of Robert Smith, assuring the world he was a love cat, filled her ears. The Cure were her current go-to – their brand of whimsical misery really appealed to her. She'd pointedly avoided mentioning it in the office as any of the olds getting excited about her listening to something they recognized would ruin it.

Stella had been terrified of being unmasked as a fraud until Reggie, Hannah and Ox had sat her down the night before uni started and given her a pep talk. It had gone along the lines of, don't worry about it, everyone starting university thinks they're a total fraud. People use it as an opportunity to 'reinvent' themselves all the time and—

Someone grabbed Stella's forearm from behind and she whirled around, crouching into a defensive stance, every sinew tensing. She felt 'the thing' inside her surge forward; that sickening crackle of power.

She was confronted by a startled Yvette – a girl from her course with a round cheerful face framed by blonde locks – standing there with her hands up, looking utterly mortified.

'Shit! Sorry, sorry, sorry,' Yvette apologized. 'I'm a total lemon. Didn't mean to startle you. Christ, good one, Yvette. Go around scaring the hell out of people.'

Stella took a step back and drew a deep breath to calm herself. 'Sorry,' she echoed, 'my bad. I'm very jumpy.'

'No, totally my fault. Shouldn't be grabbing women from behind like a muppet. I was lucky I didn't get a front-door key in the face. That was one of the things they mentioned in that self-defence session for female-identifying freshers last week. It was good, but also bloody terrifying. I mean, Jesus, right? Unbelievable. There are some scary people out there.'

Yes, thought Stella, and I'm one of them. An image flashed into her mind, unbidden, of a massive wave of blue energy surging out of her and ripping a scar in the earth, but she pushed it away.

'Don't worry about it. Too much coffee,' said Stella, trying to muster a smile. She didn't actually drink the stuff, but had learned it was an acceptable excuse for all manner of jumpiness. Her heart rate was slowing down, still punk speed, but now at the more melodic end of the spectrum.

'Right, well, I just wanted to catch you because a couple of us are heading up to check out Canal Street this evening and we wondered if you wanted to join? I mean, it's the Gay Village but you don't have to be – although obviously great if you are. Aisha is, and she's coming, I think. Plus Bea reckons she might be bi. I mean, not that any of it matters. It's more, yeah, y'know, just wanted to see if you'd fancy it?'

Yvette talked like that all the time. Just a stream of consciousness babbling forth before she finally hit the buffers of a question. She asked a lot of questions. Stella suspected she used them as a braking mechanism.

'I'd love to,' said Stella, 'but I'm afraid I've got to get back to the office. Publication night.'

'Right,' said Yvette. 'Yeah, of course. They keep you busy.'

Stella stretched her face into a mock grimace. 'Deadlines.'

'God, yeah, you're doing, like, proper journalism. Amazing.'

What had helped with Stella's imposter syndrome was the first few practical sessions they'd had, where she'd edited copy and then formatted pages using Adobe InDesign. Stella had actually shown her lecturer, John, a couple of easier ways to format articles across two pages. She'd honestly not been trying to show off. It was all just stuff she'd picked up through work and hadn't thought it was much of a big deal, but John had been blown away.

Her plan had been to try to keep *The Stranger Times* thing quiet, but once she was asked directly where she'd gained her experience, she'd had to fess up. The other students had seemed mostly impressed, but it was hard to tell. Stella had little experience with people her own age. Or, rather, people she thought might be her age.

Yvette gave a disappointed nod. 'Sure, some other time, then? We could do something earlier in the week, when you haven't got that deadline monkey on your back?'

'Yeah, that'd be good. Enjoy your night out.'

They said their farewells and Stella moved off, heading out onto Oxford Road. She hadn't eaten, and she wanted to pick up some snacks from the SPAR before heading back to the office and facing whatever inevitable last-minute changes Banecroft wanted to make.

On the very first day of class, Yvette had plonked herself beside Stella, opened with 'you weren't at induction', and started talking a mile a minute. She was chatty with everyone, but she seemed determined that she and Stella should be friends. A part of Stella wondered if maybe this was a blonde girl from the home counties looking to snap up a Black friend to show how cool she was on the all-important Instagram feed. That was probably unfair. Stella just wasn't good at trusting people.

The SPAR was busy with students stocking up on booze for pre-loading. Stella had read about the concept in an article. Apparently, the way some younger people were economizing during the cost-of-living crisis was by getting hammered before they went out. Getting thrown out of a club before you'd even got in was a thing now. As was not drinking at all, increasingly. Two very distinct approaches to life. Stella was definitely in the second camp. Getting out of control was her idea of hell. It wasn't Hallowe'en until Tuesday, but fancy dress was already heavily in evidence. Last night, she'd seen a White girl who had blacked-up as Crazy Eyes from *Orange Is the New Black*. She didn't even know where to start with that.

Bag of Revels, bottle of PRIME, sweet chilli crisps and egg mayo roll purchased, Stella headed off down Hulme Street.

She had yet to figure out how to cope with all of this. She hadn't gone to university to 'reinvent' herself, largely because she was still trying to invent herself. That's why Yvette freaked her out. The girl was a never-ending stream of questions, and Stella didn't have good answers.

'So, where are you from, Yvette? Surrey? Cool! What, me? Oh, no idea. I mean, I know I was being kept in a sort of boarding-school-cum-prison, then I busted out, got on the first train I found, then another one, and then I was in Manchester. I headed for a weird old church building because, I dunno, something drew me there, and I'm pretty sure someone was chasing me, but don't ask me who. The old church turned out to be the offices of *The Stranger Times*, which I discovered when the editor pointed a blunderbuss at me as I was trying to climb in his office window in the middle of the night. Then they took me in like a lost cat and I sort of live/work there now.

'That's not even the weirdest part, because I don't know my age, birthday, where I was born, who the hell my parents are – essentially who I am. None of it. I don't even have a full set of memories. It's like I didn't have a childhood. Not in a chained-to-a-radiator, raising-seven-siblings way, more in a there's-a-great-big-gaping-hole-where-a-life-should-be way, and I've got nothing but a few snatches of random memories that could all come from the same couple of weeks.

'Even weirder, it's only really dawned on me recently how strange that is. Like I didn't know what I didn't know. Like I wasn't properly alive. As if I don't really exist, or at least I didn't until about a year ago when I hopped on that train. And, oh yeah, I killed a man a couple of months ago at a disused golf course because I have this massive, terrifying, uncontrollable power inside me that freaks everybody out, most of all me, and I know nothing about it. I was acting in self-defence as the arsehat in question was trying to, I guess you'd say, drain me of my power or something, before inevitably killing me and a few of my friends, but yes, it does still mean I wake up screaming and I have far more golf-course-related issues than you'd expect from a girl my age, which reminds me, did I mention I don't know my age? Anyway, enough about me. What bands are you into?'

Yeah, as much as Hannah's heart was in the right place, telling Stella to go and have a normal life, that wasn't happening anytime soon. She hadn't gone to that self-defence class Yvette had mentioned because she didn't have to worry about defending herself in the way other women did. Heaven help any sex pest who came at her, because if she let rip what was inside her, they'd end up a pile of randomized rapey atoms floating away in the light Mancunian breeze. Not that Stella wasn't in danger; she'd been kidnapped twice in about six months, after all. The second time had been by Banecroft, her mentor, because the aforementioned golf-course homicidal arsehat had got inside Banecroft's head and weaponized his grief following his wife's death. Banecroft hadn't known what he was doing. Stella knew that on an intellectual level, but it hurt her emotionally. It was still a betrayal, albeit an understandable one. She knew it haunted him too, judging by the gross over-compensation of the vague promise of her receiving a couple of days' training being upgraded to a three-year degree course she had not even applied for.

Still, for all that, and for all the anxiety, Stella was happy to be there. She was a student, almost. She was doing what other people her age did, assuming the estimates of her age actually were accurate. As Ox had helpfully pointed out, Black don't crack – Stella could be thirty-four for all they knew. Regardless, perhaps things were finally calming down. Maybe, just maybe, she could start living a somewhat normal life.

Admittedly, it would be a certain approximation of normal. In the last six months, when not being kidnapped, she'd also discovered that magic was real, that there was this whole other world that existed just below the surface of the one most people knew, and it was populated with all manner of weird and wonderful creatures and characters, a lot of whom could kill you. And there really was a cabal of mega-powerful monsters who secretly ran the world, aka the Founders, although there was one less of them now since the incident just off the fourteenth fairway of Swinton golf course. All that, plus her job required her to write articles about a man from Bradford who claimed UFOs had stolen his dog and replaced her with an identical copy, a bunch of people in North Wales who had started a cult worshipping Tom Jones, and some dude who came into the office every Loon Day who was sexually attracted to cigarette machines.

Stella shoved a handful of Revels into her mouth. Yes, things were looking up. She decided to make a conscious effort to be more positive and see where it took her. Maybe she could start enjoying life and, who knew – a half-decent guy might fall from the sky and she could take a crack at having one of those relationship things she was always hearing about. Stranger things had happened, certainly to her. Not unlike Yvette's friend Bea, Stella had recently done a self-audit and had come to the conclusion that she was regrettably heterosexual, which was a pain as men seemed to come in a few unimpressive variations on the same basic idiot model.

At a junction up ahead, she noticed a group of half a dozen students talking excitedly and waving their phones about. Stella had to admit that the cliché that people her assumed age were constantly taking selfies and filming themselves held a lot of water. Talk about obsessive behaviour. You couldn't walk through campus without passing somebody videoing themselves on their phone, sharing their every unfiltered thought with the world. She was not a fan of the digital part of the journalism course she was on. *The Stranger Times* didn't even have a website, which was weird but also kind of retro cool. They had a big old printing press, run by a stoned Rastafarian, which would rumble through the night, making the building shake as it pumped out the physical sheets of paper that was their product. She probably should hate the machine for keeping her awake, but it was in its way the most reassuring sound in the world to her. Another edition of *The Stranger Times* was almost out, and everything was right with the world.

As she approached the junction, the crowd grew bigger, with more people joining it. Stella had initially thought the students were holding their phones up searching for that perfect selfie angle, but that wasn't it. Their attention was fixed on something up in the sky. She tapped her headphones to pause the track and was just about to follow their gaze when the screaming started. Stella tried to focus on what they were looking at in the dark sky, but she couldn't. Belatedly, she realized it was because the object was coming rapidly towards her.

She froze as people scattered in every direction. With a blur of motion, something passed a couple of feet in front of her face before hitting the ground with a stomach-turning squelch and the shattering of bones. Thick wet matter splashed across her cheeks as she stumbled backwards. Blue lightning crackled around her fingers as her panic stirred the beast. She started to fall but hands grabbed her, holding her up.

Stella looked down at the ground.

A half-decent guy had fallen from the sky.

3

Hannah watched the whole thing develop from where she stood, on the corner of Hulme Street and Oxford Road: the crowd of onlookers gawping, the figure somehow hovering in the sky above the next junction, Stella walking towards it all, headphones on, in a world of her own, utterly oblivious to her surroundings.

A chill of dread passed through Hannah, and she clutched her handbag as she broke into a run. She'd realized later it must have been the body language of the flying man that had so alarmed her. It was like how when you're on an aeroplane, the very last thing you want to hear in your pilot's voice is any hint of doubt. Nobody wants to be told, 'I'm going to take a crack at landing this thing, let's see how we get on.' That figure in the sky, even from a distance, gave the distinct air of being as shocked as the onlookers at what he was doing. As Hannah ran down the street, his arms flailed. The only effect this had was to make him gain altitude, which was obviously not his intention. A random memory of a scene from *Willy Wonka & the Chocolate Factory* popped into Hannah's head: Charlie and Grandpa enjoying flying until they realize they are floating into a massive extractor fan.

There was no fan above this figure though, just more and more cloud-filled night sky.

The sound of the onlookers rose in pitch and a few of the sharper ones moved backwards.

Hannah stepped into the road to dodge a group in fancy dress who were blocking the pavement, having turned around to watch. She hurried between two parked cars, banging her shin on the tow bar of one of them as she passed. She yelped in pain but kept moving, stumbling into the slow-moving traffic, running hard now. In front of her, Stella, with her head firmly down, was still striding forward, clearly seeing the crowd as just another obstruction to negotiate on her route home.

Hannah looked up. The airborne figure was rising faster now, waving all of his limbs in blind panic. He was shouting something that Hannah couldn't make out, but there was an unmistakable edge of terror to his voice. A hair's breadth from screaming.

And then, he hung there for a long dreadful moment of Wile E. Coyote stillness before whatever had been holding him up deserted him. As he hurtled towards the ground, he didn't even scream. Others certainly did. People ran in all directions, leaving Stella standing suddenly alone. She stopped, her attention drawn by the sudden movement around her. Hannah was a matter of yards from her now. Close, but not close enough.

The man landed a few feet in front of Stella, hitting the road with a nauseating noise that would stay with Hannah for ever. Stunned, Stella staggered backwards and fell into the arms of her oncoming colleague. They both tumbled to the ground, blue energy crackling around Stella's hands, which sent a wave of panic crashing against Hannah's soul. Hannah tried to push her thoughts away but visions of the recurring dream she'd been having for the last couple of months – the one with Stella standing only a few hundred feet from this spot, at the junction of Oxford Road and Whitworth Street, wreaking havoc – played out in her mind. Hannah had stood at that junction several times over the last few weeks, convincing herself that a silly dream was all it was. A perfectly rendered, finely detailed, silly dream.

The blue light disappeared, and Hannah regained her feet first. Stella looked up at her, confusion writ large across her face. Hannah helped her to her feet as bedlam broke out around them. She grabbed Stella's headphones off the ground before they were trodden on by the returning tide of spectators coming to satisfy their morbid curiosity with a better look at the poor unfortunate.

She propped Stella up against a nearby lamp-post as people ran back and forth, unsure what to do. Hannah held Stella's head in her hands. 'Are you OK?'

'Guy. From the sky.'

'Yes, I saw, but are you OK?'

Stella tried to push Hannah away. 'He needs help.'

Hannah moved herself as best she could to block Stella's view. 'He doesn't, unfortunately. But are you OK?'

'I . . .'

'Are you hurt at all?'

'No.'

'And you're . . .' Hannah couldn't think of how to put into words what she wanted to say next, so she went back to, 'But you're OK?'

'I'm fine,' said Stella, moving away slightly. 'I'm not the one who . . .'

Hannah glanced at the window of the Chinese restaurant on the corner behind them, where ogling faces were pressed up against the glass. She tried to block them out as Stella lurched for the gutter and threw up the contents of her stomach.

'What the hell are you doing?'

Hannah looked up to see that the voice had come from a policewoman in a hi-vis jacket who had arrived on the scene with her colleague. She was standing in front of the body, obstructing the view of some people who had taken out their phones to film it.

'Get out of it, you vultures. You should be ashamed of yourselves.'

Her colleague finished talking into his radio mic and approached Stella and Hannah. He spoke in a strong Mancunian accent. 'Is she all right?'

'Yes,' said Hannah, rubbing Stella's back. 'Just shocked. She was right beside the . . . Where the poor guy landed.'

'Right and . . .' He stopped talking, recognition breaking across his face. 'Oh, hang on – you're that woman from the loony paper, aren't you?'

Hannah didn't like his tone. 'If by that you mean *The Stranger Times*, then I am, yes. I was just passing.'

'Oh no, this is weirdy bollocks, isn't it?'

'Excuse me?'

'We got a call saying a bloke was floating. This is some of that weirdy bollocks you lot are involved in, isn't it?'

'We are journalists and this has nothing to do with us. Although' – she lowered her voice – 'yes, it was, from what I saw, something that could be described as an unexplained phenomenon.'

He nodded and turned to his colleague, who was attempting to push people back in several directions at once, while repeatedly making the clearly false statement that there was nothing to see here. 'Marcy, this woman is from the loony paper and confirms it's weirdy bollocks. Says we should call in Sturgess.'

Hannah's eyebrows shot up in alarm. 'I didn't actually say . . . Don't tell him I said . . .' She heard exactly how stupid the rest of the sentence was going to be and thankfully stopped herself.

'Control,' said the PC into the radio mic strapped to his chest, 'confirm this is a status forty-two. I repeat, a status forty-two. We're going to need an ambulance and anyone you can spare for crowd control. We'll need to close off the street. And screens – we're going to need lots of screens.' He looked up at the people now standing on the balconies of the surrounding apartment buildings, peering down. 'Make that a tent. If Forensics aren't going to be here ASAP, then we'll need to source one from somewhere else. This thing is drawing a bigger crowd than City in the Champions League.'

Stella, seemingly now empty, got to her feet.

'Right,' said Hannah. 'Well, I think I need to get my friend home.'

'Oh no,' said the PC, 'you two are going nowhere. You're witnesses.'

'Look around, officer – there's no shortage of those. I really didn't see much at all, to be honest.'

'That's as maybe, love, but she clearly did.'

'What do you . . .' Hannah looked at Stella and immediately plunged her hand into her handbag. 'Right, just a sec, Stella.'

Stella's expression was blank. 'What?'

'I've . . .' Hannah produced an opened pack of tissues and pulled one out, before moving towards Stella. 'Let me just . . .'

Stella put her hands up to stop her. 'What the hell are you doing?'

'I just . . . You've . . .'

'You've got dead guy all over you, love,' chipped in the PC.

Stella turned and found out she had not in fact thrown up all she could.

Hannah glared at the PC. 'Did they send you on a special course to learn that kind of bedside manner, or does it just come naturally?'

The PC shook his head as he turned away. 'Weirdy bollocks. I knew it.' He jabbed a finger at someone standing on the pavement about ten feet away. 'You, get out of here right now or I'll arrest you for trying to extract a mobile phone from your arse in public.'

'But my phone isn't—'

'It will be in a second!'

How Go Glasgow?

Experts have been left befuddled by the ongoing random appearance of people from Turin, Italy in the Scottish city of Glasgow. Over the last six months, there have been forty-seven reported incidents of confused Italians being picked up by police, all with the same story. They all reported that they were in Turin, turned a corner and found themselves inexplicably in Scotland.

The most recent case was that of Mr Giuseppe Borgo, who explained, 'I was going to the *negozio di formaggio* for some nice cheeses and then suddenly, I am in something called Soggy Hall Street and a man is saying he is going to give me "a puss full of headers for looking at his burd". I asked what he meant and then I woke up in the hospital.'

One theory, developed by Dr Wilbur Flake at University of Glasgow's School of Physics & Astronomy, is that the two cities are linked by a wormhole that instantly transports people from one location to the other. 'Experts have long questioned the point of twinning cities, such as Turin and Glasgow, and it may turn out that the surprising reason is that they are linked by rips in the space–time continuum. What makes this harder to prove conclusively is that neither end of the wormhole seems to stay tethered in one spot for very long.'

Glasgow Council have put a rapid response team in place to deal with the issue, following an incident whereby an Italian gentleman suffered frostbite, having been unexpectedly transported to Glasgow in September. Meanwhile, officials have appealed for calm after significant numbers of Glaswegian families with suitcases have been found roaming their home city, running around corners in the hope of a cheap holiday.

4

Stella and Hannah sat on the rear step of the ambulance and watched as the Greater Manchester Police put up barriers to hold back the tide of Thursday-night revellers. The crowd, in various stages of inebriation, had grown steadily over the hour, as people strained to get a look at what was going on. Thankfully, someone in authority had shown up pretty quickly with one of those crime-scene tents, so there wasn't actually very much to see. It hadn't stopped people trying, though. One idiot dressed as Wally from *Where's Wally?* had hopped the barrier, and Hannah had the guilty pleasure of watching the female PC who had been first on the scene detain him with an assist from a nearby wall. As he'd been led away, he looked dazed enough that he might have some trouble finding himself.

To the left of where Stella and Hannah were sitting, an interesting discussion had broken out between a guy with long black hair up on the fourth-floor balcony of the apartment building and one of the PCs on the ground. It related to what the guy was and was not allowed to film under UK law. There was mention of freedom of speech, the Magna Carta – which seemed to be getting shout-outs in all kinds of weird places these days – and the assertion that if the guy didn't go back inside, right this minute, his door was getting booted in and he could film that too.

'This is taking a while, isn't it?' said Stella.

'Yeah,' Hannah agreed. 'It really is.' She opened her handbag and looked inside. 'I think I've got some mints here somewhere, if you'd like one?'

Stella put her hand over her mouth. 'Shit, is my breath bad?'

'No, no, not at all. I just, y'know – the taste.' Hannah pulled out a small plastic box of Tic Tacs. Stella took a couple, and they both sat there for a while, sucking in the minty flavour.

After a minute, Hannah spoke in a lowered voice. 'Look, I know you've been asked this several times already by me, that idiot policeman and the ambulance guy, but are you OK?'

'Well, some poor sod fell out of the sky right in front of me,' said Stella. 'That sucked.'

'It was pretty horrible,' agreed Hannah.

'Mostly for him.' Stella shifted herself around and ran her fingers through her hair, which she had recently changed to a dark red. 'I mean, don't get me wrong, it's awful and I feel terrible for the poor guy, obviously, but' – she lowered her voice slightly – 'I didn't kill him and that's not something we can say about everybody we've come across recently.'

Hannah patted Stella's arm. 'That was self-defence, and you know it. In fact, you saved me and Banecroft.'

'Christ, don't remind me. That gets out and I'll be up in front of The Hague, charged with human rights violations.'

A laugh escaped Hannah's lips as, with pinpoint timing, DI

Tom Sturgess walked around the side of the ambulance and stopped in front of them.

'Nice to see you're having a good time,' he said, not unkindly. 'You asked to see me?'

'Hi, ehm, actually no,' replied Hannah. She pointed in no direction in particular. 'The officer asked what this was, and I said it was an unexplained incident, and then he . . .'

'Right,' said Sturgess, fishing a notebook from his inside pocket and flipping it open. 'And how did you two just happen to be here?'

Hannah didn't appreciate his tone. 'Stella was walking home after her lecture. She's studying journalism at Man Met now.'

'Congrats,' he said, turning to Stella. 'And you were just on your way home?'

'Yes,' said Stella.

Sturgess raised his eyebrows. 'That's pretty convenient.'

'No,' snapped Stella, 'it really isn't. I got covered in dead guy. Have you ever been covered in dead guy? It's not nice. Not nice at all. You have no idea how much I want to have a shower right now.'

Sturgess held up his hands. 'OK, sorry. I didn't mean to . . . I have to ask.'

Stella jutted her chin and folded her arms grumpily.

Sturgess turned back to Hannah. 'So how did you end up being here?'

'I was, erm . . . just passing.'

Hannah was painfully aware of how unconvincing she sounded.

'She was following me,' said Stella.

'Excuse me?' said Sturgess.

'She was following me,' repeated Stella. 'Every time I leave the office, either she, Banecroft, Ox or Reggie follows me. They're a little over-protective.'

'No kidding,' said Sturgess.

'It's . . .' started Hannah, before realizing she did not know where she was heading with that sentence. After an awkward pause, she settled for, 'We just want to make sure she's safe.'

'Me, or everybody else,' muttered Stella under her breath.

'I see,' said Sturgess. 'And you didn't know the guy?'

'Honestly,' said Hannah, 'I saw him floating around and then he fell to the ground. That's it.'

'And I didn't even see that,' said Stella. 'First I knew about it was when he landed right in front of me. Otherwise, I'd have got the hell out of the way.'

'OK,' said Sturgess. 'So he was . . . Even I can't believe I'm asking this question but, he was flying about?'

'Sort of,' said Hannah. 'Quite a lot of people were already watching him before I turned the corner, and they can probably give you a better account, but from what I could see, it could more accurately be described as floating, and he seemed to have no control over it. I mean, it looked like he was flapping around in a panic and then, well, you know what happened next.'

Sturgess jotted a couple of quick lines in his notebook, then flipped it closed and stuck it back in his pocket.

'So,' said Hannah, 'who was he?'

He seemed to consider the question. 'Off the record?'

Hannah tilted her head in slight exasperation. 'Of course.'

'We believe he was a student staying in the apartments just up the road. At least, the initial reports suggest he was seen above there first. I've got officers knocking on doors now. We're still waiting on a definite ID, but student makes sense.'

Hannah noted the end of the sentence. 'Makes sense?'

'There have been a few other incidents. Not . . . not like this, but, well, it's hard to explain.'

'Try us,' said Stella. 'We're pretty used to having to understand the hard-to-explain. Comes with the job.'

Sturgess glanced over his shoulder. 'Not now, but I might need your help as you've got connections in the' – he looked around, fishing for the right word – 'community that I don't have.'

'Well,' said Hannah, 'I think I speak for all the staff at *The Stranger Times* when I say we would be delighted to offer any help we can to the Greater Manchester Po—'

Some form of kerfuffle had just broken out at the crowd control barrier. After a few seconds, a voice they all recognized rose above the din. 'Let me through this instant, you cloth-eared, flat-footed automaton. Two of my journalists are in there and I demand to see them, or are the Greater Manchester Police now detaining members of the free press in the course of performing their duties?'

'I say all the staff . . .' began Hannah.

'Say what you like,' offered Stella, 'but the man can project.'

One of the PCs gave Sturgess a plaintive look.

The DI sighed and gave a beckoning wave. 'All right. Let him in.'

The barriers parted and Vincent Banecroft strode through, wearing a green overcoat that had seen better days and a brown suit that hadn't. As he got closer, it became clear that, in fact, the jacket was from one brown suit and the trousers were from another. It was not a pleasing effect. The blue trainers weren't helping either.

'Christ,' said Sturgess as they watched him heading towards them, 'is it laundry day?'

Hannah shook her head. 'That would involve him doing laundry.'

As Banecroft reached the trio, he turned to DI Sturgess. 'Under what charges are my journalists being detained?'

'Hello to you too,' said the DI, 'and in answer to your oh-so-politely worded question, no charges. They are witnesses and are helping police with their inquiries.'

'About what?' asked Banecroft.

Sturgess answered by gesturing at the bustle of activity around the crime-scene tent. 'Hard as you may find this to believe, I have better things to do than bringing you up to speed.' He looked down at Hannah. 'Will you be in your office tomorrow?'

She nodded.

'In which case, if you wouldn't mind staying here for a few minutes, DS Wilkerson will be over to take your formal statement presently and then you can go.'

'They will go now if they so wish,' said Banecroft.

'It's fine,' said Hannah, holding up her hand. 'We'll do the statement thing.'

With a resigned shake of his head, Sturgess turned and headed off in the direction of the tent.

'I don't have the time for you two to be lollygagging around here all evening,' said Banecroft. 'If they want a statement, they can read it in the paper.'

'We're fine, by the way,' said Stella.

Banecroft looked at her. 'Course you are. I can see that. So, what's the headline?'

'It's raining men,' supplied Stella, which earned her an admonishing look from Hannah. 'What?' she said, sounding defensive. 'It's gallows humour. I'm the one in shock here.'

'No kidding.'

'So,' interjected Banecroft, 'some poor sod jumped off a building?'

'No,' said Hannah. 'Well, technically, probably yes – but unless the law of gravity has been repealed, he didn't come down as you'd expect. He was floating up there for quite some time.'

'Really?' said Banecroft, sounding suddenly more interested. 'I find it hard to believe this is a story suitable for *The Stranger Times*.'

Hannah and Stella exchanged a confused look before Hannah responded. 'What are you talking about? This is exactly our kind of story. It pretty much fell into our lap.' She caught Stella's look. 'That was accidental. Not the same thing.'

'When I say it isn't a *Stranger Times* story, I was basing that on the fact that I appear to have not one but two journalists at the scene, and they're sitting here flapping their gums instead of going around getting statements.'

'Oh, give it a rest,' said Hannah.

'Journalism isn't something you just do when you feel like it.'

He looked down at Stella. 'You need to be out there now, getting fresh, on-the-scene, visceral reactions.'

'I've still got bits of the guy in my hair. Is that visceral enough for you?'

'Well, I . . .' Banecroft suddenly trailed off. 'He's back.'

'Who's back?' asked Hannah.

'There's a man over there.'

'Where?'

'Don't look, don't look, don't look!'

Hannah bit her lip. 'Well, why tell me, then?'

Banecroft straightened his coat. 'Just act natural. Pretend I said something funny.'

Stella squinted. 'We're calling that a natural everyday occurrence now, are we?'

'That's it,' said Banecroft, 'keep talking. You two stay here, I'm going to . . .'

Without another word, he turned and headed back in the direction he'd come from, away from where he'd been looking.

'Is it me,' said Stella, 'or is he getting odder?'

'It's hard to quantify that,' said Hannah as she drew her compact out of her bag. She flipped it open and, after some adjustment, saw in it the crowd behind the barrier on Hulme Street, where she assumed whoever Banecroft had spotted was located. 'I can't see who the hell he's talking about.'

'Still,' said Stella, 'nice to see him getting out of the office for something other than following me.'

Hannah clicked the compact closed. 'You really knew we were following you?'

'I did,' confirmed Stella. 'If it's any consolation, you're better at it than Reggie or Ox.'

'Well, there's that.'

'The rankings are . . .' Stella held her hand out at chest height. 'Banecroft.' She lowered it. 'You.' She lowered it again. 'Reggie.' She held it just above the ground. 'Ox.'

'Really?'

'Yeah. Ox got into a screaming argument with one of those charity muggers while following me the other day. James Bond hardly ever does that. So, you see, you're in the top half of the table.'

'I'm not, actually,' said Hannah.

Stella raised an eyebrow at her.

'I'm surprised too, but . . .' She placed her own hand above head height. 'Grace.'

Stella's mouth dropped open. 'You're joking?'

'You're the one who didn't see her.'

'I assumed she wasn't involved or . . .' Stella shook her head in disbelief. 'Really?'

'It is surprising,' agreed Hannah. 'The woman has hidden depths.'

'No kidding.'

They sat in silence for a few moments before Hannah spoke again. 'You know we're doing it because we care, right?'

'I know.'

'I mean, we all want you to have a normal life but . . .'

'Yeah, some complicating factors there. I'm not sure following me about is a workable long-term solution though, is it?'

Hannah shrugged. 'Meh. It's not like any of us has much of a social life.'

'Things between you and the detective inspector seemed pretty frosty. What's the deal there?'

Hannah opened her mouth to say something then shut it again.

'What?' asked Stella.

'Nothing.'

'By any chance were you going to make some remark about personal boundaries and then remembered that you were talking to someone who you just got busted for following around?'

'Maybe.'

'So?'

'Well,' said Hannah, 'it's complicated.'

'Cool. I love complicated. You should see my Wordle stats.'

Hannah puffed out her cheeks. 'We were, you know, almost in a relationship, and then in order to sell the lie, I had to pretend to break up with him to pretend to get back with my ex-husband for . . .'

'Your super-secret badass mission infiltrating a cult with Mrs Harnforth.'

'I'm not sure I'd put it quite like that, but yes. Anyway, I got back, told Tom I had been pretending, only it turns out if the other person doesn't know you're pretending then you're really not. Still, I told him what I'd been up to and why – well, some of it, anyway. And . . .'

'And what?'

Hannah shrugged. 'And I don't know what. I guess we missed our moment or something. I did mess him around.'

'With good reason.'

'Yeah, but . . . It still isn't the best of starts, is it? Nobody likes to feel expendable.'

'You also saved his ungrateful arse from a vampire. Like an actual pointy-tooth, bloodsucking monster. That should count for something.'

'To be fair, it was actually Banecroft who killed the vampire and saved him.'

Stella pursed her lips. 'Hmmmm. That does explain the obvious sexual tension I was picking up between the two of them.'

Hannah laughed. 'Wow, how weird are our lives?'

'Amen, sister.'

'For the record, none of us would mind at all if you found yourself a someone, you know.'

'Sure,' said Stella. 'Dating with Banecroft sitting in the row behind us at the cinema would be quite the experience.'

'We could . . . I mean . . . Don't feel you can't . . .'

'Oh, don't worry,' said Stella, 'I'm on all the apps, hunting high and low. Won't be long now. Men are literally falling at my feet.'

'Oh, Jesus, Stella!'

'What?' she protested. 'It's a coping mechanism.'

'You are not well.'

'Who isn't well?'

Hannah turned to the source of the voice and gasped.

'Sorry,' the man apologized. Chiselled features, delightfully messed-up hair, sparkling blue eyes, soft pillowy lips that a teen-aged Hannah may have kissed on a poster a time or two. 'My name's Cillian Blake. I'm a lecturer at the university. I heard this tragic incident might involve some of our students so . . .'

Hannah let out a girlish giggle, which earned her a baffled look from Stella. She could feel her cheeks burning bright red. 'Sorry,' she said. 'I just . . . You caught me off guard. I . . . I saw you play the Hammersmith Apollo. All four nights. Big fan.'

'Ah,' said Cillian Blake, offering a winning smile, 'thank you. Careful, though – you're showing your age.'

Hannah laughed far more than the comment warranted. 'I'm . . . yes, I . . . Me and my friend Carol saw you in concert seventeen times, in fact.'

'Wow.'

'She's an estate agent now.'

'OK.'

'I mean . . . Can I say I'm so sorry about Nigel's death?'

'Thank you,' said Blake. 'It was a great tragedy. Losing my best friend like that. It's part of what inspired me to get into lecturing and working with young people. Make sure they're coping with the stresses of modern life. That's why a tragic suicide like this is so upsetting.'

'Oh no,' said Hannah, 'this isn't a tragedy – I mean, a suicide. It isn't a suicide. It was . . . is obviously a tragedy. I just meant, sorry – he was flying and then he fell.'

Cillian Blake narrowed his eyes and pointed in the direction of the tent. 'He was . . . flying?'

'Yes,' said Hannah. 'I know it sounds crazy. True, though.'

'It does sound crazy.'

'There's a lot of crazy going around,' said Stella pointedly.

'We see a lot of it in our line of work,' offered Hannah, seeing some kind of port in the storm of conversational disaster. 'We work for *The Stranger Times*. I'm the assistant editor.'

'The weird newspaper thing?'

'Yes,' said Hannah, blushing again. She was somehow simultaneously thrilled and embarrassed that he'd heard of them. 'It would be great to get a quote or an interview or something?'

'Hmmmm,' said Blake. 'Not sure that would be appropriate. I should probably talk to the police. See if I can help.'

'Sure, absolutely. Big fan of the solo album too, by the way. I don't care what anyone says, I liked it.'

Blake gave just the slightest hint of a wince.

'I mean, also, sorry about the . . .' Hannah found her hands were flapping about, making gestures completely independently of her mind. Then again, her mouth seemed to have gone off on its own long before she managed, 'Terrible tragedy. Tragedy. Nice to meet you.'

With a dip of his head, Cillian Blake moved off.

Hannah watched him go then tried to shove her entire fist into her mouth.

Stella put an arm around her shoulders. 'So, that went well.'

5

If there was one thing Vincent Banecroft didn't like – and, to be clear, there was considerably more than one thing, but if pressed at that particular moment to name just one – he would plump for being messed with.

If given the option to name two things, the second would be idiots in fancy dress. In his opinion, anyone who took dressing up in costumes seriously was desperately trying to make up for a chronic lack of personality. Batman was exactly what happened when someone dreadfully dull had too much disposable income.

Seeing as Banecroft was currently being messed about by someone in fancy dress, he was really having quite the evening.

This had all started on Tuesday morning. In accordance with the rota that Grace had drawn up based around Stella's university schedule, he had been following Stella to her lecture in something called 'new media'. Upon discovering what it meant, he'd made the case that giving lectures to young people about how TikTok worked was the ultimate example of teaching your granny how to suck eggs. Stella had ignored him and was attending anyway. In fact, so far, she had attended every class and lecture, demonstrating that she had yet to develop the proper instincts of a student.

Truth be told, Banecroft would have preferred to have enrolled Stella on a 'proper' journalism course, but it had taken every favour he could pull in to get her on this one. He owed her a debt, one greater than he could ever repay, and if someone had asked him before this evening if there was one thing he didn't like, it would have been that – being for ever in someone's debt. His actions, while under the sway of one of those bastard Founders who'd got inside his head and weaponized his grief, had been both understandable and unforgivable. The fact that everyone else was at least acting as if he was forgiven was irrelevant – he couldn't forgive himself. Which was why he was currently bobbing and weaving across St Peter's Square, following some idiot in fancy dress.

Back on Tuesday morning, Banecroft had been trailing Stella from a distance as she'd walked along the Bridgewater Canal towpath when he'd first seen the man. She'd been taking the scenic route to her classes, preferring a slowly rolling canal and the threat of being attacked by territorial Canada geese to the more direct route that involved four lanes of slow-moving, ill-tempered traffic. She was not difficult to follow – first, because he knew where she was heading and she was actually going there, and second, she put headphones on as soon as she left the office and seemed to ignore her surroundings utterly. It was that kind of blinkered vision that resulted in you not noticing things such as men falling from the sky. It was also something he made a note to bring up with her when the moment was right.

The man had been standing on one of the bridges, watching them pass beneath. Banecroft had noticed him because a heavy-set man of about six feet eight with long white hair, wearing an all-black outfit complete with a wide-brimmed hat that gave him the air of a seventeenth-century puritan crossed with a nineties wrestler, was noticeable. A vivid scar also ran down the left side of his pock-marked face. He had impassively watched Stella pass but did not follow. Banecroft had been surprised when this pilgrim character had appeared again near the car park on Cambridge Street, standing statue-still, watching. He hadn't made any effort to hide his interest, either. His steely-eyed stare followed first Stella and then Banecroft as they walked by. This time, Banecroft had deliberately caught the man's gaze and held it. He had neither attempted to look away nor changed his expression. Beneath the ludicrous hat lay piercing black eyes that bore into you. Banecroft had always considered himself to be in possession of an intimidating stare, but he'd more than met his match.

He hadn't done anything about the man at the time because the guy hadn't actually been doing anything wrong. Yes, he was oddly dressed, but then, this was Manchester. It wasn't short of unusual 'characters'. There was the man who cycled up and down Oxford Road with a boombox in the basket of his bike, playing his eclectic music so loudly it was distorted to the point of being almost unintelligible. Then there was the woman in a wedding dress who chained herself to a bridge every second Wednesday of the month for two hours, before calmly unlocking herself again and going to the pub. 'Characters.'

Banecroft had checked with the others when he'd got back to

the office and nobody had seen a man that matched the description. He'd been inclined to chalk it up to coincidence until the man had reappeared that evening, standing behind the barrier, staring at where Stella and Hannah were sitting at the back of the ambulance. The trick with coincidence was being able to tell when something no longer was one. Whoever this man was, he was taking an unhealthy interest in Stella, and Banecroft was therefore about to take an unhealthy interest in him. The girl had nearly been hit by some poor bastard falling from the sky, and he was damn well going to make sure he found out why, and who was behind it. If anyone was going to throw people at his staff, it would be him.

It had been his intention to work his way to behind where the man was standing and, having gained the element of surprise, confront him. That plan swiftly went out the window when, while making his way around the block, Banecroft spotted his target walking along the pavement on the far side of Oxford Road. He'd set off in pursuit.

The ensuing chase, if you could call it that, had been odd. Disconcertingly odd. The Pilgrim, as Banecroft now thought of him, was walking with a purposeful stride, but not fast, and yet, somehow, Banecroft kept losing him. This should not be this hard. The streets were busy, but the man stuck out like a sore thumb. Banecroft had followed more than his fair share of people in his time, especially back in his beat reporter days, and he'd either completely lost his touch or something else was going on here.

The chase followed a pattern: Banecroft would be trailing the man, turn a corner then the Pilgrim would disappear into thin air. Banecroft would turn around and try to determine which way to go. Just as he'd make up his mind and pick a direction, he'd glance back to see the man walking in the other direction. The Pilgrim never looked back, never acknowledged Banecroft's presence, and yet Banecroft felt sure he was being messed with.

And so, this bizarre game of cat and mouse had continued up Oxford Street, through St Peter's Square and up past the Royal Exchange. Banecroft wondered if there were multiple people dressed like this, interchanging, but to what end? Just messing him about? It seemed like an awful lot of hassle for an odd practical joke. Mind you, fancy dress was the first step to becoming the kind of tedious buffoon who invested time and effort in practical jokes in lieu of having a personality. Such people either fell into doing that or joined the Flat Earth Society. It was hard to say which was worse.

At some point in proceedings, Banecroft's desire to confront the man had morphed into a curiosity to simply follow him. He, more than anyone, knew that information was power. Perhaps he'd fallen into the trap of giving his opponent more credit than he was possibly due. The figure had never looked back, never directly seen him. It was still conceivable that he didn't even know Banecroft was there.

He was surprised when the Pilgrim walked into the Market Street entrance of the Arndale shopping centre. Something about the guy's outfit didn't give the impression of a man hoping to pick up some late-night bargains. Having said that, he could certainly do with updating his wardrobe. Banecroft himself had recently acquired some suits from a charity shop, following the fortunate event of someone his size dying.

The Pilgrim navigated his way around the kiosks offering TV packages and a vast array of customizable mobile-phone cases and kept going. He didn't even glance in the window of Build-A-Bear. What kind of a monster didn't look at the teddy bears? Instead, he headed straight for the escalator outside the Döner Shack, which led to the first floor. Banecroft stepped onto the bottom step just as the Pilgrim was getting off at the top.

The place was still a hive of activity despite it being almost seven thirty. All around, shoppers were sauntering along, chatting happily in duos or trios, having completed their missions; other lone individuals were dashing past, clearly still trying to achieve some objective before the eight o'clock closing time. Banecroft watched the Pilgrim head up the concourse and past a large group of teenagers without any of them commenting on his unusual attire. Banecroft was not so lucky.

'Nice suit, mate – lose a bet?'

The Pilgrim was definitely travelling somewhere with purpose. Banecroft allowed himself to get closer because, for the duration of the trail, the man had never looked back once. He strode through a walkway between some banks of lifts and past Waterstones. Banecroft was now no more than fifteen feet behind.

In his mind, Banecroft hadn't pictured where he thought the Pilgrim was heading, but what happened next was a surprise. His quarry made a quick right turn and, without breaking stride, walked straight into Victoria's Secret. Banecroft, while no prude, had never actually been inside such an establishment, but he had a fair idea of what the place sold. The window was full of mannequins sporting various colours and styles of lingerie, and he noted that an effort had been made to make the dummies multiracial. Inside, he assumed there would be what was euphemistically referred to in a recurring advert in *The Stranger Times* as 'implements of romance'. Or perhaps not. It was a brand from the US, after all – a nation with prudish peculiarities, seemingly more alarmed by the proliferation of drag queens than automatic weapons.

Banecroft darted forward to keep the Pilgrim in view as he entered the shop and walked by the shop assistants, who seemed to fail to register his presence entirely. Clearly, a six-foot-eight man in retro fancy dress frequenting their shop was a regular occurrence. The Pilgrim then marched straight down to an area at the back of the store and disappeared behind a curtain. Banecroft stood outside for a long moment staring in, quite possibly looking like a married man who'd decided to get the wife something racy for her birthday, and who was now feeling like he might be out of his depth.

This was ridiculous. He was Vincent bloody Banecroft. When in doubt, he needed to be Vincent bloody Banecroft. Recent events had caused him to lose some of his nerve, and it was relying on that which made him who he was. 'Screw it.'

He walked in and also made a beeline for the rear of the store, following in the Pilgrim's footsteps.

One of the sales assistants looked up from the display she was adjusting of things that were edible but probably wouldn't go well with a Sunday roast, and gave him a sceptical look. 'Can I help you, s—'

'No, thank you, I'm with him,' he said, nodding towards the back of the shop.

'Who, sir?'

'Oh,' Banecroft said with a chuckle, 'you know very well who.'

Now that he was closer, he could see that the area at the back was the changing rooms. The curtain behind which the Pilgrim had disappeared was a heavy black velvet. As evil lairs went, this was an unusual one. Banecroft would give him that.

He pulled the curtain back with a flourish and then . . .

That was when the screaming started.

6

It said something about Hannah's mental state that she allowed Stella to guide her to the sofa in the reception area of *The Stranger Times* without putting up a fight. Nobody who had ever experienced sitting on this particular couch would ever wish to do so again. It was less a piece of furniture and more a place where self-esteem went to die. There was no comfortable way to perch on it. What's more, there was no way to remain seated on it without looking incredibly uncomfortable. Bits of it sank, poked out, slipped, unexpectedly rose, sagged and sloped in several directions at once. You could plonk a supermodel on the thing and they'd end up looking like a pubic-lice sufferer with one leg shorter than the other who shouldn't be let out on their own.

Not for the first time, Hannah said, 'Oh God,' in a mortified groan.

'OK,' said Stella, 'at the risk of taking a leaf out of Grace's book, I'm going to make you a nice cup of tea.'

'Oh God,' she repeated.

Stella looked up at the sound of raised voices coming from the bullpen.

'No, absolutely not,' said Reggie. 'I forbid it.'

'You forbid it?' countered Ox, sounding equally outraged. 'And exactly who are you to go around forbidding stuff? Who died and made you God?'

'Do not take the Lord's name in vain!'

That was Grace. And by the sounds of it, she was at her wits' end.

'Or maybe,' said Stella, 'I should go find out what that is?'

'Vincent did not approve the changes,' said Grace.

'But he didn't forbid them either, and he's not here, is he?' responded Ox.

'Yes, Ox, but the pertinent fact you are forgetting,' said Reggie, 'is that at some point he will be here, and at that point, he will pick up the biggest object he can find and bludgeon you to death with it, and I'm worried that object could be me.'

Before Stella could move, the double doors flew open.

'The problem with you people,' said Ox as he stormed through, 'is that you can't handle the truth.' He strode towards the top of the stairs, with Grace and Reggie trailing in his wake, but stopped when he noticed Stella and Hannah. 'Oh, look who's finally come back. Had a nice night out on the beer, have we?'

His comment earned him a clip round the ear from Grace. 'Ouch, what was that for?' He then looked back at Stella and the realization spread across his face. 'Oh, or I mean, whatever you were up to.'

'As it happens,' said Stella, 'we were helping the police with their inquiries.'

'What?' asked Grace, suddenly concerned. 'All because you

went for one drink? Alcohol is truly the devil's mayonnaise.' She blessed herself twice.

'Mayonnaise?' echoed Reggie.

'He puts it on everything. Like the French.'

'Drink?' repeated Stella. 'What are you . . .' A thought struck her. 'Ah, hang on. When we were late back, did Hannah text Grace that I'd gone for a drink or something? To stop you worrying?'

The other three exchanged glances.

'Relax. I'm fully aware you've all been following me.'

Ox pointed at Hannah, who was still sitting on the sofa looking stunned, her legs at an awkward angle that made it look as if she were attempting to lay an egg. That sofa never disappointed. 'Did she tell you that?'

'No. I spotted all of you. Well, all of you except Grace.' She turned to her. 'I'm genuinely impressed to find out you were on the squad. You're a ninja.'

'Well . . .' Grace wore a facial expression that was somewhere between pride and worry that this was a trap.

'Relax,' said Stella. 'I get it.'

'It's only because we care, sweet child,' said Reggie.

'Appreciated.'

'So, if you weren't out boozing,' said Ox, 'where were you?'

'Long story short, a man fell out of the sky.'

Grace blessed herself for a third time. 'You mean an angel?'

'No, I mean fell hard, unfortunately. The poor guy is dead now. He was floating about Hulme Street and then, well, he wasn't.'

'Floating?' asked Reggie.

'Apparently. I didn't see it personally. All I saw was him hit the pavement in front of me.'

Grace's hand flew to her mouth. 'Oh no! You poor girl. Are you OK?'

Stella held up her hands to prevent Grace from going into full mother-hen mode. 'I'm fine. I mean, it was absolutely horrible. I'm probably going to have nightmares and I could definitely use a shower, but other than that . . .'

Reggie stepped forward and studied Hannah. 'And what exactly happened to our dear assistant editor?'

'I don't want to talk about it,' muttered Hannah.

Stella patted her on the shoulder. 'I'm afraid that's not happening. Best rip off the band aid.'

Hannah closed her eyes again. 'Oh God.'

Stella turned back to the group. 'Hannah here is suffering from a social-embarrassment overdose.'

'I don't want to talk about it.'

'She really doesn't,' agreed Stella. 'As evidenced by the fact that all she said on the way home was that and . . .'

'Oh God,' moaned Hannah again.

'Yep, that,' said Stella.

'Was this, by any chance, brought on by a certain detective inspector?' asked Reggie.

'Excellent guess,' said Stella, 'but no. Although he was there, and while that was awkward in its own right, it was merely the aperitif. Which is a French word, by the way – one of the few I know.'

'Yeah,' said Ox. 'Apparently, it means summat covered in mayonnaise.'

'I think I'm going to be sick,' said Hannah.

'Oh, that's new,' said Stella. 'Excellent. I'm taking that as a sign of progress. See? Talking about it is helping already.'

'Talking about what?' said Grace irritably. 'You have not actually told us anything.'

'Like I said,' continued Stella, 'Han isn't talking so I've pieced this together from my first-hand observation of the conversational car crash in question and a quick bit of googling on my phone on the way home. She met a guy called Cillian Blake, who was in a band called Herschel's Garden in the late nineties and is now a lecturer at the uni.'

'I remember them,' offered Ox. 'Some melodic twee southern crap.'

This slap in the face of her fandom appeared to be enough to rouse Hannah. 'Crap? How dare you? They were incredible. *Flowers of Tomorrow* is one of the all-time great albums.'

'Wait,' said Reggie, 'I thought that Blake chap was dead?'

'Ah,' said Stella, 'no. You're thinking of Nigel Stay, the other member of the band. McCartney to Cillian Blake's Lennon.'

'You're not comparing them to The Beatles?' scoffed Ox.

'Better than the stupid Beatles,' countered Hannah.

She sounded remarkably like a petulant teenager and her comment resulted in raised eyebrows all around.

'OK,' said Stella, 'well, you see my point. Our Hannah is a big fan and, well, her teenage rock-star crush appeared out of nowhere and it didn't go well.'

'When you say . . .' started Reggie.

'She sort of compared his solo album to the poor guy falling from the sky.'

'I didn't,' said Hannah, looking as if she might cry. 'Oh God, did I?'

'The point is,' said Stella, 'she's not having a good night.'

Hannah was now banging the heels of her hands into her eyes repetitively. Stella reached out to stop her. 'That's not helping.'

'Nothing is,' said Hannah in a soft voice.

Manny appeared at the top of the stairs. 'Wha' g'wan?'

'Hey, Manny,' said Stella, before addressing the room. 'Guys, Manny is here, and he's wearing trousers.'

The group duly applauded. It had been Hannah's idea. Manny's memory was flaky when it came to certain things – remembering to wear trousers, in particular – and rather than have people remonstrate with him, Hannah had hit on the idea of applauding him whenever he remembered to dress, as a sort of positive reinforcement. She'd got the idea while watching one of those dog-training programmes on TV.

Manny duly bowed and took his ovation in good spirits. He then nodded towards Hannah. 'What wrong with her?'

'It's a long story,' said Stella. 'Don't worry about it.' She looked at her watch. 'How are things looking for getting the edition out?'

'Ah,' said Ox, 'about that. I was going to make a minor alteration to an article on page three.'

'Minor?' said Reggie, his voice laced with disbelief. 'You're going to use a story about ritual sacrifices in the Amazon to put in a scathing review of our local curry house.'

'It's a fun aside – people love that kind of thing.'

'The Tiger's Palace will sue us into oblivion.'

'They gave me the worst case of the trots I've ever experienced.'

'I know,' said Reggie. 'As your flatmate, you woke me up at four in the morning to give me a progress update.'

'I could have died.'

'That, my friend, we agree on, but not for the reason you think.'

Reggie and Ox both began to talk at once, growing louder and louder as they did so. Their argument increased in volume for about thirty seconds until everyone ducked at the sound of Grace blowing a whistle. Everyone, that is, except for Manny, who spun around twice and nearly fell over before somehow regaining his footing in an almost balletic motion. It reminded Stella of a clip of Charlie Chaplin she'd once seen.

'Holy crap,' said Stella, her hands clamped over her ears. 'Where did you even get a whistle from?'

'I picked one up from my friend Kofi's new sports shop. I was saving it for a special occasion.'

'That was special, all right,' said Hannah.

Stella looked at their assistant editor. It turned out neither sympathy, tough love nor talking it through had been able to bring her round, but a madwoman with a whistle had done the trick.

'OK,' said Hannah, clapping her hands. 'Ox, you're not making any changes to the article.'

'But there was so much poo,' he said plaintively.

'I know,' said Hannah. 'I was in the WhatsApp group you created to immortalize it. Your misery loves company. I say this with love, but you need to get over it.'

'Says the woman mooning over some has-been.'

'I was just . . . caught off guard is all.'

'So was I,' said Ox. 'And when I complained, they never offered me a free meal or anything.'

At the other end of reception, the phone started to ring. Grace tutted and went to answer it.

'Only you,' interjected Reggie, 'would angle for a free meal from a place that made you volcanically ill.'

Ox shrugged. 'Bargain's a bargain. What are the odds of it happening twice?'

'A lot higher than the odds of Vincent Banecroft letting you get your revenge via the medium of his newspaper,' said Hannah. 'Although, feel free to take it up with him.' She looked around. 'Come to that, where is he?'

'I thought he went to see where you were?' said Reggie.

'He did,' said Hannah, looking across at Stella, 'but then he . . .'

Grace walked back to the bullpen, looking stunned as she held up the phone. 'It's Vincent. He's been arrested.'

7

Vincent Banecroft awoke with a start to find DS Andrea Wilkerson looking down at him, Styrofoam cup in one hand, laptop in the other.

'What the hell are you doing in my bedroom?' he asked.

She rolled her eyes. 'You're not in your bedroom, Mr Banecroft. You've been arrested for public indecency. You're in an interview room at Stretford nick, remember?'

He looked around. She wasn't wrong. The room was about five metres by four, utterly unremarkable save for the table at which he was sitting with a digital recorder on it, and a camera positioned in the far right-hand corner of the ceiling.

'I do. I was just resting my eyes and having a little daydream about what to spend the money from the wrongful arrest lawsuit on.'

'Were you?' she said, without enthusiasm. 'Well, it's one way to pass the time.'

'Has your boss put in an appearance yet?'

Wilkerson sat down in the chair opposite, opened the laptop she had brought with her and began to type. 'No, for the last time, DI Sturgess is dealing with the Hulme Street incident . . .'

'The man floating around before crashing to earth?'

'The Hulme Street incident,' repeated DS Wilkerson. 'He is a detective inspector who would not normally deal with stuff like this. To be honest with you, as a detective sergeant, nor would I, normally, but seeing as it's you, we've made an exception.'

'Don't I feel special.'

'You certainly act like you do.'

'Before we get started on you giving me a full and unreserved apology, can I ask – is this the same interview room I was in the last time you falsely arrested me?'

This prompted Wilkerson to glance up briefly from the screen. 'I'm not sure. I know we discussed putting up a plaque to commemorate your visit, but sadly, budget cutbacks scupper many of our well-intentioned plans.'

'I ask,' said Banecroft, 'as you've redecorated since then.'

'Yeah, I think it was around the time a smackhead covered all the walls in his own excrement.'

'And you went with brown paint?'

'At a guess, it cuts down on cleaning. I can't say I was involved in the decision-making process.'

'Shame. The place could really use a woman's touch.'

Wilkerson sat back in her chair. 'Sexism too. Is there no end to your skills?'

'I just meant—'

'Whatever. Speaking of yearning for "the woman's touch", let's get back to it, shall we?'

She leaned across the table and pressed the red button on the digital recorder. 'This is DS Andrea Wilkerson, 452318, recommencing interview with one Vincent Banecroft at 11.17 p.m., October the twenty-sixth. Mr Banecroft is being detained under Section Five of the Public Order Act, is under caution and has waived his right to legal representation. Is all that still correct, Mr Banecroft?'

'Yes. I'd also like to state for the record, I've yet to receive my promised cup of tea.'

Wilkerson pushed hers across the table. 'Here, I haven't touched this one. You can have it.'

'Thank you.'

'Don't thank me yet, you haven't tasted it. Now, when we last spoke, you were explaining to me that when you ran into Victoria's Secret in the Manchester Arndale shopping centre this evening, you were pursuing an individual. Is that right?'

'Yes. A tall man, long white hair, dressed all in black, including a ridiculous wide-brimmed hat, who I'd noticed in the crowd at what you are referring to as the Hulme Street incident.'

'And you decided to chase him around Manchester?'

'No. Having seen him behaving in a suspicious manner earlier in the week, I initially wanted to confront him, but he took off and I decided to follow him.'

'All the way to the Arndale?'

'Yes.'

'Did he stop to do any shopping?'

'He didn't go in anywhere . . .'

'Until he got to Victoria's Secret. Funny that.'

Banecroft folded his arms. 'Look, can we stop pussyfooting around? If you check the CCTV . . .'

He trailed off as DS Wilkerson smiled at him. 'Oh, we have. I happen to know the head of security at the Arndale, and he was kind enough to get one of his people to stay late and pull it off for us.'

Banecroft had a sudden sinking feeling.

DS Wilkerson turned the laptop around to face him. 'For the tape, I am now showing Mr Banecroft footage I have received electronically from the Arndale security team, taken earlier this evening.' She hit play. 'There's you walking in via the Market Street entrance . . .'

'Yes, but he was ahead of me, so . . .'

The footage cut to showing the main concourse as Banecroft came around the corner. The Pilgrim was nowhere in sight.

'But . . .'

He watched the rest of the footage in silence. Him riding the escalator, walking around the first floor, passing the crowd of kids, before eventually stopping in front of Victoria's Secret and, after a few seconds, rushing in. He would say chasing a shadow, but there wasn't even one of those.

'But he . . .'

'Yes?'

'That's been doctored.'

'Really?' said Wilkerson. 'So, your contention now is that the Arndale has its own special effects department?'

'I . . .' Banecroft paused.

'Yes? You've gone rather quiet, Mr Banecroft. How very unlike you.'

Banecroft cleared his throat. 'I now wish to engage the services of legal counsel.'

'Very well. I am therefore terminating this interview at' – she checked the clock on the wall – '11.20 p.m., owing to the accused's expressed desire for legal representation.'

DS Wilkerson stopped the recorder.

As soon as she did so, Banecroft jabbed a finger at the laptop screen. 'You know this is bullshit.'

'Do I?' she said. 'I'm afraid in boring old police work, Mr Banecroft, we have to go by what we can see and, well, you've seen that.' She got to her feet. 'It's a busy night. I'll let you know when we can get you processed.'

'Whoop-dee-doo!'

She closed the laptop and picked it up. 'So, would you say this is going better or worse than your last visit?'

'The night is young.'

She nodded. 'Not if you've been on since nine this morning, it isn't. Good luck with that cuppa. The nickname for the machine is Ice-T.'

'Because it's cold?'

'No, because it's got a real "cop-killer" vibe.'

As the door closed behind her, Banecroft stared dolefully into the Styrofoam cup. The tea was considerably greyer in colour than was traditional.

Damn it, he'd been played. Whoever the Pilgrim was, he'd been messing with him the whole time. More than that, he was clearly something other-worldly to boot. Banecroft admonished himself. It's not as if that should come as a total surprise by now.

Lesson learned. He nodded to himself. He'd be ready next time. And there would definitely be a next time.

Banecroft lifted the cup of tea for a cursory sniff and proceeded to throw it in his own face. His subsequent yelp was more from surprise than anything to do with its mercifully lukewarm temperature.

His yelp of surprise was because there, standing in the corner of the room, smiling at him, stood the Pilgrim.

8

Dr Carter kept her face in the practised listening pose she had perfected over the years, nodding at appropriate intervals, as her boss ranted on and on. Every time she heard someone banging on about patriarchy, she had to laugh. Oh, sweetie, try dealing with the Founders, an organization that was ninety-five per cent male, most of whom had been alive for centuries, and then come talk to me.

Her role, though not defined in such modern terms, was crisis management. Traditionally, it was not a job you held for long – you were either made into a Founder yourself and joined the select group of actual immortals, or you met one of many possible gruesome ends. Dr Carter had stepped into a literal dead man's shoes to take on the role. Smoking footwear had been all that had remained of her predecessor. It was a little on the nose, but the higher-ups do so enjoy sending loud and clear messages. She was still alive because she was very good at her job, or at least she was when people let her get on with doing it.

Her direct superior was the kind of man who would host a one-way video conference and leave you sitting there for twenty minutes, staring at the red light above a black screen while he ranted at you about an issue, rather than let you get on with fixing said issue. She couldn't ask, of course, but by the way he talked, she genuinely wondered if he thought any and all problems were somehow her fault.

It was as if he felt that in a world where magic existed and its existence was kept secret from the population at large, every incident of it spilling out was preventable. The Council of Founders was made up of the most powerful magical practitioners there had ever been, and they, more than anyone, knew that magic was, by definition, barely controlled chaos. That was one of the many reasons they were so utterly paranoid. They were immortal but not invulnerable, and after decades of war, they were now in a state of truce held together by the Accord, which supposedly kept them safe, but also constrained their ability to use their power. It also forbade them from procreating, which really didn't go down well with the boys. These were people who were not used to showing restraint. They had clawed their way to where they were by having none. By being willing to do what others would not. Their reward was immortality, yes, but there was also the cast-iron certainty that should they die, they would spend eternity trapped in a never-ending hellscape. Life does not like those who defy its natural order, and it is willing to be patient to exact its revenge.

Despite all she knew, Dr Carter had long since decided that she wanted to be one of them. A Founder. Since she'd been a child, death and decay had terrified her. If she was honest, getting old bothered her as much as, if not more than, dying. She'd watched her own mother be diminished by illness, and swore it would never happen to her. Now, she was so close to removing herself from both the Grim Reaper's and Time's clinging grasps in one fell swoop, she could almost taste it.

A fundamental part of the Accord signed with the Folk, and which brought the senseless war to an end, was that no new Founders could be made. Or, to be more precise, there was to be no increase in their numbers. The maintenance of current numbers had been a critical point, as it discouraged the Folk from trying to take one of them out. This way, any such action would lead to the sacrifice of more Folk to create a new Founder. It was very much a one-in, one-out system.

This meant that, theoretically, Dr Carter could be waiting for the rest of her life, but even paranoid immortals got careless. They also got into fights with other paranoid immortals. A decade ago had seen the incident where Lords Stringer and Cavendish had got into a feud over a horse, of all things. After a ferocious battle, Stringer had killed the other man. The rest of the Founders had then killed Stringer because the first guiding principle of the Founders was that causing the death of a fellow member was the most unforgivable of sins. It was mutually assured non-destruction. For reasons Dr Carter had never understood, the Founders also killed the horse. With those two gone, the queue had moved on. Since the death of Dominic Johnson a couple of months ago, it had moved again, and Dr Carter finally found herself at the front. That was the good news. The bad news was what it had taken to get her there.

Johnson, arrogant even by the high standards set by the Founders, had been given clearance by the Council to exact his revenge on Vincent Banecroft, believing it not to contravene the terms of the Accord as it was deemed a 'personal matter'. The fact that the 'personal matter' stemmed from Banecroft and the staff of *The Stranger Times* having thwarted Johnson's illegal attempt to make his son a Founder was conveniently forgotten. He wanted his vengeance, let him have it. It had ended in Johnson's death at the hands of a teenage girl.

Unfortunately for Dr Carter, she had previously promised Banecroft that the Founders would show no interest in the aforementioned girl. This was a problem. Ironically, the second guiding principle of the Founders was your word was absolute. Again, unfortunately for her, she knew that in rooms she wasn't in, the discussion was being had about whether this agreement existed with the Founders or with just her. The first rule of survival in this world was never allow it to be your death that solves a problem.

It wasn't that anyone had liked Johnson. He'd been widely regarded as a monumental arsehole, but it was the principle of the matter. That, and the Founders didn't like the idea of the existence of a girl with some undocumented power that could take one of them out. Dr Carter had been against Johnson's stupid plan at the time and had pushed back, but ironically, its failure now put her in a precarious position. She'd never been closer to her final goal and never in more immediate danger of not reaching it.

In light of the above, her boss's bloviation was an unwelcome distraction, but it was a source of information in itself. He was an unwitting barometer of the state of play in the Council, and the fact that he had been banging on for as long as he had was a good indicator of his level of stress. He was one of the 'lesser powers', hence why he faced the indignity of dealing with underlings such as her. Him being this tense meant the Council was tense, which was very bad news.

She refocused herself, as he seemed to be finally coming in for a landing.

'The smooth running of things day to day is of vital importance to our ongoing mission and, all things considered, Doctor, I am very disappointed that you let this happen.'

In spite of herself, Dr Carter allowed an eyebrow to rise at this ridiculous assertion. 'Respectfully, my lord, I didn't allow anything to happen.' She looked at the screen of her phone. Doing so while he was speaking was a mistake you didn't make twice. 'I have now had the identity of the individual who fell from the sky confirmed and he was indeed a first-year university student, one Wayne Grainger, recently moved to the city and not a registered member of any Folk clans. That means either he is an anomaly or else this was an act carried out by a third party.'

'Another bloody anomaly.'

And didn't the Founders really hate those. Yes, they, the Founders, by their nature, were the alphas of the magical world. Their natural ability and tenacity in the field were what got them to that peak position, and their aggressive acquisition of power over millennia ensured they stayed there, but they were by no means alone in being magical. The Folk was the loosely defined title given to all people of a more magical bent, which could take many shapes and forms. Generally, it ran along family lines. Anomalies, however, were ordinary people who, despite having no fae bloodline, developed magical ability. They presented many types of problem, not least the tendency to draw attention to themselves, like a baby left in charge of a handgun.

'Yes, it appears the individual in question, Wayne Grainger, is from Portsmouth. Mother a dentist, father a town planner, no Folk ancestry that we know of.' It was always possible, of course, that the dentist had been playing away from home, but now was not the time to bring that up.

'There have been far too many of these recently,' huffed the voice.

On that point, he was not wrong. There had been several reports in recent weeks of peculiar occurrences that were relatively minor in nature. One possibility being considered was that this was a side effect of what the Folk had termed the Rising. For decades, the amount of background magic in the world had been steadily fading away, and then, suddenly, it wasn't any more. It was another of many current sore points for the Council. This particular magical tide raised all boats, and they very much wanted anyone who wasn't a Founder to drown.

'And the damn footage is all over the internet!'

If Carter ever found the person who set up Google alerts for this man, she would take great delight in ramming her high heel directly through their eye.

'Yes, Your Lordship. As you know, in this day and age, everyone has a camera phone and access to the bullhorn of social media and—'

'And you need to stop it.'

Sure, let's hold back that tide. 'I am putting a strategy in place to deal with this incident.' *Or at least I was until you decided to monologue at me*. 'And—'

'What about your associate – Baladin? Isn't she supposed to be good with this stuff?'

Carter was secretly delighted. She had been hoping to deflect a little blame. Tamsin Baladin was becoming a problem. It wasn't so much the naked ambition of the woman – they looked for that in an acolyte after all – but she was something else. Thanks to her company, she had the kind of money that could buy shortcuts, and she was looking for them all. She had hired the finest teachers money could buy to train her in the ways of magic, and she had teams hunting high and low for all forms of magical artefacts in an effort to increase her power.

On cue, the door to Dr Carter's office opened and Tamsin Baladin, looking like she'd just stepped out of hair and make-up, came striding in. You had to be really paying attention to notice how she held her right hand ever so slightly differently, a hangover from the broken arm she sustained in the Johnson debacle.

'Ah, Tamsin,' said Dr Carter, 'good of you to finally join us.'

Baladin ignored Carter and favoured the screen with that dazzling smile of hers. 'Apologies for my lateness, Your Lordship.'

'Not good enough,' barked the voice. 'When we say jump, you say how high. Or are you too busy with other projects?'

'Not at all, Your Lordship, I was dealing with this one.' She turned and pointed at the large screen on the wall behind Carter. 'If you will direct your attention here . . .' She clicked a device between her fingers and a video recording instantly filled the screen. How the hell did she do that?

They watched as the footage Carter had already seen a dozen times played out before them. The figure floating in the air before plummeting to the ground.

'This was filmed in Manchester just over three hours ago,' Tamsin announced.

'Yes,' said Carter. 'We've—' She stopped talking as a second clip filled the screen.

'This,' continued Tamsin, 'is from New York an hour ago.'

A similar figure floated in the air before hurtling to the ground. The screen then split and showed multiple occurrences of the same phenomenon, all playing out with different figures, different buildings, some at night, most in daylight. 'And Hong Kong, Sydney, Toronto, Stockholm, Cape Town . . .'

'This is a nightmare,' wailed the unseen voice.

Tamsin turned on her heel with a flourish. 'Quite the opposite, Your Lordship. This is our solution. You see, these clips are fake. Effects generated by a new app called Long Way Down, which just became available on all mobile platforms. Users can generate these effects within minutes. It's spreading like wildfire.'

Carter was struck by a deeply unpleasant sinking feeling.

'B-but . . .' stammered the voice. 'But the Manchester footage is real, isn't it?'

'Yes,' clarified Baladin, 'but it will be lost under a tidal wave of the other clips which are already going viral on all platforms, thanks to a little push from my team. A broadsheet journalist of our acquaintance is already writing a piece that will run tomorrow condemning this kind of morbid entertainment, and so on and so on.' It was all the woman could do not to finish with a bow. 'The problem is contained.'

'My word,' said the voice. 'This is excellent work, Ms Baladin.'

'Yes,' said Dr Carter, trying for sincere.

'You could learn a lot from her, Doctor.'

Ouch, direct hit.

'There is, however, something else,' said Baladin.

Dr Carter tried to shoot her a warning look not to overstep the mark yet further, but Baladin avoided meeting her eye.

'I don't know if you are aware of this,' Tamsin continued, 'but the girl from *The Stranger Times*, Stella last-name-unknown, was involved in the incident.'

'What?'

Dr Carter leaned forward. 'There is no evidence of that, my lord. She was just near by.'

'It's a rather big coincidence,' Tamsin went on. 'She was right beside the man when he fell.'

Dr Carter turned to her. 'When you've been doing this job for more than a few months, Tamsin, you will come to realize that coincidences happen with alarming regularity. The key is not to overreact.'

'If this girl had anything to do with this . . .' growled the voice.

'Absolutely, my lord. If' – Dr Carter laid heavy emphasis on the word – 'that's the case, then that will be something we must deal with, but, as I know you appreciate, we need to tread carefully here.'

'The girl is a danger,' insisted Tamsin.

'Only because she was made into one. Johnson's foolish plan, which you were privy to, resulted in his death and riled up the Folk yet further, after his previous unsanctioned efforts to smash the Accord to pieces.'

'The man was a damned fool,' agreed the voice, having rewritten his attitude towards Johnson's plan now that it had failed, 'but that girl is a danger.'

'As,' interjected Dr Carter, 'is any attempt to seek vengeance on her. Leaving aside the massive damage it would do to the already strained relationship with the Folk, *The Stranger Times* has been useful to us.'

'And you,' said the voice, 'guaranteed the girl's safety for some unfathomable reason.'

'I agreed we would not take an interest if she did nothing, and she hasn't.'

'She killed a Founder,' protested Tamsin.

'She defended herself. Attacking her was never signed off by the Council.'

'She wasn't technically attacked,' said Baladin. 'That Banecroft fool offered her up.'

'Not of his own free will,' countered Carter.

'It was still a ridiculous promise to make,' said the voice.

'Respectfully,' said Carter, 'if you remember, sire, I made the promise when we had no idea what the girl was. And, more importantly, we did so at the time because we had certain creatures running around Manchester causing us considerable problems. An issue, need I remind everybody' – Dr Carter threw out a hand – 'that was entirely created by Tamsin's brother.'

'That is not—' started Baladin.

'Enough!' shouted the voice.

Carter and Baladin glared at each other before turning their attention back to the black screen.

'Sorry, my lord,' said Carter.

'We do not have the time for petty squabbling. Dr Carter, get to the bottom of this matter immediately. Ms Baladin, excellent work.'

Baladin jutted her chin. 'Thank you, sire.'

'Now that the matter has arisen, I'm reminded that I have been asked to obtain an update on your brother's, let us call it "condition".'

'He is progressing well, sire.'

'We are reaching the point where such vague assertions are losing their impact. He is an issue that needs to be dealt with one way or another, and soon.'

'I—' Tamsin cut herself off as the red light on top of the screen flicked off, indicating that the meeting was over.

The two women turned to one another. The undercurrent of hostility had been building, but it was now finally out in the open.

'You are playing a dangerous game, Tamsin.'

She stiffened. 'I am merely trying to fulfil my role to the best of my abilities.'

Dr Carter regarded her for a long moment. 'Yes . . .'

Her attention was diverted by the ping of an incoming message on her phone.

She read it, and a smile played across her lips. 'Now, if you will excuse me, I think it's time I caught up with an old friend.'

9

Standing in the corner of the room as if he'd always been there, the Pilgrim favoured Banecroft with a humourless grin, his yellow-toothed smile a festering wound in his pock-marked nightmare of a face. When he spoke, it was with an American Southern drawl that sounded like its owner's mouth had been previously used to mix cement.

'Why, Mr Banecroft, I do so hope that I did not startle you.'

'Not at all,' said Banecroft. 'I just thought one of the shit stains on the wall had come to life.'

The smile slipped into a disapproving sneer. 'Always such vulgarity.'

'Says the man perving his way around lingerie shops.'

The big man took a few steps into the centre of the room, his size all the more imposing in such a confined space. Banecroft glanced down at the floor. There was indeed no shadow.

'It is odd you should accuse me of that. You are the one currently in jail for the offence.'

'Not exactly. And while I'm enjoying the Foghorn Leghorn tribute act immensely, would you like to get to the point of this little visit?'

'Always so disrespectful to your betters. The sign of an inferior upbringing.'

'I assume that's your version of "your ma", so let me save you some time. I'm going to guess you aren't showing up on the camera there in the corner, so no, I shall not be attempting to swing for you, just in case you were hoping to get a video of me fighting air for *You've Been Framed.* The only reason I am speaking to you now is that I'm expecting you to explain the point to this dog and pony show, so get to it or I shall start ignoring you entirely.'

'I'd like to see you try.'

'Happy to,' said Banecroft. 'Your face is reminiscent of a camel's scrotum, so I'll be delighted to close my eyes and catch up on some sleep. I'm currently running at a deficit of about three years.'

'Unfortunately for you, I am the stuff of nightmares.'

Banecroft rolled his eyes. 'Oh, please, you're a walking cliché. Having said that, most of my nightmares comprise being chased around by a giant flaccid penis, so that checks out.'

The Pilgrim clenched his fists and took a step towards Banecroft. 'You are an impertinent wretch.'

'Easy there, Bubba. Don't go forgetting you're a ghost and—'

He was interrupted by a right hook making contact with his unprotected face. Banecroft, whose career had featured him taking more than a few punches, found the experience of this one unpleasant in different ways to the usual blows. It had weight behind it but not in proportion to the figure who'd thrown it. Along with the feeling of the fist meeting his cheek and nose, there was the sensation of the ghost of a fist passing right through his head. As the physical contact sent him backwards, the wall saved him from tumbling off his chair.

He looked up to see the Pilgrim divided. It was like watching a 3D movie without the proper glasses, with various iterations of the same image superimposed over each other but a fraction out of alignment.

Banecroft held up his hands in front of his face, but no follow-up came. Instead, the Pilgrim stood there and appeared to literally pull himself together, all the misaligned carbon copies drawing back into one.

There was a moment's pause before the man spoke again, his voice less strident. 'I . . . I don't know what happened.'

'What happened,' said Banecroft, 'is that I've got a key to the front door of our office in my pocket, which is supposed to protect me from magic. Seeing as you're, whatever the hell you are, looks like I got half-credit.'

The Pilgrim straightened. 'That is not what I meant. I apologize, sir. That act was beyond my remit and beneath my station.'

Banecroft raised a finger to his nose and drew it away to confirm a slow but steady trickle of blood was coming from his left nostril. 'Well, on the upside, at least I've finally got some physical evidence. Was a little worried my mind had gone off on safari again.'

'It has not.'

'Thank God,' said Banecroft. 'So, what was it like fighting Hulk Hogan? I've got more respect for wrestling now you've sucker-punched me.'

The Pilgrim scowled at this remark but said nothing.

'Now that you've got that out of your system,' continued Banecroft, 'do you want to enlighten me as to the point of all this woo-woo nonsense? Starting with why you went to such lengths to get me arrested?'

The Pilgrim raised an eyebrow. 'Can I not enjoy seeing you making a buffoon of yourself?'

Banecroft regarded the man for a moment. 'Nah, you don't strike me as the prank sort, so let's cut to the chase. I'm guessing you wanted me in here' – he then pointed a finger at the world in general – 'so that I'm not out there. Rest assured, I'm going to be out of here fast, and whatever interest you have in Stella, I will move heaven and earth to stop you. She is under my protection.'

The Pilgrim tilted his head. 'Excuse me?'

'You heard me loud and clear.'

'I have no interest in the girl.'

'Bullshit. I saw you following her.'

The Pilgrim gave a soft shake of his head and a chuckle that sounded like a coffin lid opening. 'I wasn't following her; I was following you.'

Banecroft considered this. 'While I'm flattered by the interest, I'm not really dating right now.'

'I'm finding your insolence increasingly dull, Mr Banecroft.'

'Sorry to disappoint. So, if you're not interested in Stella, why . . .' Banecroft left the thought hanging.

'We needed to have an undisturbed tête-à-tête.'

He remembered the man standing on the bridge, beside the car park, in the crowd on Hulme Street. Banecroft slapped the table in front of him. 'And whoever, whatever you are – you can't enter our offices, aka the Church of Old Souls, can you?'

There was a moment of delicious joy as the Pilgrim shifted awkwardly on his feet.

'That's it, isn't it? Is it the Rastafarian and his little friend, or are you just not allowed on holy ground?'

'How dare you, sir. I am a man of unimpeachable faith and character.'

'Who just sucker-punched an unarmed man. Mother Teresa you ain't.'

'Your impudence is insufferable.'

'Good. Perhaps you should toddle back to tell whichever member of the Founders you work for that this isn't the gig for you.'

The Pilgrim scoffed. 'You think you're so smart? You do not know what you're dealing with. I care not a jot for the petty squabbles of your living world.'

Banecroft folded his arms and leaned back against the wall. 'OK, Rhett Butler, what do you give a damn about, then?'

'An appropriate choice of words as, you see, Mr Banecroft, you – are truly damned.'

His condemnation was met with a shrug. 'No arguments here. This could be hell right now. It'd certainly explain the decor.'

'Silence,' growled the Pilgrim. 'I represent an entity you may refer to as the Guardians of the Dead. It is our role to protect the spirit world, and you have been involved in the most heinous of violations.'

Banecroft said nothing to this.

'Your silence does you some small credit. I speak of one Simon Brush and your part in the desecration of his spirit.'

Banecroft eventually stepped into the pause that followed, his eyes fixed on the table. 'The instigator of that whole thing was not me—'

'No,' interrupted the Pilgrim. 'We are aware of that, and the individual in question has been dealt with. Still, you knew that when the spirit of Simon Brush came to you, he was in pain, being used as an unwilling proxy for what you believed to be your dead wife. And, because it suited you, you ignored his suffering to further your own ends.'

Banecroft kept his eyes on the table. His head was filled with memories that had played in his mind again and again over the last few weeks. It wasn't just Stella whom he had hurt. There was a hitch in his voice as he spoke again. 'That's fair.'

'That it is,' confirmed the Pilgrim. 'Personally, having observed you and judged you irredeemable, I wish nothing more than to serve righteous punishment upon you. Nothing would give me greater pleasure.'

Banecroft shrugged. 'I wouldn't be the first person to die in police custody.'

'Die?' echoed the Pilgrim, scorn lacing his voice. 'It is the curse of the living to be so blinkered as to believe that death is the worst thing that may befall them.'

Banecroft looked up at the man. Up close, there was something more about his eyes. The pupils weren't black so much as absent of all colour, light, hope. They were the void staring back.

The Pilgrim gave the slightest nod of his head and suddenly

the room was transformed into a writhing mass of ethereal flesh, blistered faces screaming, hands reaching out desperately to Banecroft from all sides, clawing at his skin.

The apparition disappeared as quickly as it had materialized, Banecroft's scream dying in his throat before he could give full voice to it.

'That,' said the Pilgrim, 'should be your fate for all eternity, for your part in this defilement. You are both unworthy and irredeemable, in my humble opinion.'

Banecroft licked his lips and tasted the blood that was flowing down from his nose. He wanted to close his eyes and wish it all away, but he worried that to do so would invite the hellish vision back in. 'You may well be right.' He blinked a couple of times in an attempt to bring himself back to the now. His skin was covered in a cold sweat that trickled down his back in icy rivulets. He tapped his trembling fingers on the tabletop, somehow reassured by its solidity. He cleared his throat as he gathered his thoughts. 'Still, there's something in the way you said it makes me think that your humble opinion isn't carrying as much weight here as you'd like it to.'

The Pilgrim ran a finger over the scar on the side of his face, the undertone of a growl in his breathing before he spoke again. 'There are those who believe you are worthy of a second chance. Fate has put you within the orbit of a greater defilement. Prove yourself by righting that unspeakable wrong and we' – he almost spat the words – 'will let bygones be bygones.'

'And what if I don't want to jump through your hoops?'

A broad smile broke across the man's weathered face. 'I would be delighted.'

'Well, that doesn't sound like something I'd enjoy. So, what is this defilement exactly?'

'Exactly? You don't get exactly. All you get is a name – William Ignatius Campbell.'

'I'm going to need more than that.'

'Good. I cannot wait to see you fail.'

'By any chance, were you a career guidance teacher in a previous life?'

'Hide behind your silly japes and smart words, Mr Banecroft. They will do you no good. Judgement is coming. You have until midnight on All Hallows' Eve.'

'Hallowe'en? Really? Bit of a . . .'

Banecroft's eyes darted to the far wall at the sound of the door opening. He never actually saw the Pilgrim disappear – it was more he was there one second and gone the next.

The door opened to reveal the rather pissed-off-looking figure of DS Wilkerson. 'Were you talking to yourself?'

Banecroft stretched out his arms. 'If you must know, I'm working on a one-man play. I'll let you know when it's on.'

'Thanks,' she said. 'I'd hate to catch it accidentally. Your brief is here.'

'I don't have a . . .'

At the sound of the irritating, high-pitched laugh, DS Wilkerson stepped back to reveal Dr Carter standing behind her.

'Vincent, sweetie, are you all right? You look like you've seen a ghost.'

Agog at Mogg

Red faces all round in Westminster today after it emerged that the MP for North East Somerset and former government minister, Jacob Rees-Mogg, is in fact the ghost of Victorian landlord Arthur Wassenstack.

Rees-Mogg, a man renowned for opinions so far right they are unviewable without a pair of binoculars and a vomit bucket, has long been a darling of 'grassroots activists' – a euphemistic term for people who have to get up an hour early every morning just to have more time to hate things. However, it is unclear what his supporters will make of him now he has come over here from the other side and is taking one of our jobs. In his defence, the job of being Jacob Rees-Mogg is not one that many other people would want.

Arthur Wassenstack, for his part, was described in *Twerp's Peerage* back in 1895 as 'a man behind the times, mean-spirited but coming from the right family and owning an acceptable number of slaves'. Sources claim that rumours about Rees-Moggs' ethereal truth have long circulated in the political sphere. One source said, 'We probably should have asked more questions when he just floated through the wall in the middle of a cabinet meeting but, to be honest, we were just all really glad he'd left.'

10

Doug 'Stink' Stankovitch would say this for Dr Emma Marsh – when she lost it, she really lost it. In his expert opinion, her tantrums were right up there with the very best of them, and seeing as he'd once toured Asia and Australia with Sir Elton John, that was really saying something. She wasn't quite at the Rocketman's level when it came to bombastic rhetoric, but then there was something about the guy who wrote 'Your Song' threatening to hunt down your entire family with a pack of rabid chihuahuas if his decaf latte was cold again that really stayed with you. What she lacked in delivery, she more than made up for in the follow-through stakes, though, because you knew Elton John would eventually calm down and almost certainly not attempt to carry out his threats. Dr Marsh, on the other hand . . .

'You are without doubt the most incompetent, imbecilic buffoon I have ever met. I'd say I'm amazed you can feed yourself but, in my experience, it's the thing you seem to spend ninety per cent of your time doing. I mean, how could you let this happen?'

'Well,' said Doug, trying to sound calm, 'I didn't let it. It happened. We knew something like this was always a risk.'

Dr Marsh was a small, wiry woman with a petite face, but then it wasn't as if her power were physical. He wouldn't put it past her to hit him, far from it, but that didn't worry him. Quite the opposite. It was the other stuff that terrified him. Her glasses, framed by her long black hair, were steaming up. She really was mad.

'If by "always a risk" you mean inevitable because you'd screw up, then yes, it was entirely predictable.'

He was sitting at the kitchen table of the farmhouse they had co-inhabited for the last few months. She was standing in the middle of the floor, flailing her arms, while her brown-and-black tabby cat, who she only ever referred to as Kitty, stretched out on the table in front of Doug, enjoying his discomfort.

'No,' he said, doing his best to sound reasonable, 'but the drugs have side effects and, y'know, they can be extreme. And besides, it's not like this is the first kid to die from thinking he could fly.'

For a second, Doug really thought she was going to hit him. Most people went red when they got angry, whereas Dr Marsh became weirdly paler than she was to begin with. He wasn't sure, but he thought some of her freckles might have disappeared. Was that even possible?

She moved closer and shouted directly into his face from a foot away. 'Yes, but he's the first kid to successfully do so before leaving a messy hole in the ground! Have you seen the footage?'

'I showed it to you.'

'Then you know. Or at least you would do if you weren't an idiot.'

Kitty rolled over, his paw swatting leisurely at Doug's hand. Kitty was an odd name for a male cat, but this didn't seem like a good time to bring that up.

'I really don't think we've got anything to worry about,' said Doug. 'The police can't trace it back to us.'

Dr Marsh stood completely still in a way that made him incredibly concerned about what was coming next.

'The police?' she repeated in a near whisper. 'You think I'm worried about the police?' She raised her voice to answer her own question. 'I couldn't give a damn about the police. They're almost as incompetent as you. But *they* will take an interest now.'

Doug knew he should keep quiet, but his curiosity was getting the better of him. 'Who are the "they" here?'

'They,' snapped Dr Marsh. 'Them. When people say the big scary "they" or "them", it's the people who they mean, even if they don't know they mean it.' She lowered her voice and over-enunciated her words. 'The Founders.'

'Who are the—'

'I don't have time to educate you. We've got to move up the schedule dramatically. Get rid of the rest of the stock tonight.'

'Tonight? But—'

'But nothing. I'm in charge here. Get it done and then I need more test subjects.'

'I already said—'

'I don't care what you say, I only care what you do, you—'

She broke off and took a couple of steps back, a look of revulsion rapidly appearing on her face.

'What?' asked Doug.

Without lowering her gaze, she jutted her head in the general direction of his crotch. 'What is going on down there?'

Doug looked down and gave her an apologetic smile. 'Oh, yeah. Sorry about that. I . . . get sort of, y'know . . . when attractive women scream at me.'

She made a retching face. 'Oh God.'

'I'm not doing it deliberately.'

'You disgust me,' she spat.

Doug leaned forward. 'Oh, jeez, don't say that – you're only going to make it worse.'

Dr Marsh clenched both her fists together and pressed them to her forehead. 'You are without doubt the most loathsome human being I have ever met.'

'Funnily enough, Elton John said—'

Doug didn't bother to finish as Dr Marsh had left the kitchen, slamming the door behind her so hard that the crockery in the cupboard rattled.

Doug looked at Kitty. The cat opened his mouth in what looked a lot like a mocking smile. For a brief moment, Doug considered shoving the animal off the table, but instantly thought better of it.

That really would be more trouble than it was worth.

11

Dr Carter stood there in a burgundy suit that cost more than the average monthly salary and flashed Banecroft a high-wattage smile.

He scratched his chin. 'I have a very vivid memory of firing you as the lawyer for *The Stranger Times*.'

'You did,' admitted Dr Carter. 'But I didn't want to embarrass you at the time by pointing out that you don't actually have the power to do that.'

'I beg to differ.'

'I know,' said Dr Carter. 'Begging to differ is very much your thing, isn't it, Vincent, darling? Still' – she nodded towards DS Wilkerson – 'let's not argue in front of the children. We have much to discuss.'

There was something in the way she said the last bit that made him pause. 'All right, fine, let's make this quick. If I keep having meetings in here, they're going to start charging me for the room.'

Dr Carter looked at DS Wilkerson. 'Honestly, it's all wham-bam-thank-you-ma'am.'

'I just need you to—' started DS Wilkerson but Dr Carter

ushered her unsubtly out of the room. Whatever else the DS was going to say was cut off by the door slamming behind her despite it not having been physically touched.

Dr Carter strode across the room, her high heels clicking on the floor as she casually twirled a finger in the direction of the camera in the corner.

'I'm going to guess,' said Banecroft, pointing up at it, 'that isn't working any more.'

'Oh,' said Dr Carter with a dismissive shrug as she pulled out the chair opposite him to sit down, 'it's Greater Manchester Police. There's every chance it wasn't working in the first place. They are criminally underfunded. So, Vincent, sweetie. Bum-rushing the changing room at a Victoria's Secret. Is this what you've reduced yourself to now in order to get my attention?'

'I didn't—'

The joviality dropped from her voice and she tilted her head. 'Are you bleeding?'

Banecroft self-consciously touched his nose again. 'It's nothing.'

'They roughed you up? How very nineteen eighties. I'm guessing that camera really wasn't working.'

'It wasn't like that.'

She produced a handkerchief from somewhere and handed it to him. 'What was it like?'

'Let's go with I slipped in the shower.'

She shrugged. 'Have it your way. Although I do wish you'd take another run at showering. Do I get to hear what possessed you to charge into a Victoria's Secret?'

'No, it's a secret.'

'Oh, Vinny, darling, you're better than that.'

'It's been a rough day. Speaking of which – a hypothetical question. If I were to say to you – big man, all in black, wide-brimmed hat, long white hair and a scar on his face?'

She pulled a face. 'Are you suggesting a little cosplay? Doesn't sound like a great look, but I'm sure you could make it work.'

Banecroft nodded. If Dr Carter knew anything about the Pilgrim, she hid it well. 'So, Doctor, why are you here?'

'Well, I heard you'd been arrested and I came rushing over.'

'And how exactly did you hear that?'

She let out a burst of that annoying high-pitched giggle again. 'Oh, come now. The organization I represent, we have more than a few chatty little birdies on the payroll.'

'You own the police?'

'We rent the parts worth bothering with.'

'Reassuring. So, you're here out of the kindness of your heart?'

She smiled. 'Well, I think you and I have been due a little catch-up for quite some time, don't you? Ever since your little protégée took out a Founder.'

'That was self-defence, and you know it.'

'Maybe I do,' conceded Dr Carter, 'but perhaps it's not me you have to worry about.'

'We have an agreement. You sat in my office and said that if I did what you wanted, Stella wouldn't be touched.'

Dr Carter rubbed one hand against her forehead and tapped her fingernails of the other on the tabletop irritably. 'Do try to pay attention, Vincent. There is some reading between the lines required here. Hard as you may find this to believe, I had nothing to do with what happened a couple of months ago . . .'

'But I bet you knew about it?'

Dr Carter's eyes darted away for a moment, telling him all he needed to know before they met his again. 'It's complicated.'

'It seems pretty simple from where I'm sitting.'

'I bet it does,' snapped Dr Carter. 'But perhaps you're guilty of rendering these things in black and white. Given your role in proceedings, I'd have thought you might be a little more circumspect.'

It was Banecroft's turn to stay silent now.

'My point is,' said Dr Carter, her tone measured, 'now is not a good time for your protégée to be near men who fall out of the sky, so you need to tell me what happened.'

'I honestly have no idea,' said Banecroft. 'I was going to ask you.'

'Despite what you may think, we play little or no part in most of the things that happen in this town. Most of my job is maintaining the status quo. Whereas yours appears to be attracting trouble.'

Banecroft withdrew the handkerchief from his nose and studied the spots of blood on it. 'That comes with the job, but this time, Stella really was just walking home. I think it might be a case of pure bad luck. Wrong place. Wrong time.'

'You're kidding?'

'So much insanity happens around us. Do you think a coincidence like that is so hard to fathom?'

Dr Carter exhaled loudly. 'Stranger things have happened, but you proving that would be extremely helpful.'

'And how do you suggest I do that?'

She waved a hand dismissively. 'Journalism?'

He sat forward. 'So, is our agreement still in place? Regarding Stella?'

Dr Carter rolled her head around her neck, and to Banecroft's eye, she looked suddenly tired. 'Between you and me, what happened on that golf course is a terrible look for my employers. The Folk are pissed and, frankly, not without justification. The Accord is under strain from all sides, and there are factions in my organization that are egotistical enough to think there are better ways to do things. That they have given up too much and have somehow been diminished. Like how a teenager can kill one of them and not face repercussions.'

'She didn't—'

'I know, I know, but it isn't me who needs to be convinced of that. Those of us trying to hold it all together have a thankless task, and the last thing we need is more random variables, exactly like your associate. Word to the wise, she needs to keep as low a profile as possible.'

Banecroft gave a mirthless laugh. 'Don't you think she's been trying?'

'Try harder. If this really is all one big coincidence, then you finding out what is behind it, and fast, would be a very good idea. I'm trying to hold back the tide here and my tootsies are getting wet.'

Banecroft shifted in his chair and gave her an assessing look. 'I think I've just had a revelation.'

'Is that so? Please let it involve deodorant.'

'You're not one of them, are you?'

'Excuse me?'

'The Founders. I just noticed. You refer to "they", "them", "my employers". I can't believe I didn't notice it before. You're not actually one of the' – he gesticulated in the air –'immortals.'

She gave him an unmistakable look of annoyance. 'What's your point, Vincent?'

'What's in it for you?'

She slid her chair back and got to her feet. 'We don't have that kind of time, sweetie.'

There was a knock on the door.

'Just a second,' she trilled before turning back to Banecroft. 'That will be DS Wilkerson reluctantly coming to inform you that you're to be released without charge. I made a call on the drive over. Consider it a freebie.'

'I didn't ask for your help.'

'No, but you need it.'

'Hello?' called DS Wilkerson from outside the room.

'No, thank you,' said Banecroft, folding his arms.

'Oh, do shut up. Have you not heard anything I said? You don't have time to wallow in here. Stella needs you out there, finding answers.'

'But—'

Wilkerson was pushing against the door. 'Is this locked?' asked the annoyed-sounding DS. 'How is this locked?'

'And you just expect me to trust you now?'

Dr Carter groaned. 'No. At least part of my point is that you shouldn't trust anybody.'

Banecroft nodded. 'Way ahead of you on that one.' He held out the handkerchief. 'Do you want this back?'

'Absolutely not,' she snapped, all joviality gone from her voice. 'And for God's sake, never voluntarily give something with your blood on it to a practitioner of magic.' She shook her head. 'How have you stayed alive this long?'

'Mainly by luck and charm.'

'Be careful,' she warned as she walked across the room. 'Both of those things run out, eventually.'

She gave a swift wave of her hand and the door flew open, sending DS Wilkerson hurtling through it and stumbling to the floor.

Dr Carter stepped nimbly over her prone form. 'Are you all right, Sergeant? You seem a little frazzled?' She waved again without looking back. 'Toodles, Vincent. Do try to stay out of trouble. There's a good boy.'

12

It was amazing how something could be both over and, at the same time, never-ending.

Marcus raised his eyes and looked around the shed. Abandoned farm equipment, broken furniture and random detritus. The kind of stuff that people could not throw out and yet would never use again. It sat here largely forgotten, wrapped in stale air and coated in dust. If only he too could be forgotten. Then perhaps he could just die.

It wasn't as if they were doing much more than the minimum to keep him alive. He had lost all concept of time. He'd been both tied and otherwise bound to this chair for so long that everything in his life before it seemed like a dream. Still, he was pretty sure that the short, bearded guy's appearances with food and water were sporadic. He had long ago passed through hunger, thirst, rage and come out the other side. Gone too was the idea of escape. He now lived in a state of stasis, the only dream being that of death. He ran the bone-dry tip of his tongue over his chapped lips. Maybe they had forgotten him. Finally.

He'd fought, though. By the gods, he had fought. She had

calmly explained what she wanted him to do and he had refused point blank. It was a truly appalling idea.

In one way or another, Marcus had been fighting his whole life. Against his demons, often against the people trying to help him, and mostly against the 'gift' he had been given. Irony of ironies, he'd only recently, after so long, found a way to a place of relative peace. And then this had happened. He'd been taken before he'd known what was happening, and since then, the chair. He'd fought with every inch of himself, every last scintilla of his soul that he could muster, everything – and it had not been enough. What had broken him were the eyes. She had spent what felt like an eternity torturing him in an array of precise and carefully judged ways, and he'd resisted. Then, one day, he'd looked up into her eyes and realized what was staring back at him.

Nothing.

She would never stop because she felt nothing, and she was too good at this to mistakenly cause him to die. That was the point he realized it was over. When he'd known there was no point fighting it any more. He had done what she had asked. He'd even tried to explain that he couldn't generate enough energy to manage it, but that had just led her to reapply her oh-so-precise methods to dredge it out of him. Leaving him a hollowed-out husk, devoid of all hope.

The door at the far end of the shed opened and sunlight streamed through, so bright in the gloom that it hurt his eyes. Let it be him and not her. Him and not her. Him meant food and water. Her meant . . .

His eyes adjusted and he watched her calmly stride towards

him, the dusty sunlight bouncing off her black hair, a large tray in her hands. His body shook but no tears came. The woman – she had never told him her name – was what could have been called petite in another context. Not much more than five foot, a hundred pounds soaking wet. Not that it mattered; her power was not physical. In fact, she had not touched him once.

She placed the tray down in front of him, pushed her glasses up her nose and said in a cheery voice, 'Now, Marcus, we've got an awful lot to do this evening, so I hope you're feeling helpful. We don't want any silly tantrums, do we?'

Both over and never-ending.

13

Hannah caught her head dipping to one side, the need for sleep lying heavy on her eyelids, and shook herself awake. She sat up and looked around the bullpen, where Stella, Reggie and Ox, all looking knackered, were plonked behind their desks, browsing the web or, in the case of Ox, doodling aimlessly.

'Right,' she announced, 'this is absurd. There is no reason for all of us to be here this late. It's well past midnight.'

She looked pointedly at Stella.

'What?' Stella replied. 'I actually live here. What are you three doing here?'

'I'm here,' said Reggie, deliberately avoiding looking in Ox's direction, 'to make sure someone doesn't do anything stupid.'

'I'm here,' responded Ox, 'as a protest against my rights of free expression being curtailed by the fascists in charge of this paper.' He looked at Hannah. 'Why are you still here?'

'I'm here because I'm a senior-ranking member of the aforementioned fascists and I need to make sure the paper actually goes to print.'

'And we here' – Hannah nearly fell off her chair in surprise as

Manny spoke from his position just inside the double doors – 'for them tea and biscuits.' He waved a mug he held in one hand and the stack of six chocolate biscuits he held in the other.

'How come he gets access to Grace's good biscuit stash?' whined Ox. 'I've looked all over and I can't find them. Why's he special?'

Manny tapped the biscuits against his head. 'She like them chocolate.'

Ox was incredulous. 'Hang on, the angel thingy that lives in . . . Ouch!'

The 'ouch' was because Reggie had just kicked Ox under the desk.

'What was that for?'

'It was because,' said Reggie, 'there are certain things you do not ask.'

Ox rubbed his leg. 'We're journalists. Finding out stuff is supposed to be our job.'

'Still, let's not risk annoying the thing that protects us while we're doing it.'

Reggie had a point. Hannah was fascinated by the terrifying angelic entity that co-habited Manny's body, but there were some questions it was probably best not to ask.

'Guys,' said Stella, 'you're all missing the bigger picture here . . .'

The other three turned to her in confusion.

'Manny?'

They looked at each other in confusion now too.

'He's wearing pants?'

'Ohhhh!' said Hannah, before joining in as all four of them applauded.

Manny duly bowed and shoved a whole biscuit in his mouth.

'I was just wondering, Manny,' ventured Hannah, 'how much longer it would be before we could start the presses rolling?'

He slurped his tea loudly before answering around his mouth still full of biscuit. 'We ready when you are.'

'We've been ready for over an hour,' said Stella. 'Remember? I came down and told you?'

Manny looked at Stella as he chewed his biscuit and swallowed. 'We no remember that.'

Stella sighed. 'I definitely did, but you were enjoying a . . . cigarette break at the time.'

Manny's facial expression was that of a stoned guy who'd just been presented with a bill. 'Ohhhh, we sorry.'

He closed his eyes and swayed for a couple of seconds. The other four looked at each other.

'Ehm, Manny . . .' began Hannah.

Before she could say anything else, a familiar thunking noise echoed through the building along with the rumble of the printing press on the floor below as it began to roll into action.

'How did he— OUCH!' yelped Reggie.

Ox shot him a pointed look from across the table. 'There are certain things you do not ask.'

The two men pulled faces at each other.

'Right,' said Hannah, keen to move on. 'There's even less reason for you all to be here now.'

'Yeah,' said Ox, 'I'm still not leaving until the moody git gets back.'

'Look at that,' said Stella. 'He's worried about Banecroft.'

'Worried me arse. He got arrested in the changing rooms of Victoria's Secret. I'm looking forward to ripping the piss out of the dirty old sod.'

'Sorry to disappoint,' barked Banecroft from the doorway.

This time, Hannah actually jumped out of her chair in surprise.

Grace was standing behind him, having offered to be the one to go to the police station and wait for him to be released.

'I have been completely exonerated and all charges have been dropped,' he announced. 'I was engaging in actual journalism, which I appreciate may be a foreign concept to some of you, but that's what it looks like.'

'It looks like—' started Ox, in a futile attempt to rally.

'Charging into a Victoria's Secret's changing room and getting slapped by a buxom lady endeavouring to fit into a corset I estimate to have been two sizes too small for her? Yes. Yes, it does.' Banecroft looked around the room. 'And may I say how inspiring it is to see the staff of this newspaper so hard at work in my absence.'

'It's almost one in the morning,' pleaded Reggie.

'News does not sleep.'

'We are literally printing this week's edition now,' said Hannah.

'Which means we're on to next week,' said Banecroft.

'I nearly got hit by a guy falling from the sky,' said Stella.

'And you should be writing that up.'

'I would like to do a restaurant review column,' ventured Ox.

'Hard no.'

'We wearing pants,' said Manny.

Banecroft looked at him and nodded. 'Between that and the presses rolling, you are fulfilling one hundred per cent of your remit, Manny. The rest of this rabble could learn a lot from you.'

Grace rolled her eyes. 'I'm going to pop the kettle on.'

'Excellent,' said Banecroft, 'it could be a late night.' He pointed at Ox. 'William Ignatius Campbell.'

'Nope,' he replied. 'Ox Chen. We've met before.'

'And your record for being consistently hilarious remains intact. Find out everything about Mr Campbell immediately.'

'Who is he?'

'That is exactly what I need you to find out.'

'But it's—'

'Right now.' He jabbed a finger at Hannah and then at the door to his office. 'A word.'

Hannah started following him as requested. 'I have a name, you know.'

'I know,' said Banecroft. 'But due to your on-again, off-again marriage, I wouldn't like to risk offending you by getting your second name incorrect. I'm nothing if not considerate.'

He shoved his way through the door and into his office.

'Yes,' said Hannah. 'Your tact is rightly legendary.' She closed the door to the office behind her. 'OK, you seem a tad wired. Do you want to explain what the hell happened?'

Banecroft went straight to his desk and, in one fluid motion, picked up a glass with one hand while extracting a half-full bottle of whiskey from the bottom drawer with the other. 'I was pursuing a figure which turned out to be a sort of ghost, although rather solid when he needs to be. No charges are pending as that Dr Carter woman made it go away.' There was a pause as he lit a cigarette with one hand while bringing the suicidally large measure he'd just finishing pouring to his lips with the other.

'Wait. What, how, who?' asked Hannah.

Banecroft smacked his lips, having finished his drink, and proceeded to pour another while puffing away on the cigarette. 'All excellent questions, no time to answer any of them. Here are the headlines: we have two problems. First, and most importantly, we need to find out what the hell was going on with your minimalist skydiver, and fast, because the Founders think Stella has something to do with it.'

'But she was just—'

'I know,' interrupted Banecroft. 'But, given recent events, they're rather interested in her, and this might be all the excuse they need.'

'Dr Carter—'

'She's on our side. Actually, no – that's a ridiculous statement. She is on her side, but it is sort of pointing in the same direction as our side right now, and we probably need to keep it that way. So, you are in charge of investigating that. Liaise with Detective Inspector Nice-but-Dim, and if you need to make a man of him to get what you need, well, I for one will think none the less of you.'

'Stop trying to be revolting.'

'Who is trying?' He grabbed another quick mouthful of

whiskey. 'I, meanwhile, have another issue to deal with. This . . . I don't actually know his name. Big fella, all in black, ridiculous hat, face like a camel's scrotum—'

'Wait, that's the man you asked if anyone had seen earlier in the week.'

'Yes, him. Looks like a pilgrim, talks like Elmer Fudd after he's found both Jesus and smack. Apparently, I've got until midnight on Tuesday to solve this William Ignatius Campbell thing or I'm going to be dragged to a terrifying eternal hell for my part in the defiling of Simon Brush's ethereal spirit.'

'Oh my God,' said Hannah. 'But that's . . . You can't. How did . . . Don't they—'

'Again, those are several excellent questions you've almost asked there, but I don't have time to deal with them. We need to get back out there and get moving. Time is of the essence, and if I've got a long weekend left of living, I'd like to make the most of it.'

He tried to move past her and head back out the door, but Hannah stepped into his path and stood in front of him. 'Hang on a second.'

Banecroft huffed in frustration.

'Look me in the eye.'

After a moment, Banecroft did so.

'You're going to be, what was it, "dragged to hell"?'

Banecroft shrugged. 'To be fair, *a* hell. I don't know if it is *the* hell, or if indeed there is an actual one. There may be several. From the brief glimpse he gave me, this is one of the less fun ones.'

Hannah held his gaze. There was something else there behind the bluster. Fear. Genuine fear.

'This is real, isn't it?'

'Very.'

'OK,' said Hannah, 'we will sort it out.'

She was surprised when Banecroft's response came out in a snarl. 'No, you will protect Stella. *That* is the most important thing.'

'All right, then – we'll do both.'

'In an ideal world,' said Banecroft, 'but if the existence of vaping proves anything, it's that we don't live in one of those. I have made my priorities very clear. It's why I don't want anyone else knowing about this.'

'But—'

'It's my life. It's my decision. Protect Stella at all costs and the other thing we will deal with as best we can.'

'And you really believe this, whatever it is, could happen?'

'I do.'

'Why?'

'Two reasons. One: he gave me a brief but very vivid taster, and believe me, it felt exceedingly real.'

'And two?'

'I sort of have it coming.'

'That's crap.'

'Is it? When all the stuff with Simon was happening, I knew something was very wrong, but I decided to ignore it to suit my own agenda.'

'You weren't in your right mind. And besides, Simon himself forgave you.'

'Maybe that's not his decision to make.'

Hannah threw up her hands. 'So this is what, your way of punishing yourself?'

'Oh no, I'm going to damn well try to beat this thing, not least because I'd like to rub this big ugly bastard's pompous nose in it, but let's just say I see no benefit in trying to appeal the decision.'

Hannah puffed out her cheeks. 'OK, fine.' She jabbed a finger at him. 'But you're letting me help.'

Banecroft went to speak, but she cut him off.

'We can do the Stella thing at the same time. We can multitask. Also' – she waved a finger at his face – 'why is there blood around your nose?'

'The ghost bloke punched me in the face.'

'That is a very human response to meeting you.'

'Actually, before I forget, never give anything with your blood on it to a practitioner of magic.'

'Right,' said Hannah with a nod. 'Well, there's most of my ideas for Christmas presents out the window.'

'Speaking of which,' said Banecroft, 'while getting arrested earlier, I couldn't help but notice, have you seen how many edible clothing options are available now? Imagine trying to explain those to someone in a famine.'

'I'll do everything you ask on the condition that we never discuss edible underwear again.'

'You drive a hard bargain. Done.'

Hannah stepped aside, Banecroft opened the door and strode back into the bullpen. 'Right, give me answers.'

'Well,' said Ox, while staring at his screen, 'assuming it's the same fella I just found and, given the relative obscurity of Ignatius as a name, I assume it is, does a forty-three-year-old software engineer, single, with no kids sound right?'

'No idea,' said Banecroft. 'Tell me more.'

'Homeowner. Address in Chorlton. Solvent. All in all, remarkably dull.'

'Excellent, well, his life is going to get considerably more interesting, as he will be talking to you and me first thing in the morning.'

'That'll be tricky,' said Ox. 'He's dead.'

14

Doug 'Stink' Stankovitch sat in the front seat of the van and diligently worked his way through the last survivor from the box of a dozen doughnuts he'd picked up on the way there. It had been a rough day and he was eating his emotions. He sneezed violently and failed to cover his mouth in time, which resulted in the inside of the windscreen taking some friendly fire. Kitty, the cat who was lounging on the passenger seat, lifted his head from enthusiastically licking his nether regions for just long enough to shoot Doug a dirty look.

'Don't gawp at me like that. I'm allergic to you, you little sod.'

The cat shifted to give Doug a better view of his arsehole in a way that didn't seem like a coincidence.

Doug hated cats. In truth, he hadn't had much experience of them prior to meeting Kitty, but that had been more than enough. He was well used to dealing with all manner of highly strung and demanding individuals, but the cat and its owner might just be the worst.

Doug had been a roadie since birth. His dad had been on the road crew for Zeppelin's last tour when he and his mum hooked up. They'd both been drunk. She later claimed she'd thought he was Robert Plant. He even less convincingly claimed he'd thought she was the woman he'd been married to at the time. They'd ended up together and inexplicably stayed that way, with his mum and Doug following whatever tour his dad was on. The 'together' here was in the broadest sense of the word. They had what could be termed an 'open relationship' or, more accurately, a 'never-ending fight with the occasional screwing of other people thrown in'. Doug's mum would often get work on the tour too – in costumes, catering or, if she was really lucky, doing the occasional bit of backing vocals. And so, Doug had spent his childhood wandering around backstage, largely unsupervised, on some of the biggest tours in the world, a snotty little kid with his finger up his nose. It was less raised by wolves and more raised by road crew, which was arguably far more dangerous.

He didn't have a conventional education, but he did learn a lot of things that money couldn't buy and therapy couldn't fix. Most people in his situation, spending their lives surrounded by music, would probably have come out of it being able to play the guitar like a rock god. Not Doug. In a weird twist of fate, he was tone deaf. Couldn't play a lick or hold a beat to save his life, and boy he'd tried. Wasn't even able to tune a guitar. It turned out, though, that he had other skills. He was prime tour-manager material. He could get you from A to B, from backstage to onstage, and from sober to stoned really well. He was the oil that made the wheels of the rock 'n' roll machine turn.

Tonight was a long way from being his first drug deal. Admittedly, he was usually on the requisition side of things instead of the supply, but still, it all counted. What was interesting about the whole situation was that he himself didn't do drugs. Didn't even drink. None of it did anything for him. He was like the Obelix character from those Asterix comics that one of Pink Floyd's crew had given him when he was a kid. Like he'd fallen into the magic potion from birth and so it had no effect on him. Doug was a facilitator for other people's delectations. The man who could get you anything and get you out of any jam. A large part of being able to do that was the ability to be morally flexible. Morals were like maths to Doug – something he hadn't encountered until remarkably late in life and which had never really stuck.

He reckoned he'd bought drugs in every country on earth that a music tour could conceivably pass through, and a few more besides. In the 1990s there'd been that warlord in Somalia who'd been a big fan of hair metal and had decided to throw himself the mother of all money-is-no-object birthday bashes. Bands who'd had their careers killed overnight by grunge held their noses and took the payday in a belated effort towards the pensions they forgot to take out. It had ended up being like a festival of has-beens who weren't long enough gone to be retro. The subsequent party had gone on for two days and, even by Doug's lofty standards, had been quite the Bacchanalia of debauchery. AA lost a lot of members that weekend. He'd watched a guy, who name-checked Jesus every chance he got, blow up a cow with a grenade launcher. A bass player who now sold holistic sweatpants or some such crap on the Shopping Channel had availed himself of an invitation to behead a guy. The guy in question had already been sentenced to death, so it wasn't like he was killing him – technically. At least, that's how he'd explained it. Having said that, he'd enjoyed it so much that the warlord had offered to sentence a few more for him.

People always said to Doug that he should write a book, and would invariably come back to him the following day to make sure he definitely wasn't going to. He wouldn't. Doug believed that what went on tour stayed on tour, and he'd been on tour his entire life. At least, he had been up until twelve years ago.

He'd been there the night Nigel Stay had died. Doug had sourced him the gear. He'd also driven him to hospital and tried to save the guy's life. He'd got no credit for that, though, did he? No, instead, people blamed him for the bad batch the kid took. Like it was the first time that had ever happened. Doug felt incredibly bitter about the whole thing. How was he responsible if a grown-up asked for something and then it went badly? He was a facilitator. Nothing more, nothing less. People drove their cars off cliffs every day – did you blame the mechanic?

Besides, people got way too precious about rock stars dying. Dying is what rock stars do. Have you seen what happens if they don't? Butter-selling shills, cheese-making Tories, or vegan racists. Better to burn out than to fade away. Cobain had it right. At least, Neil Young had, but the cover version had been spot on. Nobody wants to see their misspent youth selling timeshares in Florida.

Still, after all that, Doug couldn't get arrested. Suddenly he was everything that was wrong with rock 'n' roll. What people didn't realize was that he was the beating dark heart of it. Great music was made by arseholes. You want nice people, join a gospel choir. Amplification makes everything better and everyone worse.

Doug not being able to get arrested turned out to be a misconception, though, as evidenced by the Met booting in his door. The inquest had wanted someone to blame, and he fitted the bill. Luckily, while he'd never intended to write a book, he did have what he termed his 'rainy-day fund'. It wasn't actually a fund. It was a collection of photographs. Lots of photographs. The rich and powerful were just like everybody else, in that they wanted to party with rock stars. Doug, being the only one in the room with his wits about him, had taken the odd picture. One image in particular had made most of his legal troubles go away, thank you very much, Your Majesty. He'd taken the twelve months in minimum security as it was just long enough for the press to move on and forget about him. Besides, he'd needed somewhere to stay anyway, and everywhere that wasn't on tour felt like a prison, whether it was one or not.

When he got out, he'd found himself, for the first time in his life, a tour manager without a tour. He also discovered that he was in possession of an extremely non-transferable skill set. The odd bit of occasional work had come and gone, but nothing worth mentioning. Job centres were grim places that left him feeling broken. He often caressed his dear old dad's Colt .45 but he never had the balls to do it. So, life had gone on, despite his feelings on that matter. Each day a slightly shittier photocopy of the last. At least, that was until an ex-employer had rung to offer him a little unconventional work. To this day, he wasn't sure he'd made the right choice. He'd seen a whole lot of weird stuff in his time, but this was on a different level. He couldn't pretend it bothered him morally, because nothing did, but he wondered whether he'd live through it. It was like being on a never-ending long weekend with the Somali warlord, and you just had to hope the party didn't turn against you.

Still, at the end of it there lay the chance to get his old life back, and what wouldn't he give for that? He only ever slept well on the back of a moving bus, and something in his heart hurt every time he woke up in the same room, morning after morning. All of this he could write off as one strange long nightmare if he could just get back on the road again. Promises had been made. Normally, he had a hard and fast rule about never believing anything the talent said, but this time he'd had to make an exception. All of this was why he now found himself in the car park of a B&Q at midnight, continuing the latest twist in his drug-dealing career by becoming the supplier instead of the receiver.

He watched a vehicle as it pulled into the car park, stopped and flashed its lights twice. He flashed his in return and it drove towards him.

'Would you look at that?' he mused to the uninterested cat. 'Who brings a bloody people carrier to a drug deal, I ask you? Where's the sense of style?' As the people carrier pulled up ten feet in front of him, Doug shook his head and grabbed the holdall from the back seat. 'This should be straightforward. Stay here.'

He opened the door to get out and Kitty leaped over him, disappearing into the night.

'Fine,' he sighed. 'Have it your way.'

A guy with a head of floppy red hair in the style that went in and out with nineties Madchester got out of the front seat of the people carrier and regarded Doug. 'Y'all right there, pardner? Your cat ran off.'

'Don't worry about it,' said Doug. 'It's a blessing.'

People often assumed incorrectly that Doug was American. The reality was he'd never really lived anywhere, and his accent was an odd mishmash of whoever was around him. He was also not the most physically imposing of men. He was just over five feet in height, and not far off that in width. He'd shaved twice in his life and not cared for it on either occasion, so his beard was extensive to the point of covering a large part of his face and reaching down to his belly button. He only ever trimmed it when it started to interfere with his enjoyment of pizza. Doug considered personal hygiene to be similar to income tax, in that he knew about it but regarded it as something that happened to other people.

His heart sank when the back door of the people carrier opened and a second man got out.

'We said only you and me.'

'Relax,' said the floppy-haired one. 'He's a mate.'

'He's your mate, not mine.'

The other guy stepped forward. His hair was tightly cropped and he wore a suit, in contrast to the other guy's baggy jeans and T-shirt. Management. 'I'm everybody's mate.'

'I ain't here to make friends.'

'All right, then – I'm Spam's boss.'

'I didn't want to know his name and I don't want to know about your org chart.'

'Yeah, well, *my* boss wants to know about you. Wants to know where all this new merchandise is coming from. He says you're flooding the market, and that's bad for business.'

'I'm selling them to you.'

The man tilted his head and ran a finger along his jawline. 'Yeah, but it's not just us, is it? You're spreading it around. We know you've been supplying all these amateurs, and we don't like that.'

'Then you shouldn't have accepted the deal. So, are we doing this or am I getting back into my van and driving away?'

When the guy pulled out the gun Doug could see he had been expecting more of a reaction. He took it out in a way that looked as if he'd practised it a few times.

Instead, all Doug did was sigh. 'Believe me, you don't want to do that.'

'Are you threatening me?' asked the man, with a big artificially whitened grin.

'Warning,' Doug clarified.

This garnered a laugh from the man in the suit, who looked across at his colleague, who then joined in.

'Seriously,' said Doug, 'you really don't want to do this.'

The smile dropped from the suit's face, and he took a couple of steps towards Doug. 'Don't bother pretending you've got back-up. We've been watching. You're here alone. You should never let the other side pick the spot.'

'Good advice,' said Doug, with a roll of his eyes. 'Thanks for that.'

'You'd want to mind your manners. You're on our patch, and we want to know what some smart-arse Yank midget is doing here, bunging out gear at near cost price.'

'If it makes you feel better, I could charge you more.'

'Funny man.' He waved the gun in the direction of the people carrier. 'Get in the back.'

'Nope.'

'I wasn't asking.'

Doug puffed out his cheeks and folded his arms. He looked at the floppy-fringed dude. 'I want you to remember that I tried.'

'What's that supposed to—'

The suit swivelled round as, from the darkness behind him, came a sound he'd undoubtedly never heard in his life before. The closest thing Doug could liken it to was if a lion could roar and giggle at the same time.

'What the fuck was that?'

'Back-up.'

The suit swung the gun back in Doug's direction. 'Stop fucking about.'

'I came here to do a deal. You're the ones fucking about.'

'Anything happens to me, and I'm shooting you.'

'I wouldn't do that,' said Doug. 'I'm its lift home and you don't want to piss it off.'

Another growl-cum-giggle and Doug caught a hint of red eyes flashing in the darkness.

The suit whirled around wildly, attempting to point the gun in every direction at once.

'That's your cat,' said the ginger fringe. 'It's just his cat.'

'Nope,' said Doug. 'Wrong on two counts. One, you know that old pub joke about does your dog bite? Well, this ain't my cat. Belongs to the woman who thinks she's my boss.'

'Where the fuck is she?' hissed the suit.

'She's not exactly what you'd call a people person, which is why I'm here.'

The suit spun around again, convinced he'd heard movement to their right now.

'And two,' continued Doug, 'as your colleague has rightly surmised, it ain't just a cat.'

'Call it off,' ordered the suit.

'It doesn't listen to me. Nobody listens to me. If you'd listened to me, you wouldn't be in this predicament.'

'Shut up with—'

Doug ducked as the suit, convinced he'd identified the source of the noise, whipped the gun to the left and squeezed off three shots into the darkness.

'I think I got it!' he shouted excitedly.

'Nope,' said Doug as a mass of fur, claws and teeth flashed briefly across his vision from right to left, and then the suit was gone.

In the darkness, half a blood-curdling scream stopped abruptly, to be replaced by a wet munching noise.

The ginger mop-top crumpled wide-eyed and shaking to the ground beside the front wheel of his people carrier.

Doug walked over to where the man was now babbling to himself. He kicked his feet. 'Oi, Ham or whatever your name is, get it together.'

'I . . . There was . . . He . . .'

'Yeah, and if I was you, the main thing I'd be focusing on is that it wasn't you. Concentrate on that. Focus on getting out of here in one piece because fuck that guy. That guy got what was coming to him.'

The mop-top nodded. Somewhere in the darkness, the sound of bones being crunched between powerful teeth could be heard. It wasn't a sound that anyone would soon forget.

'Now – and for your sake, I really hope you've got the right answer to this question – did you bring the money?'

The man nodded furiously while his eyes scanned the darkness. He pulled a wad of fifty-pound notes from the front pocket of his jeans and held them out to Doug.

Doug bent down, sniffed at the wad, then reluctantly took it between two fingers. 'For Christ's sake, if you've got a propensity for pissing yourself, don't keep the money in your front pocket. That's just common decency.'

'Sorry.'

'Yeah, you're not the one who's going to have to hold a hairdryer to this mess. Is it all here?'

Mop-Top nodded.

'It'd better be.' Doug dropped the holdall on the ground in front of him. 'There, as agreed – two thousand pills.'

'No,' protested Mop-Top, 'you don't need to . . .'

'Oi,' snapped Doug, kicking the man's leg again, 'listen up.

This is important. I *do* need to.' He pointed at the bag. 'You're taking them, you're going back to your boss and you're telling him that they need to be gotten rid of fast – in Manchester, in the next week. It's sale-of-the-century time and everybody must get high. We clear?'

Mop-Top scanned the car park again as a noise came from a different part of the darkness.

'Focus,' snapped Doug, prompting the man to look back up at him. 'Are. We. Clear?'

His question was met with more nodding.

'Repeat it back to me.'

'All the pills have to go. Sell 'em all.'

'In Manchester,' added Doug.

'Yeah, yeah. In Manchester. No worries.'

'Good. Because I'll be coming to check,' said Doug, before pointing at the darkness, 'and I won't be alone.'

With that, Doug turned and headed back to his car.

'W-wait,' stuttered Mop-Top, just as Doug reached the front bumper. He turned back around.

Mop-Top pointed a finger about. 'Should I . . . Should I pick up the body?'

Doug shook his head. 'There won't be one.'

As he opened the car door, the figure of an ordinary domestic cat zipped out of the darkness and hopped nimbly into the passenger seat.

Doug sat down, tossed the damp wad of money onto the dashboard and wiped his hand on his jeans with a look of disgust.

Through the foggy windscreen, he could see Mop-Top

scrambling back into his people carrier and zooming away at the highest speed such a vehicle was capable of reaching.

Just as Doug turned the key in the ignition, his phone pinged with a text alert. 'Looks like it's going to be a busy night.'

He released the handbrake. On the seat beside him, he could hear the cat licking itself enthusiastically once again. 'And as for you, didn't anyone ever tell you not to play with your food?'

15

Bea was freaking out.

She fell through the doors of the club, and her shoe caught on something on her way out.

'You all right, love?' asked one of the bouncers as she stumbled onto Canal Street. It was thronged with people, but she managed to regain her footing and avoided crashing into anyone.

As the cold night air hit her, Bea realized that her jacket was still in the cloakroom. She didn't care. She needed to get out of there right now.

She was not all right. She was a long, long way from all right. She didn't know what the hell was happening to her, but the one thing she knew she definitely wasn't was all right.

She'd been standing at the bar chatting with a girl called Laura. Well, chatting wasn't the right word for it. They'd been taking it in turns to shout in the other's ear, but still. It was less about the words than the easy physical contact, the looks, the smiles. Bea wasn't that experienced in all of this, but it had felt as if it had been going really well. Up until the point when it hadn't.

Laura had a fluffy pixie hairstyle with an undercut. Bea knew that because she'd been thinking of getting one herself but had chickened out. Seeing it look so good on Laura made her regret the decision. It complimented Laura's flashing green eyes and elven features. She was sexy as hell and she seemed to be interested in Bea, which had come as a surprise. At first, she had thought Laura was just chatting, but then Laura's two friends had moved off and she had stayed. Bea's friends had moved off too, and then it had been just them, albeit with Yvette none-too-subtly watching them excitedly from the other side of the dance floor. She'd only known the girl for a couple of weeks, but she had a serious mother-hen vibe going on.

Laura hadn't asked her to dance – she'd said it wasn't her kind of thing – which was perfect for Bea. Being tall always made her feel awkward on the dance floor. She was athletic, sort of, but she'd never kidded herself that she was within an arse's roar of graceful.

She'd felt great. Elated. Maybe it had just been the pill kicking in, but it seemed like more than that. As a rule, she wasn't big into drugs. Joints made her sleepy, but the couple of times she'd taken ecstasy it had somehow got her out of her own way. Freed her from her inhibitions, so she didn't have to spend so much time worrying about what other people thought. That crappy little voice in the back of her mind could take a break.

Still, she and Laura had talked, and the contact levels had steadily grown. Unspoken lines had been crossed, signals received, all of that.

Bea had been shouting in Laura's ear asking if she wanted

another drink when it had happened. At first, as she'd withdrawn her hand, she'd thought Laura had been messing with her. All of a sudden there were flowers in her blonde hair that hadn't been there a second ago. Daisies.

Laura had touched her hair, grimacing at having found something unexpected, and pulled it out. They'd both looked down at the flowers in her hand in confusion, neither of them knowing what was happening.

Bea had looked around. Maybe someone else was messing with them? The rest of the club seemed to be carrying on with its night, unaware and unbothered by their existence.

Laura had leaned forward and shouted something in Bea's ear that she didn't catch. She'd cupped her hand around Laura's ear to respond and then pulled away in horror. As soon as she'd touched the other girl's hair, flowers had started sprouting from her fingertips. Buttercups this time. They were thick in Laura's hair and, as she'd stumbled backwards, pulling at the flowers in alarm, the look in her eyes had changed from confusion to anger.

Bea had looked down at her own hands, with no idea what the hell was happening. She'd reached out to touch Laura, but the other girl had pulled away. Her eyes had grown wide as she'd stared at Bea, confusion and fear etched across her face. People started looking at them, picking up on Laura's body language. Bea had taken a couple of steps back to lean against the bar but as soon as she'd touched the brass railing that ran the length of the counter, tendrils of ivy had sprung out of her hand and started to wrap themselves around it.

That was when she'd legged it. Straight for the door, moving as fast as possible among the throng, doing everything she could to avoid touching anyone.

Out in the cold air, she took off at a run. She didn't know or care in what direction she was headed. What mattered was that she was moving away from people. As she dodged groups of revellers, a man made a joking remark that she couldn't make out, accompanied by laughter from his friends. Behind her, Bea thought she might have heard someone calling her name, but she didn't look back. Her heart was pounding in her chest, her mouth was dry and her body felt like an electrical current was being sent through it. Every fibre of her being felt like it might be ripped asunder at any second.

Before she knew it, she found herself out in the road. The loud blare of a car horn made her spin around. A black taxi screeched to a halt a foot away from hitting her. Automatically, she threw out a hand and watched in horror as purple flowers spread across the bonnet of the car. Its engine cut out and as the driver, looking mystified, started to open the door, she ran again.

Another screech of tyres, but she didn't look around. She ran and she ran. She kept her eyes trained on the ground in front of her, whatever concentration she could muster focused on keeping herself upright and moving forward, while avoiding touching anyone or anything.

She only stopped when she turned a corner and found herself alone in an alley. In a bustling city, she had finally come across a pocket of almost unnatural silence.

She bent over. Her lungs were on fire now too. She studied her hands again, turning them over at arm's length. It was a trip.

That was it. A bad trip. Hallucinations. People on drugs experienced this kind of stuff all the time. Her brain was playing tricks on her. It made sense. The putrid smell from the large wheelie bin beside her seemed real enough though.

Bea tried to settle her breathing. She was having a panic attack or something, and she needed to regain control of herself. That was all.

Deep breaths. She'd be OK.

'Are you OK?'

It was a female voice she didn't recognize. She spun around to see a figure standing at the mouth of the alley.

'Who are you?' Bea asked.

'I'm here to help. I imagine you're having a pretty weird night.'

'You have no fucking idea.'

'Can I come towards you?'

'No. Sorry. I don't know you and . . .'

'No problem. That makes sense.'

'Sorry, I'm . . . I'm freaking out. Just give me a second.'

Bea turned to the wheelie bin and slowly reached her hand towards it. Her fingers were shaking, a fact that had little to do with the cold.

She placed a fingertip against the cold steel and held her breath.

Nothing happened.

She watched it for a couple of seconds.

Nothing continued to happen.

Bea let out a ragged breath and, with it, much of the tension left her body. Her heart started to slow.

'Are you OK?' asked the figure again.

'I'm fine,' said Bea. 'I think I just—'

She heard the noise first and turned to see the lid of the bin fly open and a holly bush emerge from it, racing towards the sky.

Bea turned around and threw up the contents of her stomach. At least she tried to.

All that came out were pink roses.

16

Today was a new day. Most importantly to Hannah, as she walked through the bright early morning sunshine towards the Northern Quarter, it was no longer yesterday. That had not been one of her best. She hadn't handled meeting DI Tom Sturgess for the first time in a couple of months very well, but that paled into insignificance compared to how badly she'd handled Cillian Blake appearing out of nowhere. She had spent most of the night lying awake, re-living events, and the memory was not improving with age. In her defence, it would have been hard to deal with even without some poor guy having just fallen out of the sky in front of her. The last thing she'd needed in that situation was her indie-rock teenage crush strolling into her life.

Yes, she'd known Cillian Blake was based around Manchester these days. How could she not? It had frequently been discussed on the Herschel's Garden forums. He was a lecturer in English at Man Met and he was running his drug charity, aimed at 'starting a new conversation' about the topic. He'd come out in favour of legalization a few years ago, and it had made all the newspapers in a weird combo of drugs-policy rehashing meets the much-loved 'where are they now' angle on an ex-rock star turned academic. So yes, of course she'd known they lived in the same city, but it was a big city. She'd resisted the temptation to check on the forum if anyone knew exactly where he lived, as there were lines you shouldn't cross. Besides, the forums were proving less and less appealing these days. Since relinquishing her role as an admin, after what was now euphemistically referred to as 'the schism', she hadn't been on there anywhere near as much. There were now, inevitably, two forums – the new one took the view that the band's songs being used to sell tampons and toilet cleaner was a great betrayal; the original Herschel's Garden forum considered it cringeworthy but forgivable and, all in all, best ignored.

The point was, today was a new day, and Hannah was going to bounce back. There were urgent matters that needed her immediate attention. They had to prove that whatever the hell had happened yesterday was nothing to do with Stella. Then, there was the other thing with Banecroft. She'd wondered if it was possible that he'd somehow imagined the whole episode where a mysterious figure had given him a few days to avoid being dragged to hell. It sounded far-fetched, but only if you hadn't lived Hannah's life for the last six months. These days, not only was anything possible, but almost everything was far too believable.

And so, first thing this morning she'd texted DI Sturgess to suggest they meet to exchange information at his earliest convenience, and that she would go to him. The reasons for this were twofold: first, she was being proactive, and second, not meeting at the offices of *The Stranger Times* meant that she wouldn't have to deal with Grace appearing constantly in her eyeline, the office manager's eyebrows dancing a Macarena of encouragement.

She'd also texted Reggie in the hope that he would accompany her, to smooth out the inevitable awkwardness, but she had yet to hear back. It had been a late night for them all, and he was a man who loved his sleep.

She'd expected Sturgess to suggest a breakfast place, but instead he'd sent her an address on Oldham Street, with instructions to press number three on the buzzer. It was the heart of Manchester's trendy Northern Quarter. In the evenings, it would be bursting at the seams with life. At eight twenty on a Friday morning, it was full of semi-conscious people making their way to their offices, often stepping over other semi-conscious people waking up from the night before. Recently, the district had been written up in the *Guardian* as the hippest area outside of London, which felt a little like a southern journalist had got on a train for the first time and was stunned to find that cocktails were available north of Watford. Hannah had lived in Manchester for less than a year, but something about the place made the chippiness seep into your bones remarkably fast.

Number ninety-eight Oldham Street had a battered blue door that had seen better days and at least one kicking-in. There was no signage to be seen, just a set of well-worn buzzers. She pressed number three and, after a wait of a few seconds, a distorted voice that could have been anyone from Sturgess to Mariah Carey said a few words.

'Hi,' responded Hannah, 'it's me. Hannah Willis.'

The voice that probably wasn't Mariah said something else, and the door buzzed open. Hannah pushed her way through. As welcoming committees went, the smell was quite something. It held hints of organic matter, with strong overtones of petrol and a redolence of curried chips. Hannah slammed the door firmly behind her, lest the smell escape into the wider world and go on an olfactory rampage.

The stairs were narrow, and the paintwork was so worn, chipped and stained, it was hard to tell which, if any, of the numerous regrettable shades of yellow in evidence was the original colour. The one thing you could say for the paint was that it was at least better than the carpet. The whole place was in dire need of a clean, and the water running down the walls in several places would come in handy should anyone ever decide to take up that Sisyphean challenge.

Hannah, being careful to not touch the walls, started to climb the stairs. She was working on the assumption that three on the buzzer meant she'd need the third floor. As she ascended, the stench of stale cigarettes was added to the heady olfactory mix. The stairs themselves managed simultaneously to feel sticky, creaky and about to collapse. Finally, there on the landing of the third floor, stood Tom Sturgess, looking rather awkward. In contrast to his surroundings, he was well-groomed and immaculate, possibly all the more so given said contrast.

'Welcome to my new office,' he announced.

'Oh,' said Hannah, as she climbed the last few steps. 'It's very, ehm . . .'

'Yes, isn't it just?'

He showed her into a room that was a mild improvement on what she'd seen so far, but wouldn't be featured in a double-page spread in *Interior Designer* any time soon. It was an office with several mismatched metal filing cabinets shoved anywhere there was space. The 'feature wall' hosted a hodgepodge of printed-out photographs and documents Blu-tacked to it. Sturgess noted her scanning it.

'If you could please avert your eyes – some of that is classified, and all that.'

Hannah raised her hands in mock surrender. 'Sorry, I'm developing the journalistic bad habit of being curious.'

'Be careful – you know what it does to cats.'

Two similarly cluttered desks were arranged opposite each other under what could laughably be called the room's window. It was about two feet by three, and featured an exciting view of the wall and a small window of an adjoining building. Sturgess pulled out a chair from behind one of the desks, directed Hannah to it, and then sat down behind what she was guessing was his desk.

'So,' began Hannah, once duly seated, 'can I just check – are you still a member of the police force?'

'I am,' confirmed Sturgess. 'Though I can see how you might be confused.' He leaned back in his chair. 'Seeing as I am now working full-time on what at least one of my bosses delights in referring to as "weirdy bollocks"—'

'Ah, I hate to be the one to break it to you, but it's not just that boss. The PCs at last night's incident referred to it as that too.'

'Excellent. It's always good to see the police lexicon being broadened. So yes, seeing as I am duly engaged in the aforementioned, it was decided that I would benefit from having my own off-site facility.' He waved his hands around expansively. 'As you can see, no expense was spared.'

'Congratulations.'

'Yes. Not every detective inspector has a radiator of his very own that he has to hit with a hammer to get heat out of. And we have an inexplicably good view of the record shop next door's toilet. I made eye contact with the proprietor last week while he was in there and he's now, thank God, installed a lace privacy curtain, but some things you can't unsee. In summary, my career is going from strength to strength.'

'Sorry,' said Hannah.

Sturgess brushed away her sympathy. 'To be honest, while I appreciate it doesn't look like it, this is a huge improvement. Out of sight is out of mind, and if the higher-ups don't want to deal with me, believe me, the feeling is more than mutual. As things are now, I've got the freedom to actually investigate what I need to investigate, and I have a wall I can stick stuff to, which you are not allowed to look at.'

'I'm not going to lie,' said Hannah with a smile, 'if we stay here much longer, I'm going to damage a muscle in my neck from trying not to turn my head.' She nodded down at the spare desk. 'Have you got company?'

'DS Wilkerson is here three days a week, sort of. There's also talk of a uniform getting seconded to me at some point. I assume they're just waiting for someone to piss off the chiefs enough to warrant it.' Sturgess sniffed. 'Sorry about the smell, by the way. I'd say you get used to it, but you really don't.'

'It is . . . something.'

'Oh yes, probably several somethings, all of which smell like they died a long time ago, and badly. I've brought it up with the landlord and, incredible as this sounds, he claims he can't smell anything, which is comfortably the most outrageous lie I've been told in my entire career in law enforcement. Speaking of which, we should probably get on with doing some of that.' He moved a couple of sheets of paper and consulted his notepad. 'I should ask, now that we're alone and you've had some time to reflect, is there anything about last night's incident you might have remembered that you didn't recall at the time?'

'Honestly,' said Hannah, looking him dead in the eye, 'both Stella and I were there entirely by accident. It had nothing to do with us. I hope you believe that because apparently the bloody Founders don't, which is why I'm so keen to find out what happened.'

It was only after she said this that Hannah belatedly remembered that you had to assume everything Sturgess heard was also known by the Founders, owing to what she internally referred to as 'his thing'. It was easier to call it that than the terrifying eyeball on a stalk that lived in his head, unbeknownst to him, and which was some form of parasitic spy – one that could kill him if he found out about it. More than almost anything, Hannah wished she didn't know about it.

Sturgess gave her an assessing look. 'Why do you care what the Founders think?'

Hannah shifted in her seat a little. 'You know. It's the principle of the thing.'

'Would now be a good time to ask you about a mysterious incident that happened on an abandoned golf course around about the time you departed and then dramatically returned to Manchester, and which was definitely not a meteor strike?'

'I don't know anything about that.'

He nodded. 'Sure. And you're all taking turns following the young girl who works in your office everywhere she goes because . . .'

Hannah decided to redirect in lieu of answering. 'Like I said, there's nothing I can tell you about the thing that happened to that poor guy yesterday, but we are happy to help you in any way we can.'

Sturgess nodded again, this time in resignation. 'OK. Well, the guy's name was Wayne Grainger, and he was a first-year film student. I met his distraught parents late last night, and from what little I could get out of them, they didn't seem to understand how he could possibly have ended up flying high over Manchester.'

'God, that must have been awful.'

Sturgess chewed his lip for a moment. 'Yeah, those talks are always horrible, and God help you if you get used to them. That'd mean you didn't feel anything any more. Still, the best thing I can do is get justice for their son.'

'So you think someone was responsible for this?' asked Hannah. 'Like, it wasn't an accident?'

'Yes and no.' Sturgess opened a couple of drawers in his desk before finding what he was looking for. 'Over the last few months there's been a steady increase in the number of incidents of what I guess we can call a paranormal nature.'

'Or you could go with "weirdy bollocks".'

'That I could,' conceded Sturgess. 'But while they've been inexplicable, there's been a pattern, we think.'

'Inexplicable?'

'A guy fell through a solid wall. Somebody – we're not one hundred per cent certain who – froze the toilets of a pub in Cheadle. I mean, like a solid block of ice, and then legged it out the window. A lot of attendees at an illegal rave claimed an invisible person was running around screaming and walloping into people.'

'We heard about that one too,' confirmed Hannah.

'I know. "Invisible man wrecks everyone's buzz" was quite the story.'

'That was Ox,' said Hannah.

'The point is,' continued Sturgess, 'we are fairly confident that those pretty dramatic incidents are extreme examples of something a lot more common. Individuals are experiencing bursts of something that they can't control, and we think it's connected somehow to these . . .'

Between his thumb and forefinger he held up a small plastic bag containing four blue tablets.

'Drugs,' said Hannah.

'Drugs,' confirmed Sturgess. 'In particular, methylenedioxymethamphetamine aka ecstasy, or molly if you're of an American persuasion.'

'But surely if ecstasy caused stuff like that to happen . . .' started Hannah.

'Exactly,' said Sturgess. 'We'd be aware of it a long time before now. It's not like the fine folk of Manchester just started taking Es. Lest we forget, this is the town that produced the musical powerhouse that is Bez from the Happy Mondays, who I've always suspected might have dabbled in narcotics on occasion.'

'And Bez has never flown or . . .'

'Or done any of that other stuff. Not that I'm aware of, no.'

Hannah pointed at the tablets in the bag. 'So, there's something different in these.'

Sturgess leaned back in his chair. 'You'd think so, wouldn't you? These particular ones, which we confirmed have been involved in a couple of these incidents at least, are, get this, sold under the name Merlins.'

'Subtle.'

'Exactly. Only I've had them tested, and the only thing unusual about them is the fact that there's nothing unusual about them. A lot of the time, when people think they're getting ecstasy, they're getting it mixed with caffeine or synthetic chemical substitutes or, frankly, whatever some dealers have lying about the place, but this stuff is pure ecstasy. There's nothing in it that should cause stuff like that to happen.'

'Oh.'

'Yeah,' said Sturgess, tossing the bag onto the desk. 'So, whatever it is, it's either one massive coincidence, something else that's somehow interacting with the drug, or there's something about these pills that science isn't capable of discerning. Still, they were on my radar before last night, poor Wayne Grainger had one in his pocket and a preliminary blood test confirmed that there was ecstasy in his bloodstream.'

'Didn't I see something in the paper about there being a big drug taskforce thing in Manchester at the moment?'

Sturgess pulled a face.

'What?' asked Hannah. 'Am I wrong?'

'No, there is. It's being run by a DI Sam Clarke, who is living proof that ineptitude is no barrier to career success.'

'Friend of yours, is he?'

'Oh, yeah, we get on great.' Sturgess nodded at the tablets. 'And I did try to get him interested in this, but he's not exactly one of life's creative thinkers. He and that taskforce are only interested in heroin and coke, because that's how you get on the news and, call me a cynic, but that's the main purpose of that taskforce. Make some headlines and get pictures of armed-response guys kicking in some doors and dragging people out in handcuffs.'

'Is that a bad thing?'

'Not necessarily, but it's just knocking 'em down so someone else can take their place. I mean, you could—'

He stopped as Hannah could hear a voice loudly shouting, 'One . . . two . . .'

'Oh no,' said Sturgess in a glum entreaty delivered to the ceiling.

'Three . . . four!'

On the next beat the entire room started to vibrate to enthusiastically delivered funk metal.

Sturgess grimaced and grabbed a pile of papers on his desk to stop them from falling off.

Hannah looked at him with raised eyebrows.

'Manc Funk Express,' he shouted over the din. 'Their practice room is downstairs.'

'Right,' Hannah shouted back. 'That's fun.'

'Yeah, in a makes-you-want-to-eat-your-own-ears kind of way.'

'They practise this early?'

'Yes,' said Sturgess with an exaggerated nod. 'They're very dedicated.'

'What?'

'Sorry,' he said even louder. 'I thought they wouldn't be in for a while. They just fired their drummer.'

Hannah pointed at the floor. 'They got a new one.'

Sturgess nodded. 'Fourth one. The bass player can't keep a beat, but his uncle owns the building.'

'Ahhhh,' said Hannah, because words didn't seem to be entirely possible.

As if on cue, the band stopped playing and the bass player started a solo.

'Nobody needs that much bass,' complained Sturgess after a few seconds.

'So,' said Hannah, hoping to take advantage of the relative reduction in volume, 'what's our next step?'

'Well,' said Sturgess, pointing to the pills, 'any chance you know someone we could ask about these?'

'I know just the man,' said Hannah, although the last bit of her sentence was lost as a drummer attempted to join back in with a bass player who wasn't willing to share the spotlight.

Hannah and Sturgess both winced as three different musicians went off in three different directions before eventually, and mercifully, they all stopped.

'Let's get out of here,' said Sturgess, as he stood up and grabbed his coat. 'Do you really think this guy will help us?'

'I'm not sure, but whatever he tells us, I can at least guarantee it'll be true.'

Book Bites Back

Greater Manchester Police are stumped after the disappearance of a van from outside the independent bookstore Tea Not Dinner Books in Ancoats. The vehicle, which belonged to the world's largest online retailer, was parked for five minutes while the driver took his weekly designated comfort break. Upon his return, the driver found nothing but the van's rear axle remaining. More peculiar is the fact that the shop now possesses a DIY section and a coffee bar that wasn't there yesterday.

This is not the first time that concerns have been raised about the shop's unusual expansion. Three weeks ago, the owner of a neighbouring vape shop reported his premises 'missing' after he arrived one morning to find it had vanished, but the bookshop was sporting a rather good sci-fi and fantasy section.

A representative from Manchester City Council said, 'We are launching a full investigation, as while there are probably loads of bookshops in the city, vapers having to walk almost twenty metres to find the next available vape shop is a serious risk to public safety.'

17

Hannah was finding it a challenging facial-expression situation to master. She was attempting to look both happy to be patiently waiting as DI Sturgess took a call while simultaneously not being overly interested in the details of said call.

They were standing outside a lighting shop on Commercial Street, having walked there from Sturgess's new office. The conversation between the pair had been relatively stilted, and notable for what was not being said.

'OK, Andrea,' Sturgess was saying. 'Keep me in the loop. Thanks.' Then he hung up and gave Hannah an apologetic smile. 'Sorry about that,' he said as they resumed walking. 'DS Wilkerson just accompanied the drugs squad on a raid of Wayne Grainger's dealer.'

'Oh,' said Hannah, 'that's exciting.'

'Not really. He got the drugs from a mate, who in turn got them from a postgrad student who has already confirmed she got them off the dark web. There's going to be no trail to follow, and she'll have picked them up from somewhere innocuous with no CCTV, like a park. This is the third arrest of a source for Merlins – all small-time amateurs who decided to dabble, none of whom met anyone in person and did the whole thing online. None of it leads us anywhere useful.'

'That's a pain,' sympathized Hannah as they negotiated their way around a trio of men who'd stopped for a chat, then entered a walkway between buildings.

'Welcome to the joys of modern policing. For every small advantage technology gives us, the criminals get it tenfold. It's almost like the entire internet is driven by criminals and everything else that happens is a by-product of that.'

'Stop it, or you're going to ruin my ability to enjoy cat memes.'

They emerged from the walkway with the Bridgewater Canal to their right.

Sturgess stared at two pissed-off-looking swans that were gliding past serenely. 'Not that I'm not enjoying the stroll, but where exactly are we heading?'

'Just up here,' said Hannah. 'Cogs is a bit unusual, but he's been an invaluable source.'

'And you're sure he won't mind talking to me?'

'No,' said Hannah, who hadn't stopped to consider that, 'I'm sure it'll be fine.' She added the last bit as much to herself as for his benefit, as uncertainty started to creep into her mind.

They walked under the railway bridge and re-emerged into the bright autumn sunshine. 'Call it a hunch,' said Sturgess, 'but is the guy we're meeting the fella on the boat, by any chance?'

In the middle of the canal sat the *Nail in the Wall*, Cogs's boat, moored in its usual position. On the bow, the man himself was standing with his back to them, naked from the waist up and wearing a bandana, engaged in what looked like tai chi or, at the very least, what someone who didn't actually know tai chi but who wanted to give it a go would be doing in lieu of it.

'What gave it away?' asked Hannah.

'It was less the tai chi,' admitted Sturgess, 'and more the fact that the bloke's dog appears to be doing it with him.'

As they got closer, Hannah could indeed see that Zeke the bulldog was sitting on the deck beside Cogs, practising his own canine equivalent of the discipline.

'About the dog,' said Hannah. 'His name is Zeke and he can talk.'

'I'm sorry, the dog can—'

'Talk, yes. But don't make a big thing out of it. He gets annoyed.'

'Right,' said Sturgess. 'Well, if the fact that he can talk comes up in conversation with the talking dog, I'll try not to mention it.'

'Good,' said Hannah, stepping onto the nearby pedestrian bridge to get her closer to the boat. 'Also, Cogs is cursed to only tell the truth, so we can totally trust what he says.'

'Now that really *is* handy. How do you get such a curse?'

'He got his from winding up a river goddess, I think.'

'I've often said the Greater Manchester Police should be recruiting more of them.'

Having now reached the middle of the bridge, Hannah leaned over the railings and started to pull up the rope with the bell attached to it. She spoke in a whisper. 'He's a little temperamental, so best let me do the talking.'

'The dog?'

'No. Cogs.'

'Right,' said Sturgess, nodding. 'Starting to wish I'd had my morning caffeine before we did this.'

Hannah rang the bell.

'Bugger off,' said Cogs, his back still to them. 'I'm aligning myself with the cosmic whatchamacallit.'

'Cogs, it's me.'

Without turning his head to look at them, Cogs changed position, extending his hands in both directions, as if he were trying to keep two invisible people from having a fight.

'I don't care who "me" is, darling,' he shouted, 'because *me* me is not open for business. I'm trying to achieve inner bloody peace here.'

'It's important.'

'It's always bloody important,' he snapped, sounding less and less at one with the universe. 'What people fail to understand is that "important" is a relative term. Whether or not I've taken a dump in three days is important to me, but I don't feel the need to share that information with everybody, do I?'

Cogs continued to ignore them, but Zeke had clearly grown bored of the tai chi, as he gave up and shuffled around to face them. He favoured Hannah with a canine smile, his tongue lolling out.

'Don't mind him,' said Zeke. 'He's in a mood because of the constipation.'

Beside her, Hannah heard Sturgess make a little gagging noise. Even being forewarned couldn't prepare you for some things.

Cogs threw up his hands and turned around to glower down at Zeke. 'What are you doing telling people my personal business like that?'

'Because maybe they'll go and get you some of them tablets.'

'I don't need any tablets. I'm going to resolve my issue in a natural manner.'

'Serves you right for eating all that steak,' said Zeke.

'You ate it too!' protested Cogs.

'Course I did – I'm a dog.'

'You only claim that when it suits you.'

'I've been having lovely shits personally, mate.'

'Oh, that is a low blow. Do you want to talk about what I had to do for you when you ate that rubber ball that time?'

Zeke, despite the limited range of facial expressions of a dog, still managed to look embarrassed. 'We said we were never going to discuss that again.'

'And I wasn't gonna, was I?' said Cogs, waving his hands about as he spoke. 'But apparently bowel movements, or the lack thereof, is now something we discuss with all and sundry. I mean . . .' Cogs gesticulated in the direction of the bridge then stopped himself. He looked at Hannah and then pointed at Sturgess, his facial expression suddenly very serious.

'Ehm . . . sweetheart, who is your friend there?'

Hannah had a sudden sinking feeling.

'This is . . . Tom.'

'And what does Tom do for a living?'

Hannah gave a tense smile. 'He is . . . He is a . . . OK, look – you don't need to worry about it . . . but, he is a police—'

Hannah didn't manage to finish her sentence before Cogs slammed his hands over his ears.

'Code red! Code red!'

He and Zeke both attempted to run in every direction at once.

'No,' pleaded Hannah, 'it's OK. Honestly. We just . . .'

Cogs dived below the deck before re-emerging wearing a pair of industrial ear protectors. Zeke, meanwhile, was gnawing at one of the ropes that was mooring the boat to the shore.

'Seriously, it's . . .' Hannah stopped and looked down. On what had been a previously clear morning, fog was suddenly starting to gather on the surface of the water. She ran down the far side of the bridge, waving her hands in a desperate attempt to attract Cogs's attention. 'Honestly, it's fine. He'll go away.'

The fog was rising rapidly now, so much so that she could barely see the boat, despite it sitting only a dozen or so feet away.

'I promise,' she cried forlornly. 'It is going to be . . .'

The fog that now enveloped her was of a pea-soup thickness, and she was scarcely able to make out her hand in front of her face.

'I am sorry,' she shouted into the all-consuming whiteness, her voice sounding oddly muffled.

She stood there for a full three minutes before the fog began to fade away. The *Nail in the Wall* was nowhere to be seen. As it continued to clear, she eventually saw DI Sturgess standing on the bridge, looking over at her.

He pointed down at the water. 'I don't think he wanted to talk to me.'

'Yes,' said Hannah, wishing the ground would open up and swallow her, 'I got that impression too.'

18

Before today, Hannah had been only dimly aware of the Peacock Lounge. She remembered reading an article, back when she'd first moved to Manchester, about some fringe religious group attempting to whip up a moral panic about it. Men were taking their clothes off! She recalled thinking that the newspaper had reported it with an appropriate degree of dismissive snarkiness. It helped that when the journalist had joined the four people who claimed they represented the 'silent moral majority' for a morning's protest, they'd been met with nothing but scorn from passers-by. The anti-protest had culminated in three homeless men performing an impromptu striptease that caused the four horsemen of the moral majority to call it quits.

Drag acts. Male strippers. Karaoke. That was what the Peacock Lounge offered. It wasn't exactly subtle. There were twenty-foot signs outside advertising it all. The venue was situated right beside the entertainment hub that was the Printworks. And if the Northern Quarter was where the indie kids hung out, then this was the area where people of all ages came to get smashed. There was plenty of currently dormant neon in evidence, and countless sandwich boards advertising drinks promotions that involved jugs and other inadvisably large receptacles.

When DI Sturgess had mentioned that he had a friend who might be able to help them, she hadn't expected they would end up here. Mind you, if the morning so far had proved anything, it was that she was no expert when it came to sources. The Cogs incident had been mortifyingly embarrassing. What was worse, Sturgess had even tried to warn her subtly, but she'd been too excited to show off that she had a source. *Ohhhh, look at me, I'm a proper journalist doing proper journalistic things who doesn't mind that you no longer want to go out for dinner.*

In hindsight, she could also see how someone who was cursed to tell only the truth might not want to have a chat with law enforcement. If Cogs had just let her explain. Instead, he'd taken the nuclear option and disappeared. Admittedly, it had been an impressive disappearing act, presumably achieved with the assistance of the river goddess or water spirit or whoever it was that Cogs had pissed off in the first place to end up trapped on water and unable to lie. She could only hope that Banecroft wouldn't find out, or she'd never live it down. The man was irritating enough when he didn't have such juicy fruit to throw.

Unsurprisingly for 11 a.m., the Peacock Lounge wasn't open properly, but there was still someone behind the counter in the reception area. Hannah and Sturgess walked in to find a young man with tightly cropped hair and remarkably good skin standing nervously behind the desk, while a middle-aged woman with a black bob and a Gucci bag stood on the other side glaring daggers at him.

'Hi,' said Sturgess. 'I'd like to have a word with Toni, please.'

'I was here first,' barked the woman, redirecting her daggers towards Sturgess.

'Nobody said you weren't,' replied Sturgess calmly, 'but I still need to tell the gentleman who I'm here to see.'

The man behind the counter gave Sturgess an awkward smile. 'She's on her way down.'

Sturgess thanked him, then he and Hannah took a seat over by the far wall. Just as they sat down, a tall woman made taller by an impressive beehive wig and six-inch heels strode through the open door behind the counter. Her right eye was covered with a diamond-encrusted eyepatch. She clocked Sturgess immediately and gave him a wave of a finely manicured hand, every finger of it adorned with rings.

'Hello, handsome. I was wondering when you were going to pop in.'

'Are you the manager?' barked the angry woman.

The woman with the eyepatch turned to her, looked her up and down, then gave her a smile that was notable for its lack of warmth compared to the one Sturgess had just received. 'Manager, owner, Svengali, proprietor, North West Business Awards 2023 entrepreneur of the year runner-up. I'm the whole package, sweetheart. Toni LeGrange at your service.'

'I wish to make a complaint.'

Toni leaned against the counter. 'Well, colour me shocked.' She placed a hand on the young man's shoulder. 'Ricardo, sweetheart, pop off and get yourself a cuppa, love.'

Now released, the young man bolted for the door behind reception as if fleeing an active shooter situation.

Toni regarded her nails carefully as she spoke. 'So, what, pray tell, is the nature of your complaint?'

'I was here last night on my sister's hen do—'

'And was the show not as advertised?'

'No,' said the woman. 'I mean, I don't know. We didn't get to see it all.'

Toni nodded. 'Was that because, by any chance, you and your drunk mates got thrown out?'

'It was outrageous,' said the woman loudly, slapping the counter with her hand to emphasize her point.

'Yes,' said Toni, in a saccharine voice, 'it was. Have you come back to apologize?'

'Apologize?' If the woman's voice went any higher, only dogs would have been able to take her complaint.

'That's right,' said Toni. 'For your appalling behaviour towards my staff.'

'How dare you! We did nothing except attempt to enjoy your tawdry little show.'

'Tawdry?' echoed Toni, raising her uncovered eyebrow archly. 'Well, somebody's education wasn't wasted.'

'You're not taking me seriously. Is there someone else I can talk to?'

Toni drew herself up fully. 'What? Do you mean the man of the house? It's been a few years, but I could probably still do the voice for you.'

'My husband knows someone very high up in the council.'

'Oh, fabulous,' said Toni. 'Tell him to sort out the potholes up on Shudehill, will ya, sweetie? They're diabolical. Pinged the suspension on the Lexus last week.'

'I have a serious complaint. You ruined my sister's hen do!'

'Did we?' said Toni. 'How about we look at the tape and see exactly who ruined what?'

This caused the woman to pause. 'Tape?'

'Oh, yes, darling,' said Toni in a sing-song voice, waving her hand about for emphasis, 'we have CCTV throughout the establishment for just this kind of eventuality.' She pointed at a large screen behind the counter. 'Give me two ticks and I can get it up here for you.'

'That won't be . . .' The woman cleared her throat. 'We were enjoying the show and your security was very heavy-handed.'

'Do you think so? Would you like to see the bit where your sainted sister rushed the stage and attempted to grab the genitalia of one of my performers? How do you think hubby's pal on the council would feel about sexual assault?'

The woman barked a humourless laugh. 'It's hardly that.'

'Really?' asked Toni. 'I'm pretty sure it is. I think her shouting "that is what one is supposed to look like" as she does it doesn't make it not sexual assault, and yes, we do have the audio. However,' she continued, batting her large eyelashes, 'I'm just a simple country gal unfamiliar with your big city ways, so if you'd like me to double-check, as luck would have it, the handsome gent sitting over in the corner is a detective inspector in the Greater Manchester Police. We could ask him. Yes, I can get the tape up on the big screen in two shakes of a lamb's tail.'

The complainant spun around, her previously red face now looking considerably paler.

Sturgess gave her a nod and a smile.

'That will not be necessary,' the woman sniped.

'Have it your way, love. And, not that I'm an expert, but speaking as a divorcée, if, days before her wedding, your sis is trying to grab the first cock she sees like it's the last lifeboat on the *Titanic*, I don't think her hen do not going to plan is her biggest issue. Now, would you like us to move on to the footage I have of you clearly assaulting one of my security guards with your fake-assed Gucci bag, or would you just like to fuckity-fuck off now?'

The woman stood there for a few seconds, her lips flapping open and closed as her brain overruled every response her mouth was coming up with. Eventually, she snatched her bag off the counter and stormed towards the door.

'That's what I thought,' said Toni.

As the woman pulled open the door, she whipped around, determined to have the last word. 'I am never coming here again!'

'You're damn right, sweetheart,' replied Toni, with a mock-theatrical series of finger snaps. 'Ya barred!'

Sturgess and Hannah got to their feet and watched through the window as the woman marched off down the street.

'I see you haven't lost your customer service skills,' observed Sturgess drily.

Toni giggled. 'Oh, love, I have to deal with one of those basic bitches a week. It's really helping me cut down on caffeine.' She smiled at Hannah. 'Present company excepted of course, but a lot of these straight women do not know how to behave in polite company. I mean, let your hair down, girls, but try to keep it in your pants. Come to that, keep your pants on. I've had one of my boys off sick for two weeks – some skank's knickers hit him in the face and gave him an eye infection.'

'Oh dear,' said Sturgess.

'Never mind all that,' said Toni, 'stop being rude and introduce me to the lady, Detective Inspector.'

'Sorry,' said Sturgess. 'Toni, this is Hannah; Hannah, Toni.'

'That's Toni with an i,' said Toni cheerfully, extending her hand to shake Hannah's warmly, 'because I will insist on making a disability into a brand. So,' she said, wiggling a finger between Hannah and Sturgess, 'I like this. What's going on here?'

Hannah tried very hard not to blush.

'Nothing,' said Sturgess, sounding equally embarrassed. 'Hannah is just assisting me with . . . helping with, I mean . . . We're doing an investigation together.'

Toni pursed her lips and rolled her eye to the heavens. 'Oh me, oh my, you breeders are straight up ridiculous. Say what you want about the gays, at least we know how to send out some clear signals.'

'OK, Toni,' said Sturgess, 'I'm here because—'

'Oh, shush,' said Toni, slapping him on the arm. 'We'll get to that.' She turned to Hannah. 'Has strong and silent here told you how we met?'

'There's no need to . . .'

'Yes,' insisted Toni, 'there is. It's a good story and you come out of it very bloody well.' She turned back to Hannah. 'This man is my hero. Seriously.'

'You're being a bit overdramatic.'

'Me?' said Toni, clutching her hand to her chest for effect and raising her voice. 'Being overdramatic? HOW. DARE. YOU!'

Hannah couldn't help but laugh.

Toni tapped her on the arm. 'I like this one. Good laugh on her.' She leaned forward. 'So, bit of backstory here. Before I was Toni with an i, I was Tony with a y – a brickie from Bolton leading one of those lives of quiet desperation you hear so much about. I'm sitting there one night, on the sofa with dear Doreen, my ex-wife, and we're watching *The Birdcage*. Have you seen it?'

'Yes,' said Hannah. 'Wonderful film.'

'Oh, yes. The sublime Nathan Lane and poor sweet Robin Williams, God rest his tortured soul. A tour de force and inspiration for this place. I mean, all right, we're mainly entertaining hellish hen dos, but we got voted the most popular club in the Gay Village a couple of years ago, despite not even being in the Village. They appreciate our services in keeping tourists out of gay spaces and we're taking one for the team.' Toni gave a mock salute. 'The first line in the gay defences. And hey, hen dos are people too. Well, mostly . . .' She stopped and looked at Hannah in confusion. 'Wait, what was I saying?'

'*The Birdcage*,' Hannah prompted.

'Right,' said Toni. 'So I had me one of those honest-to-God epiphanies. I turned to dearest Doreen and said, "I'm not happy."'

'Oh,' said Hannah, 'did she not take it well?'

'No,' said Toni. 'Well, I mean, she didn't at first, but she said later on she'd sort of always known. You can ask her yourself – she runs the box office upstairs. She's getting hitched next month to a lovely landscape gardener called Craig. I'm giving her away and I'll tell you something for nothing, she's not having her hen do here.' Toni leaned closer. 'Doreen was fine with it; other people, not so much. Now, back in the day, I was a big fella, so I could handle myself, but I got jumped by my brother, her brother and a couple of their mates, because our Keith has always been a cowardly little swine. They kicked seven kinds of shit out of me. Broken ribs, smashed ankle it's how I lost my eye.'

Hannah gasped and held her hand to her mouth. 'That's awful.'

'Yeah,' said Toni, 'not the best. Law enforcement wasn't overly keen to get involved either' – she nodded in Sturgess's direction – 'except for my white knight here. Fresh out of training, still on probation, when everyone else isn't bothered, he goes out on his own time and finds the CCTV footage to smash the alibi the four big brave boys had concocted, and I got my day in court. Only Keith got time and the whole process was a shit show, but . . .' Toni's eye was wet with tears now. 'This fella stayed by my side through the whole thing.' She patted Sturgess on the arm affectionately. 'He is one of the good ones.'

Sturgess cleared his throat. 'I don't know why you insist on telling people that story.'

'Oh, shut up,' said Toni. 'We both come out of it great. You're a bloody hero and I am the phoenix that rose from the ashes. Get this – Keith's wife came in and asked me for a loan a few months ago, can you believe that?'

Sturgess shook his head. 'No.'

'What's even more bizarre is I gave it to her. Their father is a piece of shit, but those kids are little sweethearts, and if Wendy wants to get her hairdressing qualifications, she's going to bloody well get 'em. I'll even give her a job after. I'm not giving up my family just because we've got an arsehole or two.'

Toni rapped her knuckles on the top of the counter. 'And here is me harping on.' She stood up and smoothed her hands over her hair. 'You are here, dear Detective Inspector, because I promised you a little something. *Un momento, señor.*'

She turned and started tapping away at the computer behind the desk.

Sturgess looked at Hannah. 'I asked Toni to keep an eye out for anything unusual.'

'Poor choice of words,' warbled Toni.

'Shit,' said Sturgess, looking mortified. 'Sorry.'

Toni cackled. 'You're too easy.' She glanced up at Hannah. 'Anyway, I told him we get unusual all the bloody time. But he said I'd know what he meant if it happened and, last Sunday, it did. Apologies for not texting sooner, but I was away, and they don't like to bother me when I'm having one of my two weekends off a year.' With a flourish, she walloped a couple of keys on the keyboard. 'Let me pop it up on the big screen. Don't worry, nobody can see it from outside.'

After a second, the screen behind the counter was filled with the image of a large room with a stage at its centre. Groups of people sat around in cabaret-style seating – fours, sixes, the occasional eight around a table, watching a trio of drag acts performing 'Lady Marmalade', complete with scantily clad dancers.

'Yes,' trilled Toni, 'we really are that obvious. Give the people what they want.'

'What am I looking for here?' asked Sturgess.

'Patience, Tommy dearest. As a great man once said, you'll know it when you see it.'

'OK, but just—' Sturgess cut himself off as a red-headed woman stood up from one of the tables and stumbled towards the back of the room. They watched in silence as she staggered and placed her hand on the back of the chair belonging to a woman from another group. She stood there, trying to breathe, then looked as shocked as everyone else when the back of the chair she was leaning on burst into flames.

Patrons started to scatter and a couple of members of staff rushed forward, guiding people away from the blaze, but Hannah's eyes remained fixed on the redhead, who was looking at her own hand as if she'd never seen it before in her life.

'I take it this is—' started Toni.

'Yes,' said Sturgess.

'I figured.'

They continued to watch as a member of staff rushed onscreen with a fire extinguisher to put out the blaze, then the footage froze.

'I would go for a fiery-redhead quip normally,' said Toni, 'but that poor girl looked horrified, didn't she?'

'Yes,' agreed Hannah.

'By the way, I think it's safe to assume she was also responsible for the fire damage we suffered in one of our cubicles about five minutes later. We don't have any cameras in there because – well, the obvious reason.'

'Sure,' agreed Sturgess. 'Do you get many people taking ecstasy here?'

Toni arched an eyebrow. 'Is that an official question?'

'Of course not.'

'Just checking. And honestly, not a lot. Probably less than most places. My security is pretty hot on it. Bar anything else, high people aren't drinking and I'm running a business here. Glasses of tap water doth butter no parsnips.'

Sturgess pointed at the frozen image on the screen. 'That group . . .'

Toni nodded. 'I spoke to the staff after, when you mentioned it. They said they hadn't seen anything but there had been a lot of high spirits and hugging.'

Sturgess bobbed his head, lost in thought. 'It would be a massive help if we could speak to that woman.'

Toni didn't say anything, just smiled.

Sturgess looked at her excitedly. 'You're kidding?'

She gave a coquettish grin. 'How good do I look to you right now?'

'Spectacular. Toni?'

She turned to Hannah. 'He is a gem, but he does need to learn a little in the foreplay department.'

'Don't they all,' muttered Hannah.

Toni laughed. 'Seriously, I bloody love her,' she said to Sturgess before turning back to Hannah. 'I'd offer you free tickets, but I like you too much. You deserve better than this place.'

'Toni?' pressed Sturgess, failing to keep the irritation from his voice.

Toni picked up an envelope from beside the PC and held it up. 'Took me absolutely ages this, scanning the CCTV and then credit-card receipts. Finally got her paying by card at the bar.' She proffered the envelope to Sturgess, only to pull it away as he tried to snatch it. 'Uh-uh, you know I'd do anything for you, my sweet Tommy, but if someone could clarify with the fire inspector that this incident doesn't need to be followed up . . .'

'Consider it done.'

She handed him the envelope.

Sturgess opened it, read what was inside then slipped it into the inside pocket of his suit jacket.

'Toni, you are one in a million.'

'Oh, at least,' she responded. 'Now, if you'd like to make it up to me, how about you take this lovely lady out to lunch because none of us are getting any younger and I've got some spectacular hats that need a day out.'

19

'Found it!'

Stella stood there, looking down at the plain wooden cross. She, Ox and Banecroft had split up to try to find the plot, Southern Cemetery being exceedingly large. They'd spent the first half-hour wandering around on the old side, before crossing over Nell Lane into the new part. Logically, you'd think that all the newer graves would be here, but there were several different areas dotted around both sides where piles of freshly dug earth were in evidence. Several religions had their own sections, there were family plots, and even an environmentally friendly meadow, for people who wanted the planet to live on after they'd gone.

It was only Stella's second ever visit to a graveyard, and the first in daytime, and she was finding the whole experience rather depressing. She knew they weren't supposed to be cheerful places for the most obvious of obvious reasons, but she reckoned the visit was hitting her in a different way than it did most people.

Seeing gravestone after gravestone, listing years of births and deaths, names of loved ones left behind – the fundamentals of life. All those simple facts were missing from her own. Here lies Stella, no second name, no idea when or where she was born, nobody to leave behind. To be fair, this particular grave in front of her didn't yet bear those details either. All the newer graves were without stones. Banecroft had mentioned something about having to wait six months before a gravestone could be erected, hence the temporary wooden crosses.

Ox walked up to her, gasping for breath. 'Damn it, you were strolling about while I was running, and you still found it first.'

'That was running?'

'Yeah,' said Ox, sounding slightly offended. 'I mean, not *running* running, but I was . . . I'm trying to get . . .' He swung his arms a bit to make a point he lost faith in halfway through. 'D'ya know what, never mind.'

Stella held up her phone. 'There's a searchable map online.'

Ox looked around. 'Ah right, I guess that does make sense.'

He turned his attention to the cross. 'So, this is him, then – William Ignatius Campbell.'

'Looks like it.'

The grave had no flowers on it. Not even grass. It was just loose soil.

Stella squinted into the distance. 'Where's Banecroft?'

'Dunno, but the way he was moving, I suspect he's gone for a wee.'

'Do graveyards normally have toilets?'

'Nope.'

'Oh,' said Stella, before thinking it through. 'Oh!'

'Yeah. I'm sure he'll go behind a tree, at a respectful distance. Even Banecroft isn't going to wazz on somebody's grave. Well, probably not.'

'Thanks for that image, though,' said Stella.

'So,' said Ox, lowering his voice despite nobody being near them, 'do you have any idea what we've been doing all day?'

'As in?'

'As in,' continued Ox, 'sifting through the entirely unremarkable remains of this poor sod's life. Banecroft comes in last night, straight from the clink, and with no explanation starts barking about this guy. I don't get it.'

Ox did have a point. William Ignatius Campbell had died of a heart attack four weeks previously while cycling home from work. Born and raised in Glasgow, he'd come to Manchester to study at university and had stayed on after graduating. They'd spoken to the doctor who had certified his death, as well as to his rather confused boss at his old job (as an actuary), who was deeply suspicious as to why anyone was interested. They'd also met with the organizer of his board-gaming group, which had been the only evidence they'd found of a social life. The lady had been more embarrassed than anything, feeling guilty that the group didn't really know anything about one of their oldest members, save that he drank bitter, in moderation, and which board games he enjoyed.

They'd visited his former house, too; it was up for sale with the proceeds going to his only surviving relative, his mother, who was in a home just outside Glasgow suffering from what sounded like rather severe dementia. They'd managed to convince the estate agent they were cash buyers with money to burn and had been shown around by a guy called Jase, who spent a lot of time looking at his phone. The house had been incredibly ordinary. The furniture was still in place, but Jase had been quick to point out that they could get rid of it if they liked. It had a basic functionality, as if it belonged to someone who knew a coffee table was necessary, but also knew that nobody apart from them would be seeing it.

Similarly, the results of Banecroft calling in a favour and having William Ignatius Campbell's bank records and so on checked revealed an utterly unremarkable life. He was paid well, and was relatively frugal in his expenditure, with the exception of paying a lot for his mother's care. His will had left everything towards continuing to provide for her as long as required, with the remainder to be split between a dog shelter, a refugee charity and a mix of other charitable organizations scattered between Manchester and Glasgow.

All this leg work had revealed was an ordinary bloke who liked playing Carcassonne, Risk, and a bit of something called Bolt Action, which was a Second World War tabletop battle re-enactment game. He'd cycled everywhere, was 'popular' at work – in the sense that he was a quiet guy who did his job – and nobody seemed to have a bad word to say against him. The digging around in his online presence revealed nothing of any interest except the fact that he seemed to really dislike the historical documentaries presented by the comedian Al Murray. His life was not only quiet but also rather depressingly empty.

Stella shrugged. 'I've got no idea what we're doing,' she confessed, 'but Banecroft seems very wound up about it.'

'Yeah,' agreed Ox. 'I mean, I know this is a bit "this water is rather wet", but he's been in a right strop all morning. We haven't found anything, but he won't tell us what we're looking for.'

Stella spotted their boss in the distance. 'Here he comes.' She waved at him and pointed at the grave. He proceeded to stomp in their direction.

'Do you think after this,' said Ox, 'we can call it a day? I mean, it's Friday, it's the closest we get to a slow day any more and I've got some stuff I want to catch up on.'

'Why are you asking me?' said Stella. 'I don't know any more about what goes on in Banecroft's head than you do.'

'Yeah, but you're his favourite.'

Stella shook her head in disbelief. 'Are you still annoyed about the car?'

'I am a bit, yeah,' said Ox, folding his arms. 'I mean, when he asked me if I've got a full licence, I thought I might finally get to drive his Jag – instead, you drive us everywhere and he says if any cops stop us, we're to swap seats. It's a bit rich.'

'Don't blame me. I didn't want to use the day as a driving lesson. I've got him barking instructions from the back seat and you making various "oh" and "ah" noises from the passenger seat every time I try to change gear.'

'Just saying, you don't even have a provisional licence.'

'I know,' snapped Stella. 'It's just one of the many, many fun perks of not actually existing. Thanks for bringing it up, though.'

Ox turned and looked sheepish. 'Sorry, I didn't . . . I just—'

The apology hadn't got off the ground before Banecroft reached them. 'This him?'

'Yes,' confirmed Stella.

Banecroft stood there and stared at the grave. 'Right. Anyone notice anything?'

Stella and Ox looked at each other warily. Banecroft's little pop quizzes always had a point to them and, more often than not, the point was that you were an idiot.

'Ehm . . .' said Ox, 'the details on the cross thing are consistent with what we know?'

'Yes,' said Banecroft. 'Mainly that he's dead. Anything else?'

He looked at both of them pointedly.

Stella couldn't think of anything, and she resisted the urge to guess, as that always made things worse. Eventually, after a torturous pause, Banecroft shook his head in disappointment. 'Old Willy, God rest him, has been dead for a month . . .'

They both nodded, and Stella tried and failed to determine the shoe that was about to drop.

Banecroft poked at the loose earth with the toe of his shoe. 'So why does this grave still look freshly dug?'

'Can I help you?'

Stella spun around. She'd been so focused on trying and failing to answer Banecroft's question that she hadn't noticed the shaven-headed woman in blue dungarees who had walked up behind them.

'Yes,' said Banecroft. 'Do you work here?'

The woman nodded.

'And what can you tell me about this grave?'

She eyed him warily. 'What do you mean?'

'I think you know exactly what I mean.'

'You family?'

'Worse,' said Banecroft. 'Press.'

The woman whipped around and threw her hands up in the air. 'Oh, great, just great. This is absolutely great!'

The trio exchanged looks but said nothing.

'Who tipped you off? Was it Greg?'

'I can't say,' said Banecroft.

'I bet it was Noel?' she ventured, addressing the universe as much as Banecroft. 'Could be any of them, to be fair. This is the old boys' club in action, that's what this is. Oh, yeah, a woman can't be a gravedigger. It's the glass whatchamacallit?'

'Ceiling?' offered Stella.

'Yeah,' she responded, 'but, y'know, six feet under ground. The glass earth? Permafrost? Crust? There should be a good word for it. Course, now they'll make it look like all of this is my fault.'

'In which case,' said Banecroft, 'why don't you give us your version of events.'

'Events?' she echoed. 'Events? There was no event. I dug that grave, one of my first, all good and proper. I remember it got filled in fast as there wasn't much of a service. All done by the book, though, and then, Monday, I come into work and I notice the bloody thing has been disturbed.'

'What?' said Ox.

She paused. 'You knew that, didn't you?'

'Of course we did,' said Banecroft, shooting a look at Ox. 'And how was that allowed to happen?'

'Allowed?' said the woman, looking outraged. 'How are we supposed to stop it? We don't have twenty-four-hour security. It's a graveyard. Somebody comes in here and does that, what can I do? I brought it up at the regional meeting on Tuesday and they said to ignore it. Got all shifty about it if you ask me. I mean, it's not right, is it? Grave-robbing. Lowest of the low. It happens more than you'd think. There was a thing online I found. You've got people selling real skulls on some of these websites. Not right, is it?'

'No,' said Ox, in an effort to contribute.

'No,' she confirmed. 'And the looks between them at the meeting. I think it happens a lot more than anyone lets on and they're just not saying. Y'know – wink, wink, nudge, nudge. Ask-me-no-questions-and-I'll-tell-you-no-lies sort of thing. Thing is, I'm a questioner, me. Always have been.'

'But you didn't get any answers?'

'No,' she said. 'Not from them. Just kept saying it was probably moles. Moles, I tell you! I wasn't going to swallow that nonsense.'

'So, you took steps?' said Banecroft.

'I did,' she confirmed. 'I ignored what they said and dug the thing up. On my own time, mind you. Stayed late and did it Tuesday evening.' She looked nervous at admitting to this. 'I know that's against the rules, but I had to know.'

Banecroft nodded. 'Quite right. And what did you find? Had something been taken?'

'Something? No. Someone. The bloody coffin was empty.'

They all looked down at the grave again.

Stella pointed at it. 'So there's . . .'

'Just an empty coffin down there. I called the police, and they came around, eventually. Didn't take it serious enough though, if you ask me. Took some notes but they said, "Well, we've got missing people who are still alive, but if any dead ones show up, we'll let you know." Then Mr Douglas rings me, screaming down the phone, tells me to fill it in and say nothing to no one. He's coming over Monday. Reckon I'm for the chop.' She looked off into the distance, her eyes suddenly wet. 'I bloody love this job and all. Outside. Peace and quiet. You get to fulfil an important role in providing people with a dignified repose and all that. Plus, you get to use a mini digger, and those things are the dog's bollocks.'

'I'm sure,' said Banecroft. 'So, the police are doing nothing about this?'

The gravedigger shrugged. 'Not as far as I can see. I even said to them, you want to ask that sniffy fella.'

Banecroft furrowed his brow. 'Excuse me?'

She dipped her head and looked around. 'Sniffy fella. That's what we call him. He goes around all the Manchester graveyards, every bloody day. Proper weirdo.'

'Could he just be a taphophile?'

The woman reared back and gave Banecroft a horrified look. 'Whoa, whoa! I didn't say that. Don't put that in the paper. I mean, he's weird, but . . .' She made a retching face.

'It just means someone who is interested in cemeteries.'

'Oh . . .' mused the woman. 'Them people. We get lots of them. Second-largest graveyard in Europe. We're like Woodstock for those nut— I mean, enthusiasts. Doing rubbings of gravestones and all that. They're mostly harmless. Weird. But harmless.'

'What makes this man different?'

'He's a freakish-looking fella. Weird head. Tall. Gangly.'

'So far,' said Ox, 'this just sounds like that comedian Stephen Merchant.'

'No,' said the gravedigger. 'I mean, real creepy, like.'

'Again,' said Ox, 'co-creator of *The Office*, Stephen Merchant.'

'Does this Stephen Merchant fella go around sniffing . . . like, proper sniffing graves?'

'No, I do not believe so.'

'Probably not him, then,' said the woman. 'It's not natural, though, is it? Not natural. I said about him to the police, but the fella said sniffing wasn't against the law.'

'And how would we find this individual?' asked Banecroft.

'Find him?' she said. 'You only just missed him.'

Banecroft looked around. 'He was here?'

'Yeah,' she said. 'He's here every day. Aren't you listening? Come back tomorrow and you'll catch him.'

Banecroft clapped his hands. 'Excellent.'

'I suppose this means we're working the weekend, then?' asked Ox glumly.

'Don't think of it as working,' said Banecroft, slapping him on the back. 'For a start, you won't be getting paid for it.'

20

Reggie patted Hannah on the shoulder encouragingly. 'Look at it this way, my dear – this can't possibly go any worse than your first attempt at information-gathering.'

'Thanks,' responded Hannah. 'That's really helpful, Reginald. Remind me to let you do all my pep talks from now on.'

He wasn't wrong, though. After the disaster that was trying to ask Cogs for information, Hannah had realized that she did have a Plan B. Seeing as Plan A had gone so monumentally wrong, she'd decided to keep it largely to herself. The reasons for this were twofold. First, if the Cogs incident had proved anything, it was that bringing a detective inspector from the Greater Manchester Police with you when you were endeavouring to acquire information from sources might not be the best idea. Second, if this plan was to go as badly as the first, she'd really rather that DI Sturgess wasn't there to witness it. There was only so much humiliation even Hannah could take in a day. She did, however, bring Reggie along, both for moral support and the very practical reason that'd he'd been here previously.

She stepped through the doors with as much confidence as she could muster, and Reggie followed behind her. Friday lunchtime was a busy time for pubs – well, most pubs. The Kanky's Rest wasn't exactly doing a roaring trade. She'd never been here before, but it tallied with the description Reggie had given her: opaque windows and guttering candles dotted around the tables in defiance of the time of day; a faint aroma of cigarette smoke, despite a smoking ban having been in place for nearly a couple of decades now. Everything in the room looked as if it predated it, including the clientele.

What atmosphere there was took a noticeable dip when Hannah walked in. It was like something from a movie. Everyone in the room stopped talking and stared at her as she stood in the doorway. The man in a remarkably thick overcoat sitting in the corner even stopped the animated conversation he'd been having with himself. A red-headed woman laconically launched dart after dart directly into the bullseye of the pub's well-worn dartboard, despite her eyes being fixed on Hannah.

Reggie spoke under his breath as he fixed a smile to his face. 'I think word might have got around about you.'

'Oh God.'

Hannah was relieved when the familiar figure of John Mór, wearing a black sleeveless T-shirt, appeared behind the bar at the end of the room. 'All right, you lot, you can cut out the stranger-walks-into-a bar-in-a-western routine.'

The patrons, with a low level of grumbling permeating the air, all resumed their activities. The two women who'd been knitting the two sides of a garment that looked as if it was intended for something with enough limbs to qualify as a member of the octopus family, and enough heads probably not to get invited to any family reunions, went back to clacking their needles at a frightening speed.

Reggie nudged Hannah in the back. 'Move,' he urged. 'You remember how walking works.'

'Right.'

She started to make her way down the room towards John Mór, trying to smile at everyone as she did so. Nobody smiled back. Hannah was aware that she was a chronic people-pleaser, and she was finding this experience extremely unsettling. She was ninety per cent certain one of the sweet old lady knitters hissed the word 'narc' as she passed.

John Mór stood and watched them approach, slowly giving the bar a clean it didn't need with a dirty rag that wouldn't do the job. 'Afternoon, Ms Willis. Reggie.'

The pair nodded their hellos. 'I get the feeling I'm not terribly popular,' said Hannah.

'You'd be right. News of your visit to Cogs has got around.'

A woman with long black hair and impossibly long nails was standing at the bar, a half of bitter on the counter in front of her. Hannah looked her way and wished she hadn't. The woman's stare was of the kind that could skewer you to a wall.

Hannah turned back to Mór. 'I'm really sorry,' she apologized. 'I didn't know. DI Sturgess is a good guy. He's helped us out a lot in the past.'

She glanced back at the space the black-haired woman had been occupying to find it suddenly empty, with no evidence of where its erstwhile inhabitant had disappeared to.

'That's as maybe,' said John Mór, 'but, respectfully, you ain't the Folk. To us, the police are just a weapon of the Founders, used to keep us in our place.'

'OK, but DI Sturgess isn't . . .' Hannah didn't finish the thought. She threw a look at Reggie beside her and could tell he was thinking the same thing. Sturgess might be trustworthy, but the same couldn't be said for whatever the hell that thing living in his head was. 'I'm really sorry,' she finished weakly. 'If you can get a message to Cogs, please tell him I'm sorry.'

'Ah, don't worry about it. He'll calm down, eventually. He was about due to find a new spot soon, anyway.'

Hannah tipped her head to the room behind her. 'Am I going to be *persona non grata* with the rest of the Folk now, too?'

'Nah,' said John Mór, before raising his voice pointedly, 'I'm sure some of these folks will remember that *The Stranger Times* has been doing a good job for us recently, and that you saved my life not two months ago.'

'The crossword is very hit and miss,' said the redhead in a surprising Spanish accent, without looking up from tossing nothing but bullseyes.

'We are addressing that,' said Hannah quickly.

'It has been much better in the last few weeks,' confirmed Reggie, 'and that is this woman's fault. I mean, it's thanks to her.'

John Mór ran his hand over his immense beard that stretched all the way down to his navel. 'I'd have focused more on the saving-my-life bit personally, but sure, go with the crossword thing if you like.'

Hannah lowered her voice and leaned in. 'I wouldn't say I saved your life.'

'You don't have to. I just did. Now, I take it you haven't come here just to soak up the ambience.'

'No,' confirmed Hannah.

He nodded. 'I'll save you a bit of time, then. That poor lad who fell yesterday – he wasn't one of us.'

Hannah scrunched up her brow. 'When you say "one of us"?'

'Most of the Folk is made up of clans, you see. Sort of like families, only a lot bigger.' Both Hannah and Reggie leaned in further to hear him better as his sonorous voice dropped yet lower. 'As part of the Accord, the peace agreement between us and the Founders, each clan has to pay its part of the Cost . . .'

Hannah nodded; she knew about this. The Founders remained immortal by being rejuvenated by the very life force of members of the Folk. In the past, that had involved the Folk being hunted down and killed for it; now it involved some method of extraction she didn't understand.

'So, as a part of the deal, every clan keeps track of its members.'

'And this boy,' clarified Reggie, 'wasn't a member of any of the clans.'

'That's right,' confirmed John Mór.

'But I don't understand,' said Hannah. 'He showed obvious magical abilities. I mean, he couldn't control them but . . .'

John Mór nodded. 'It's not unheard of. While generally, members of the Folk have what I'd guess you'd call natural abilities with magic, the odd ordinary person can develop them too. They refer to them as anomalies.'

'And these anomalies – is it possible that drugs could cause these abilities to appear?'

John Mór shook his head. 'I shouldn't think so. Never heard of anything like that before.'

'It's just,' said Hannah, 'there's been quite a lot of incidents recently – of people apparently taking something, and then powers suddenly manifesting themselves.'

John Mór cracked his knuckles and circled his head around his neck. 'That would be a new one on me. It's not how it works. Folk like a drink or whatever else as much as ordinary people – if not more so – and powers, or whatever you want to call 'em, don't start popping up when they're off their faces. It takes most people an awful lot of training to get close to being able to use their power.'

'If it isn't a terribly rude question,' began Reggie, 'what's your power?'

John Mór favoured him with a smile. 'I mix a mean martini.' He looked up as the doors at the far end of the room opened and a quartet of suited men entered the pub, chatting happily. 'Oh, lunch-time rush.'

'I don't suppose,' said Hannah, aware that she was very probably pushing her luck, 'that there's anyone who could tell us a bit more about anomalies?'

'Funny you should mention that,' he said, his smile broadening. 'The Sisters Divine want to see you. Eleven o'clock, Sunday morning.'

'Who are—'

'I'll let them explain,' said John Mór. 'Good news, though – not only will they not mind you bringing your policeman friend with you, they're insisting on it.'

21

'Signal. Manoeuvre. Signal. Manoeuvre!'

As Banecroft's Jag swung into the small car park beside the offices of *The Stranger Times*, Stella redoubled her grip on the steering wheel. 'For the last time,' she yelled over her shoulder, in the direction of the back seat, 'stop shouting those two words over and over again. They've lost all meaning.'

'You learn through repetition,' said Banecroft.

'That means that people learn by practising, not by you repeating something ad nauseam.'

'You say potato, I say tomato. Now, reverse-park the car into the garage.'

'You say tomato, I say park your own bloody car.'

Stella turned off the engine and tossed the keys into the back seat before shouldering open the driver's door and stomping off towards the main doors.

Ox turned around and looked at Banecroft.

'I can park it if you like.'

'Good God, no. I wouldn't trust you to do that.'

'Right,' said Ox, 'but you've had an unlicensed teenager driving it all day.'

'Yes,' said Banecroft, 'and I think she's coming along well, don't you? In my experience, people learn a lot quicker under pressure. Lumps of coal turning into diamonds, et cetera.'

Ox shook his head. 'Unbelievable. Absolutely unbelievable.'

He exited the car and followed Stella.

'Dear oh dear,' muttered Banecroft as he clambered over the centre console and into the driver's seat, 'why is everyone around here so dramatic? I mean . . .'

He broke off at the sight of the figure standing by the main doors.

As a matter of principle, he took his time parking the car then slowly walked towards the entrance of the former church that was now both his work and home. 'Haven't you got anything better to do than stand around on street corners?'

The Pilgrim favoured him with his dentist's nightmare of a grin. 'Mr Banecroft, I just wanted to see how you were getting along. After all, the clock is ticking. Tick-tock. Tick-tock.'

'Yes, thank you, I know how time works.'

The Pilgrim withdrew a pocket watch from inside his coat and consulted it. 'I make it you have precisely one hundred and one hours left until you are mine.' His eyes lit up on the word 'mine', or at least somehow the darkness within them shone.

'What exactly is it you have against me?'

The Pilgrim tucked his watch back in his coat pocket before answering. 'You remind me of every arrogant son of a bitch I had to deal with in my life, and I shall rejoice in seeing you punished for your sins.'

'It's nice to see a man who enjoys his work,' said Banecroft.

'Sorry to disappoint you, but I've already figured out what has happened to William Ignatius Campbell. You really should have picked a harder clue.'

'You know nothing,' said the Pilgrim. 'And you undoubtedly never will.'

'If you don't want me to succeed, why did you give me the opportunity, then?'

'That was not my decision.'

'That's right,' said Banecroft. 'I've been thinking about that. What was it you said?' He broke into a parody of the Pilgrim's accent, '"Fate has put you within the orbit of a greater defilement." Lordy be and heavens to Betsy.'

The Pilgrim's top lip rose into a snarl. 'Enjoy your mockery while you can.'

'Oh, I will. But the thing I realized – "the orbit of a greater defilement"? Makes me think that whatever this is, it's linked to that silly sausage dropping out of the sky last night. That's right, isn't it?'

The Pilgrim said nothing, but his facial expression spoke volumes.

'I knew it,' said Banecroft, striding past him and turning around in the entrance to the Church of Old Souls. 'Thank you so much for the invaluable assistance.'

'You're going to burn in the fires of a righteous hell,' growled the Pilgrim.

'Yes, yes, so you keep saying. Anyway, I think we've got off on the wrong foot. Would you like to come upstairs for a cup of tea?' He slapped his forehead. 'Oh, that's right, you—'

He broke off as the Pilgrim disappeared.

'Something I said?'

Banecroft turned on his heel and walked up the stairs. As he neared the top, he was met by Grace staring down at him. 'Who are you talking to?'

'Myself,' said Banecroft. 'Accept no substitutes.'

Grace shook her head. 'I can't tell if you are getting weirder or just even more obnoxious.'

'Can't it be both? And yes, to the cup of tea you're about to offer me.'

'As it happens, I was going to the kitchen anyway, but I would prefer if you asked nicely.'

'Let's assume I did. Where are the lesser members of my staff?'

'It is not that big a building. I am sure you can figure it out for yourself.'

'I could or I could just . . .' As he turned and backed through the door that led into the corridor that was a direct line to his office, he cupped his hands around his mouth and shouted, 'Hannah!'

Hannah walked through the bullpen door into Banecroft's office at the same time as he entered via the other one. 'There's no need to shout,' she said.

'How else would I get you in here?'

'You could, I don't know, walk into the room I'm in and ask me to come in here.'

'That doesn't seem like something I would do,' he said, throwing himself into the chair behind his desk. 'So, how are investigations coming along?'

Hannah then proceeded to give Banecroft a potted account of her day, featuring Sturgess's explanation of the unusual occurrences related to the consumption of Merlins, the incident at the Peacock Lounge, and John Mór's explanation of the anomalies. She skipped over the trip to Cogs's houseboat for obvious reasons.

'So,' summarized Banecroft, 'people are getting more messed up than usual on drugs. Doesn't tell us much, does it?'

'Well,' she said, trying not to sound defensive. 'It's my first day on it. How much progress did you make on your thing?'

'Someone has stolen a body out of his grave, and we will all be staking out the graveyard tomorrow to find the culprit.'

'How's that supposed to work?'

'Apparently, the culprit turns up there every day and sniffs about while looking, and I quote, "tall and weird".'

'That's very convenient of him.'

'Yes,' agreed Banecroft. 'It is rather.' He pulled a bottle of whiskey out of the bottom right drawer and looked around the desktop, pushing aside a couple of piles of paperwork so that they avalanched onto the floor. 'Grace,' he bellowed, 'where is my drinking glass?'

'I threw it away,' came the hollered response. 'It was disgusting.'

'Did you get me a new one?'

'No. You drink too much.'

'I'm not sure drinking directly from the bottle is going to slow that down.'

Hannah put her hands over her ears. 'Do you have to shout? Don't you have an intercom?'

'Grace,' roared Banecroft, 'Hannah wants to know why I don't have an intercom any more.'

'You blew the speaker by shouting into it.'

Banecroft pointed at the door. 'See? Not my fault.'

'How do you think that is not your fault?'

'Shoddy workmanship.' He raised his voice again. 'Where's that cup of tea?'

'I'm not giving it to you if you're going to use the cup to drink whiskey.'

'Fine,' snapped Banecroft. 'I won't.'

'Really?'

'I promise.'

No response followed this, so Banecroft returned his attention to Hannah. 'Where was I? Oh yes, something that occurred to me. This Pilgrim fella – I just remembered today that he said fate had put me into the orbit of a greater defilement than what I've been judged guilty of.'

'What is that supposed to mean?' asked Hannah.

'I'm not sure,' he admitted, 'but it does raise the possibility that your thing and my thing might be related.'

'How?'

'I don't know.'

The door flew open and Grace walked in, carrying a cup of tea and a plate with four digestive biscuits on it. 'You promise you will not drink whiskey out of this cup?'

'I promise,' vowed Banecroft.

Grace looked him in the eyes for a long moment. 'Lies make baby Jesus cry.'

'I thought Jesus was dead?'

'He is alive in our hearts and in heaven.'

'But he's still a baby?'

'What?' said Grace.

'I thought he was a thirty-three-year-old man when he died. How is he still a baby?'

'He's not. I just meant . . .'

'Is it the holy quartet? The Father, the Son, the Holy Spirit, and then the son as a baby? Bit of an odd mix.'

'Right,' said Grace, plonking the cup down. 'There is your tea. Your biscuits have been withdrawn because of your blasphemy.'

'How did I—'

He was interrupted by the slam of the door that followed Grace on her way out.

He tutted as he kicked off his shoes. 'She's rather temperamental these days, isn't she?'

Hannah shook her head. 'Why do you feel the need to wind her up?'

'Keeps her young,' he said, throwing his socked feet up on the desk before picking up his cup of tea. 'So, what's your next action point?'

'Do you mean other than trying to block out the unpleasant stench of your socks?'

'Yes, besides that.'

'John Mór says he's going to take me to meet somebody who can help on Sunday morning. I'm about to ring DI Sturgess to tell him.'

Banecroft nearly choked on the tea he was knocking back

remarkably quickly. 'Are you mad? First rule of journalism is never ever take a copper with you to meet a source.'

Hannah nodded. 'Yes, obviously, I know that'– she mentally added the word 'now' – 'but whoever we're meeting specifically asked for him to come.'

Banecroft puffed out his cheeks. 'I still don't like it.' He reached down to the bottom left drawer in his desk and pulled out a second bottle.

'You said you weren't going to use that teacup.'

'To drink whiskey,' said Banecroft, turning the second bottle around. 'This is rum.'

'Since when do you—'

'Since I picked up some by mistake. Never go shopping while drunk.'

'Excellent advice.'

'Hannah,' shouted Grace from outside the door.

'Yes?'

'Is he drinking whiskey?'

Hannah looked at Banecroft, who was pouring himself enough rum to cure an entire ship of scurvy. He raised an eyebrow at her.

'No,' she said, before adding at a considerably lower volume, 'technically, he isn't.'

'Good. Do you know a man called Cillian Blake?'

'What?' she said, her voice rising an octave involuntarily. 'Erm . . .' She was standing now. 'Yes, I . . . Well, I . . . Obviously, I . . . Could . . .' She realized she was hopping from foot to foot.

'Is the toilet broken again?' asked Banecroft.

'Shut up, Vincent. I . . . Oh God. Erm . . . Could you take a message?'

'OK,' said Grace. 'I suppose I could. Mr Blake, she is in a meeting. May I take a message?'

Hannah's knees almost buckled when she heard the voice. 'Sure, or . . . I could wait.'

'Sorry,' said Hannah, 'he's here?'

'Yes,' said Grace through the door. 'Did I not mention that?'

Hannah bit her own knuckle. 'No. No, you didn't. I'll be right out.'

She turned around, then back again, then around, then back again.

'This is like watching a one-woman performance of a Marx Brothers movie,' chirped Banecroft, drink in hand.

Hannah stomped over to his desk and, for reasons even she didn't understand, grabbed his socked foot. She spoke in a hiss. 'So help me, Vincent, I put up with a lot from you, but I swear to God, you embarrass me now and I will never ever forgive you. Is that absolutely clear?'

Banecroft raised his free hand. 'I'm not going to say or do anything.'

'Right,' said Hannah, looking down at her hand and then pulling it away in horror when she realized what it was touching. She wiped it on her jeans and a small part of her made a mental note to amputate it later.

'Ah, I thought I was in for a foot massage there.'

'You're not supposed to be talking!'

'Sure, you engage in inappropriate touching in the workplace and I'm supposed to keep quiet about it?'

Hannah said nothing, but her look was enough.

'Right,' said Banecroft. 'Shutting up now.'

She walked over to the door to the bullpen, paused and tried to neaten herself up. She then took a deep breath, attempted a relaxed smile and opened the door.

Grace was standing there, while Reggie, Ox and Stella all sat behind their desks, studiously pretending not to look while watching events unfold with a palpable air of intensity. Reggie's right ear was somehow managing to stare intently at her.

'Mr Blake,' said Hannah, 'apologies. I didn't realize you were actually here.'

'Sorry,' he said, flashing the same dazzling smile, 'unforgivable of me, I know, dropping in unannounced. I just wanted to follow up on what happened to our poor student last night, and I'm afraid the police aren't being very cooperative.'

'I see,' said Hannah, nodding. This was going OK; she was sounding like an adult human being who could string sentences together. 'Well, I don't know much but if you'd like to step out into the reception area, I will give you what information I can.' Yes, and that way, she wouldn't have four people staring at her as she spoke. This was good. This was very good.

Hannah pointed towards the double doors. 'If you'd just like to . . .'

It was then that Manny walked in with a 'cigarette' in one hand, flicking an unresponsive lighter with the other. 'We lighter no work no more. We need fire for we . . .' He looked up and noticed that everyone was looking at him. 'Wha' up?'

Stella found her voice first. 'Manny, you know how you just walked into the room?'

'Yes.'

'Have you noticed how nobody is applauding?'

He studied her for a long moment and then glanced down. 'Ohhhh.'

'Yeah,' said Stella. 'That.'

The Bard Takes It Hard

Patrons of the Bard's Tale pub in Stratford-upon-Avon have reported that the behaviour of the resident ghost of William Shakespeare has taken a turn for the worse.

Landlord Roger Wilby stated, 'Previously, old Willy would only pop up every now and again, and he was mostly harmless. He'd recite a line from a play at someone while they were playing the fruit machine, try to throw in a joke with one of the new barmaids – which nobody would get as we don't speak Ye Olde English – or often, he was found wandering about the ladies loo while pretending to be lost, the dirty old sod. Then, somehow, and don't ask me how, he got online, and now all he does is stomp about the place, screaming and howling while reading out his one-star Amazon reviews.

'Just last night we had the pub quiz, and people couldn't hear the questions for him shouting about someone called Clint007, who said the film was better than the book. Last week, plates full of Sunday roast were thrown about the place when someone gave him a one-star because his complete works didn't fit through their letterbox. One review accuses him of stealing famous quotes and lazily bunging them in his scripts, and I actually applied to Amazon to get that one taken down, because he ripped out one of the urinals after that. I swear to God, we're one more "not as good as *Twilight*" away from him burning the entire building down.'

22

This was getting ridiculous. Hannah needed to calm the hell down. For God's sake, she was an intelligent woman. An assistant editor no less, of an esteemed publication – well, a publication, at least. She was annoyed at herself, and frankly, if she could, she'd take herself outside and give herself a damn good talking-to.

Here was the problem: while yes, she was a strong, independent woman and all that, none of us is just one thing. While we'd like to believe otherwise, we don't entirely shed our teenaged selves like a skin as we evolve. It all stays in there. It's like how addicts, even those who have managed to turn their backs on their addictions, still describe themselves as addicts. Hannah had been a devoted follower of Herschel's Garden ever since they'd released their first single. Her and Carol's first ever gig – like, a proper gig on their own, as opposed to the Spice Girls with Mum – had been Franz Ferdinand at the Hammersmith Apollo when they were becoming fully fledged indie kids, and they'd both fallen in love with the first support act. Nigel, the intense multi-instrumentalist, and Cillian, the charismatic frontman.

And so it had gone on. As Hannah had grown from awkward teenager to, well, slightly less awkward uni student, over the course of two albums the band broke through from indie darlings to the cusp of real mainstream success. 'Your Smile', their most poppy of pop songs, had cracked American radio and suddenly, they were expected to step into the role of global phenomenon. Then, tragedy had struck, and Nigel had become another victim of rock 'n' roll excess. As Cillian had so memorably put it at the memorial organized for fans, 'He'd been a sensitive soul who couldn't find easy ways to cope with the world.'

Hannah distinctly remembered bawling her eyes out at university the night she'd heard the news. She'd rung Carol but had only received a text message a couple of days later. They'd been growing apart by that point, and she was with Darren, a man with no music in his soul and nothing but greatest hits albums in his VW Golf.

Life had gone on because that is what life does. The band had remained a part of her, but inevitably that part had grown smaller. Cillian's solo album had been, well, to put it kindly, 'missing the magic'. It had sounded like a bunch of songwriters had been hired to recreate what they thought Herschel's Garden should sound like and they'd totally missed the point. Hannah had even been at the show at the Hammersmith Apollo where Cillian had made the decision to play only tracks from his new album and none of the HG classics. Some people had booed, others had quietly walked out. Worse than that had been those who'd stayed and laughed. Some of them might have worked for the music press, judging by the reviews that appeared over the next couple of days. There was blood in the water, and they had been vicious. Hannah's now ex-husband Karl had point-blank refused to come with her, and so she had stood alone at the back of the venue and watched. At the end, she'd left quietly and saw some familiar faces on the way out, each of them sharing that same look. As Cillian Blake had left the stage without an encore being requested or given, he'd shared it too. It was over.

Karl and Hannah had never had one of those jokey laminated lists some married couples have, of famous people they are allowed to sleep with. In hindsight, that was probably for the best, as Karl undoubtedly would have got his own laminating machine and worked both it and the definition of the word famous to the brink of exhaustion. Still, if they had done, Cillian Blake would have been on Hannah's list. Which meant that yes, it was weird to be sitting there that evening in the Admiral's Arms, quite possibly the worst pub in Manchester, while Cillian Blake was standing at the bar buying her a vodka tonic.

He'd suggested they go for a drink, and she'd said yes, because almost anything would be better than her co-workers finding reasons to walk in and out of reception in order to spy on them. In the two minutes she and Cillian Blake had stood there, after Manny had gone downstairs on the epic quest to find his trousers, which he realized also contained his spare lighter, the reception area had been remarkably busy. Grace had sat behind her desk doing the worst impression imaginable of conducting a fake phone call. She had started by pretending to be ordering printer paper and then had clearly lost focus, which was why she'd subsequently enquired about train times to Glasgow and finished by explaining how they were happy with their broadband supplier – which they definitely weren't.

Cillian had asked where the nearest pub was, and Hannah had quickly identified it as the Admiral's Arms before trying to discount it even more quickly. Alarmingly, he'd gone with, 'Oh no, I love a bit of local colour,' and so here they were. It was Friday after work, but the Admiral's didn't experience any form of early evening rush. The same old man who always sat at the bar was there, staring into a half-pint of Guinness like it had burned his house down, while his dog – the only cheerful presence in the place – sat patiently under the man's stool. Two women were sitting in the corner knitting and . . . Wait a second. They were the same two women Hannah had seen earlier in the Kanky's Rest. What the hell were they doing here? One of them looked up at Hannah and she swiftly averted her eyes. Something about older northern women was properly terrifying. It was as if they'd seen everything the world had to offer and were not only unimpressed, but also keen to tell it so.

Hannah diverted her eyes back to Cillian Blake at the bar. He was talking to Dennis, the landlord, and it was a fascinating battle. Blake was a charming man and Dennis was the least likely man in the world to be charmed. Every time Hannah had been in here, invariably for a quick lunchtime drink as time never allowed her and her co-workers to venture further afield, Dennis had acted as if their presence was as welcome as a barbecue truck at a bar mitzvah. At first, she'd assumed he didn't like the staff of *The Stranger Times*, but after a few visits, she realized this warm welcome was extended to everybody. Dennis looked at anyone trying to purchase drinks as if they were guilty of murdering his entire family until proven otherwise. It was an almost admirable level of visceral antipathy to maintain, especially for one who ostensibly worked in the service industry. You had to respect his commitment while also doing everything in your power to get away from him before he remembered somewhere he could bury a body.

Hannah looked away again as Cillian returned with the drinks.

'Sorry,' he said, as he deposited Hannah's vodka tonic in front of her, 'I got chatting to Dennis, the landlord. Real character. He used to be in the merchant navy until his leg got trapped under a crate while he was strapping down cargo in a storm.'

'Really?' asked Hannah. 'Wow, I didn't know that.'

'Yeah, great guy. Gave us these on the house.'

'On the . . . on the house?'

'Yes,' said Cillian. 'That's a common phrase, isn't it?'

'Not in here.'

Cillian raised his drink in a toast. 'Cheers.'

'And can I just say again – sorry about before.'

'About what, exactly?'

'Mainly the naked Rastafarian.'

Cillian laughed. 'To be fair, he was wearing a beaded bracelet and a T-shirt.'

'Yes,' said Hannah, with a laugh, 'an unfortunately rather short T-shirt.' She steadied herself. 'And while we're on the subject, when we met yesterday evening . . .'

Cillian waved away her second apology. 'Forget that. You'd just been through a terrible experience, and I popped up and started to ask you questions. Absolutely unforgivable.'

'No, but . . . I was just caught off guard. And I . . . I'm actually a big fan of your solo album.'

'And now I know you're definitely lying. I haven't been able to listen to it in ten years. Biggest mistake of my life.'

'Oh no, I wouldn't say that.'

'Well, that and the two months with the ponytail.'

Hannah put her hand to her mouth and laughed. 'Oh God, I do remember that.'

'Why didn't you warn me?'

'I was too busy screaming at you from the front row.'

'Ha! Well, that's a long time ago now,' he said as a look came over his face.

'Do you miss it?' The question popped out before Hannah could think to stop herself.

Cillian shrugged. 'I mean, it was a great time up until . . . well, you know. I mean, more than anything, I miss my friend.'

Hannah shifted in her seat. 'Right. Yes. Of course. Sorry, I didn't mean to—'

'Oh no,' said Cillian, favouring her with that smile again, 'it's good to talk about it. The stuff I do with my charity – we tell people, you need to talk about your pain. Locking it away doesn't help anyone.'

'Nigel was very talented.'

Cillian nodded. 'He was. He truly was.' He raised his glass again. 'Gone too soon.'

She joined in the toast and took a sip of her drink. It had a slice of lemon in it. Hannah had once seen Dennis bar someone from the pub for asking for such a thing. His line about how the customer could 'bugger off somewhere else to get their five-a-day' had made her feel so relieved that she'd never dared to ask.

'So,' said Cillian, 'you were a big fan, then?'

Hannah nodded. 'I mean, I know I should try to play it cool here, but yes. I once bought a blank CD off the internet because someone swore it contained the mythical lost album.'

Cillian winced. 'Me too.'

An enduring part of the Herschel's Garden mythology was that they'd already secretly recorded their third album but Cillian had made the decision after Nigel's death never to release it.

Hannah opened her mouth to ask about it but decided not to. Instead, she went with, 'So, how are you finding being an English lecturer?'

'It's good,' he said with a nod. 'I mean, nothing makes you feel old quicker than seeing freshers every year,' he continued, laughing, 'but I enjoy the work. Plus, Manchester is a good place to do work with my charity. There's a lot of students here, and young people in general. It's all well and good telling them to just say no to drugs, but people have been saying that for decades and it hasn't worked. Maybe time to try something else.'

'Is the university OK with your work?'

He shrugged. 'Yes and no. They would rather I didn't talk about the subject at all, but on the upside, Herschel's Garden fans are now at the point in their lives when they've got kids reaching uni age and, apparently, I'm a' – he made bunny-ears quotes in the air – 'useful recruitment tool.'

'God,' said Hannah, 'that's depressing.' As Cillian pulled a face, she slapped a hand over her mouth. 'I meant for me, not you. For me!'

He laughed. 'Both of us. Anyway,' he said, shifting about,

'apologies for messing up the jovial mood, but one thing about being a loud voice in favour of legalization – it doesn't make you popular with the police.'

'I can imagine.'

'Actually, to be honest, quite a few of them agree with me, but it's career-ending to say so. They also aren't going to tell me anything about what happened to poor Wayne Grainger.'

Hannah bit her lip. 'To be honest, like I said, I can't tell you much either. I mean, I assume you've seen the footage?'

'I have, but then, there's all that other footage. Like it's from some app or something.'

'Yeah, Stella mentioned something about that. Weird, and rather . . . mawkish.'

'That's a very polite word for it. But, I mean, the whole thing was some kind of special effect or something, wasn't it?'

Hannah shook her head. 'I can only tell you what I saw, and the poor guy was, well, not flying. I think flying implies control. Floating is more accurate – at least, until it really wasn't.'

'Right,' said Cillian. 'I mean, I guess . . . doing what you do for a living, you probably see a lot of weird stuff.'

'Yes, although nothing quite like that before.'

'What could cause that?'

Hannah shrugged. 'They don't know, but . . .'

'What?'

'Well . . .' Hannah hesitated and looked into those sincere blue eyes. 'They think it's possible it has something to do with drugs.'

'Oh no.'

'Maybe,' she added.

'This is the problem, though,' said Cillian. 'Right here. Because everything is illegal, it's unregulated and there's no real way to warn people about dangerous side effects. Is there anything else you can tell me?'

'Not really. Like I said, we have to deal with a lot of insanely weird stuff, but this is something new.'

'Sounds dangerous.'

'Can be.' Hannah tried to look nonchalant as she shrugged. 'But we're good at what we do and the office is protected.'

'Protected? Protected how?'

Crap. What the hell was she doing? Running her mouth off, saying things she shouldn't, to try to sound impressive. 'Ehm . . .'

It was at that moment that Hannah looked up to see Ox, Reggie, Stella and Grace piling in through the far doors of the pub, doing a terrible job of looking surprised to see them.

'Looks like the gang is all here.'

'Yes,' said Hannah, through gritted teeth. 'What are the odds?'

23

Cillian Blake hit the button to turn off his electric SUV and took a deep breath. He had been summoned back to the farm, and this time, there was no way of avoiding it.

Emma Marsh had always been difficult. He'd known her since they'd been children, when they'd attended the same grammar school. Her brilliance had been matched only by her unpopularity with her classmates. Recognized as a genius at a particularly young age, she had never been shy about rubbing other people's noses in it. Not just other pupils' either. The staff's too. It was as if she'd been born smart and somehow hated the world for it. Cillian, on the other hand, as well as being a good student had always been popular. Into music, the arts – the charming young man with the dazzling smile. The pair of them moved in completely different circles – if you could even say Emma had a circle – but they'd overlapped in one area: the school debating team.

Cillian had signed up for it as he'd always enjoyed performing. Emma had joined because she was being encouraged to take up more 'social' activities; and she did enjoy beating other people to a pulp with her intellect. He had been captain, focusing on charming the judges, whereas Emma had obliterated the opposition with her relentless verbal assaults. Their teacher had referred to them jokingly as his good-cop, bad-cop combo. Circumstance had made Cillian the closest thing that Emma had to a friend. In truth, he'd known she was obsessed with him, but that was fine, a lot of people were, including a couple of the teachers. He'd grown used to it. Admittedly, the way she had tried to impress him had been remarkably different to anything else he'd experienced. He'd later captured it in the lyrics of 'Dark-eyed Girl'. The critics had fallen over themselves to pick apart the song's terribly clever central metaphor, much to Cillian's amusement. The real trick was that there hadn't been one.

They'd both gone on to achieve big things: Cillian met Nigel Stay at university and formed Herschel's Garden, releasing two critically acclaimed albums and on their way to being the next big thing before tragedy struck; Emma completed a medical degree in record time and became *the* bright young thing in the field of medical research, blazing a trail before her controversial attitudes to certain ethical questions made her a pariah.

It was classic Emma – entirely convinced she was right and other people were fools. She had no time for rules she didn't agree with. The rules in question concerned testing on humans, and her attempts to circumvent them got her not only struck off the medical register, but she'd also spent three years behind bars. Rather than serving as a chastening experience or a wake-up call, the prison sentence had served only to poison the well of resentment Emma already held for the rest of the world.

The pair had inevitably fallen out of touch once they'd left school, but she'd found Cillian again, by breaking into his house.

He'd been at a real low point, and she'd woken him up at four in the morning with a dead badger. After that, one thing had led to another and . . .

He closed his eyes and gathered himself. They were almost there now. Success was so close he could taste it.

He'd been doing his best to avoid Emma, not least because of her incessant demands, but steering clear of her was no longer possible.

He looked at the farmhouse through the rain-splattered windscreen. It had taken him months to find somewhere with everything they needed. The space. The privacy. He'd invested everything he had into this, and quite a lot he didn't. He'd signed a deal to write a book he hadn't even started, and had long since blown through the advance. He'd taken out every loan he could, and when that still wasn't enough, he'd sold his soul or, to be more precise, the rights for Herschel's Garden's songs to be used in adverts. Nigel's money-grabbing sister had been delighted after Cillian had previously blocked her attempts to do the exact same thing for so long. It had been quite the humiliating climbdown, and the fanbase had been duly appalled. This needed to work. He was out of other options.

He could see the warm glow of the kitchen lights through the curtains. She'd be in there now, waiting for him. Stewing. There was no point waiting for Emma Marsh to calm down. It simply never happened.

He jogged across the large yard through the light smattering of rain, cursing as his right shoe found a puddle. When he entered through the door, Emma was indeed sitting at the kitchen table waiting for him, as he'd known she would be. The place was all rustic charm – at least in here. The outer sheds and the workshop were a very different story.

A half-finished glass of red wine sat on the table in front of her, the bottle nowhere to be seen. She was always worse when she'd been drinking. Her long black hair framed a thin face and the kind of wiry physique that was the result of your brain running so hot that at times you forget to eat for days on end. She wasn't unattractive in absolute aesthetic terms; it was just that her face frequently fell into a scowl of embittered rage that did nothing for her.

She looked up at him, her hair shielding her right eye, the left one shining bright with accusation. 'You took your time.'

'I'm sorry, Emma. I got here as soon as I could.'

'I know you were busy – out with one of your whores!'

'What?'

'Don't lie to me,' she snarled.

'You had me followed?'

'Yes, and don't you dare start talking about invasion of privacy. Not when you've been caught red-handed.'

'What are you talking about?' asked Cillian, crouching down beside her. 'I took that silly Hannah girl out for a drink because I needed to find out what the people at the paper know.'

'Oh, yes – pumping her for information, were you?'

He tried to touch her knee, but she jerked away. 'Sugar plum, it's not like that. This was just work. I'm doing all I can to protect you. We need to know what they know.'

'Why?'

'Why?' repeated Cillian. 'Because a kid fell from the sky.'

She shrugged. 'So? Can't make an omelette without breaking some eggs.'

He winced. The woman never even pretended to care.

'So,' she said, her curiosity temporarily peeking through her anger, 'what do they know?'

'Not that much, as far as I can tell, but I think they're chasing down the drug angle, and I think they might be working with the police.'

He was interrupted from saying anything more by her kicking the chair opposite. 'Jesus Christ, this is a disaster.'

'Let's just—'

'Don't you dare tell me to calm down.' She jabbed the tabletop with her finger. 'This is what happens when you rely on an incompetent buffoon to manage important parts of a project.'

'Doug is doing his best, I'm sure.'

'His best,' she scoffed. 'He's an incompetent degenerate. I don't know why we have him.'

The answer, which Cillian didn't want to acknowledge, was incredibly simple. Despite the impression given by the worlds of politics, sport or motorway driving, finding someone utterly devoid of morals was a remarkably difficult task. Such people should be avoided at all costs, unless you are engaged in an activity that is entirely outside the realm of moral acceptability, then they become invaluable. Step forward Doug Stankovitch. In the depraved world of rock 'n' roll touring, you don't get given a nickname like Stink lightly, and it had nothing to do with his admittedly questionable standards of personal hygiene.

Cillian looked around. 'Where is Doug?'

'Your hairy little friend is out, theoretically doing something useful for a change. Sorry, I know how much you hate being alone with me.'

Cillian moved around the table. 'Darling, it's not like that.'

He placed his hand on her shoulder, but she shrugged him off. Her eyes were wet as she looked up at him.

'You've been avoiding me.'

'Of course not.'

She raised her voice. 'Don't lie to me!'

He lowered his, trying to defuse her anger. 'I'm not, sweetheart, but you know we have to be careful.'

'Careful?' she mocked, with a bitter laugh. 'I've got that idiot as my only help. I'm having to use knock-off supplies because we don't have any money.'

'I've given you everything I have.'

'Well, it wasn't enough.'

He paused. There was something in her words that set an alarm bell ringing. 'Wasn't? What did you do?'

She folded her arms, the anger in her voice simmering down a little. 'I handled the situation. I would have talked to you about it but, like I said, you've been avoiding me.'

He moved into her eyeline. 'Emma, what did you do?'

'The good news is, I don't have to scrape by on the pitiful budget you gave me any more. We have a benefactor now.'

Cillian couldn't believe what he was hearing. 'What are you talking about? Nobody can know about this work.'

'Relax. This person contacted me, and they already knew everything.'

'Oh God,' said Cillian, pulling out one of the kitchen chairs and slumping into it, 'we're ruined.'

She waved a hand dismissively across the table at him. 'Oh, grow up. This person was extremely well informed, and if they wanted to ruin us, they would have already.' She preened a little. 'They are an admirer of my work. Someone who truly gets it and who wants to support it.'

'Who are they?'

'Who cares,' said Emma. 'It was all done over email and encrypted chat. They are providing us with a substantial budget and all they ask in return is access to my research. Thanks to this latest fuck-up, we need to move fast. We need more of everything.'

'But isn't it dangerous to—'

'Dangerous?' she shouted. 'Not for you. I'm doing all the work here. Soon, you'll get what you want out of this.'

He leaned across the table and placed his hand on hers. 'What *we* want. This has always been *our* plan.'

'But you haven't been pulling your weight. I told you that we needed more.'

'I know,' said Cillian, 'but it takes time for the pills to trickle through.'

'Not any more,' she said with an alarming grin. 'I acquired a bigger batch.'

'What? You can't do that without—'

'I can do what I like!' she yelled. 'I'm in charge here. You weren't getting it done. You use and abuse my brilliance, but you act like all of this is somehow beneath you. I'm combining magic and science in a way nobody has ever dreamed of, and you treat it like I'm unblocking a toilet. I'm doing all of this for you, you ungrateful bastard, and I know that as soon as we're done, you'll up and leave me.'

And so they were back to this. 'Emma, stop. Baby, I will never leave you. You mean the world to me, and you're giving the world to me. I owe you everything.'

'You've got a funny way of showing it.' She got to her feet abruptly, sending her chair toppling onto the tiled floor. 'Upstairs, now. I want to have sex.'

Cillian steadied his face, as he knew she would be studying him for a reaction. 'Could we just—'

'No.'

'It's just I'm—'

'I don't care. Take one of those pills I got you.' She gave a bitter laugh as she moved towards the stairs, taking off her cardigan as she went. 'Better living through chemistry.'

24

Hannah stood with her umbrella over her head and watched as the steady rain came down around her, puddling in places between the gravestones. She was standing in the lee of one of the chapels, giving herself a moment out of the squalling wind to try to encourage some warmth back into her bones. While it felt like a lifetime ago now, the morning had started brisk and sunny, but this was Manchester, and the meteorological mood had taken a turn for the worse as the day developed.

Despite the weather, Southern Cemetery was still quite busy. It was a mix of relatives visiting graves, Saturday-afternoon tourists and mourners at the three different services that were taking place. There was a smattering of famous graves to be found, although some of the most ostentatious belonged to former mayors of the city who might well have been something in their day but now attracted little interest from passers-by.

Hannah was no expert but, as far as these places went, the cemetery seemed to be quite nice. It was divided into two halves by a road. Certainly, the older area had plenty of trees, and all of it was rather neat. There were signs for nature trails that children could follow, and plaques describing the different trees and birds. The other side was more functional and newer looking. Fewer trees and more open spaces, waiting to be filled in. It also contained the most upsetting graves.

The resting places of the long dead were interesting, but they were history. Even the memorials to young men from all over the commonwealth who'd lost their lives in the world wars, while of course sad, were now snapshots of a different world, a level of detachment granted by time. In contrast, the thing that hit Hannah the hardest was, of all things, the YouTube logo. She guessed the rules here were more flexible than in most cemeteries. They allowed gravestones with mentions of YouTube, *Fortnite*, Harry Styles – stone renderings of PlayStations, which seemed silly until you realized they were there to represent the passions of the departed. Young children. Every time you passed something like that, it drew the eye and took the wind right out of you. Some pains were too great to contemplate, and just knowing they were out there affected everyone who passed within their orbit.

Banecroft had decided that, given the size of the area to be covered, the entire team was required for this surveillance operation. Everyone except Manny, who got a pass on the grounds that he literally could not leave the grounds of the offices. On days like this, Hannah rather envied him. She'd been dealing with Ox, Reggie and Stella all grumbling about this assignment, and seeing as Banecroft had elected to explain its importance only to Hannah and nobody else, all she could do was sympathize and theorize that it probably wouldn't be much longer.

Grace was the only member of staff who didn't seem to mind

being there. She was spending her time visiting graves that were obviously neglected. She had accidentally pressed the button on her walkie-talkie at one point, blocking the channel, and all anyone could hear was the sound of her reading off the names of the departed and praying for their souls.

The walkie-talkies were proving invaluable. Hannah hadn't even known they'd had them until Ox had produced their box. When she'd asked what they'd needed them for previously, she hadn't received an answer, but Reggie and Ox had shared a look.

The team had initially split up to cover more ground, but that had been back at 8.30 a.m. when morale had been high. It was now 2 p.m. and, even allowing for the rolling thirty-minute breaks Hannah had implemented to keep people sane and allow them to get something to eat and take care of other needs, it was fair to say the entire crew was showing signs of irritability. Over five hours of mindless circling will do that to you.

Reggie and Ox were now walking around together, as always, seeming to prefer squabbling with each other to silence. Stella had her headphones on. It was Grace's turn to trek over to the drive-thru McDonald's on the Princess Parkway to use the facilities. It didn't help that all they knew about the person they were looking for was that it was a man who was 'tall, weird-looking and sniffy'. Apparently, when Banecroft had pressed the woman who had given him that description, she'd assured him they'd know him when they saw him.

There had been a few false sightings, which had mainly comprised them following lone men in anoraks as they either walked to visit a grave or just passed through on their way to somewhere else. As it was late October, people with a case of the sniffles were not an entirely uncommon thing. Ox had even tried to convince them that their suspect must be the man who'd turned up wearing a Liverpool football shirt: 'I'm telling ya, it's not right. Matt Busby is buried here. It's bleedin' sacrilege is what it is.'

To be fair to Ox, both in terms of logos on gravestones and floral arrangements left in front of them, there was no shortage of City and United colours. This was Manchester, after all. While the cemetery was divided into Church of England, Catholic, Jewish, Muslim and non-denominational areas, it was really football that was the one true religion, and there were only two acceptable churches.

Banecroft's voice came through in Hannah's earpiece. 'I've got him.'

Her head snapped around. She'd seen Banecroft only a few minutes ago, skulking at the west end of the cemetery. She began to scan between the trees to locate his distinctive figure, but her eyes stopped on another man making his way between the gravestones. The gravedigger had been right – they would know him when they saw him. He wore a distinctive green mac over a brown jumper and tatty jeans. He was tall but stooped, with an odd gait, and his back was curved. His skin was of a hue that reminded Hannah of bad cheese, and his black hair was not slicked back, but clung to his head, his scalp visible through it. While how he looked was odd, it was how he moved that really stood out. He scurried at a near run, darting forward, stopping, sniffing the air, one of his long-fingered hands caressing gravestones as he passed, before he'd stop suddenly, smell the air and then dart forward again.

Hannah whispered into the walkie-talkie tucked inside her coat. 'I see him. West side of the old cemetery.'

While he was a man, she found the word 'creature' forming in her mind. She tried to look casual as she moved parallel with him, three rows away, watching him as he continued to make his way between the gravestones. She noted Banecroft doing the same a few rows on the other side of him. They needn't have worried about being stealthy. The man seemed entirely unconcerned with the living, at one point even pushing past a couple of older women who were dawdling in front of him on the narrow path. One of them said something to him, but he ignored her.

Hannah watched as, eyes closed, the man's head spun round, and an off-coloured tongue flicked out between his thin pale lips, as if tasting the air. He dashed forward again until he emerged on the main footpath that paved the way towards the chapel from the gate on Nell Lane, the road that divided the cemetery.

The man stopped, sniffed the air again and then turned abruptly towards the Nell Lane entrance where Stella stood, headphones still on, a look of shock on her face as he stared directly at her. A couple walking their dog made their way around her and continued up the path, eyeing the man and then Stella, clearly wondering what this was. They weren't alone in their unease. Hannah, a heavy feeling in the pit of her stomach, started walking forward quickly, moving parallel to the path but heading towards Stella. When she grew level with the man in the mac, she could see his face again. He was studying Stella intently, sniffing the air around her, a crooked grimace smeared across his face. Closer now, she could see that his eyes were unnaturally wide and bulging.

As the dog-walkers passed him, their Yorkshire terrier snarled and started to yap aggressively, straining at his leash to get to the man. Its owners apologized profusely as they dragged their suddenly incensed canine away. All the while, the man never took his eyes off Stella. Instead, he slowly raised his hand, and Hannah watched in horror as he pointed a bony finger directly at her younger colleague. Stella took a couple of steps back and was preparing to turn the other way when the man broke into a lolloping run towards her.

Hannah yelped and set off towards Stella, but she'd only gone a couple of feet when Banecroft, waving his closed umbrella like a fiery sword, jumped into the man's path.

'Oh, no you don't. You shall not pass!'

The man pulled up and reared back, his eyes darting left and right, suddenly confused by what was happening.

'I want a word with you, sunshine!'

Before Banecroft could say anything else, the man took off like a startled deer. He turned and, his eyes wide with panic, ran straight at Hannah.

'Stop him,' roared Banecroft.

Hannah held out her arms and saw the wild look in the man's eyes as he hurtled towards her. She opened her mouth to speak, but the man didn't stop. Instead, he attempted to leap over her, and he almost made it, but one of his feet caught Hannah in the chest and sent her sprawling backwards onto the wet ground.

As she began to pick herself up, Banecroft rushed by. 'Come on, lazy bones. The game is afoot!'

25

Vincent Banecroft was dying.

Chest heaving, bile clawing at the back of his throat, his life may well have been flashing before his eyes, but he couldn't see it for all the bright amoebous blobs that were bumper car-ing off each other in his field of vision. He was vaguely aware of someone behind him tutting, but it was hard to be sure over the sound of his own blood rushing in his ears, possibly seeking some way to leave his body. He couldn't blame it. His forehead was pressed against the cold wet granite of the gravestone to which he was clinging, having stumbled into it. He turned his head slightly and, between gasping breaths, threw up what he'd drunk for breakfast.

'Pathetic.'

He didn't need to look up to know who the voice belonged to.

'Oh, good,' said Banecroft as he glanced up into the sneering face of the Pilgrim. 'You're here. I was worried you'd miss this low moment.'

'Such a pitiful wretch.'

'I've got it. You were a personal trainer in a past life.'

'As if you could sink no lower, you now defile this grave with your noxious expulsions.'

'With apologies to' – Banecroft pushed himself back so he could focus on the headstone – 'Mrs Amanda Bakingstoft, who died in 1905, I was in hot pursuit of a suspect.'

'Pursuit?' echoed the Pilgrim, the word dripping with scorn. 'You ran all of three hundred feet before collapsing.'

Banecroft glanced over his shoulder. 'I'll admit, my physical conditioning isn't what it once was.'

'Would this be before you were a drunken unworthy sop destined to burn in hell for all eternity?'

Banecroft spat on the ground in a futile attempt to clear the taste from his mouth. 'I'm not sure this isn't hell already.'

He was given a millisecond to regret his choice of words before all around him transformed into a writhing mass of flesh, flailing limbs and screaming faces. One of the faces came within inches of his, the abject terror in its eyes burning into his.

And then it was gone again.

'Thank you for that,' muttered Banecroft, standing upright without having made any conscious decision to stand. His feet were once again running in the direction he'd last seen the man in the green mac heading, rushing between the gravestones.

As he ran, he heard the mocking voice of the Pilgrim carrying after him. 'Three more days, Mr Banecroft. Enjoy them.'

He certainly wasn't enjoying this one, but somehow his body had found a second wind he was unaware it possessed. The man in the mac should have been long gone but Banecroft caught a flash of bright green fabric through the trees, on the pavement outside the cemetery. Banecroft pushed through the bushes, and he was finally able to get a clear view of his quarry through the wrought-iron railings. What seemed to have slowed the man down was the combination on a bike lock, for a bike that looked unworthy of such security. It possibly started life red in colour, but was now so rusted it looked more brown. The man's big, wet, fishlike eyes stared back at Banecroft, his face contorted as his long fingers fumbled with the lock.

Banecroft looked up and down the length of the railings. The nearest gap was about thirty yards away in the wrong direction. He briefly considered trying to climb over the top but the best-case scenario was he'd fail; the worst-case was that he'd impale himself in the attempt. With one last look at the man in the mac, he set off back towards the pedestrian entrance. Just as he reached it, a large man with four small yappy dogs on leads entered, blocking the path.

'This is a graveyard,' hollered the man, 'not the Olympics!'

Banecroft pushed past the harrumphing dog-walker and emerged onto the pavement just in time to see the man in the mac releasing his bike from the lock. Despite it being an entirely futile endeavour, Banecroft rushed towards him, getting within thirty feet before the man pushed off on his bike and pedalled away through the Saturday-afternoon traffic.

'Wait!' Banecroft shouted forlornly, as if that was ever likely to stop him.

Doubled over, Banecroft leaned against the railings and pressed his hand over the stitch he now had in his side. He was probably going to throw up again, just as soon as he had enough air in his body to do so.

He was disturbed from his reverie by the loud honking of a car horn. With great effort he re-focused his eyes to see his Jag pulled up at the kerb, Hannah in the driver's seat and Stella with her head out the passenger-side window.

'Get in the bloody car.'

26

Dr Marsh watched the large monitor on the wall in front of her and resisted the urge to scream. There was no point in her losing her temper, there was enough of that going on already.

'Mr Campbell,' she said into the microphone on the table in front of her, 'if you remain calm, I can explain everything.'

The subject, who was well beyond any capacity to comprehend reason, snarled and gnawed at the air like a rabid dog. Much like a rabid dog, he was now nothing but a danger that needed to be dealt with.

With a sigh, Dr Marsh flipped up a cover and pressed the big red button beneath. After a couple of seconds, the screen of the monitor duly filled with flames, then she clicked it off.

Kitty lay stretched out on the table beside her. 'What the hell am I going to do, Kitty? We're going around in circles here. We have a rage problem.'

Ironically, she had no one except a cat with whom to share her personal rage.

Kitty gave her a look that displayed concern only for where his next meal was coming from. Dr Marsh scratched his belly then remembered she did, in fact, have somewhere to vent her rage that was truly deserving. She hit speed-dial on her phone and of course, as always, it went straight to voicemail.

'Doug, you useless piece of crap. Clean up the containment chamber. I need more subjects. I don't know how many more times I need to tell you that, you worthless fool. Do your job!'

She stabbed at the phone to sever the connection then tossed it onto the table, causing Kitty to flinch.

Since Doug had told her that he, the grubby little pervert, got off on being abused, she had to admit to herself that she'd started to lay it on a little thicker. He was undeniably deserving of it, the incompetent halfwit, but she knew vaguely that there was a part of her that seemed to take pleasure in the idea that he liked it. She pushed that thought away. What an odious little worm he was. Still, it was nice to feel appreciated.

While she had always been special, she was so rarely treated as such. The word 'special' covered a multitude of things here. There was the obvious: at the age of twelve her mother had sat her down and explained that they were Wiven, blessed with magical abilities. Then followed the first in a long line of rambling speeches on 'responsibilities' and 'restraint'. The sheer insanity of such a notion – 'Here are these incredible things you can do, don't do them.' She'd also been a 'special' student; although, as she put it, the word 'genius' really just meant you were one of the few people who could walk and talk at the same time. She'd never fitted in simply because she'd never wished to sink down into the swamp of ineptitude in order to make other people feel better.

In fact, other people had so often been the problem. Whether it be their lack of understanding of her brilliance, or the ludicrous criticism of her attitude towards them. This over-sentimentalized bullshit about the sanctity of human life. Never mind that it ran contrary to the entirety of human history. Generations had walked into both metaphorical and actual lines of fire to achieve objectives determined by those in power. Every day human life was sacrificed in a plethora of ways. Take speed limits. If life is so precious, reduce the motorway speed limit from 70 mph to 50 mph. Not one expert wouldn't admit when pressed that this would save a significant number of lives. They wouldn't do it, though, because people had places to be, things to do. Ergo, human life is sacrificed for the greater good. You try to explain that to someone, though, and they'd start huffing and puffing before inevitably resorting to name-calling.

Emma was 'special' because she had never fallen for that crap. Human life had a price and a purpose, and she wasn't squeamish about using it to achieve her ends. To her, magic could be a science and vice versa, but you had to approach them both with a clear mind. Combining the two would lead to the next great leap forward in human evolution, and the prize far outweighed the price. It infuriated her that people who could appreciate that – and, consequently, her – were so few and far between.

Speaking of which, as if on cue, the encrypted chat client on her PC pinged. She moved the mouse to rouse the screen into life.

V Tepes III was the screen name of her mysterious benefactor. Infuriatingly, it was all she knew about him. Even that part – believing it was a him – was pure conjecture, but she was almost certain of it. She looked at his message.

V Tepes III: How is everything going?

She studied the flashing cursor and considered her response before typing. This man, person, man, had already invested quite a bit into her and her work. She was aware that careful phrasing wasn't her greatest skill. Eventually, she plumped for . . .

Re Annie-May: Slowly.

V Tepes III: How so?

Re Annie-May: As you know, I have found a way to reanimate consistently.

V Tepes III: Yes. Brilliant work.

Emma found herself blushing. It really was nice to be appreciated.

Re Annie-May: Thank you. However, I cannot get past the rage problem. They all start off cogent, but they degrade too quickly.

V Tepes III: That is tough.

Re Annie-May: Frustrating. I've tried every combination of drugs I can think of, and nothing is working. My rage problem is giving me a rage problem.

V Tepes III: LOL

Emma smiled to herself. Normally, nobody ever got her jokes.

V Tepes III: Don't let it get to you. You have done incredible work so far.

Re Annie-May: Yes, but I'm stuck now.

V Tepes III: I believe in you.

Another little glow of warmth.

V Tepes III: Your idea to use anomalies as a source was excellent, and your solution for how to find them was nothing short of genius.

Re Annie-May: You're full of flattery.

V Tepes III: I'm serious. Revolutionary work. I hope you understand how special you are.

Re Annie-May: I don't feel very special right now.

V Tepes III: Well, you are. I am awed by your brilliance. How are your supplies of anima by the way?

Emma looked over to the shelf in the corner on which sat most of the clay pots they used for storage after extraction.

Re Annie-May: Better than my supply of subjects. Thank you for the tips on the different pot design by the way. It has reduced wastage.

She didn't know how whoever this was knew about anima storage, and it felt like an overstep to ask. Clearly, they were a researcher of some form themselves. They had to be in order to understand the complexities of her work. Nobody else did.

V Tepes III: About your rage problem . . .

Emma paused, and then, after tapping her forefingers together, as she always did when she was excited, she took a deep breath and typed . . .

Re Annie-May: Are you going to suggest something to relax me?

She debated adding an emoji but decided against it. She was relieved she hadn't when the response came back.

V Tepes III: I mean with the subjects.

Oh.

V Tepes III: Have you considered a non-scientific solution?

Feeling slightly embarrassed at misreading the intent, she typed quickly.

Re Annie-May: Of course, but nothing can be done.

V Tepes III: What if you had a necromer?

Re Annie-May: I don't.

Re Annie-May: Nobody does.

Re Annie-May: I'm not sure they even exist.

Emma's eyes widened as she read the next responses.

V Tepes III: They do.

V Tepes III: And I know where you can get one.

Re Annie-May: Are you pulling my leg?

V Tepes III: No.

V Tepes III: I have too much respect for your work.

V Tepes III: I don't have the necromer but I have something I think you could trade for it.

Emma chewed on her lip, her mind racing. This could be the solution. The solution to everything but it came with risks. She had been doing everything to stay off the radar of the Founders for obvious reasons.

Re Annie-May: What about the F problem?

V Tepes III: LOL

V Tepes III: I won't tell them if you won't.

V Tepes III: And I guarantee the current holder of it doesn't want them to know either.

Emma leaned back in her chair and gazed up at the ceiling. In her experience, things that were too good to be true invariably were. This could be a trap, but to what end? She didn't know how, but this person already knew all about her work, and had made it clear that he/they knew where she was working from too. In fact, as part of their deal, she had given them access to all her records. What did they have to gain by screwing her around now? If she failed, her work was far less valuable to them.

She sat back upright, cracked her knuckles and typed.

Re Annie-May: OK. Go ahead. I'm listening . . .

Horny Hell

There has been yet another shocking development in what the tabloid newspapers have regrettably dubbed the 'Horny Killer' saga. The murderer – so named owing to their propensity for using what forensic specialists have hypothesized is some form of antlers as a murder weapon – has been responsible for the deaths of three people. Greater Manchester Police have recently determined that there is, in fact, a link between the individuals who were previously thought to have been selected entirely at random. Detective Inspector Jonathan Freckles explains, 'It turns out that all three victims not only visited Lyme Park in recent weeks, but may also have all been guilty of littering while there.' Lyme Park, a National Trust estate and deer sanctuary is renowned for its natural and largely unspoilt magnificence.

DI Freckles went on to say, 'As it happens, I regularly walk the dog there, and yes, while littering in such a wondrous bounty of natural beauty is of course unforgivable, it is no reason to go around killing people. I mean, definitely not three of them. Maybe one to send a message, at most, but even then, a light goring would've probably done the trick. Ehm . . . no further questions.'

After speaking to the press, DI Freckles has been placed on gardening leave to spend more time with his dog. Meanwhile, local self-proclaimed white witch and Zumba instructor Yvette Sorbet has come forward claiming that the killer is 'the spirit of Herne the Hunter, awoken from his slumber and hellbent on wreaking vengeance on those who bespoil his kingdom'. Park patrons have been advised not to approach anything with horns that looks like it might be in a mood, and to remember to pick up after yourselves, idiots.

27

Stella had to admit that, as car chases went, theirs was pretty anti-climactic. It helped that the person they were chasing was on a push bike and also, thankfully, seemed unaware he was being chased. For the first few minutes, Banecroft lay down on the back seat, breathing in such a way that indicated his no longer being able to do so was entirely a possibility. Hannah, meanwhile, calmly guided the Jag through the traffic. As luck would have it, the congestion was just the right density that matching a bike for speed wasn't that much of a challenge.

Eventually, Banecroft sat up, his breathing returned to within acceptable parameters for a human, and he unfortunately regained the power of speech. 'What the hell are you doing?'

'Well,' said Hannah, 'seeing as if we chase a guy on a bike, he'll get away from us incredibly easily if he goes anywhere that isn't a road, I thought it might make sense to follow him and see where he's going.'

'What happens if you lose him?'

'Then you'll be in exactly the same position you were in when we picked you up. Seeing as you'd already lost him.'

Stella and Hannah shared a smirk while Banecroft sat back in his seat, mumbling something about how he'd only been catching his breath, which even he didn't really believe.

'By the way,' asked Stella, 'when you shouted "you shall not pass" back there, were you deliberately quoting Gandalf?'

'Come to that,' chipped in Hannah, 'before you ran for about a hundred yards and collapsed in a heap, were you doing a Sherlock Holmes impression when you shouted "the game is afoot"?'

'The two of you watch entirely too much of the boob tube.'

'The what?' asked Stella, confused.

'He means television,' said Hannah.

'We don't even have a TV,' said Stella.

Banecroft waved this away. 'YouTube or Tisk Tosh or whatever else your generation are rotting your brains with.'

'I'm not from the same generation as Hannah.'

'Hey!' said Hannah, offended.

'No, I didn't mean . . . I just meant . . . Having said that,' continued Stella, 'we don't know what age I am. I could be older than both of you combined.'

'In which case,' said Hannah, 'you really should give skincare tips on the boob tube.'

Stella giggled.

'Most amusing,' growled Banecroft, 'Need I point out, we wouldn't have to chase or follow this individual if you'd just tackled him like I asked.'

'Tackled him?' repeated Hannah. 'Did you not notice the bit where I was standing fully upright and he almost leaped over me?'

Stella nodded. 'That was not human.'

'I know. And he really does look odd,' said Hannah. 'All that sniffing.'

'And those eyes,' agreed Stella.

'Why do you think he went for you?' asked Hannah.

'No idea,' said Stella. 'Other than the fact I'm becoming quite the weirdo magnet.'

'Oh, love,' sympathized Hannah, 'wait until you've had my dating history before you think that.'

'Could we keep our focus, please?' snapped Banecroft.

'We are,' said Hannah. 'He's stopped at the lights, and lucky for us, it hasn't occurred to him that we could be following him. He's obeying every rule of the road.'

'Exactly,' said Banecroft. 'And when have you ever seen a cyclist do that? There's something very peculiar about this guy.'

'Sure,' said Stella. 'Never mind the bulging eyes and sniffing around a graveyard. It's the stopping at traffic lights that's weird.'

They shadowed the man in the mac all the way down the Princess Parkway and into the city centre, where it became decidedly trickier to continue their pursuit. At one point, Hannah had to run a light up on Deansgate Locks to stay within sight of him. Luckily, the green fabric of the man's coat was unusual enough to stand out even on crowded streets.

They tracked him all the way to the Northern Quarter, where he dismounted on Tib Street and chained his bike to a lamppost. Hannah pulled over, but someone behind them swiftly honked.

'Right,' said Banecroft, kicking open the back door of the Jag, 'I'll follow him. You two go and park the car.'

Stella pushed her door open and got out too. 'Screw that. I'm coming with you.'

'But . . .' started Banecroft, before realizing he had no reason to object.

As it happened, it was the shortest trail in history. They hadn't walked six feet before the man in the mac disappeared into a doorway. They walked past the pair of double doors through which he'd disappeared but, thanks to the frosted glass, they could see nothing other than the sign outside.

'The Victory Hotel,' read Banecroft.

'Looks like our boy is a guest in this fine city,' said Stella.

'Right, I'm going in.'

'Don't you mean we?'

'No,' said Banecroft firmly. 'We don't know why this guy was so interested in you, and until we do, you're staying out of his way. Take up position on the far side of the street and text Hannah what's happening.'

'But—'

'No buts.' Banecroft was resolute. 'I am your editor.'

Reluctantly, Stella did as she was told, and made her way to her position outside the entrance to the car park opposite. She studied the building while she waited – it was three storeys high and, in Stella's limited knowledge of these things, looked a little art deco, with cornicing around the narrow windows and faded red and gold paint. The whole thing looked badly in need of some TLC.

She waited for ten minutes before Hannah turned up.

'Ah, crap,' said Hannah as she noticed the car park. 'I didn't know this was here. I ended up parking up at the Arndale.'

'Banecroft has been in there quite a while,' said Stella, nodding across the road at the Victory. 'Maybe we should . . .'

Before she could finish her suggestion, Banecroft re-emerged from the doors and looked around, as if dazed by the light. He continued to look left and right until Hannah gave him a tentative wave, which prompted him to walk slowly over to them.

'Well?' asked Stella.

'They don't have any rooms and they suggested we try the Premier Inn. The staff were friendly.'

'Right,' said Hannah, 'and what about the guy you followed in there?'

Banecroft gave her a blank look.

'The tall guy in the green mac? The one with the weird eyes, sniffs a lot, remarkably good at jumping?'

Banecroft parted his lips to speak then looked around again, as if the world were a room he'd walked into, and he couldn't remember why he was there.

Hannah clicked her fingers excitedly. 'I know what this is. Someone messed with your mind. The woman at the thing did it to me and to everyone.'

'The woman at the thing?' echoed Stella.

'When I was away investigating the place.'

'Thanks for clearing that up,' said Stella flatly.

Hannah ignored her and looked intently into Banecroft's eyes. 'Do you remember anyone spinning something in front of your face?'

'No.'

'No,' said Hannah, 'I guess you wouldn't.'

Banecroft jabbed a finger at the Victory, his hackles rising. 'Are you telling me someone in there hypnotized me?'

'Yes. Well, sort of.'

'Right. We'll see about that.'

Hannah grabbed Banecroft's arm before he could storm back across the road. 'Hang on, hang on. Think it through. If you go back in there, they'll know something's up.'

'I want to give them a piece of my mind.'

'Sounds like you already have,' said Stella, which earned her a look from her two colleagues. 'What? Only he gets to be sarky? And do I have to be the one to point out the obvious?'

Her question drew nothing but blank looks.

'Apparently so,' Stella said with a sigh. 'The key to our office is supposed to stop people from being able to do their hocus-pocus stuff on you.'

Banecroft came the closest Stella had ever seen to blushing. 'I . . . I may have left it back in the office.'

'Really?' said Hannah. 'The man who spends his time berating everyone else about any minor error makes a whopper like that?'

'If I didn't have to spend so much time correcting the rest of you, maybe I wouldn't have forgotten.'

Stella and Hannah shared a look.

'That is seriously weak, boss,' said Stella.

He jabbed his finger irritably at Hannah. 'Have you got your key?'

'No,' said Hannah, 'because I don't have my own key. There are three and I share one of them with everybody else. This week is Grace's week to have it.'

She and Banecroft looked at Stella, who rolled her eyes and pulled out the key on the chain she wore permanently around her neck. 'Happy?'

'Let's go with satisfied,' said Banecroft. 'Happy isn't really my thing.'

'Ain't that the truth,' muttered Hannah. 'Right, I'm going in.'

'Take my key,' offered Stella.

'No,' said Hannah and Banecroft in perfect unison.

'You never take that off,' said Banecroft. 'Never, ever.'

'That rule is so dumb,' said Stella, then lowered her voice and spoke in a hissed whisper. 'I'm the one with the actual power. I'm the only member of staff who doesn't need protecting. Well, me and Manny.'

'We're not having this discussion again,' said Banecroft. 'You wear that all the time. The. End.'

Stella folded her arms huffily and stared at her feet.

'I don't need it,' Hannah reassured Stella, and gently patted her elbow. 'Forewarned is forearmed.'

'That is such a stupid phrase,' said Stella. 'We all have forearms.'

'I just . . . Never mind,' said Hannah with a shake of her head. 'Stay here and give me a few minutes.' With that, she hurried across the street and in through the hotel doors.

'So, what do you remember?' Stella asked Banecroft after a few seconds.

'I went in there and I' – the confidence drained from his voice – 'politely asked for a room.'

'That doesn't sound like you at all.' Stella fished her phone out of her pocket and started to work away on it industriously. 'Damn, this place has some shocking reviews. Pubes on the bed-sheets . . . no hot water, damp on ceiling, walls, floor. "The dead mouse was the only thing in the room that slept." Pillow had a knife in it. Wow! I mean, complimentary pillow knives. Fancy.'

Banecroft continued to say nothing, which Stella was finding increasingly unnerving. This was the longest she'd seen him not talk. 'Are you feeling OK?'

'No.'

'Want to talk about it?'

'No.'

'Cool. Cool, cool, cool.'

Stella turned her attention back to her screen and continued reading. '"Reported someone strangling a cat. Turns out that's the sound the pipes make when anyone flushes the loo." "Room was somehow colder than the world outside . . ." "I have been homeless; this hotel was worse."' She shook her head. 'How is this place still in business?'

Banecroft continued to stare at the doors. Much to Stella's relief, Hannah re-emerged.

'Here she is,' announced Stella before her heart sank as Hannah simply stood there, looking confused, just as Banecroft had done. 'Oh, shit.'

Hannah waved hesitantly before making her way across the street.

'Let me guess . . .' began Stella.

'They said they were full,' said Hannah, 'and that we should try the Premier Inn.' She rubbed her hand against her forehead. 'I don't feel so well.'

'Yeah,' said Stella, 'I'm thoroughly sick of this myself. C'mon. We're all going in.'

Before anyone could say anything, Stella was halfway across the street. She pushed through the double doors with the frosted glass to discover a reception that looked relatively smart, considering what the reviews were like. Mind you, going by the reviews, she'd have expected it to be on fire, flooded or both. The sofas to the right of the front doors were empty. A woman in her forties with dyed orange hair wearing a blue smock was standing behind the desk on the left. She gave Stella a broad welcoming smile, and when she spoke it was with what even Stella knew was a strong West Country accent.

'All right, love, can I help you?' she asked. Her smile dropped as Stella heard the doors open behind her, which she assumed was Hannah and Banecroft following her inside.

'Yes,' said Stella, 'I'd like to talk to whoever is messing with the minds of my co-workers, please.'

She gave Stella a wary look. 'I don't know what you're talking about.'

'Really?' asked Stella, as she leaned on the counter. 'I'm guessing you do. I'm guessing you . . .'

She broke off as the woman reached for one of those old brass call bells – the kind normally to be found on a counter, but this one was definitely behind the desk, out of the reach of customers.

Stella and the woman locked eyes. Then, when the woman

spoke, all her words came out in a rush. 'You didn't find what you were looking for. You won't be coming back.' And she rang the bell.

The last thing Stella saw before she blacked out was the look of horror on the woman's face.

28

When Stella came to, she was lying on the floor, with Hannah, Banecroft and the woman from the hotel reception standing over her. From this angle she could see a prominent damp patch on the ceiling, which looked a bit like Jesus riding a giraffe. Banecroft and the receptionist were arguing.

'She should have said something,' protested the woman.

'Said?' snapped Banecroft. 'Said what? Don't ring that bell to try to mess with my mind or it'll go badly for you?'

'If she doesn't come round,' said Hannah, 'I'm going to . . . I'm going to complain to your manager.'

Banecroft threw her a look of undisguised disgust. 'Easy, tiger.'

Hannah shrugged awkwardly. 'I'm not very good at confrontation.'

'I am the manager,' said the receptionist-cum-manager, apparently.

'Excellent,' said Banecroft, before jutting his chin at her name badge. 'Well, Janice, I hope your sprinkler systems have been serviced recently, because if she doesn't come to in a minute, I'm going to burn this place to the ground.'

The manager turned to Hannah. 'He, on the other hand, seems to like a bit of the old confrontation.'

'Oh, you have no idea,' said Hannah.

'Put away your matches,' muttered Stella, sitting upright. 'I'm fine. I mean, I . . .'

The weird ringing in her ears was forgotten as she caught sight of the reception desk – at least, what remained of it. It looked a lot like a flaming bull had charged through it. A shattered PC monitor lay on the floor and a smouldering office chair with half its back missing was rotating slowly close by. There was also now a large hole in the wall behind the desk, through which a confused-looking woman was peering at them. The woman in question had a blue face – as in, her skin was entirely blue, with a series of odd ridges across it. She looked as confused as Stella felt.

'What the hell happened?' asked Stella.

'You did, my love,' said the manager, not unkindly.

Hannah knelt beside Stella, pushed her younger colleague's hair behind her ear, and ran a hand gently over the back of her head. 'Any bumps? Are you sure you haven't banged your head or . . .'

Stella pushed her away and pointed at the smoking remains of the reception desk. 'The key did that?'

'What key?' asked the manager, but *The Stranger Times* staff studiously ignored her question.

'Not exactly,' said Banecroft in answer to Stella. 'I don't think it was that thing so much as the other thing. Your thing.'

'Oh,' said Stella.

'Yeah,' said Hannah. 'This lady rang that bell and then your thingy went off. It appears you've got some form of in-built defence mechanism.'

'Oh, super,' said Stella, continuing to stare in horror at the devastation she'd wrought. 'That's good to know.'

Hannah offered her a hand to help her up.

'Sorry,' said the manager. 'If I'd known you were a . . . Wait, what exactly are you?'

'That's a very good question,' said Stella, taking Hannah's hand and easing herself up from the floor.

'But more importantly,' redirected Banecroft, 'what the hell is this place and what makes you think you can go around messing with people's minds?'

Before the manager answered, she made her way over to the main doors and locked them. As she turned, she noticed the blue woman still looking through the hole in the wall. 'Sorry, Agnes, everyone all right?'

Agnes responded in a strong Scottish accent. 'Aye, nae too bad, Janice. Where's me wall gone?'

'Sorry, I'll get the boys right on it.'

'Nae bother, hen,' she said mildly, before disappearing from view. Stella thought she was taking it rather well, considering.

'Who are you exactly?' asked Janice.

'None of your business,' said Banecroft.

'We work for *The Stranger Times*,' supplied Hannah, before catching Banecroft's scowling face. 'Subterfuge went so well I thought I'd give the truth a crack.'

'Oh,' said Janice, visibly relieved. 'You should have said. I'd have assumed you already knew about the Victory. I mean, we've advertised in your paper for, like, twenty years.'

'No, you haven't,' said Banecroft.

Stella clicked her fingers excitedly. 'Let me guess. "Need a place to stay? Call this number."'

The woman nodded and gave a grin. 'That's us. I'm surprised you've never wondered about it.'

'We have a man who offers to both exorcize and exercise your dog in one session, and a woman who will knit you anything you like out of your own body hair,' explained Hannah. 'We leave the small ads well enough alone.'

'Fair dos,' said Janice, before pointing at the sofas. 'Do you want to take a load off?'

Hannah stood on Banecroft's toe before he could say anything.

Once they'd all taken a seat, Janice continued. 'We've existed for . . . well, I don't know how long, to be honest. We were set up by Henry Franklin as a shelter for members of the Folk who've fallen on hard times. You know, people who can't go anywhere else.'

'Who is Henry Franklin?' asked Hannah.

The manager pulled a face. 'Do you lot not know anything?'

'We know you're harbouring a fugitive,' said Banecroft.

'Who?' asked Janice, in a way that suggested to Stella that she was not entirely surprised by the notion.

'I don't know his name, but he walked in here about a quarter of an hour ago. Tall, green mac, weird looking.'

'Brian?' said Janice, sounding surprised. 'What's Brian done?'

'Hang on a sec,' said Stella. 'That dude's name is Brian?'

'Well, it's what I call him. We don't know his real name.'

'I'm sorry,' said Hannah, 'you don't know his name?'

Janice nodded. 'He can't speak, and I don't think he understands much English.'

'But he stays here?' asked Hannah.

'Oh, yeah, for over a year now. He's one of our long-stay guests. Got nowhere else to go, what with him being a ghoul and all.'

'A what?' said Banecroft.

Janice looked at all three of them. 'Bloody hell, you lot really know nothing, do you?'

Banecroft clasped his hands in exasperation. 'Probably because people keep messing with our memories. Speaking of which, what makes you think you've got the right to go around doing that to people?'

Janice stiffened. 'We've got people in here that need protecting. Every now and again we've got to wipe the memory of them who come in here looking for more than a room. The bell doodah is a . . . Call it a magical protection device.'

'Which apparently,' began Banecroft, pointing at Stella, 'doesn't work on her.'

'No shit, Sherlock. I've got a wall that can attest to that. So, back to Brian. What do you think he's done?'

Banecroft paused for a second. 'Hard as it may be to believe, we think he robbed a body out of a grave.'

Stella wasn't sure exactly what response to expect, but the laughter took her by surprise.

'I fail to see how that is funny,' Banecroft sniped.

'He's a ghoul, you numpty. I'm going to assume you don't know what one of them is neither.' She shook her head in disbelief.

'I don't suppose there's a book we could buy with all this in it?' ventured Hannah.

'A book! I'm having a hard time figuring out which of you three is the least mad. So far, I'm going with the girl what blew a hole in my wall.'

'So,' said Banecroft, 'what is a ghoul?'

'Seeing as you asked so nicely, they're the keepers of the dead. It's an old thing. Dying out. Most of the clans don't do it no more. Pretty brutal, to be honest.'

'But what is it?' persisted Banecroft.

Janice's nostrils flared. 'I'm tryna explain that, ain't I? In the old days, when families had more kids than they knew what to do with, they'd offer one up to be a ghoul. It was . . . It's hard to explain in modern terms without it seeming awful, but it was considered an honour and, y'know, a career for the child. Sorta like joining one of them religious orders, only they're not so pious nor judgy, and there's a lot less bell ringing. They're charged with protecting the dead, y'see? Living near graveyards to watch over 'em. Dedicate their lives to it.

'It was a serious thing back when graves needed protecting. Different times. People who don't understand the old ways think ghouls are some horrible sort of necromantic cannibal, but that's all bunk. It's people getting everything arse-ways around and jumping to conclusions because these folk look a little odd. Like I said, having one was an honour for the family. They'd bring 'em gifts on certain days, all that.'

'You keep saying old times,' said Hannah in a soft voice, 'but this guy you call Brian is here now.'

Janice shrugged. 'I dunno what to tell you. Got brought in here last year, half dead he was. Injured, starving. All we know is, he don't speak and, like I said, don't understand much English, as far as we can tell. My guess is he got brought here from another part of the world with family or, well, your guess is as good as mine. I can tell you, soon as he was well enough, he went out patrolling the graveyards. Visits each one in Manchester, every day, like clockwork. I gave him that bike when someone left it behind. Recently he's been coming back very agitated but I can't tell you why.'

'From what you said, he should be living in a graveyard?' asked Banecroft.

'Well, yeah. This day and age, though, you think it'd be possible for someone like him to live in a graveyard and have nobody notice? He's in and out all hours of the day, though. And the very last thing he'd be doing is messing with graves, I can assure you of that.'

Banecroft nodded. 'But I bet he wants to find out who has been. Sounds like Brian and I might have something in common.'

29

The four of them walked mostly in silence as Janice led them up to the third floor of the hotel. She apologized for the lift being out of order and them having to take the stairs instead. The place had a musky smell to it and the corridors Stella glimpsed looked rather dark and unwelcoming. On the stairs, they passed a couple with a young child, who Janice greeted warmly but only received a curt nod in reply.

'What are they?' Hannah asked in a quiet voice after they'd passed.

'Tourists, I'd imagine,' answered Janice. 'French, if memory serves.'

'Oh,' said Stella, 'I wonder if they need to know where the library is? Wait, where is the nearest library?'

'But what are tourists doing staying here?' asked Hannah.

'We don't just host members of the Folk as guests,' Janice clarified. 'We're an ordinary hotel, too. Admittedly, we only have so many rooms available and we don't really want people staying here regularly in case they start noticing stuff. Besides, can't keep using the bell on people or they go a bit funny.'

'That's very reassuring to hear,' said Banecroft.

Janice waved away his concern. 'Relax. You've only been dinged the once.'

'Disconcertingly,' said Banecroft, 'I'm going to have to take your word for that.'

Janice pushed open the third-floor stairwell door and led them into the hallway.

'Ah,' said Stella, 'I get it. That explains the online reviews.'

'What's that?' asked Janice.

'All the reviews – they're to discourage people from staying here.'

She stopped in front of a door and gave Stella a most perplexed look. 'What are you talking about? Are there reviews of us on the internet?'

'Ehm . . . yeah.'

Janice's face lit up. 'Ohhhh, fancy. I don't really go online and all that. I'll have a looksee, though.'

'I—' started Stella, feeling suddenly terrible as she looked into Janice's friendly face. 'I wouldn't bother.'

'Anyways,' Janice said, pointing at the door to room sixty-seven. 'This here is Brian. He'll have no doubt smelled us coming from a long way away. I'll go in first and calm him down as best I can and then you can come in.' She looked pointedly at Banecroft. 'Be gentle with him. He's a sensitive soul.'

An upward jut of his chin was the only acknowledgement Banecroft gave to this request. Janice studied him for a long moment then turned and knocked on the door.

From inside the room came the distinct sound of scurrying feet.

'Brian,' said Janice in a raised voice. 'It's Janice here, from reception. I have some people with me. I think you and them got off on the wrong foot, but they're actually nice' – her eyes darted to Banecroft briefly – 'mostly, and they want to help you. OK? I'm going to come in now.'

Janice looked back at Hannah. 'God knows how much of that he understood. Stand back until I say.'

She slowly opened the door.

Stella caught a brief flash of a face inside the room, two big bulbous eyes looking out, and then it was hidden from view as Janice moved inside. From what Stella could make out, the room was about six feet by ten feet in size and didn't appear to have a window. She guessed the off-yellow flock wallpaper wasn't popular even back in the 1970s when it was probably first put up. She also spotted a painting of a window, which seemed more like mockery than a conscious interior design choice.

Janice placed her hand in the pocket of the blue smock she was wearing and produced a muffin. 'See? Everything is OK. Nobody is angry. Look, I brought you a muffin.'

Stella watched as a bony hand with long dirty fingernails reached out and snatched the muffin from Janice's grasp.

'There you go,' she said in a cheery voice, over the sound of the muffin being quickly devoured. 'You're not supposed to eat the paper , though . . . Know what? Never mind. You do you, my love. You do you. Now – these three people are from *The Stranger Times*. It's the newspaper. I appreciate you probably don't know what that is, but they're friends, OK? Friends. They say they're worried about people messing with a grave, and I know that's your thing. So, they're going to come in now.'

Janice turned to the door and nodded at Hannah, who moved inside slowly. Banecroft followed, with Stella bringing up the rear.

The ghoul, Brian, was sitting on one corner of the unmade single bed, his long bony arms wrapped around himself. His wide eyes, which had previously seemed terrifying, now looked only terrified. As Stella entered, his lips curled back and he made a guttural noise. One of his long-nailed fingers jabbed in her direction and then at the wall behind the door.

'Oh dear,' said Janice, sounding concerned. 'He doesn't like you. Maybe you should wait outside?'

Stella turned to leave, but caught sight of the wall where he'd been pointing and stopped. Around fifty Polaroid pictures were stuck to it in a grid formation. Suddenly, she got it.

'Hang on,' she said. 'I know what this is.'

She could feel the rest of the room tense as she took a step towards the bed and held out a hand.

Brian hissed but Stella spoke in as calm a voice as she could muster. 'It's OK, Brian, I get it. I understand why you're angry at me, but let me explain.'

She took a couple of steps sideways until she was standing beside the tiny desk with the Polaroids arranged on the wall above it. Each one was of a grave. She scanned them all and found the one she was looking for near the top. With a nod to Brian, she carefully raised her hand to take it down, trying not to think about what had been used to stick it up there.

She turned and held out the image in her hand. 'This is the grave of Simon Brush.' She then brought the picture to her chest.

'He was my friend. My friend.' She nodded at Hannah and Banecroft, who were watching her nervously. 'Our friend. I dug up his grave, but we did it to help him. OK? I was helping him. Bad people were hurting him, and we made it stop.' Brian's enormous eyes darted from her, over to Banecroft and Hannah, who were nodding in agreement, and then back again. Stella pointed at the picture again. 'Friend. I promise.'

There was a palpable easing of Brian's demeanour. He blinked a couple of times, pointed at the picture and then at Stella.

'That's right,' she said. 'Friend. He is . . . he is safe now.'

He nodded slowly. It was impossible to tell, really, but Stella thought it was making some kind of sense to him.

'Right,' said Janice in a cheery tone. 'Well, now that's all been sorted out, I'll leave you lot to get acquainted.'

'But . . .' started Hannah warily.

'Busy day, Saturday. And I've got to go clean up reception. You know where I am if you need me.' And with that, she pushed past them and closed the door behind her.

An awkward moment descended as the three of them stood there, with Brian looking up at them, nobody knowing what to say.

Eventually Hannah went with, 'You have a lovely room.'

'All right,' said Banecroft, 'let's not undo Stella's good work by lying to the chap.' He edged past his colleagues to the wall of photographs and studied it carefully. After a few seconds, he pulled one off and held it up. 'That's what I thought. This is the grave of William Ignatius Campbell. Look, it's got a date on it. The twenty-second of October. That tallies with what the grave-digger said.'

Stella peered at the Polaroid of Simon's grave she still held. A date was written at the bottom in a scrawling, slanted hand. 'I'd have to check, but I'm pretty sure this was the date Betty and I dug up Simon's grave.'

'That means . . .'

Hannah took a step forward for a better look at the wall. 'All of these pictures have dates on them, too. There must be over forty of them.'

Banecroft moved his hand around to indicate the photographs and looked pointedly at Brian. 'Have all these graves been interfered with too?'

Brian gave an emphatic nod.

'Christ,' said Banecroft, looking back at the wall, 'we've got a bloody epidemic of grave-robbing.'

Stella flinched, as did Brian, as Banecroft clapped his hands together. 'OK, here's the deal. You want to stop whatever this is. So do we. What do you say we work together and find the monumental shitheel behind it all?'

Banecroft, Hannah and Stella moved back as far as was possible in the small room as Brian scrabbled across the bed and disappeared into the bathroom, slamming the door behind him.

'Something I said?' asked Banecroft mildly.

'Maybe he just needed—' started Hannah, but she was interrupted by the bathroom door flying open once again. Brian re-emerged with a rather ratty-looking toothbrush in his hand. He then bent down and picked up his green mac from where it lay on the floor in a crumpled pile.

The Stranger Times trio looked at each other and then back at

Brian, who had now scrambled back onto the bed and was withdrawing a pair of socks and a pair of underpants from the bedside-table drawer.

Stella gave a wry smile. 'Looks like he's packing to come with us.'

A minute later, once Brian had gathered up his meagre possessions, including each and every one of the Polaroid pictures from the wall – all of which he was able fit into the pockets of his mac – he was clearly ready to go. Nobody was more surprised than Banecroft when Brian reached out and grasped his hand.

'Erm . . .'

Stella and Hannah failed to suppress smiles.

'Right,' said Banecroft, raising his eyebrows, 'time to go.'

The newly formed group walked down the stairs again, led by Brian and Banecroft, walking hand in hand, and re-emerged into reception.

Janice was sitting behind the desk, which had somehow been fully restored to its former glory, peering at her PC. The hole in the wall was also gone. In fact, there was no evidence whatsoever of the earlier incident.

'Oh, wow,' said Hannah, spinning around. 'This is the same way we came in, isn't it?'

Janice looked up from her computer screen, a look of horror on her face. 'Never mind that. Have you seen these reviews?'

Stella winced. 'Oh, no.'

'"I flushed the loo to get rid of a poo,"' read Janice, '"but when I looked down, there were two poos."'

'So, Brian and us are going to—' started Hannah, but Janice was entirely lost in the content of her screen.

'"This place is brilliant,"' continued Janice. 'Oh, that's good . . . Wait a sec, which film is *Saw*? Oh, hang on, that's not a compliment at all . . .'

Stella attempted to wave, but poor Janice was not in a waving mood.

They all made their way back outside through the frosted glass doors. The last thing they heard as they left was Janice's mortified voice, which followed them outside. '"This place doesn't have rats, thus proving that even rats have standards!" How dare they – we bloody well do have rats!'

30

Ox leaned against the reception desk of *The Stranger Times* and finger-drummed the beat of 'I'm Free' by the Soup Dragons, which was currently playing on a loop in his head. He stopped at the sound of Reggie sitting in Grace's chair and pointedly clearing his throat. Ox mumbled an apology and shoved his hands into his armpits to keep them away from stray beats.

'All I'm saying is this is bloody typical,' he moaned. 'The three of them running off, doing something exciting, while we get left doing the boring work.'

'First,' said Reggie, glancing up from the book he was reading, 'neither one of us is actually doing any work at the minute. And second, I have quite enough danger in my life already, thank you very much.'

'Yeah, but, like, we gave up our Saturday to stake out a graveyard, Banecroft didn't even explain what it was all about, and then the three of 'em run off somewhere.'

'They ran off after the person we were there to find. It was a sort of' – Reggie waved a clenched fist awkwardly in the air – 'a mission-accomplished thing.'

'I'm just saying,' continued Ox, 'I could do with a bit more excitement in my life.'

'We both got taken prisoner by armed storm troopers a couple of months ago. That was pretty exciting.'

Grace returned from the kitchen, carrying a tray bearing cups of tea and some biscuits. 'What is exciting?'

'Ox says he doesn't have enough excitement in his life,' said Reggie, who started to get up from Grace's seat, but she waved him back down.

'Did you not get chased around a park in the middle of the night a few months ago by some magical crazy person with weird face paint on who was trying to kill you?'

Reggie took his mug off the proffered tray. 'Thank you, Grace, dear. Not to mention the werewolf that attempted to attack us all about six feet from where we are currently sitting.'

The memory of that moment prompted Grace to bless herself.

'Is it possible,' continued Reggie, 'that as a recovering gambling addict, this is more about your perpetual need for excitement?'

'No, I don't think it is,' said Ox, taking his mug off the tray. 'Cheers, Gracie. I'm just saying, Banecroft makes us work Saturday, traipsing around in the pouring rain, and then doesn't tell us what's going on.'

'I am sure he had his reasons,' said Grace, taking her own mug before perching on the edge of the desk.

'Still,' said Ox, 'I might've had plans for today.'

'You didn't, though,' said Reggie. 'As tragic as it sounds, you and I were going to spend our Saturday night binge-watching *The Last of Us*.'

'What is that?'

'TV show,' said Ox. 'Zombie Gary says it's the greatest thing that has ever been on TV.'

'You have a friend called Zombie Gary?' asked Grace.

'Yeah, he's not actually a zombie, though. He just walks like that because he broke a bone in his foot and it didn't heal right. But, going back to my original point, I could have had plans.'

'I have plans,' said Grace, blowing on her mug of tea.

'Do ya?' asked Ox.

'Yes,' said Grace, looking offended. 'Is that so surprising?'

'I just meant—'

'As it happens, a lovely gentleman from my church called Richard has offered to take me out to dinner.'

'Ohhhh,' said Reggie, raising his eyebrows, 'where is he taking you?'

'A place called Hawksmoor.'

This elicited a low whistle from Ox. 'It's nice there, I hear. Dead expensive.'

'The reviews are very good,' confirmed Reggie. 'You don't need to cancel, Grace. We have everything covered here.'

She shrugged. 'I will see what happens. If I am busy, I am busy. If he wants to go out, I am sure he will ask again.'

Reggie applauded. 'I like it, Grace – know thy worth. Very well played, madam.'

Grace tried to hide it, but she gave a little smile.

'Yeah,' said Ox, 'treat 'em mean, keep 'em keen.'

The sound of footsteps on the stairs caused them all to turn around.

'Sounds like the hunters have returned,' said Reggie.

First Hannah and then Stella appeared at the top of the stairs.

'So,' said Ox, 'did you catch the weirdo?'

He immediately winced as Banecroft appeared at the top of the stairs, hand in hand with the aforementioned weirdo.

Banecroft scowled at Ox. 'This is Brian.'

Brian, for his part, looked around nervously, his large eyes taking everything in. To Ox's mind, he looked like a chimp crossed with Gollum, if Gollum had been better built for basketball.

'Oh, right,' said Ox awkwardly. 'Y'all right, Brian?'

'Brian doesn't speak,' said Hannah measuredly.

'As far as we know,' added Stella.

Reggie got to his feet and smiled at Brian. 'That will be a refreshing change from the rest of the occupants of this particular asylum who frankly never shut up. Welcome.'

'We are also not entirely sure how much he understands of what we say,' said Hannah.

Banecroft walked across reception with Brian, still holding his hand, trailing behind him. 'More importantly, Brian here shares our desire to find out who is digging up dead bodies as he is a ghoul.'

'Vincent!' scolded Grace. 'Don't call the poor man names.'

'I'm not. That's what he actually is. He can smell lots of things, apparently – especially dead bodies or, indeed, their absence.'

'Oh,' said Grace, clearly unsure what to make of that. 'That is . . . interesting.'

'Yes,' said Banecroft. 'Speaking of which . . .' He turned to Brian and held out his free hand. 'May I have the photographs?'

Brain looked at him for a long moment then slowly put his hand into his pocket and withdrew a stack of Polaroid pictures.

'Yes,' said Banecroft, nodding, 'that's them.'

He went to take them but Brian pulled away.

'It's OK,' said Banecroft. He pointed at Ox, Reggie and Grace, and spoke more loudly. 'These three are going to help you find the bad person or people behind it.'

Brian gave them a wary look and dropped the grip he had on Banecroft's hand.

'Poor Brian looks famished,' said Grace, cocking her head. 'Maybe we should feed him first?'

She took the plate of biscuits off the reception desk and held them out to Brian, who looked up at Banecroft. Banecroft gave him a nod and Grace yelped and dropped the plate as Brian sprang forward. Unperturbed, he fell to his knees and started to shovel the biscuits into his mouth with his free hand, like Cookie Monster gone feral.

'Oh my,' said Grace, holding a hand to her chest, 'the poor chap must be starving. I will nip home. I've got some jollof rice in the freezer and some chicken I can heat up.'

'But, Grace,' said Reggie, 'what about your—'

She waved him into silence as she picked up her car keys.

Once Brian had finished the biscuits, he picked up the plate, licked it thoroughly, then handed it back to Grace.

She smiled and took it. 'Thank you very much.'

'Right,' said Banecroft, holding out his hand to Brian again, 'can we have the pictures? We will give them back and it will help us find out what's going on.'

Brian considered the Polaroids in his hand, then tentatively handed them over. 'Thank you,' Banecroft said, before passing them on to Ox. 'They've all got dates on them. Take a look through, see what you can find.'

At the sound of creaking floorboards the group turned as one as Manny appeared at the top of the stairs.

'We lighter disappeared again.'

'Guys,' said Stella, 'Manny is—'

She didn't get to finish as Brian sprinted across reception and threw himself prostrate on the ground at Manny's feet. He then proceeded to rock up and down, arms outstretched in worshipful reverence.

'What the hell?' said Banecroft.

Everyone else looked at each other, mystified.

The Rastafarian himself looked bemused, which was not exactly an uncommon occurrence. He looked down at Brian and blinked a couple of times. Ox saw a change in his eyes, as if they had clouded over.

A wisp of smoke emerged from Manny's fingers and seemed to form itself into a hand. Brian stopped moving and looked up, tears in his big bulbous eyes and a look of ecstasy on his face as the ghostly hand stroked the top of his head.

The entire team stood in silence as this carried on for about a minute before the ghostly hand drew back and Manny shook his head, as if waking up.

'Well,' said Reggie in a soft voice, 'even for here, that was a little odd.'

'Right.' Banecroft slapped his hands together, causing everyone to jump. 'To be honest, if we're going to worship a member of staff as a living god, then I'd prefer it if it were me. But failing that, let's all stop standing around with our fingers up our you-know-wheres and get to work.'

And with that, he stomped off.

Manny wandered off towards the kitchen as Brian sat on the floor and watched him go. The rest of the staff exchanged looks again.

'I don't know about anyone else,' said Ox, 'but I'm really glad Manny was wearing trousers for that.'

31

Doug pulled the van into his usual parking spot on Arrowfield Road and stopped. Blake and Marsh had made a big deal about never parking in the same place twice and all that, but they weren't the ones having to shift a dead body back into the van. Sure, he had the trolley, but it was still a bloody tough job. People didn't talk about dead weight for nothing.

That was always the way, though – the 'talent' didn't give a crap about how awkward or otherwise it was for the grunts to do their bidding. They just wanted you to get it done. He was out here, night after night, all weathers, in the wee small hours and nobody gave a monkey's. He said 'on his own' but Kitty, the bloody cat, insisted on coming. He was sitting there now in the passenger seat, looking up at him, waiting to be released. Doug didn't know what he got up to out there in the dark on these nights and he didn't want to know.

He opened the door and without so much as a by your leave, Kitty hopped out and disappeared into the darkness.

'You'd better be there if I need you,' said Doug, towards the last known sighting of the little psychopath.

He got out of the van and stretched out his back. At least the gap in the fence was still there. He could, and would, make a new one if he had to, but it would just be additional hassle. He made his way around to the back of the van and loaded up the trolley. To be fair, seeing as some of the kit was a bit magical and that, it wasn't as much hassle as it could have been. It made what would've been at least a two-man job that would take most of the night into just a really awkward one-man job that took half of the night. He finished loading the big chest onto the trolley, picked up his crowbar, locked up the van and headed off.

The trolley more or less drove itself, Doug just needed to be there to direct it. These days, he knew the grid locations of Southern Cemetery off by heart, so he knew where he was headed without needing the assistance of a map. The torch was on mainly to make sure he wasn't walking into any particularly muddy bits. That and, as he'd discovered on one of his first nights doing this, you had to keep an eye out for graves that had been dug for use the next day. There was that time he'd ended up having to call Blake to help him get the bloody chest out of the hole it'd fallen into. He'd still not heard the end of that one.

Previously, Doug had done Blackley, Agecroft and Bury cemeteries, but they were a lot smaller, which made them more awkward to get in and out of. Sure, he had a considerable advantage in that area, but it still helped to have a bit more space. Less chance of people wandering by while you were working. It might be two in the morning, but people were still plenty nosy.

'Check out this fucking weirdo.'

Doug jumped. Shit. He'd forgotten to do the most important thing.

A couple of teenagers were standing in front of him, eyeing him up. The boy was pointing the light on his phone at Doug, while the girl cowered behind him, looking like she wanted to run, but the lad was big and stood with his legs spread, chest puffed out like he wanted to be all impressive.

'I work here,' said Doug.

'My arse,' came the response. 'Nobody works here in the middle of the night. Check this freak out, Katy. He's got a big box and a crowbar. What the actual fuck? Are you a vampire?'

'C'mon, Jason,' said the girl. 'Let's get out of here.'

'Nah. This dude is a wrong'un and I reckon he needs to be taxed.'

Doug shook his head as he pulled the hourglass from his coat pocket. God save the world from young idiots. Why couldn't the lad just do what young couples have been doing in graveyards for centuries. A large section of the population had been conceived in places like this. Circle of life and all that. But no, Jason here had to be an awkward little sod.

'Boo!' said Doug.

Jason laughed. 'You ain't scaring me, man.'

'No?' said Doug, before turning the hourglass over. 'How about now?'

There was an awkward moment before Jason looked back at Katy and shrugged. 'Still no, you hairy little freak.'

Shit. 'Give it a second.' Doug tapped the hourglass then felt that familiar sensation as the bubble enveloped him. He didn't know how it worked, obviously, but he knew what it did. When it was activated, everything within eight feet of the hourglass was rendered invisible. It wasn't a force field or anything like that. A few weeks ago, a fox had wandered into Doug's little bubble by accident and totally freaked out. Speaking of freaking out . . .

Katy screamed and ran off into the darkness. Jason did a double take between the point where Doug had – from his perspective – just disappeared from, and the departing figure of his soon-to-be ex-girlfriend, then sprinted after her. 'Katy! Babes, wait for me!'

After a few seconds, Doug heard the gratifying noise of Jason colliding with a gravestone and coming off much the worse, before limp-running away as fast as his one good remaining leg would carry him.

'Young people today,' muttered Doug, giving the trolley a nudge in the right direction. 'I do despair.'

Dr Marsh was a pain in his arse right enough, but her little toys came in handy all the same.

It didn't take him long to find the grave. It had been dug that day. Ideally, Doug tried to get to them as soon as possible. Get 'em while they're still fresh, so to speak, and nobody noticed if the grave was disturbed so soon after being filled in. He played his torch across the marker. 'Elizabeth Jane Harper' – this was the one, all right. One of the many things Dr Marsh didn't understand was that it was her requirements for the subjects that made the acquisition of them so tricky. If he could just bring her any old corpse, then this would be a doddle.

He stopped the trolley and opened the chest. The four weird little brass gnomes were remarkably heavy for their size. He placed one in each corner of the grave plot. Then, he took out the two ordinary electric lanterns that he'd thankfully remembered to charge this time and placed them on either side of the grave. That done, he pulled out his deckchair, copy of *Spin* magazine, packet of sandwiches and flask of mushroom soup. Once he'd got himself into a comfortable position, he said three words in a language he didn't recognize but which Marsh had taught him to say phonetically, and the brass gnomes sprang to life instantly, digging away in a criss-cross pattern and tossing the earth into four remarkably neat piles. For the first few times, Doug had stood there and watched in wonder. Now, it would be like sitting there watching in awe as the washing machine did its thing. Actually, given the scant amount of laundry Doug did, that would have been a more exciting experience.

He confirmed they were working as they should be, then he flicked open his magazine.

'Oh, look at that,' he said to no one, 'Queen are touring again. Now there's a group that hasn't let a little death get in the way of a good thing.'

32

Hannah awoke with a start, which was quickly followed by a moment of panic before she snatched the blindfold off her eyes. She was greeted by the sight of DI Tom Sturgess sitting beside her in the back seat of a jeep and the immense form of John Mór behind the steering wheel in front, both men looking at her with concern.

'You OK?' asked John Mór.

'Course,' said Hannah, running a hand across her mouth self-consciously.

'You fell asleep,' said Sturgess. 'Kind of impressive to be blindfolded in the back of a strange man's car and still be able to fall asleep.'

Hannah sat upright. 'John's not a stranger.'

'Don't mean I'm not strange,' said John Mór, before adding, 'We're here.' He opened his door and gave Sturgess a pointed look. 'Behave yourselves and remember our agreement.'

'Agreement?' repeated Sturgess. 'I just remember a series of demands.'

'That you agreed to, Inspector.'

'Detective Inspector.'

John Mór rolled his eyes and started to get out of the vehicle.

It had not been a fun morning. Clearly, John Mór had been asked to include DI Sturgess on the invitation to whatever this was, and he was doing so against his will. For Sturgess's part, he had not been wild about the arrangement either.

'Let me get this straight,' Sturgess had said. 'As a serving member of the Greater Manchester Police, you'd like me to surrender my phone and then get in the back of your jeep, where you're going to blindfold me and drive me to an unknown location.'

'If it was a known location,' John Mór had replied, 'there'd be no need for the blindfold, would there?'

'Did you seriously expect me to agree to this?'

'I was told to bring you,' John Mór said, with a shrug of his colossal shoulders. 'To be honest with you, I'd much rather spend my Sunday morning out fishing, but I do what I'm told. If you don't want to do what you're told, that's absolutely fine. I'll just bring Hannah here and you can go harass someone, or whatever it is you do with your time.'

'It's mainly protecting and serving,' said Sturgess.

'Who exactly?' responded John Mór. 'Nobody I know, that's for sure.'

'OK,' said Hannah, 'if we're all done with the antler-bashing, Tom, I'm sure John is only asking for these security arrangements because they are the wishes of whoever is at the other end.'

Sturgess had gone to speak, but Hannah had kept going before he could.

'I appreciate it's unusual, but then what isn't about this case?

For what it is worth, I trust John completely, and if we just go along with these requirements, we'll hopefully get the answers we're looking for.'

Sturgess had grumbled something and nodded.

The atmosphere in the jeep had been tense, and Hannah had discovered how very hard it is to make small talk while blindfolded. And then she'd fallen asleep. In her defence, she had been up all night in the office, working away with the rest of the team.

Her phone vibrated in her pocket and, without thinking, she took it out and looked at it. Stella. Again.

'Hey,' said Sturgess, 'how come she got to keep her phone?'

'I trust her,' said John Mór. 'Now, do I need to blindfold you again or can you walk the fifteen feet to the front door without making a full-on inquiry out of it?'

'Of course you can,' said Hannah, fully aware that the question wasn't meant for her. 'C'mon, Tom, let's go.'

Hannah glanced around quickly as she exited the vehicle. They were in a garden surrounded by high coniferous trees on all sides, which belonged to a picturesque thatch-roofed cottage. It appeared to be on a hillside. The freshly whitewashed stone walls and the garden's array of carefully manicured flowers and bushes gave it a slightly surreal picture-postcard vibe.

John Mór, crouching down to avoid hitting his head on the doorframe, led them inside and through a wooden door. It brought them into a living room that had been transformed into a waiting area, with two rows of mismatched chairs facing each other.

Hannah, John Mór and Sturgess sat down on one side. The room's only other occupant was an old man wearing sunglasses sitting at the end of the row opposite. Hannah wasn't one hundred per cent certain he was alive. At least, she wasn't until he spoke.

'John.'

'Lenny,' responded John Mór. 'How's life?'

'Still happening.'

'That it is.'

'How's Margo?'

'Same.'

'Tell her I asked.'

'Will do.'

This was seemingly the end of the exchange.

Now seated, Hannah availed herself of the opportunity to look at all the memorabilia in the room. It was primarily pictures and posters on the walls for a band called the Sisters Divine. In the centre of all the other photographs was a larger one of a trio of glamorous-looking women who looked like the Supremes with their beehive hairdos and matching outfits, although they were White, Black and Asian. They stood arm in arm on stage, beaming smiles while preparing to take a bow. Arranged around the central photograph were smaller images of the sisters meeting various individuals. Hannah didn't recognize most of them, but some she did. She was pretty sure the distinguished-looking gent on the top left was a famous music producer. There were a couple of others who looked like boxers or famous footballers. The person in the second-largest photograph was Aretha Franklin.

Hannah had never been good with silence, so she racked her brain to think of an ice-breaker. Then she realized there was something she had actually meant to ask. 'Oh,' she said, turning to Sturgess who was sitting to her left, 'how did your interview go with the woman?'

'The woman?'

'The woman from the Peacock Lounge.'

'Oh, yes,' said Sturgess. 'Didn't get anything. It was a bit odd, actually. She didn't remember the incident at all.'

'Really?'

'Yeah. I mean, she thought she'd got drunk, been unwell and then gone straight home.'

'So no memory of . . .'

'Setting a drag club on fire? No. I showed her the footage and she was horrified.'

'Oh.'

'She's off work – some virus, according to the doctor – so I don't know if her recall was the best, but I'm pretty sure you'd remember something like that. Mind you, she seemed a little out of it. And she claimed she'd had no' – he glanced around awkwardly – 'unusual powers. Seemed horrified by the very idea.'

'Do you think she was telling the truth?'

Sturgess ran a hand over his immaculately trimmed beard. 'If she was lying, she's one hell of an actress. Her memory of the night was, like I said, getting drunk, being unwell, then grabbing a taxi.' He paused. 'And then, oddly, staying up watching *Lawrence of Arabia*, which she hadn't seen before but she was very impressed by.'

'Right,' said Hannah, before silently considering this for a bit. 'Come to think of it, I've never seen it either.'

'Nor me.'

'It's a classic,' offered John Mór, giving the first indication that he'd been paying attention to the conversation. 'Peter O'Toole was apparently so afraid of falling off his camel that they had to get him blind drunk and strap him onto it.'

'Fascinating,' mused Hannah.

'So,' said Sturgess, in a grinding change of conversational gear, 'when do we get told who we are here to meet?'

John Mór gave him a look and then pointed at the largest picture on the wall. 'You have been granted an audience with the Sisters Divine.'

Sturgess laughed. 'You're kidding?'

Hannah could feel John Mór tensing in the seat beside her. 'Mind your manners.'

'I think what Tom is trying to say,' interjected Hannah, 'is who are the Sisters Divine?'

John Mór scratched at his beard before answering. 'They were a musical group. Wonderfully talented, too. I mean, not my type of music normally, but being in the same room as the three of them when they performed – it was something magical.' There was a genuine sense of awe in his voice. 'I mean, not *magical* magical, but, well, you had to be there . . .'

'Amen,' said Lenny, with a nod.

'The Sisters also have a very special gift. They've had it since they were born.'

'Hang on,' said Hannah. 'They're actually sisters?'

'They are,' confirmed John Mór.

'Adopted or half-sisters?' asked Sturgess.

'Neither.'

'That isn't possible.'

'Maybe in your world.'

'All right, then – explain it to me?'

'What you want to know and what you get to know are two very different things.'

The two men locked eyes.

'What is this gift?' asked Hannah, keen to move the conversation on.

'Their gift,' said John Mór, 'along with being blessed with a great deal of wisdom, is that they can show other people their gifts. They're like . . . to put it in crude terms, amplifiers.'

They all looked up as the door at the far end of the room opened. A grumpy-looking kid of about twelve years of age emerged, followed by his parents. The mother was in tears but smiling, and the father had his arm around her.

As the kid stomped out, the parents stopped to shake hands with John Mór.

'John,' said the father.

'Yussef. How was it?'

'Tiki is a pass.'

John patted the man's arm. 'Congratulations.' He nodded at the door. 'I see he's taking it well.'

The mother laughed as she wiped her nose. 'You know how kids are.'

With a smile at Hannah and Sturgess, they followed their son out the door and closed it behind them.

After a minute, Hannah spoke again. 'Can I ask what that was about?'

John Mór stroked his beard for a long moment, long enough for Hannah to wonder if her question had been rude, but then he started to speak. 'How much do you know about the Cost?'

'Not much,' admitted Hannah. 'I mean, I know it's part of the Accord, which is the peace deal between the Folk and the Founders. You all stop fighting and in exchange for that, the Folk provide the Founders with the' – this was the point at which Hannah's knowledge ran out – 'energy that keeps them alive.'

John Mór nodded. 'Anima. It's the stuff of life and it's in all of us, to a greater or lesser degree – even the inspector here. Folk have more of it than ordinary people do, as a rule, hence their abilities in certain areas. Some ordinary people still have a considerable quantity of anima, though . . .'

'The anomalies?' said Hannah.

John Mór nodded approvingly. 'The anomalies. Young Tiki there was the opposite. He's a pass, in that it has passed him by. A member of the Folk with not much anima in him.'

'And his parents were happy about that?' asked Sturgess.

John Mór nodded. 'Delighted. It's the Cost. Each of the clans decides how they pay their share, but they all have to, however they select them. Some clans have lotteries, some have'– he paused, glancing at Sturgess – 'other systems. The point is, if you're unlucky enough to be selected, there's a very good chance the process leaves you a shell of yourself. Even if it doesn't, you always have this terrible feeling that something is missing. Wake up with it every morning, go to bed with it every night. Hard to explain to non-Folk but . . . well, the Cost is the right name for it. That's leaving aside those poor people who don't make it back at all. Now can you see why young Tiki's parents are so happy?'

'He hasn't got much to contribute?' asked Hannah.

John Mór gave another nod. 'So, at least in their clan, he will not be asked to. A young boy might dream of being blessed with magical abilities, but his parents dream of him just having a happy and healthy normal life.'

This phrase hung in the room for a long time, as they all considered it. The silence was broken by Hannah's phone vibrating again.

'You might want to turn that off,' said John Mór.

'Sorry, sorry,' said Hannah, glancing at it before doing just that. 'It's Stella. She's got a terrible idea, and she wants me to run it by the detective inspector.'

Sturgess raised an eyebrow at her.

'She's got it in her head that if people are taking these drugs and experiencing these side effects or, well, whatever we're calling them, she, as our resident student, should go out, undercover – only, well, as herself – and see if she can find out what's going on.'

'That's not the worst idea,' said Sturgess.

'Yes,' said Hannah, 'it is.'

'I mean, we'd obviously be there, monitoring her, but if she could identify a dealer, we could try to follow them back to their source.'

'Haven't you got police who can do that?'

'Yes,' agreed Sturgess, 'currently all part of the drug task-force. Would you like to guess how well that meeting will go if I go in and explain we need to find the source of some ecstasy tablets because people are developing magical abilities after taking them?'

Hannah pinched the bridge of her nose. 'Crap. I promised I'd ask on the assumption you'd say no. I'll run it by Banecroft. He, I assume, will say no.'

Sturgess shrugged. 'Your call. I'm just saying, not the worst idea we've had.'

They all looked up as Lenny cleared his throat. 'The Sisters will see you now.'

As the three of them stood, John Mór turned to Sturgess. 'I appreciate this is all new to you, so let me be very clear. These ladies are the closest thing the Folk will ever have to proper royalty. You will show respect and speak when spoken to.'

'They invited me here,' said Sturgess.

'And you'll be uninvited with prejudice if I feel it is required.'

'OK, boys,' said Hannah, 'let's not go through all this again.'

John Mór gave Sturgess a long, last look then turned to the door.

'My, my,' said Lenny, 'this is all a little tense, ain't it?'

Musk Unmasked?

A former close associate of billionaire and champion of certain types of free speech Elon Musk has shocked the world by announcing that Musk does not exist and is, in fact, an online entity entirely generated by artificial intelligence. Roger Drake, a self-described code architect (whatever that is), has claimed that Musk was created by a NASA supercomputer as a test.

'It was an experiment to see what AI could do,' Drake explained. 'We input a bunch of tech magazines, sixteen pages of *Atlas Shrugged* and a 1994 edition of *Hustler*, and Elon was what popped out. He has since run amok, building up a fortune while claiming responsibility for other people's work and telling everyone how the world should be run. I know what you're thinking – all those pictures of him in the papers? That's all generated too – just google the phrase "Matt Damon's face combined with a leg of pork".'

However, in a further twist in the tale, it has now been alleged that it is in fact Roger Drake who is a computer-generated fictitious creation, and that Elon Musk is 'just some guy, y'know?' *The Stranger Times* will monitor this story carefully while maintaining an open mind – Mr Musk's lawyers, please take note.

33

They were ushered into a room that was so warm as to be uncomfortable. A sofa was positioned at one end, with three leather armchairs facing it and a coffee table in the middle. John Mór directed Hannah and Sturgess to take a seat on the couch and then stood against the wall behind it.

The Sisters Divine, while considerably older now than they'd been in the pictures hung in the waiting room, were still very beautiful-looking women with an air of glamour to them. Each still sported an immaculate beehive hairdo and wore lashes and a full face of make-up as if they were about to go on stage. Their woolly cardigans only slightly took away from the look. Hannah reckoned they must be in their eighties now, but none of them looked anywhere close to that.

The Black sister was up making tea in the corner, while the Asian sister smiled at them over some knitting in one of the armchairs, and the White sister sat in her chair in the middle, polishing her thick glasses before setting them back on her nose. Only then did she speak, and only after giving Hannah and Sturgess a very long, assessing look. She turned her attention to John Mór and smiled.

'How've you been, John?' she asked in a soft Welsh accent.

'Can't complain, ma'am.'

'Rather be out on the river, if I'm not wrong,' said the Asian sister in a Southern American accent accompanied by a broad smile.

'You know me,' said John, 'I go where I'm pointed.'

'And a lot more besides,' said the Black woman in a Birmingham accent as she returned from the corner with a tray of teas.

Hannah moved forward to help.

'Don't you worry yourself, bab,' she said, placing the tray down on the coffee table. She then pointed at a mug and each of the guests in turn, before serving her sisters.

'I don't actually . . .' started Sturgess, before John Mór reached over and thrust the mug into his hand.

Only when everyone had been given their tea, and all three sisters had settled down in their armchairs, were they properly addressed.

'Thank you for coming,' began the Black sister. 'We are Nora, Gloria and Diane. Pleased to make your acquaintance.'

'Thank you for seeing us,' said Hannah. 'We are . . .'

'Oh,' said the Black sister in her Brummie accent, 'we know who you are, bab. Nobody gets in here if we don't. Tell me, does that fine Manny still work at *The Stranger Times*?'

'Yes,' said Hannah with a smile, 'he does.'

She nodded. 'He used to babysit us back in the day when we was only baby birds. One of my sisters here had the biggest crush on him. Won't say which one.'

The Asian sister smiled while the White one looked stern.

'Sorry,' said Hannah, 'you mean you babysat him?'

All three sisters pulled back in mock shock before the White one spoke. 'How old do you think we are?'

'No, I . . . ehm . . .' Hannah looked up at John Mór in confusion, and she could have sworn he was smirking behind that big beard of his.

'So,' said the Asian sister, 'young folk are taking drugs and then strange things are happening?'

It wasn't a question, but Sturgess answered it anyway. 'Yes.'

All three sisters nodded. 'You see,' said the White sister, who was suddenly speaking in a Birmingham accent, 'what we do is amplify someone's inherent abilities in a controlled manner. The amplification ain't the hard part . . .'

'It's all hard,' said the Asian sister, who now spoke in the Welsh accent.

'Ain't that the truth,' said the Black sister who now spoke with a Southern drawl. She stopped and looked up at John Mór. 'Sorry, we're switching, aren't we?'

John Mór nodded.

It wasn't just the accents, Hannah realized. It was the voices. It was as if there were three people there and three bodies, but they somehow swapped between them. She glanced at Sturgess who, if anything, looked even more freaked out than she was.

The Black sister turned her attention back to Hannah and Sturgess. 'Sorry about that.'

All three sisters took a sip of tea simultaneously and then the Asian one spoke once, having returned to the Southern accent. 'This OK?'

John Mór nodded again.

'Now,' she said, 'what was I saying?'

'Amplification,' prompted the White sister, Welsh once again.

'Yes,' confirmed her sister. 'These drugs, they're amplifying ordinary people. Our guess is someone is fishing to find those who have abilities they don't even know about.'

'Why would they be doing that?' asked Sturgess.

'We don't know,' said the Black, once again Brummie, sister. 'That's not what worries us. What worries us is how.'

'You see,' continued the Asian sister, 'we have a brother. Different from us, but the same too.'

'We have each other, you see,' explained the White sister, 'whereas poor Marcus has no one. It's different for him.'

The Asian sister nodded her head sadly. 'Along with the ability to amplify comes . . . other things. Things that are hard to deal with. Marcus has struggled with it throughout his life. Drink, mostly.'

'But he got himself clean,' said the Black sister, 'almost four years ago now.'

They all nodded.

'He was doing well,' said the White sister, in her soft Welsh accent. 'Really well. He was a new man.'

They all bobbed their heads again.

'Then, on the twenty-eighth of July, he left his house and never came home again,' said the Asian sister, her voice suddenly strident.

'Did you report this to the police?' asked Sturgess.

'We did,' confirmed the Black sister.

Hannah had a bad feeling about where this was heading. Her suspicions were confirmed when the Asian sister spoke again.

'Exactly how much interest do you think the police showed in the disappearance of a former alcoholic with a record of petty crime?'

Hannah could feel Sturgess shifting awkwardly on the sofa beside her. 'I'd assume that they treated it with the due diligence that any missing-person report deserves.'

All three sisters raised their eyebrows in perfect synchronicity. Then they looked at each other and Hannah suspected a conversation was going on between them which nobody else in the room was privy to.

Eventually, the Black sister turned back to them and held out her hand. 'The tablets?'

Sturgess stiffened. 'What makes you think I have some of them with me?'

'Don't you?'

He looked at Hannah and reached into the pocket of his jacket, withdrawing a small plastic bag with four of the distinctive blue tablets in it. He half stood and awkwardly handed it across the coffee table.

The White sister took the bag and spilled the tablets into the palm of her hand. Her two sisters each reached across and placed a finger on top of them before they all closed their eyes.

There was a momentary orange glow around the tablets, then the three sisters opened their eyes again. The Black sister pulled a tissue from the sleeve of her cardigan and dabbed at a tear rolling down her cheek. The White sister, with a determined focus, placed the pills back into the bag before speaking. When she did, there was a hitch in her voice. 'It's Marcus.'

'I don't understand,' said Sturgess.

Her eyes were suddenly cold steel as she glared at him. 'It's Marcus. Marcus's power has been put into these pills.'

'I see.'

She tossed them down onto the coffee table. 'We don't think you do.' She jabbed a finger at the tablets. 'Marcus would not do that, which means that someone is making him do it.'

'You're sure?'

The Black sister almost spat out her words. 'Of course we're sure.'

The White sister reached across and patted her sister's hand tenderly before continuing. 'Someone has taken our brother and is making him do this. You find Marcus, you'll find whoever is behind whatever this is.'

'I don't—' started Sturgess.

'Thank you for coming,' said the Asian sister.

'But—'

John Mór stepped forward. 'OK, that's all you get.'

'But—'

'All. You. Get,' growled John Mór. His tone gave Hannah the distinct impression that he'd happily bodily lift Sturgess out of the room given the chance.

'Thank you very much for your time, ladies,' said Hannah as she got to her feet.

'Not you, Ms Willis,' said the Asian sister. 'You stay a moment. John and the detective inspector will wait for you outside.'

Hannah gave Sturgess a nod and he and John Mór left the room, closing the door behind them.

'Don't worry,' said the Black sister, 'you won't be in here long enough for them to kill each other.'

'That's a relief,' said Hannah with a nervous laugh.

'You have a question you want to ask us,' prompted the White sister.

'I do?'

The Black sister smiled. 'You do.'

Hannah stood there, her mouth open, trying to think. She pointed back at the door. 'I . . . I can't think of anything but I'm sure DI Sturgess has lots of questions.'

'Oh,' said the Asian sister, 'he does, but some people are better when they don't have the answers.'

'Honestly,' said Hannah, 'I understand you're worried about your brother, but believe me, regardless of what happened before, DI Sturgess will not rest until—'

The Black sister waved her into silence.

'We know who and what he is. It's why he was brought here. We even know about that nasty thing in his head. But your question isn't about any of that. We're tired, so we should get to it.'

'I don't understand.'

'Let us put it this way,' said the White sister, 'when you leave here, in the days and weeks that follow, what will you regret not asking?'

An image of Stella, standing in the middle of Oxford Road, sprang into Hannah's head. She spoke before her mind had time to process it. 'I keep having this dream.'

The Black sister pointed a finger at her. 'And there it is.'

Hannah's heart was racing now. 'It isn't just a dream, is it?'

'You already know the answer to that question,' said the Asian sister, 'but you don't want to admit it.'

'We know how that is,' said the White sister.

'Precognition,' said the Black sister, giving Hannah a kind look, 'as in knowing the future, is a very rare thing. Rare . . .'

'But not impossible,' finished the Asian sister.

'Seeing it is one thing,' said the White sister, 'but understanding it is a whole other kettle of fish. You might just be seeing one possible future.'

'Yes,' agreed the Asian sister. 'Remember we saw that nice young man on the television that time, explaining how there are infinite variations on the world we know, all running in parallel, all playing out the different choices we could make.'

'He is totally wrong about that,' said the Black sister. 'I mean . . .' She considered it for a moment. 'Yeah, pretty much totally. The universe has more imagination than he gives it credit for. There are alternate whatever-you-want-to-call-thems beyond the one we know, but they aren't boring spot-the-difference variations on ours.'

'There's typically a lot more tentacles, for one thing,' said the White sister.

'And the thing with precognition,' said the Asian sister, 'is . . . Well, look at the world around you. Most people don't even have cognition. As in, they don't see the world they're already in as it actually is, never mind being able to understand what it is going to be. There are no easy answers.'

'Does that answer your question?' asked the Black sister.

Hannah ran her fingers through her hair. Her mind was racing. 'I'm still not sure what my question is.'

The sisters all laughed and then the Asian one spoke. 'Sorry, dear. Can't help you there. Best of luck to you. I'm guessing you're probably going to need it.'

34

'Hannah!'

Grace, Stella, Reggie and Ox all jumped as Banecroft came stomping out of his office. Brian the ghoul, meanwhile, dived behind a desk.

'Why on earth are you shouting?' asked Grace.

'I came out of my office shouting the name of a member of my staff,' said Banecroft. 'What possible reason do you think I could have for doing that other than the obvious? Namely, I wish to speak to Hannah.'

Grace waved a hand round the bullpen. 'Can you see Hannah here?'

'No,' said Banecroft, giving Grace a perplexed look, 'that's why I was shouting.'

'She is not here,' offered Reggie. 'As in, *à la* Elvis, she has left the building.'

'Why is she not here?'

'Because,' said Stella, 'as she mentioned yesterday, she's off following up a lead with DI Sturgess.'

Banecroft shook his head. 'Is that what they're calling it now?'

'Don't be so . . . you,' said Stella.

'Besides,' said Ox, 'it's Sunday morning, so the real question is, why are the rest of us here?'

Banecroft paused to take in the team, who were all standing around the portable whiteboard that Grace had picked up from somewhere. 'All right, I'll bite – what are you doing here?'

'Before we get to that,' said Grace, holding up a hand as she walked over to the corner where Brian was cowering. 'It's all right, Brian – out you come. Ignore the shouty man.'

Brian slowly emerged and resumed his position on the desk in the far corner. He hugged his knees to himself and watched everyone at the far end of the room.

Grace smiled at him then gave Banecroft a dirty look as she walked back across the room. 'If we could use our inside voices, please – our guest is a little skittish.'

Banecroft joined the rest of the team at the board. 'If he's going to work here, he'll have to get used to it.'

'Who on earth suggested he wants to work here?' asked Reggie. 'I have the strong suspicion he's already suffered enough in life.'

'Certainly, the poor thing was famished,' said Grace, lowering her voice. 'He ate everything I brought from home, then most of the takeaway we got at ten, and three of those awful kebabs Ox went out and got at two in the morning.'

'Awful?' repeated Ox. 'They weren't awful. They're just not designed to be eaten by sober people.'

'Poor Brian seemed to manage,' said Stella.

'Yeah,' agreed Ox, 'and before you start training him up as your next journalist protégé, there's a few other areas you might need to work on.'

Stella slapped Ox on the arm.

'What?' he said. 'It's true.'

'What's that supposed to mean?' asked Banecroft, glancing back at the ghoul.

'He seems not to be entirely au fait with all of the facilities that modern life has to offer,' said Reggie diplomatically.

'Like what? He couldn't log on to the wifi?'

'It's more to do with his logging off,' said Ox with a smirk. 'He went outside and took a shit in the car park.'

This earned him a clip around the ear from Grace.

'Ouch,' said Ox, rubbing the side of his head. 'Why are all the women in this office so violent?'

'None of them has ever hit me,' said Reggie. 'You might want to ruminate on that.'

'Hang on,' said Banecroft. 'As much as I enjoy seeing Ox being soundly beaten, could we go back to the car-park thing?'

Reggie smiled then spoke through gritted teeth. 'He did . . . well, what Ox said. But to be fair to him, he did then pick it up in a bag and put it in a bin.'

'Right,' said Banecroft. 'While that would be highly impressive for a dog, it's less than ideal from a human.' He glanced back in the direction of where Brian was sitting. 'Well, humanoid. Ox, congratulations! You're in charge of showing him how to use the facilities.'

'What? Why am I in charge of showing him how to take a—' He was interrupted by Stella and Grace hitting him simultaneously. 'Enough with the violence! This is assault in the workplace.'

'Out of curiosity,' asked Reggie, 'are you gay by choice or was it just inevitable given your way with the ladies?'

'As my employer,' said Ox to Banecroft, 'you shouldn't be allowing this kind of abuse.'

'Allowing?' said Banecroft. 'I'm positively encouraging it. If all three of them hit you at the same time, I'm going to bring in a cake.' He turned to the whiteboard, which he now saw had the Polaroids stuck to it in various groupings. 'Now, what is this?'

'This,' said Reggie, with an air of pride, 'is what we all stayed up all night doing.' He looked at Banecroft expectantly. 'Sorry. Most people would have been tempted to say something encouraging there, but I forgot who I was talking to.'

'Ox went through all the Polaroids,' began Stella, 'and figured out which cemeteries they're from.'

'Yeah,' said Ox, still looking a little grumpy. 'There's a database. He pointed at the large group. All these are from Southern Cemetery, which I suppose you'd expect, seeing as it's massive.' He pointed at the three significantly smaller groupings. 'These are from Agecroft, Blackley, and a couple from Bury. We could also tell that almost all these people, assuming the dates Brian has put on them are correct, were dug up within two or three days of being buried.'

'Then,' said Stella, 'Grace had a bit of a genius idea.'

Grace flapped a hand at her younger colleague. 'It was nothing, really. It was just like they do on all the crime programmes on TV. I said we should profile the victims and see what they had in common.'

'That's what took most of the night,' said Reggie. 'We had to go through social media, newspaper reports, obituaries. It took a long time but we've come up with a very definite profile.'

'We have,' agreed Stella, pointing at the clipboard she held in her hand. 'They were all between the ages of seventeen and forty-four. They all appear to have been in pretty good health before, well, dying. None of them died violent deaths. We've got strokes, heart attacks, a few other things, undiscovered medical issues, quite a few with no explanation, and we reckon at least six were from drug overdoses.'

'And what does that tell us?' asked Banecroft.

'Not much,' admitted Reggie. 'In the sense that we don't know why whatever beastly person is behind this is doing what they're doing.'

'But,' said Ox, 'and this was kind of a group idea' – they all looked a little proud – 'we realized that the profile meant that we could try to figure out where they might be going next.'

'Yes,' said Stella. 'There are three people who've been buried in the last couple of days who fit the profile, all in Southern Cemetery. On behalf of the group' – she took a little bow – 'ta-da!'

Banecroft nodded and looked at the board. 'This . . . is good work.'

'I'm sorry?' said Reggie. 'Could you repeat that?'

'No.'

'Only, it's the first time any of us have heard you say that,' said Ox, 'and while we're all a bit sleep-deprived, I think I speak for all of us when I say, we'd like to hear it again.'

'Oh,' said Stella, snatching up her phone, 'let me record it.'

Ignoring them all, Banecroft waved a hand at the board. 'And what is your suggestion for what we are going to do with all of this?'

'We thought we could pass it on to the police,' said Grace.

'Really?' said Banecroft. 'You're just going to explain that we have a ghoul with an excellent sense of smell who told us that all these graves had been robbed and, without asking us any further awkward questions, would you mind terribly putting surveillance on the three graves we think are going to be next?'

His outpouring of logic was met with a moment of deflated silence.

Stella let out a heavy sigh and dropped her clipboard onto a table. 'Has anyone ever told you that you really know how to kill a good vibe?'

'Many times. The good news is you all get to go home and get some sleep.'

'Oh no,' said Reggie with an air of impending doom.

'Because tonight we are staking out these graves.' Banecroft rubbed his hands together and marched off in the direction of the kitchen.

The other four, feeling suddenly exhausted, watched him go.

Ox sat down on a desk. 'Can I just point out that nobody, not one of you, hit him? There is no justice.'

35

Paulo gave a beneficent smile to hide the fact that at that very moment he was enjoying the thought of how wonderful it would be to set upon everyone currently in his shop with an axe. The problem with owning a shop that sold things like dream-catchers, salt lamps, mood balls and holistic healing pebbles was that it attracted the type of idiots who were interested in dream-catchers, salt lamps, mood balls and holistic healing bloody pebbles.

Recently, he had been discussing with his therapist his recurring dream in which he set his own shop on fire. Dr Rosenthal had kept asking Paulo what he thought the symbolism meant. He didn't think it meant anything more than exactly what it said on the tin. He wanted to burn the place to the ground.

These idiots, like the two standing on the opposite side of the counter, who were having an argument over whether a supposedly two-hundred-year-old leather pouch previously owned by Choctaw Nation Native Americans was or was not vegan friendly, drove Paulo insane. The argument, if you could call it that, was that Leeohnel felt that as the leather pouch was a part of the Choctaw culture, where they hunted for food, it could not be considered murder in the same way modern leather goods could be.

Cassandra felt that while she would never oppress anyone else's culture, any form of commercial transaction involving leather goods was a tacit approval of the meat-filled consumerist industrial complex. Something like that, anyway. Paulo couldn't get all the way through any of the tediously long sentences either of them was spewing to make their point.

This had been going on for a good fifteen minutes now, although ten of them had been taken up with some easy point scoring on Cassandra's part when dozy Leeohnel had mistakenly used the word 'Indian' instead of 'Native American'. The reality was, the pouch in question had actually come from an Indian: his name was Raj, and he was a chef down at the Taj Palace. He had a nice little side line in knocking out stuff like this pouch, complete with hilarious authenticity certificates that the nitwits lapped up. He had once offered to tell Paulo how he aged the leather, but Paulo had stopped him from saying as he had some sneaky suspicions, and he didn't want to think of them every time he touched the stuff.

Paulo dreamed of giving up the shop and doing something, anything, different from this. He couldn't, though. His customers wouldn't let him. Not the customers like Leeohnel and Cassandra. He didn't care about those customers. It was the other customers. The ones who availed themselves of what the shop was really for, behind the front of fake spiritualism and knick-knacks for people who painted their nails black and thought that made them witches, or even interesting. His true customers were very serious people.

And then there was the visit he'd received earlier in the year. He'd been in possession of a certain knife that was strictly taboo because of its use in blood magic. He'd kept it hidden away and only lent it to very specific customers for strictly agreed upon rituals that those in power weren't particularly bothered about. Then that damned Yank had come in and got it off him through a combination of the carrot and the stick. That particular individual had gone on to cause all kinds of trouble, and Paulo had received another visit. He'd been fined, warned and, bizarrely, denied the right to shut down the shop. The powers that be considered him useful, and he was told he would be given an opportunity to prove his usefulness in the future.

Just the thought of it all made his ulcer throb. His wife said he needed to learn to cope with stress. Paulo knew the reality was, if she knew what he was really dealing with, she'd run out of the house screaming and wouldn't worry about the little details like packing, saying goodbye or, indeed, taking the kids with her.

Paulo was between a rock and another rock. Both of which had faces that were glaring at him, waiting for him to screw up. They had also taken almost all of his illicit items. Those had made up his rainy-day fund, and now he was naked and it was a matter of when, not if, the rain was coming.

He looked up as the bell over the shop door rang and, sure enough, there was yet another little rain cloud. The two customers arguing in front of him were unpleasant in the simple-fools-who-liked-to-talk-too-much kind of way. The woman in the doorway was another stratosphere of unpleasantness. She had long black hair and glasses, and was now staring at him impatiently. The index finger and thumb of her left hand were tucked into her palm as she tapped the three tips of her remaining fingers three times against her forearm. Paulo shook his head slightly. She'd been in several times recently buying supplies, always complaining about both the quality and price. She had been so unpleasant to deal with that Paulo had had to take half a dozen Rennies and lie down after each visit.

'OK,' said Paulo, snatching up the pouch and tossing it behind the counter. 'I appreciate this is an emotive topic. Perhaps you two should go somewhere and discuss it further, and I shall keep it back for you, Leeohnel, if you decide you still want it.'

Cassandra wrinkled her nose in a smug little toothy grin of victory.

Good god, thought Paulo, *could the two of you just bang already? Or do whatever the hell it is you twenty-first-century hippy types do instead of shagging.*

'I'd like to discuss it further,' said Leeohnel, a man not blessed with the ability to read a room.

'I'm afraid the shop is closing now.'

'But it's only—'

'Family emergency,' said Paulo.

'Oh dear,' said Leeohnel, 'I do hope everything is—'

'So do I,' said Paulo. 'Thank you for your concern.' He waved a hand towards the door and even Leeohnel was able to read that sign.

'Namaste,' said Leeohnel.

As he and Cassandra turned to leave, Cassandra addressed the other woman standing to the side of the door. 'I'm afraid the Emporium is closing now.'

'Not for me,' she said with a remarkable absence of grace.

Cassandra shot her a dirty look as she exited.

Once they'd left, the woman gave a flourish of her hand and the door locked itself.

'Hey,' said Paulo, 'since when do you get to close my shop?'

'I don't think you want anyone in here for this conversation.'

'I don't want to be here for this conversation,' said Paulo, 'so how about we skip it entirely?'

She gave him a bitter smile. 'But I'm about to make you an offer you can't refuse.'

'Look,' he said, holding out his hands, palms facing her, 'I don't know what you've heard, but I don't deal in anything dodgy.'

'Yes, you do.'

'Not any more.'

The woman glanced around then said, 'You have a necromer and I want it.'

Paulo made a noise that he'd never heard come out of himself before. Part choke, part laugh, part his brain trying to escape out his ear. 'Are you insane? I don't have one of those. Nobody has one of those. I want nothing to do with anything like that.'

'He said you'd say that.'

'Well, whoever "he" is was dead right. Because I've no idea what you're talking about.'

She pulled out a large gold coin and dropped it on the counter. Paulo had seen one of them before. The bloody Yank had given him one. Then, they'd taken it back, along with a whole lot else. Paulo had a weirdly Pavlovian response to seeing it – part of him still wanted it even as he physically drew back as if the thing could bite him.

'Not interested.'

'I haven't finished,' said the woman. She calmly pulled out a small stoppered clay vial about two inches long and laid it gently on the table.

'It can't be!' breathed Paulo.

'It is,' confirmed the woman. 'Anima. The very life force of the world. The most important substance known to man. A nice little drop of it, too.'

'You c-can't . . .' stammered Paulo, before clearing his throat. 'If that's what you say it is—'

'It is, and what's more, you know it is.'

'Then trading in such things is highly illegal and I want nothing to do with it. Now, I will ask you to please leave. Vinny?'

A creaking of furniture sounded from the back room as Vinny stirred from where he was no doubt playing Candy Crush on his phone. He was not much more than big dumb muscle, but at least the troll's presence beside him might get it through this bloody woman's head that he was serious about not being interested.

'He said both of these things wouldn't be enough.'

'He was right again,' said Paulo. 'Not that there is anything to be right about, because I definitely haven't got anything like that thing you mentioned.'

Vinny rumbled out of the back room and Paulo was slightly

reassured by his shadow blocking out some of the light coming from behind him.

'What's up?' asked Vinny.

The woman ignored him entirely. She continued to stare at Paulo. 'He said what would get us what we wanted would be information. One word, in fact.'

'Let me guess?' said Paulo, feeling more confident. 'Shazam? Necronomicon? Rosebud? Hocus pocus?'

'That's two words.'

'Shut up, Vinny.'

'No,' said the woman. 'None of those words. To be honest, I don't even know what the word means, but he assured me you would. Maybe I'm wrong? Maybe my friend was pulling my leg? Maybe I'm about to look very foolish?'

It was the way she smiled at him that filled his soul with icicles of pure burning dread.

She licked her lips and then, calmly, spoke a word. If you'd asked Paulo five seconds beforehand, he would have assured you there was no word she could say, anyone could say, that would have the effect she was hoping for.

And then she said it again.

He stood there for what felt like a very long time, his whole body gripped with an overwhelming terror. His legs seemed like they were about to buckle. His throat was now as dry as a desert.

She waited, and then she raised an eyebrow in question.

Paulo blinked and cleared his throat. 'If you . . . If you give me a couple of minutes, *madame*, I shall get you what you require.'

She gave him a smile laced with acid. 'Thank you, sir.'

He turned and pushed past Vinny into the back room.

As bile touched the back of his throat and tears stung his eyes, Paulo heard Vinny speaking in that big, dumb voice of his. 'Can I interest you in a cappuccino?'

36

Reggie and Ox sat side by side in their deckchairs, hugging themselves for warmth as they stared into the darkness.

'How cold does it have to be before we freeze to death?' asked Ox.

'Not this cold.'

'How do you know?'

'Because it's Manchester in October, not Antarctica.'

'People freeze to death in Manchester, you know.'

'Tragically, I do. But not at this time of year, and not when I've lent them one of my very best coats to keep them warm.'

Ox sniffed and pulled at the cashmere overcoat. 'Not that I'm not grateful and that, but why does this smell funny?'

'What you are smelling there, dear boy, is clean. It's what you get when you do laundry.'

'I do laundry.'

'I meant more regularly than realizing you have to do some because you can no longer prise any items of your underwear off the floor with a crowbar.'

Ox clapped his gloved hands together.

'Will you keep the noise down?' hissed Reggie. 'We're supposed to be silently observing.'

'Why can't I look at my phone?'

'Because in the middle of a dark graveyard it's a rather big giveaway if your big daft face is lit up. Just keep your voice down and thank your lucky stars we're not both sitting doing this on our own, like the original plan called for.'

'True enough,' conceded Ox.

They had been due to stake out three different plots where someone had been buried in the last couple of days, but that plan had changed when they'd arrived.

'Bloody hell, though,' said Ox. 'Poor Brian on that grave, eh?'

Reggie sighed. 'It was rather horrible.'

As soon as they'd reached the graveyard, Brian had clambered out of the back of Grace's car and rushed to one of the graves they had been about to watch over. That of Elizabeth Jane Harper. Evidently, they were too late. When they caught up with him they'd found him lying on top of it, crying his eyes out. Grace had eventually led him away, attempting to console him.

'I feel sorry for him,' said Ox, 'but he freaks me out.'

'Really? He speaks highly of you.'

'Ha ha. Here, not that I'm not thrilled to be in your company, but why do you reckon Grace insisted on being with Banecroft?'

'Because he doesn't enjoy drinking around her and she doesn't enjoy him drinking.'

They fell into silence, both of them looking at the surrounding gravestones. They were in the old graveyard, watching a family plot where Roger James Matthews had been buried, joining his mother and grandfather, after suffering a heart attack which was the result of a congenital heart defect. Over in the new graveyard, Grace, Banecroft and Brian were keeping an eye on the freshly dug grave of Deborah Rose McCarthy, cause of death unclear.

'It's creepy this, innit?' said Ox.

'Sitting in a cemetery all night, waiting for grave robbers to show up? What makes you say that?'

'Are we sure it's grave robbers?' asked Ox, ignoring the sarcasm.

'What other options are there? It's not like these bodies are just getting up and walking away.'

As soon as the words left Reggie's mouth, he regretted them. It was a particularly unsettling image. They both looked around nervously. Their position was a copse of trees about sixty yards away from the plot. It wasn't ideal, but graveyards offered limited scope for camouflage.

'I just had a horrible thought,' said Ox.

'Worse than grave robbers or dead people digging themselves up?'

'Yeah. What if neither of those things happens?'

'Oh God,' said Reggie. 'We could be back here tomorrow night doing this again.'

'And the next night and the one after that and—'

'I get the idea,' snapped Reggie. 'Thank you, Ox.'

'I still don't get how Stella and Hannah have got out of this.'

'Something to do with their investigation into that poor lad who fell. Stella had an idea she kept bugging Hannah about and apparently Banecroft agreed with it. Hannah didn't look best pleased.'

'So where are they?'

'Some place called Smilers.'

'Smilers? The nightclub?'

Reggie shrugged. 'You're asking me like I would know about such places?'

'Are you seriously telling me we're out here freezing our arses off in a graveyard and they're out having the time of their lives?'

'Would you keep your voice down, please?' hissed Reggie. 'You'll bloody wake the dead!'

37

Stella was not having the time of her life.

This was particularly annoying, as everyone around her appeared to be doing just that.

After finally getting the clearance from Banecroft to go do some actual investigating, she'd responded to one of the plethora of texts and WhatsApps she'd received from Yvette from her class that yes, she would be up for going out. Naively, Stella had assumed that this would happen later in the week. It being a Sunday, nobody would be going out, obviously. Monday traditionally followed Sunday, and that was when people had work, and even students like Stella had a video-editing lab at ten the next morning. Yvette had excitedly informed her that Smilers had amazeballs promos on tonight and it was the best going-out night of the week. Girls got in free and pitchers were only a tenner. If almighty science could ever figure out how to turn perkiness into clean energy, they could run Wigan off Yvette alone.

And so, Stella had picked out her nicest black T-shirt, jacket and skirt to complement the best of her three pairs of DMs, and she'd gone to meet the girls. There had been pre-drinks in a bar, in which Stella had not partaken, except for a glass of Coke. There'd also been what had been referred to as 'pick-me-ups', which she'd also turned down, all while trying to give the impression she was totally cool with everyone else's choices and implying that, against all available evidence, she'd had a 'big weekend' and was taking it easy.

She'd found the pub rather overwhelming. That should have been the warning sign there and then. It wasn't as if she'd not been to one before. Well, if you counted going with Reggie, Ox and Hannah to the Admiral's, but this had been rather different. Considerably higher energy. Stella had spent virtually no time 'hanging out' until this point, and it turned out it was a lot harder than it sounded.

The girls – five of them in total – had been very welcoming, especially Yvette. A lot of the talk was about poor Bea and how they needed to get her out. Apparently, she'd been at a club in the Gay Village on Thursday and had had a bit of a freak-out. She'd been chatting to a nice girl, but then had suddenly bolted for the door like the place was on fire. The consensus was that she was struggling with her sexuality, and they all needed to rally around. Since 'the incident' she'd been saying she felt under the weather, but they'd have to try some tough love soon if she didn't snap out of it. Stella was surprised to hear that not going out in three days constituted a crisis, but then, she was being made increasingly aware that she did not know how to be someone her age, assuming estimates of said age were correct.

Then they'd headed to the club. Flashing lights, loud music – Stella felt as if she were being Guantanamo-Bay'd. She couldn't believe people inflicted this upon themselves voluntarily. She caught her own reflection in one of the mirrored walls and was pissed off by how meek she looked. The image of one of those poor bunny rabbits who'd had make-up tested on them popped into her head. She needed to get it together and fake pretending to have a good time.

In her defence, her ability to get into the swing of things was further affected by the fact that she was working. Keeping her eyes peeled for nefarious characters was taking up quite a bit of her focus. Her expectation of what a drug dealer looked like was drawn from US cop shows, and it was slowly dawning on her that they may not have been the best sources of info. Nobody was wearing a vest, gold chains and a baseball cap worn backwards.

The music in Smilers was not only loud, but also earth-shatteringly awful. The chances of them playing anything by The Cure seemed to be slim to non-existent, if one discounted the idea that Robert Smith and co had allowed anything in their back catalogue to be given a 160 bpm dance remix, and even if they had, Stella really did not want to hear it. Everyone else was out on the dance floor and she . . . she wasn't even minding the coats, as they'd left those in the cloakroom.

She was minding the drinks, though. That was important. Depending on who you asked, spiking was either an epidemic or overblown, but it definitely happened. There'd been a week of hysteria in the papers with horror stories about needles being used and everything. Stella found herself alternating between staring at the glasses intently and trying to check out the room, all while studiously ignoring the couple sitting on stools on the far side of the dance floor, who looked almost as uncomfortable as she felt.

Hannah and DI Sturgess had a rather complicated past, and the awkward body language between them did not bode well. On the upside, they looked credible in the sense that they appeared to be two people on a very awkward date, which wasn't a million miles from the truth.

Stella jumped as Yvette and the girls piled back into the booth, everyone talking a mile a minute.

'Oh my God, that guy was all up in your business.'

'Shut up, he was gross as.'

'Give it a couple more drinks!'

Laughs all round.

Yvette tapped Stella on the knee as she leaned in. 'You have got to come up for a dance next time. It's hilarious out there. I will not take no for an answer.'

'Yeah, no, I will. I will. Just, y'know. Not really my thing, but I'll give it a go.'

'You just need to let your hair down. Feel the rhythm.'

Stella nodded, smiled then excused herself to make a trip to the bathroom she didn't need.

Five minutes later, after she emerged from the cubicle, she saw the back of someone she recognized standing at the sinks where positive 'you look fabulous' messages were scrawled across the mirrors in glittery designer stencils. They were a nice contrast to the smell of vomit emanating from the end stall.

Stella took her place at the sink next to Hannah, and they exchanged a sideways look.

'So,' said Hannah, 'how's your evening going?'

'I may have made a terrible mistake.'

'I get it. Everyone says uni is all about trying new things, but nobody mentions that you'll probably end up hating most of them. There's a reason you haven't tried lots of things before. Many, many things are awful.'

Stella laughed. 'When will this end?'

'Any time you like.'

'No, we're here' – she glanced around before speaking any further, but the two women at the hand dryers were paying them no mind – 'doing an investigation. It's important.'

'Yeah,' said Hannah. 'It must be, for us both to be putting ourselves through this.'

'How's it going with D—' She glanced around again, the two women at the hand dryers having now left. 'Tom.'

'As badly as you'd expect. The awkwardness, coupled with the fact that we've both realized we're way too old to be here, has made for a truly special night.'

'Oh, God, sorry.'

Hannah gave her colleague a hip bump and giggled. 'Don't worry about it, kiddo. At least we're both having a better night than poor DS Wilkerson.'

'I don't even know who she is in there.'

'Easy,' said Hannah. 'She's the young, attractive woman on her own who is fending off advances left, right and centre. I thought she was going to put the last guy through a wall.'

They moved over to the hand dryers. 'Any leads yet?' asked Stella.

'No, but then Tom has quite the penetrating stare, and I've a sneaking suspicion nobody would feel comfortable dealing drugs within a mile of him. He might not be the world's greatest undercover.'

They paused their conversation as they both dried their hands then turned for the door. They stood to one side to avoid the inebriated trio of women who had just staggered in and, once they'd passed, Hannah leaned in to Stella. 'Look, you never have to come to a place like this ever again if you don't want to, but if you'd like some free advice from an old hag, let yourself enjoy the sheer shitness of it all. Dancing is ninety per cent jumping and screaming – there really is no trick to it.'

With a final nod, they split up and headed in separate directions back to their tables.

On the walk back, Stella told herself Hannah was right. She needed to lighten up a bit. Everyone else was having a good time and maybe if she allowed herself to, she would too. Yvette had bought her a fresh glass of Coke and Stella thanked her. She really was very nice.

It helped that when she settled into her space in the booth, Trish was telling the story of a truly awful date that was genuinely hilarious. Then the others shared similar stories of disaster dates. When asked to chip in with her own tale, Stella borrowed a version of a night out she'd seen in a Swedish sitcom that, she guessed, correctly, the others hadn't seen. Everyone hanging on her every word, laughing along as she told a story, was something she hadn't experienced before, and she found herself enjoying it. She might not get into clubbing, but she could see the upside of lying at least.

After about twenty minutes, Yvette suggested they all take to the dance floor again and, before Stella's brain had a chance to object, she found herself standing. From there, she followed the crowd and quickly found that Hannah was right – dancing really was a doddle. The rhythm literally pounded through you. You just had to let it do its work. Eyes closed, she let it take her away, allowed her body to do what it wanted to when you just let it get on with it. She found herself hugging all the other girls. They were great. No, they were her best friends. These five girls would be her best friends for the rest of her . . .

Then she felt it.

Inside her, that sickly feeling. The beast stirring. Oh no. Not now.

But it didn't make any sense. It stayed happily locked away until she was in danger, and then it came roaring out, whether she wanted it to or not. Unless . . .

Stella grabbed Yvette's arm, harder than she meant to if the girl's wide eyes were anything to go by. She put her mouth close to Yvette's ear and shouted, 'Did you put something in my drink?'

'What?'

'My drink?'

Yvette gave her a nervous smile. 'Relax. Enjoy it. You're fine.'

Stella was not fine. Not even a little.

She released her grip and spun around, taking the club in. A couple of hundred people dancing, enjoying their lives. Unaware that a bomb was standing in the middle of the dance floor and that she was it.

She headed in what she thought was the approximate direction of the front door, pushing her way through the crowd roughly. She had no time for apologies or anything else. Out. All that mattered was getting out as quickly as possible.

She stumbled over the two steps that led up from the dance floor. Her hands flailed out in front of her and met the sticky floor. Someone laughed. A hand reached down to help her up, but she shook it off. She was on her feet again, moving as fast as she could now.

She wasn't where she thought she should be. Everything was different.

Her chest was tight now. Panic was clawing at every fibre of her being.

And as it did so, the beast continued to rise. She could feel it all the more now. It was coming. A when, not an if.

She twirled around, bumping into someone as she did so. Liquid splashed against her forearm. A voice. 'For fuck's—'

But she was gone. The doors. She'd finally spotted the doors. Another stumble as she rushed up the stairs, but she regained her footing.

The cloakroom was to her right, staffed by a bored-looking girl wearing headphones and reading a book. Stella ignored it. No time for that.

As she pushed past the crowd of half a dozen boys negotiating their way in, one of the bouncers said something, but she didn't hear it. The cold rain on her face was a blessed relief.

Despite the inclement weather, the pavement was crowded with revellers. Taxis and Ubers negotiated their way around each other, dropping off and picking up.

Too many people. Stella needed to get away from people.

For the second time that night, her feet made a decision before her brain could intervene. The club was on Great Ducie Street, just around the corner from the Arena. She ran at full pelt, turning right and heading up the road. She had one idea. One hope.

Someone behind her shouted something, but she didn't look back. All that mattered was forward. Get away. Far, far away.

She rushed across the street through the stationary traffic and darted across the far two lanes, ignoring the honk of a car coming towards her.

She was on the opposite pavement now. The rain upped its intensity, battering against the exposed flesh of her arms and face. All the muscles within her were tingling in a way that had nothing to do with the cold or the rain.

She took the first left turn that presented itself and ran until her legs and lungs gave out. Time was up. She had to stop in order to do the best she could to, if not control it, at least direct it.

She looked around. She was in the middle of a large car park, which was still half full of cars. This was good. At least, it was the least bad option of those she'd been presented with. There was nobody around. This was—

She heard a voice again, shouting her name.

Stella turned to see Hannah about fifteen feet or so behind her.

'Are you OK?' Hannah shouted.

'Get back!' screamed Stella. 'Get the hell back!'

'It's going to be all right.'

'It's not. It's not. It's . . .'

Stella's body convulsed and her chest spasmed forward as if

the world had just hit the brakes and she was being thrown against an invisible seatbelt that was holding her back. Her arms flew out of their own accord and she screamed. Screamed as she never had before. A full-throated roar of terror.

In her head, one word punched its way through the panic that seized her. Up. Up. UP.

She turned her face skywards, the rain beating down heavily onto it now, forcing her eyes closed. Then everything became too much, and it was no longer possible to hold back the flood.

Then it came . . .

Her eyelids flew open as, with an immense rush, a column of blue energy flowed out of every pore of her being and ripped into the sky. The heavy black clouds were splashed in blue as the energy seemed to skitter across them as it dispersed. The surface of her body hissed as the raindrops hitting it evaporated instantly into steam. The world lit up in blue and then, as soon as it had happened, it was gone again, to be replaced by a cacophonous din as the alarms of every car within one hundred feet sprang into squealing atonal life.

Stella collapsed on the ground. The tarmac should have been wet, but instead, it was hot to the touch.

The world faded out, only to snap back into focus a few moments later when a hand slapped her across the face. She looked up through bleary eyes to see Hannah's terrified expression as she stared down at her.

'Are you OK?'

'I'm . . .'

'Stella, are you OK?'

'Tired.'

Hannah hauled her off the ground. 'Get up.'

'Just . . .'

'Get. Up.' Hannah dragged her to her feet. Then, DI Sturgess was there, and he grabbed Stella's other arm.

'Walk,' said Hannah. 'Walk.'

DI Sturgess said something that Stella didn't catch.

'No,' snapped Hannah in response. 'We need to get her away from here. Now.'

They walked. Stella was dimly aware of people running around them, this way and that. Excited chatter.

Someone said something to which Hannah replied, 'She's fine. Just drunk . . . No, I didn't see anything.'

Then they stopped, and suddenly there was a cab beside them. A blessed black cab. Hannah pulled open the door.

'Is she all right?' came a gruff voice, laced with suspicion.

'She's fine,' said Hannah, pushing Stella in.

'She's not gonna barf in the back of my cab, is she?'

'No. She doesn't drink. She's . . . diabetic.'

'Bloody hell. Do you need the hospital?'

Hannah pushed in beside Stella in the back seat. 'No need for that. We're heading home. Mealy Street, please.'

As the door was about to close, Hannah shouted, 'Hang on! Sorry. One sec.' She leaned out of the cab and grabbed Sturgess's arm. 'The CCTV.'

'What about it?' asked Sturgess.

'Delete it.'

'I can't—'

'I don't care what you have to do, Tom. Delete it. Nobody can know about this.'

'But—'

'But nothing. Do it!'

Before he could protest any further, Hannah leaned back in and slammed the door shut. 'Sorry about that,' she apologized to the taxi driver.

Stella finally felt capable of speech again. 'I haven't got my jacket.'

'Don't worry about it,' said Hannah, sounding infinitely calmer. She pushed Stella's wet hair out of her eyes.

'You're OK. You're going to be OK.'

'Are you sure you don't want the hospital?' asked the driver.

'No, honestly, she's just had a scare,' said Hannah, sounding almost chatty. 'Some insulin and a good night's sleep. She'll be fine.'

'Fair enough.'

Stella leaned against the rain-splattered window and watched as the lights of the city whirled past.

'Miserable old night,' said the taxi driver.

You've no idea, thought Stella. No idea.

38

He did not know why he did this to himself. He came to this room, his studio, night after night, whenever he couldn't sleep. He'd been doing it for years now. Ever since . . .

Cillian Blake tried to clear his mind. Cleansing breaths.

There is only this moment.

This singular moment.

No future.

No past.

No other.

He ran his fingers up and down the ebony fretboard of the guitar, a D-45 Harvey Leach Lotus Flower – the king of acoustic guitars. Spruce top and rosewood back and sides. It promised a clear and bright tone as favoured by Neil Young, to name but one of many. It was a stunning feat of craftsmanship. A true work of art that had created countless other works of art. 'Harvest Moon' had been written on such a magnificent instrument.

Cillian formed his fingers into the chord of G, as he had been doing since the age of seven years old, and strummed.

It sounded like absolute dog shit.

He knew it wasn't the guitar. He had the finest tuners known to man. The kind of kit that could tune a guitar in the middle of a concert in front of eighty thousand people in under thirty seconds and get it right, time after time, every time.

He knew what it was. He'd discussed it with enough highly trained and highly priced experts over the years. It was in his head. The sound the instrument was making wasn't the sound he was hearing. The guitar wasn't the problem. Nor was the piano, the keyboard or any of the other seven guitars in the room.

The problem was him.

Cillian had discussed a lot with the so-called experts, but some things he'd kept to himself for obvious reasons. Like, for example, the fact that every time he touched any musical instrument, Nigel was there. Not in a touchy-feely 'with me in spirit' way either. No, he was there, usually sitting in the corner of the room but occasionally standing, always with that mocking smirk on his face. Cillian had seen his fill of it in the final days of Herschel's Garden.

They'd taken a break for a few months because they couldn't stand the sight of each other. Then, they'd come back together to get to work on new material and, euphemistically, the producer had told the record company they were making 'slow progress'. What that meant in real terms was that in a band with two people in it, they couldn't spend more than ten minutes together in the same room without a blazing row breaking out. The R&D guy had eventually brought in an actual marriage guidance counsellor, for Christ's sake. All that had resulted in was more blazing rows, while day after day, highly paid session musicians played Monopoly and smoked joints in a recording studio that cost a small fortune to hire.

During those therapy sessions, it had all come out. Nigel's resentment at having found out that Cillian had been discussing a solo deal. Just discussing. Cillian knew that while they'd been on a break, Nigel had been locked away in his house in Scotland. Cillian was convinced he had a whole album's worth of material stashed away that he wasn't sharing. They were flaming out and Nige was sitting there metaphorically roasting marshmallows on the flames of Herschel's Garden, purely out of spite. From day one, they'd put both of their names on every song, even though Nigel had been the main songwriter. That had been the deal. Cillian was the frontman – he was the one with the charisma. Try getting anywhere in the music business without that. Nigel being Nigel, the little techno boffin that he was, he never confirmed nor denied the existence of 'the secret album', but Cillian had known. It had been there in the little smirk.

After Nigel's death, they'd looked everywhere. Anywhere they could think of. Nothing. They'd even found his excited texts to an old friend from his uni days, Imran Massif. Imran had been a technically gifted keyboard player who couldn't find a hook to save his life. He and Nige had always been close though, geeking out on stuff Cillian couldn't even begin to comprehend. As Cillian had suspected, Nigel had indeed built his own studio at the house. It was packed with all manner of equipment. What they couldn't find anywhere was a single note of recorded music. It was as if it had vanished into thin air.

Or, to be more exact, it was as if Nigel had taken it to his grave. They asked everyone, even Nigel's estranged sister, who, unsurprisingly, knew nothing. Imran was the only possibility, but when Cillian got in contact he'd told him exactly where he could go. Nige had seemingly confided a lot in Imran and Cillian had considered trying to approach him again several times over the years, but last he'd heard he now lived in Dubai. The idea of offering him money if he could point Cillian in the right direction soon became moot when Imran designed some encryption algorithm that was now used by most banks in the world. Never mind millionaire, he was well on his way to billionaire status if the press was to be believed.

Cillian put the guitar back down on its stand. He'd broken a lot of them in the past, but all that had earned him was piles of expensive firewood.

This time it was him who was smiling. 'You can smirk all you want, Nige. It won't matter soon. Everything that has gone between us won't matter. I've sacrificed so much. Every penny I have. Every ounce of my dignity. I've even had to screw that awful woman. I've given all of it, but it will all be worth it soon.'

He stood and looked at himself in the full-length mirror, turning this way and that. He was still in good shape for a man his age. Hell, for a man of any age. Behind him in the mirror, he saw Nigel looking at him in the reflection. That smirk.

Cillian smiled back. 'Whether you like it or not, my old friend – I'm putting the band back together.'

Carols Gonna Work It Out

The population of Belgium has shocked the world by voting to no longer have a government. The former north-west European democracy will now be ruled by what they are calling 'a council of Carols'.

Professor of Politics at Ghent University, Anders Janssens, explains, 'Really, people were sick to death of politicians. They spend all their time either trying to get elected, trying to get re-elected or in the pocket of big business, who they need in order to get elected. It was decided that just getting a bunch of regular people to have a go at running the country instead was a much more sensible proposition.'

In the end, Carols won the vote by a landslide after it was determined that Grahams keep meaning to do stuff but never actually get around to doing it; Brians are obsessed with giving long rambling speeches in meetings that go nowhere, which mean people miss lunch; and Yvonnes are just all about that drama. Predictably, Nigels are taking the case to the European Court of Human Rights to have the result thrown out, because they've always been awkward buggers.

39

Hannah looked around Banecroft's office, trying to find the most lethal object to throw. 'I'm sorry, could you repeat that?'

'I said,' said Banecroft, drink in hand, socked feet on desk, 'how the hell did you let this happen?'

'I didn't let anything happen, thank you very much. It just happened. Her friend spiked her drink.'

'Her friend?'

Hannah flapped a hand in the air. 'What do you want from me? The girl was an idiot and thought she was helping Stella relax.'

'Should she not be arrested?'

'Do you mean—'

'The friend!'

'Technically. Possibly. Probably. I don't know,' said Hannah, 'I had bigger things to worry about at the time. Like poor Stella freaking out and running away as far as she could before her, whatever the hell we're calling it, happened.'

'And we think it was one of these Merlins again?'

'We do, although we still don't have any idea why the hell someone is going to all this trouble to identify anomalies.'

'Great,' said Banecroft. 'So the whole exercise was futile, then?'

'Not exactly,' said Hannah, who was still possessed of a burning desire to hit Banecroft with something but lacked the energy.

She'd brought Stella home sometime around one and had spent most of the night checking that she was all right. Stella had been so exhausted that she'd conked out, only waking up around 5 a.m. when her brain had recharged itself enough to freak out properly.

'What do you mean, not exactly?' asked Banecroft.

'When Stella ran out, I followed her, with Sturgess following me. DS Wilkerson noticed something – namely, one of the bouncers sending a message. Turns out that quite a few of them are in a little WhatsApp group. There's a number they can text if they notice anything weird and they get three hundred quid if it checks out.'

'You're kidding.'

'No. Sturgess is looking into it but he's not overly optimistic – apparently, a twelve-year-old can get an untraceable number if they know what they're doing, and payment was all anonymous digital-currency stuff, so don't hold your breath for a big reveal on that one. Whoever the hell is behind this, they're really good at covering their tracks.'

'So,' said Banecroft, 'in summary, we know these Merlins are ecstasy that's probably been shazamed by this Marcus Divine fella, probably against his will. We also know they cause these delightfully monikered anomalies to, I don't know, anomalize all over the place, and we know that whoever is behind it is very keen to find out about it when these anomalous events happen. Christ, if this turns out to be some Elon Musk type endeavouring to assemble a superhero team, I'm going to force-feed the tragic loser his own reproductive organs.'

Hannah wrinkled her nose in disgust. 'Vivid as always, Vincent.'

'I do try.'

'The bit you've left out is Sturgess has chased down one of these anomalies – the woman from the Peacock Lounge incident – and she apparently has zero recollection of it.'

'She's forgotten about setting things on fire?'

Hannah shrugged. 'Apparently. According to Sturgess, she had no idea what he was talking about. Like it never happened.'

Banecroft shook his head. 'Even by the lofty standards of this place, this whole thing makes zero sense.'

'Indeed. Still, now we know about the hotline, and DS Wilkerson said she put the frighteners on this bouncer to keep quiet about getting rumbled. Assuming we can make sure that they don't find out we know, maybe we can send a message and get whoever's behind this to turn up and say hello.'

'Hmmmm, not the strongest of plans, given that there's nothing incriminating in just turning up somewhere.'

Hannah slumped back in her chair. 'I know, but I'm tired and it's all we've got.'

Banecroft huffed. 'You're tired? You didn't spend all night in a graveyard in the pissing rain.'

'Yeah, I hear it was grim.'

'How've you heard that?'

'Would you be shocked to discover there's a little group chat for everyone who works here who isn't you?'

'So, you're all talking about me behind my back?'

'Yes,' said Hannah. 'Saying nothing anywhere near as bad as what you say to people's faces.'

'Well,' he said, lighting a cigarette, 'none of you has my way with words.'

'Very true. Anyway,' Hannah softened her voice without realizing, 'anything to report on your end?'

'Indeed. I've seen a ghoul take a dump behind a tree, bag and bin it.'

'I really meant on your . . . problem.'

'On that, no.'

'But didn't this guy say your deadline was tomorrow at midnight?'

'Yes,' said Banecroft, flicking ash into his ashtray. 'Surprisingly, I hadn't forgotten that. You can tell your WhatsApp chums that we'll all be going back to continue our stakeout tonight, including you. I've not seen the weather forecast, but it is Manchester, so assume the worst.'

'What are you going to do if that—'

Banecroft slammed his foot down on the table, causing everything to rattle. 'What did I say at the very start of this? Don't worry about it. Your only concern is keeping Stella safe, and may I say you're doing a bang-up job.'

Hannah glared at him. 'That's a low shot, even for you.'

'Sleep deprivation makes me cranky.'

'God help us all.'

'He hasn't seemed inclined to do so up until this point. How is Stella?'

'How do you think? Freaked out.'

'Still? But it's been what, over ten hours since it happened? Has she not moved on?'

'Ox broke your favourite mug over a month ago and you still bring it up.'

Banecroft swung his feet off the desk and stood up. 'Nonetheless, time to get our girl up off the mat.' He threw open the door to the bullpen and marched out. 'Where the hell is everybody? It's ten o'clock on Monday morning. We are still a functioning business, are we not?'

'They've all been up all night and working all weekend,' protested Hannah, following him out.

'So? I'm here.'

'You live here.'

'So does Stella. And where is she?'

'In bed, I'm guessing.'

'Stella,' roared Banecroft.

'Vincent!'

'She's young. I didn't sleep at all between the ages of seventeen and twenty-eight.'

'You're an inspiration to us all.'

'STELLA!'

'You could at least go and knock on her door.'

Banecroft shook his head and stomped off towards reception. 'Fine. Throw in breakfast in bed. Turndown service, too. Why not? In my day, young people were up and at 'em at the crack of dawn. Full of beans. Raring to go.'

'Full of crap, more like,' said Hannah.

'I heard that.'

'You were meant to. That's how conversations work. I appreciate it's not something you're used to.'

Banecroft turned to where the church spire that doubled as Stella's room was and thumped on the makeshift wooden door.

'Oi, lazy bones – rise and shine.'

'Christ, you'd wake the dead.'

Banecroft and Hannah shared a look.

'Stella,' barked Banecroft.

'Stella,' said Hannah, 'we're coming in.'

Banecroft pushed the door aside roughly to find an empty room. 'Well, I take it back. She does have get up and go, as it appears she has got up and left.'

40

Stella said goodbye and closed the apartment door awkwardly. That had not gone as expected. Actually, she wasn't sure what she'd expected from it. What it had been was a really awkward conversation that went nowhere with someone looking at her like she was mad.

She'd woken up just after 7 a.m. to a deluge of texts and voice notes from Yvette, apologizing, grovelling and self-flagellating in a way only the middle class can really pull off. The girl had decided she was an unspeakable monster for dropping a pill in Stella's drink. She spent a considerable amount of time explaining and simultaneously ripping apart her own reasoning, before going on a toe-curling riff for about an hour's worth of messaging, explaining how yes, although she had technically spiked (oh gosh, I'm such a fool) Stella's drink, she hadn't been trying to have sex with her – not that Stella wasn't very attractive, she absolutely was, but Yvette wasn't a lesbian, not that there was anything wrong with it, totally onboard. Maybe she should try it . . .

At a certain point, Stella had stopped reading. Yvette appeared capable of typing faster than the human eye could read. It was quite impressive. Stella messaged back to say she was fine and to forget about it. Not that she was fine, or that any of it was fine, but she didn't have the energy to go over and over it, again and again. Besides, it was clear that Yvette was on the verge of turning herself in to the police and Stella didn't want to have to deal with all the hassle that came with that. As it was, she'd so far refrained from googling to see what reports there'd been of strange occurrences opposite the Arena.

Five minutes later, once she'd had some time to think, Stella had texted Yvette again. After she'd confirmed Stella's suspicion that Bea, her of the freak-out from the Village last week, had indeed taken a Merlin – *totally of her own free will, I swear. I'm not a monster!* – Stella had asked for Bea's address and phone number. She'd told Yvette very firmly that her presence wasn't required, and had then texted Bea to introduce herself and explain that she was coming over. She'd also ignored Bea putting her off and headed out anyway.

Hand on heart, she didn't know why she'd sneaked past Hannah without telling her where she was going. Maybe Stella was royally sick of feeling so utterly out of control when it came to her own life and body, and this – taking some form of action – felt like what she needed to do.

Bea, when she'd eventually opened the door, wrapped in a duvet, had not shared Stella's enthusiasm. She'd explained that she had a viral infection and was just taking it easy – doctor's orders. The poor girl did not look well at all. Stella, believing that they had some kinship, having suffered somewhat similar experiences, had attempted to get her to open up about what had happened the week before, but her questions had been met with nothing but confusion. Bea had felt ill that night – probably the early stages of the virus – and gone home. End. Of. Story. She'd watched a movie, gone to bed and woke up feeling rough. Stella's questioning about weird things happening, unusual powers, all of that, had been met with a mystified blank stare.

Stella found herself being somewhat politely but firmly pushed out the door of Bea's apartment, which she shared with two flatmates, and thanked for her interest in a way that strongly suggested that this had better be where her interest ended.

And so, Stella was now walking down a road in Fallowfield on a surprisingly sunny morning, having no idea what she was supposed to do next.

At least, she got to do that for all of five minutes before a jeep pulled up beside her. It was being driven by the big hairy dude, John Mór, and Hannah was in the passenger seat. Reluctantly, Stella hopped in the back.

'Have you been following me?'

'No,' said Hannah mildly.

'Then how did you find me?'

'Your phone.'

Stella was outraged. 'You've been tracing my phone? Are you kidding me? I cannot believe that!' She paused. 'All right, don't say it. We all signed up to that Find My Friend thing. I remember now. Still, though . . .' she said, folding her arms. 'Not cool. Anyway. Drive on. Let's get me back to being locked in my tower for the safety of the Great British public.'

'Actually,' said Hannah, signalling for John Mór not to drive off just yet. 'I've had an idea. There's some people I'd like you to meet.'

Stella narrowed her eyes. 'Well, this doesn't sound creepy at all.'

'It's not. They're nice. They're . . .' She looked pleadingly at John Mór. 'How would you describe them?'

'I wouldn't,' he said. 'I also wouldn't bring people to see them uninvited, but you're blackmailing me into it.'

Hannah wound her neck in. 'Blackmail is an ugly word.'

'All right,' he said, addressing Stella. 'She pointed out that both me and her would be dead if it wasn't for you. For what it's worth, she's not wrong. From the little I've been told, you had a horrible night. Might be that the Sisters are exactly who you need to talk to. If I were you, I'd jump at the chance. If I was me, I'd reluctantly agree to making it happen' – he gave Hannah a pointed look – 'although not as fast as some people think it needs to.'

'Sisters?' asked Stella. 'Like nuns?'

John Mór laughed. 'Definitely not. Although, I suppose a bit like that Whoopi Goldberg in the film, but no. They're ordinary sister sisters. Well, not ordinary.'

'And what if I don't fancy doing this?' said Stella. 'Maybe I'm sick of being treated like some freak show.'

'It's not like that,' said Hannah. 'I think this'll help.'

Stella bit her lip, considering her options.

John Mór turned around in his seat. 'Look, doing this is a pain in my arse and I'd be delighted if you sacked it off. Having said that, if you want answers, well, the Sisters are the people most likely to give you some. So, what are we doing here?'

Stella nodded. 'OK, then.'

'All right,' he said, putting the jeep into gear noisily. 'What are the chances of you wearing a blindfold?'

'Slim to no way, never,' said Stella firmly.

'I figured.'

'On the upside,' said Stella, 'I'm absolutely exhausted, so there's every chance I'll conk out before we get to wherever we're going.'

John Mór indicated and pulled out into traffic. 'Fingers crossed.'

41

This was the moment Stella resolved to give up entirely on trying to predict what happened next. She wasn't sure what she'd been expecting, but three old ladies had definitely not been it. Hannah had stayed behind in the waiting room while John Mór had walked Stella straight into an uncomfortably warm sitting room where a White woman, an Asian woman and a Black woman were sitting in armchairs, wearing dressing gowns, their hair in curlers, hands and feet stretched out to allow freshly painted nails to dry. The reek of hair spray, nail polish and heaven knew what else was so strong that it took a great deal of effort for Stella not to hold her hand to her face.

'John,' said the Asian lady with a Welsh accent, 'lovely to see you, as always.'

'Now, get the hell out and never speak of this on pain of death,' said the Black lady with an American accent.

John Mór pirouetted with a speed and grace that belied his size. 'I was never here.'

And then he wasn't.

The White lady smiled at Stella and waved a hand towards the sofa opposite the three armchairs. She spoke with a melodious Birmingham accent. 'Please, take a seat, love.'

Stella sat down.

'You'll have to forgive us,' said the Asian lady, 'we don't normally receive visitors on a Monday.'

'Monday is repairs and maintenance day,' explained the Black lady with a playful grimace. 'Never get old, dear. It's far more hassle than is worth bothering with.'

'Oh, stop it,' said the White woman. 'I'd imagine the poor girl is frightened enough without you giving her the terrors-of-time speech.'

'I'm just saying.'

The White woman turned in her chair to look over her shoulder and, for the first time, Stella noticed there was someone else in the room. 'Oh, Jackie, dear, you can take a well-earned break.'

The small blonde woman with a cheery face nodded at Stella then left through another door.

'That Jackie can work miracles,' said the Black woman, giving Stella a playful waggle of her eyebrows. 'Magic comes in many forms.'

The three sisters shared a look and an odd moment passed while they all hummed for a couple of seconds, as if deciding on a key, before turning back to Stella.

'So, dear,' said the White lady, 'what do you know about us?'

'Ehm . . .' began Stella, trying to sound calm. 'Hannah said you could help me. I mean, tell me what I am. I . . . By the way, outside, in the other room, I just saw it briefly, but was that Quincy Jones in one of the photos with you?'

Stella wasn't even sure why she was asking, but for some reason her brain had decided it was important. Not that she'd meant it as such, but as accidental good first impressions went, this was a doozy. The three women beamed at her, clearly delighted that she'd noticed.

'A very charming man,' said the Asian lady.

'And such an ear,' chimed the White lady.

'But we're not here to talk about us,' said the Black sister, 'are we?'

Stella worked the thumb of her left hand into the palm of her right. 'I guess not.'

'Normally,' said the Asian lady, 'there are tests we do. To find out what abilities, or at least capabilities, a person possesses.'

Stella tensed. 'OK.'

'But don't worry,' said the Black lady, 'the good news is, we won't be doing that with you. I'd imagine that after last night that comes as a relief.'

Stella nodded again.

'The bad news,' continued the White lady, 'is the reason we won't be doing that is . . . we can't tell you what you are.'

'But . . .' Stella faltered. 'Hannah said that you . . .'

'Normally we can do a lot of things,' said the Asian lady, 'but I'm afraid what's inside you isn't anything we've seen before.'

Stella sagged back on the sofa.

'In all honesty, child,' said the Black woman, 'we can feel the energy coming off you from here. Never felt the like of it in all our days.'

'Great,' said Stella, looking down at the ground. 'I'm a freak.'

'That is definitely not a word we would use,' said the Black sister sternly.

'Can anyone help me with this thing?'

'Oh, yes,' said the Asian woman, 'someone can, but you're not going to like the answer.'

'At the risk of sounding trite,' said the White woman, 'it's you. Heaven knows why, but someone or something made you into something different. Very different. Something we haven't seen before, and believe you me, that is really saying something. And we get it – you hate it. Having something inside you that you don't understand. It's terrifying. Trust me, nobody knows that better than us.'

All three sisters nodded again in perfect unison.

'But,' continued the Black woman, 'it doesn't define you.' Her kind eyes narrowed. 'That's something that's up to you to do.'

The Asian sister leaned forward. 'Because, you see, the scary thing about you, dear, isn't the power. There is always power. Power in itself isn't good or bad, any more than water or fire or damn near anything is. What's scary about you is how scared you are. The fear, child – the fear. It's coming off you in waves. You're so terrified of yourself, it must hurt to breathe.'

'Well,' said Stella, feeling tears pricking her eyes, 'you would be scared too if you had this monster inside you. I can't stop it. I . . . I killed a man.'

They all nodded.

'Did you?' asked the White sister. 'Or did the man kill himself by trying to destroy you and the people you love?'

'I still did it.'

'You did,' said the Black sister, 'and you're here to feel bad about it.'

'As opposed to being dead but feeling great about yourself,' finished the Asian sister.

'Is there any way of getting rid of it?' asked Stella.

'Not a good one,' said the Black sister, giving Stella a sympathetic look. 'You go looking for quick fixes in this life and you'll only find more problems. More confusion. More pain. People go looking for ways to take away the pain and pretty soon the solution becomes the problem. Trust us – doing that ain't going to solve anything, and you'd best be careful of anyone who tells you otherwise. Whether or not you like it, this is you, honey. Whatever this is. It ain't fair and it sure as hell ain't easy, but it's you.'

'You can spend your time fighting it,' added the Asian sister, 'but it'll eat you up inside. Make you someone and something you're not.'

'Your only way out is through,' continued the Black sister. 'You got to run towards it, not away from it. Instead of fighting who you are, you need to embrace it.'

'But I don't know who I am,' said Stella, wiping tears away from her cheek in annoyance. 'I don't have memories. A past. A . . . anything. I'm pretty sure Stella isn't even my name. For all I know, I picked it off the side of a beer can.'

'None of that matters,' said all three sisters in perfect synchronicity.

'In this world,' said the Asian sister, 'you are who you decide to be.'

'Actions define us,' said the White sister, 'nothing else. You know who you are. You're the people you surround yourself with. The things you fight for. The things you fight against. A past doesn't say where you're going, it's just baggage you have to bring on the trip. All you're doing is travelling light.'

'So,' continued the Black sister, pointing a blood-red fingernail towards Stella's chest, 'instead of viewing whatever is inside you as some curse, make it a gift. You're scared. Be scared, but face it. Find out who you are.'

'And what happens if I don't like who I find?' asked Stella.

'Then change it,' said the Asian sister simply, sitting back in her chair. 'Honestly, dear, we feel sorry for you. We do. But you have got to stop feeling sorry for yourself. You no longer have that luxury.'

'Now, if you'll excuse us,' said the White sister, while favouring Stella with a kindly smile, 'up next is the shaving, plucking and tucking section of events, and believe me, you do not want to be here for that.'

Five minutes later, Stella was in the back seat of the jeep, staring into nothing as the rain that always seemed to come out of nowhere hammered against the glass. She didn't feel much like talking, and Hannah and John Mór let her be. At least for a while.

'So,' said Hannah, unable to contain herself any longer, 'how'd it go?'

Stella folded her arms tightly. 'No answers, just got some advice.'

'Oh,' said Hannah.

A moment of silence stretched out between them, punctuated by the jeep's windscreen wipers working strenuously against the rain.

'If it means anything,' said John Mór as the jeep idled at a T-junction, waiting for a break in the traffic whooshing by, 'as wisdom goes, the sisters are as good as it gets.'

Stella said nothing to this, just jutted her chin. She suddenly felt tired – the kind of tired that took a lot more than a good night's sleep to fix.

They drove on in silence for a few more minutes before Hannah turned around in her seat. 'By the way, who was it you went to see this morning?'

'Oh,' said Stella, 'it was a girl who was a friend of Yvette's.'

'Was she there last night?'

'Nah. She went out with them last week and, according to what the girls said, she had a bit of a freak-out and disappeared. I thought it might have been the same thing that happened to me.'

'But it wasn't?'

Stella shook her head. 'Nope. She just got drunk then got the hell out of there because she thought she was going to be sick. Ran off home and sat up watching a movie. I thought it would help with the investigation, but it was a total waste of time. She spent ten minutes telling me how much she enjoyed some *Lawrence of Arabia* film.' She turned to Hannah. 'What? Why are you looking at me so weird?'

42

Banecroft jumped as Dr Carter sat down on the bench beside him.

'Vincenzo, sweetie, too much coffee?'

'I never touch the stuff,' he replied.

'Really? I never pictured you as the type to sit in the park staring off into the distance, contemplating life's great mysteries.'

'I'm not.'

What he didn't want to add was that he'd been trying to ignore the six-foot-eight behemoth in black who'd been delighting in reminding him that he had less than two days until he would be dragged to hell for all eternity. It was the kind of thing that could really put a crimp in your morning. Between that and watching adults fly by on e-scooters, he was starting to despair, both for himself and for humanity in general.

'So, to what do I owe the questionable pleasure?' he asked. 'Actually, before we get to that, are you aware that you're dragging a hairpiece behind you?'

Dr Carter picked up the dog. It was a Pekingese, aka a large mop of hair framing a pair of beady eyes and a mouthful of teeth that snarled at Banecroft. 'Vincenzo, meet Vinny. I named him in your honour.'

'I'm touched.'

'Don't be,' she said. 'He's incessantly aggressive, high maintenance, and he shits absolutely everywhere except outside.'

'That's unfair. I am quite the fan of the alfresco elimination.'

Dr Carter put down the dog again then yelped as it bit her on the finger.

'You weren't kidding.'

She looked embarrassed as she sucked on her digit. 'The little monster was a gift, although I'm starting to think he was more of a brilliantly executed passive-aggressive counter-attack. His only upside is that his teeth aren't that sharp. Anyway, speaking of shitting outside, would you like to explain what happened last night?'

'I don't know what you're talking about.'

Dr Carter shook her head. 'Really? Must we go through this charade every time? You know I wouldn't be here if I didn't know.'

'I was told DI Sturgess deleted all the CCTV foot— Ahh,' said Banecroft, nodding his head slowly, 'silly me. I forgot you've implanted some parasitic-eyeball thing in the detective inspector's head that sees everything he sees.'

Dr Carter pouted. 'You say that like it's a bad thing.' She tugged on Vinny's lead, as he attempted to savage a passing jogger, before speaking again. 'I thought we had an understanding? You need to keep your little protégée out of the limelight, especially after her role in the whole flying-student incident.'

'Her role was a walk-on part, and you also said I needed to find out what the hell was going on with that. Incidentally, I don't suppose you know anything about ecstasy tablets that have been magically messed with, do you?'

'I can tell you it's absolutely nothing to do with us.'

'That's a relief.'

'I'm much more partial to a mint julep myself. I should let you buy me one some time.'

'And I would,' said Banecroft, 'only I'm not sure I can claim back boozing with all-powerful entities of pure evil as a work expense.'

Dr Carter looked down at Vinny, who was now attacking her handbag.

She sighed. 'Unfortunately for both of us, I am far from all-powerful. You need to make whatever this is go away fast, and you need to keep that girl away from any further trouble.'

Banecroft hauled himself to his feet. 'I've been trying but, unfortunately for the both of us, trouble keeps looking for her. By the way, don't suppose you know anything about someone robbing several dozen graves in the last few months?'

Dr Carter raised an eyebrow. 'I don't, but I can tell you that anything involving necromancy is really frowned upon in my world.'

'Yes. This might shock you, but messing with dead bodies is considered poor form in my world too. It's one reason ventriloquists now use dummies.'

Dr Carter bent down and, with some difficulty, extracted her bag from the jaws of her permanently irate canine. 'Still, for all our sakes, concentrate on fixing the first thing.'

Banecroft noticed the smiling figure in black standing over Dr Carter's shoulder. 'I can do both.'

'Do them quickly, would you? The clock is ticking.'

A broad grin spread across the Pilgrim's ruined face.

'You've no idea,' muttered Banecroft. 'No idea.'

43

DI Tom Sturgess glanced across the desk at DS Wilkerson, who was making no effort to hide her confusion. She was halfway through her morning container of M&S pre-packaged fruit, a melon piece skewered on her wooden spork, hovering in mid-air. The last time he had seen this exact facial expression on his part-time DS was when they'd been dealing with a Manchester bus driver who'd announced he was Julius Caesar reincarnated before attempting to drive a busload of morning commuters to Chester, from where he had intended to launch an invasion of Wales. Thankfully, some commuters had technically hijacked the bus before it had reached the motorway. Sturgess and Wilkerson, as was often the case, had been called because someone somewhere deemed it 'weirdy bollocks', although it quickly transpired that a marriage breakdown and some poorly prescribed meds were more at fault than any Romans, living or dead.

Hannah Willis was not claiming to be the reincarnation of anyone, and was thankfully yet to take any hostages, but she was sounding similarly unhinged. Just a few moments ago she'd burst into their office, sweaty and out of breath, and babbling what sounded a lot like nonsense. Stella had followed in her wake and looked only marginally less confused than Sturgess or Wilkerson did.

Sturgess spoke in his calm voice, the one they teach you in basic training. 'OK. Take a deep breath and explain all that to me again.'

'The memories – they're not real.'

'Right,' he said slowly. 'You keep saying that like we're supposed to understand what it means.'

'And we definitely don't,' chipped in Wilkerson.

'OK,' said Hannah, before taking a few deep breaths. 'Sorry. There was a traffic jam on Deansgate, so we ran here. I'm a bit . . . out of puff . . .'

Sturgess didn't look at Wilkerson, but he could sense her wanting to add a rejoinder about what else Hannah was out of, but thankfully she held off.

Sturgess got to his feet to free up one of the room's two chairs. 'Do you want to sit down for a second? Or . . .'

Hannah waved him away. 'OK. Sorry. I went too far too fast there, didn't I?' She straightened up and gathered herself. 'Right.' She pointed at Sturgess. 'Your woman. The one from the Peacock Lounge.'

'I told you – that was a dead end. She remembered nothing.'

'Exactly!' said Hannah, clicking her fingers. 'As far as she recalled, she was ill, she went home and watched a film. What was it again?'

'*Lawrence of Arabia*,' supplied Sturgess.

'Shit the bed!' exclaimed Stella, who suddenly looked excited too.

'Why is that exclamation-worthy?' asked Sturgess.

Hannah pointed at Stella, who said, 'Because I talked to a girl from uni this morning, who had a freak-out last Thursday in a bar in the Village, only she just remembers feeling ill, going home and watching . . .'

Hannah joined in for this bit. '*Lawrence of Arabia*!'

'OK,' said DS Wilkerson. 'I'm still totally confused.'

'Both women,' continued Hannah, 'went home after a big night out and stayed up to watch a three-hours-and-seven-minutes-long film that, without stereotyping too much, I think it'd be fair to say you wouldn't expect them to have any interest in. That's because they didn't watch it.'

'So, they're both lying?' asked Wilkerson.

'No. They're saying exactly what they remember. It's just that the memory is fake.' Hannah looked around at the three confused faces looking back at her. 'Someone put that memory into their heads to hide what really happened to them.'

'Someone can do that?' asked Sturgess.

'Yes!' said Hannah. 'They did it to me. Well, sort of.'

'When?' Sturgess was curious.

Hannah reflexively glanced in Wilkerson's direction. 'That's not important now.'

'Hang on,' said Sturgess, 'are you telling me that someone can put something inside your head without you knowing?' A strange look came over Hannah's face that he could not read. 'What?'

'Nothing,' she said quickly, glancing at Stella. 'Nothing.'

'Wait a sec,' said Wilkerson, throwing her half-eaten fruit pot into the bin. 'So, what you're saying is that what they remember is wrong?'

'Yes,' said Hannah. 'Someone gave them a false memory.'

'The same memory?'

Hannah shrugged. 'I guess so. I don't know how they do it. Maybe it's easier to, I dunno, reuse the same one. And think about it – that's a film these women probably wouldn't have watched before, so I suppose it wouldn't clash with anything that was in their heads previously.'

'Hang on,' said Stella, 'if they didn't watch this film, then what the hell did they do?'

'Exactly,' said Hannah, throwing her hands in the air.

Sturgess looked at Wilkerson, finally understanding why Hannah was so excited. 'We need to go hunting through CCTV and follow these women from the moment they leave the venues. When exactly did your—'

Before he could finish his sentence, Stella had her phone to her ear. 'I'm finding out.'

Sturgess stood in front of Hannah. 'You're brilliant. I mean – this, this is brilliant.' He winced internally, as he could feel Wilkerson's smirk burning into the side of his face. 'If we can find out what happened in those missing hours, it'll blow the whole case wide open.'

'I know,' said Hannah, beaming. 'Not going to lie, pretty chuffed with myself.' She looked around the room. 'By the way, what happened to the band downstairs?'

'Creative differences,' said Sturgess.

'Yeah,' said Wilkerson, her desk phone now cradled under

her chin as she rang the station, 'I caught the guitarist smoking a joint out back and now they're all too afraid to come in here.'

'Well,' said Hannah, 'that's musicians for you. Untrustworthy bunch.'

44

Ox sensed Reggie opening his mouth.

'Don't say it!'

'What?' protested Reggie.

'You're about to say, "At least it's not raining", and I swear you've said that every fifteen minutes for the last four hours we've been sitting in this stupid bloody graveyard, and if you say it again, so help me, never mind us trying to find out who is taking bodies out of here, I'll be leaving an extra one behind.'

They were sitting in the new side of the cemetery, having opted to change their location from last night's. If they'd realized this would mean being so close to a bin full of rotting flowers, Reggie would have reconsidered. There were limited hiding places over here. The other two teams had installed themselves on the old side: Stella and Hannah in the Jewish graveyard area, Banecroft and Grace in the Catholic area. Brian the ghoul had something of a roaming brief, which was a polite way of saying he was weird, and they just sort of let him get on with doing his own thing. There were now three plots to keep track of, as there had been several burials earlier that day, one of which – Malcolm Jude Butler – fitted the criteria perfectly.

There was a long pause in the conversation, so long that it graduated from pregnant to married with children, before Reggie said, 'You're in a bit of a mood.'

'I just . . .' faltered Ox. 'I'm just . . . I get it – this is an investigation. I don't really understand how we got into it and why there's a weird ghoul living in the office—'

'Brian seems nice enough,' said Reggie.

'I'm sure he is, although whoever thought to call him Brian needs to give their head a wobble. He's the least Brian Brian in the history of Brians. My point is, I get why we're here, freezing our arses off, I just . . . How are we supposed to spot an invisible person digging up a grave?'

'Stella only said they *might* be invisible.'

'Great. We're hoping to catch Schrödinger's cat. And let's put aside the fact that the girl has experience in the field of supernatural grave-robbing.'

Reggie nodded. 'I'll grant you that is weird, but no weirder than Brian.'

'Nothing is weirder than Brian,' said Ox. 'Did I tell you I found him with his head in your bin yesterday?'

'No,' said Reggie, 'but thank you for the image. He's clearly had a . . . hard life up until this point.'

'All I'm saying is he appears to be living in the office full-time now, and we don't know anything about him. I mean, yeah, he seems harmless, but we don't know that for sure, do we?'

'And are you worried about the safety of your fellow employees or are you just annoyed because he ate your toy?'

'A bobblehead is not a toy. It's a collectible.'

'Yes,' said Reggie archly. 'I believe they now have a whole wing of them in the Louvre.'

'Make all the jokes you like, but we know nothing about him. He's there all hours. Could be dangerous. We don't know. I mean, three other people sleep there.'

'I see,' said Reggie. 'And who are you most worried about? The supernatural teenager with the immense, incomprehensible power? The Rastafarian possessed by a terrifying angelic spirit thing, who poor Brian appears to worship as a god? Or Vincent Banecroft, who is, well, Vincent Banecroft?'

Ox folded his arms and pushed his chin into his chest before muttering, 'That bobblehead was a present.'

★

Stella and Hannah sat huddled together in their deckchairs, sharing a blanket.

'We should have brought two blankets,' whispered Hannah.

'Or, like, a hundred.'

'Is it weird that this feels kind of fun?'

'Sitting in the dark in a freezing-cold graveyard? Yeah, super fun.'

'OK,' said Hannah, 'well, not the graveyard part. I just mean, I always wanted to go camping, and I never got to. You know, under the stars.'

'Clouds.'

'But there are stars behind the clouds.'

'"Behind every cloud there are stars",' said Stella in a teasing voice. 'You want to slap that over a cat dangling off a branch and get it up on Etsy. You could sell some serious tea towels.'

'Mock me all you want.'

'Believe me,' said Stella with a smile, 'I intend to. You should fully expect Ox to be working up posters of that by the end of the week, and we'll use them to wallpaper the office.'

'That's assuming we make it that far. I might die of exhaustion before then.'

'How come you didn't sleep today?'

'Well . . .' began Hannah.

'You were too excited about your big investigation breakthrough today, weren't you?'

Hannah gave a guilty smile. 'A bit.'

'Any—'

'Still no messages from Sturgess.' He and DS Wilkerson were checking through CCTV footage to see if they could find out what happened to Bea and the Peacock Lounge woman in their lost hours, given that they definitely didn't go home and watch *Lawrence of Arabia*. 'Do you not think I'd have mentioned if there was an update? I mean, I'm sitting right beside you.'

'Yeah, but you went for a wee an hour ago. Might have been a text then.'

'You think I'm texting Sturgess while I'm weeing?'

'I don't know what kind of kinky stuff you olds get up to.'

'Oh, don't,' said Hannah, pulling a face.

'I hate the waiting,' said Stella.

'For that, or for something to happen here?'

'Both.'

'I'm sure Banecroft would say, "Welcome to being a journalist."'

'Yeah, I've read that – journalism is mostly sitting around in graveyards, freezing your foo-foo off. We covered that in week one of the course.'

'Should have brought more blankets,' said Hannah.

'Should have brought more blankets,' agreed Stella.

★

'Are you all right?' asked Grace.

'Of course I am,' snapped Banecroft.

'It's just you're looking off into the distance and making weird faces.'

'I am not making faces.'

'You most certainly are.'

'OK, if you must know, there's a six-foot-eight man in black standing over there, with a face like a half-chewed golf ball, and he's grinning at me like he's going to drag me to hell in about' – Banecroft checked his watch – 'twenty hours, give or take.'

'I will not talk to you if you are going to be silly,' scolded Grace.

'If only I'd known that was all it would take . . . And now we're on the subject, what are you staring at?' asked Banecroft.

'The grave. The one we are supposed to be watching.'

'Meh, don't worry about it.' He nodded towards Brian, who was crouched down a few feet away. 'I've got my best man on the case. He'll smell whoever it is before we ever see them. Now, can I have my flask back?'

'No. I told you – not for at least another hour.'

'It's been at least an hour.'

'I took it off you six minutes ago.'

'It keeps me warm,' pleaded Banecroft.

'If that was the case, then poor drunken people wouldn't freeze to death on the streets.' Grace blessed herself.

'We keep this up and I might volunteer to join them.'

'I also do not approve of you allowing Stella to go to nightclubs.'

'She's a big girl.'

'She is still a child.'

'Well, if it's any consolation, I don't think she enjoyed the experience, so I wouldn't worry about her going again.'

'I worry about everything,' said Grace. 'And you should too.'

Banecroft glanced off to the side again. 'I worry plenty.'

Their attention was stolen by Brian, who had suddenly perked up and was sniffing the air.

'What is up with him?' asked Grace.

★

'I'm telling you,' whispered Ox, 'that bush over there moved.'

'Sure,' said Reggie. 'Just like that gravestone waved an hour ago, and before that, you had me convinced there was someone up in that tree.'

'That was bullshit, but this is real.'

'Yeah. Absolutely. I'm totally falling for this, Mr Boy Who Cries Wolf.'

'Fine,' said Ox. 'Be like that.' He got out of his deckchair, hunched down and started to creep forward slowly.

'Stop messing . . .' began Reggie, but Ox waved him away as he continued to move between the trees, heading towards the grave.

'He's taking the piss,' said Reggie to himself, sounding less than one hundred per cent certain. 'No, he is. He is. He's always doing this to me,' he muttered, nevertheless rising slowly out of his seat.

★

Doug finished positioning the four brass gnomes, stretched out his back and sat down in his deckchair. He needed to get some kind of fancy cushion for himself. A folding chair did not provide the type of lumbar support he needed, and he was getting steadily more sore.

Hopefully, he wouldn't have to do many more of these. Earlier on, Dr Marsh had come back from her little trip out very excited, like she'd made some kind of breakthrough. It was the closest thing he'd seen to her being in a good mood. She had still called him several names, but there'd been a twinkle in her eye. The memory of it made him shift in his chair. He thought there was something there, but he'd been wrong before. The problem with getting off on women acting like they despised you is that it was hard to tell them apart from women who really just despised you.

He uttered the phrase in the ancient language he didn't understand, and the four little diggers got going on their task. After watching them for a few seconds, he pulled out the magazines he'd picked up at the garage and studied them in the light from the two lanterns. He'd been in a rush. One of them was a gaming magazine. He wasn't big into it, but he had bought himself a PlayStation. He'd also picked up *New Scientist*, on the off chance he and Dr Marsh ever had a conversation that wasn't about how much she despised him. Finally, he had a copy of *Razzle* because a man had needs.

A slight popping noise made Doug look up from his reading matter to find an East Asian fellow with a goatee crouched a few feet in front of him. The chap looked almost as shocked to see Doug as Doug was to see him.

'What the—'

'Grave robber!' hollered the man, standing up and pointing. 'Grave robber!'

Doug attempted to get out of his chair.

A scuffle ensued, which was the kind of fight that resulted when two middle-aged men with little experience in this field of endeavour, other than watching the odd Liam Neeson film, attempted to engage in violence. As Doug stood, the other man rushed him and they both fell over in a heap. They then proceeded to flail about on the ground in an awkward, graceless wrestle that would have embarrassed two six-year-olds. Doug caught an accidental elbow in the face, and the other fella walloped his own head on a length of stone edging around the grave behind them.

Then, one of them – it was hard to tell who – kicked over the hourglass. While still engaged in this epic tussle, Doug was now dimly aware of another voice in the distance, shouting in surprise. He needed to get the hell out of there.

As the two men rolled about, his opponent gained the upper hand – probably more by luck than by any skill. Still, Doug found himself being straddled, with the other fella pinning his arms to the ground.

'You're under arrest.'

'You're not a cop,' wheezed Doug.

'Citizen's arrest.'

'This is a big misunderstanding.'

The man glanced at the gnomes, digging away beside them industriously, oblivious. 'Sure it is. You're—'

Before he could say anything else, Doug's opponent was interrupted by a massive feline barrelling into him, sending him flying into the darkness.

Now free, Doug wasted no time. He staggered to his feet and started to run as fast as he could. He wasn't worried about direction. He just needed to get the hell out of there.

Somewhere behind him, someone screamed.

★

Teeth.

That was what Ox could see in the darkness.

An awful lot of teeth.

And red eyes.

His sense of terror battled against a cloying wooziness that tried to drag him down into unconsciousness. Blood was oozing down his neck and his ribs ached. He'd crashed into someone's gravestone, breaking it into several pieces that now lay between him and the wet grass. That felt like the kind of thing that was going to lead to a lot of really bad luck. The immense shape that was slowly approaching him through the darkness indicated that all that misfortune was about to come in one big fatal dose.

Dazed as he was, Ox was still trying to piece together the salient details. For the first time in his entire life, he'd been winning a fight. Previously, he'd held a pathetic 0–4 record in that area, two of his previous 'bouts' having ended with his underwear being pulled over his head. This one had been going really well. He'd had the odd little man who was 90 per cent beard pinned down. He'd been actively considering saying something pithy and memorable that, ideally, someone who wasn't him would overhear and recount later on, making him sound cool. Then everything had gone sideways – including him, as he'd found himself flying through the air, followed by his unhappy landing.

He watched the red eyes in the darkness coming ever nearer. That was bad.

Beneath them, the white canine teeth leered at him.

That was worse.

Worse still, both of those body parts were alarmingly far off the ground, backed up by a massive form that was casually inching closer. Even in the dark, it was obvious that the creature could move much quicker than this if it wanted to, but it didn't. It was enjoying his terror.

It was welcome to it. Ox had plenty of terror to give.

The thing was only a few feet from him when Reggie stepped in front of Ox, waving his hands about with as much menace as he could muster. 'Be gone, foul beast!'

The thing made a contented purring noise. Never something you wanted to hear from an opponent.

'Get out of here, Reggie,' Ox ordered through gritted teeth.

'Never,' said Reggie. 'I can just—'

The thing moved so fast that Ox didn't even see it. It flicked out a paw and one second Reggie was standing there, the next he was swatted away, a screech tumbling through the darkness, followed by the sound of crumbling stonework meeting a soft body.

'Reggie!'

Along with the terror, Ox found a little anger now, which felt better. He grabbed on to it. 'Screw you, ya big . . . pussy. Nothing but a shitty little bully. I'm not scared of you.'

The thing padded forward on silent feet, standing over him now. A giant paw hung in the air over Ox's head, its claws somehow catching the light from the distant lanterns. No, not by accident. The creature was moving the paw that way intentionally. It was enjoying itself.

He scrunched his eyes shut. 'This is why people prefer dogs.' Not the greatest of last words, but they'd have to do.

Ox's eyes flew open again as the creature issued an unexpected yelp of pain. It no longer loomed over him. Now it was rolling around between the gravestones, hissing and clawing as it tangled with a figure.

Brian. It was Brian.

The thing was four times his size, but Brian was in there, thrashing about, fighting for all he was worth.

'Reggie!' hollered Ox. 'Reggie!'

He heard a noise from somewhere over to the right. Relief washed over him as he heard his friend's grumbling voice, 'Bloody cat!'

Ox looked on, trying to figure out how he could help. After the initial element of surprise, Brian now appeared to be struggling. The cat swung itself around and worked its claws to force Brian away from him, before pinning him to the ground aggressively. Brian wriggled, desperately trying to find some purchase on his opponent.

Then, with an awful, piercing noise that would stay with Ox for the rest of his days, Brian was in the thing's teeth, being ragdolled in the air and thumped against the ground. Limbs flailing.

A loud bang and a flash of bright light somewhere from Ox's left tore the night asunder. The cat howled in pain before dropping Brian, leaving him sprawled on the wet ground. The feline monstrosity issued a last venomous hiss then lolloped off hurriedly into the night.

From the darkness came the sound of running feet and Banecroft appeared above Ox, holding his blunderbuss. 'What the hell was that?'

'Never mind,' Ox shouted. 'Brian. Check on Brian!'

45

Panic.

It had been nothing but sheer panic.

Hannah held Brian in her arms, his green blood soaking into her coat as she carried him up the stairs to *The Stranger Times*' offices. He was so light. She'd been shocked when she'd realized she could carry him on her own.

His entire body was limp, and they'd been unable to bring him round. His skin was showing an alarming array of dark angry bruises coming up, counterpointed by several nasty-looking wounds that were oozing. Worst of all, his right leg was hanging down at a sickening angle and a sliver of bone was sticking out through his jeans. His breath was shallow. Barely there.

Grace had driven Hannah and Stella back to the office with Brian in the back seat. They'd thought of the hospital, of course, but would any doctors know what to do? Or would Brian get dragged off to some lab to be analysed? They had no idea. And so, they'd come back to the office. Hannah still wasn't sure they'd made the right call. It was the blood, the green blood, that had made them bring him here instead.

Banecroft, Ox and Reggie had sped off in Banecroft's Jag.

Hannah thought he'd said they were going to try John Mór's pub first, and then the Victory Hotel. There must be someone who knew how to help a badly injured ghoul. How to save his life. They needed someone's damn phone number. Why didn't they have anybody's bloody number?

Stella pushed some papers off one of the spare desks and Hannah laid Brian's unconscious form down on top of it. Grace ran in, carrying a jug of water and a tea towel from the kitchen.

'Brian,' urged Hannah. 'Brian, can you hear me?'

Nothing. Stella tucked a cushion from the sofa under his head.

'Is he still breathing?' asked Grace.

'Yes,' said Hannah. 'Yes, yes, but . . .' She held his hand. His skin was ice cold. 'Blankets. Maybe we should get blankets? Keep him warm.'

Grace rushed off.

Hannah moved Brian about, trying to get him into a comfortable position.

Stella threw the contents of another desk onto the floor and they shoved it beside the first one, so that none of Brian's lanky frame was dangling over the edge.

'Oh God,' said Stella, tears touching the sides of her voice, 'his leg.'

'I know,' said Hannah. 'It's bad.' She hurried over to Reggie's desk and grabbed a large pair of scissors. 'We need to cut the trousers off and . . . clean the wound. Yes, that's a thing you're supposed to do. GRACE?'

Grace was beside her, blankets in hand. 'Water. Lots of hot

water. And Stella, ring the others, see how they're getting on. And for . . .'

Hannah jumped as Manny appeared beside her, bare chested, peering down at the limp form of Brian lying across the desks.

'He's . . .' faltered Hannah, 'he's in a bad way.'

Manny touched a hand to Brian's forehead gently.

'Sorry, Manny,' said Hannah, 'but I'm going to need some room here. Could you . . .'

Stella was standing at the other side of the table, her phone pressed to her ear. 'They've got John Mór and he's ringing someone else. On their way. Couple of min—'

Stella broke off as Manny placed his hand on Hannah's arm and gently pushed her away.

'Manny, I need to—'

'No,' said Manny, in a firm voice. 'He dying.'

'What? No, he isn't.'

'No time,' said Manny.

'But—'

Hannah stopped as she noticed Manny's eyes glaze over. He placed his hands about a foot above the ghoul's supine form. Wisps of smoke snaked out of his splayed-out fingers, reaching down and caressing Brian's body.

'What in the hell . . .' began Stella.

'Language,' said Grace automatically, as she continued to stare intently at Manny.

'I've got no idea what's happening,' said Hannah, 'but . . . I guess let's let him . . .'

The smoky wisps had grown into thicker tendrils. Grace

gasped as they lifted Brian off the surface of the table. As he rose up into the air, more of the tendrils emerged from Manny's fingertips and wrapped themselves around him. They all took a step back, watching the maelstrom above their heads grow and grow, Brian's body suspended within it.

The smoke then took the form of the figure Hannah had seen once before – that of the angel. The last time, *The Stranger Times* had been under attack, and its face had been a mask of ferocious rage that chilled the soul. This time it was different. It emerged from the mist, a beneficent beauty looking down upon the world. Manny slumped forward, dangling in the air as if held up by invisible strings.

Hannah took another step back and yelped as she stumbled into someone. She turned to find Banecroft, Reggie, Ox and John Mór standing behind her, all gawping up at the swirling form that was now spreading its smoky wings, touching two of the bullpen's walls as it did so.

'What—' shouted Banecroft.

Hannah cut him off. 'No idea.'

The form of Brian began to rise further into the air, slowly spinning and twirling in the maelstrom until it ended up standing upright, its eyes still closed. The roiling cloud of smoke shrank in size as the mighty wings enveloped it. Brian's arms stretched out, joining it in a hug.

Everyone ducked their heads as it started to move.

Even later, when they spoke about it, the staff found it hard to describe, even to each other, what happened next. The angel and Brian, intertwined, proceeded to swirl around the room, like a couple of graceful ballroom dancers in the air. Hannah noticed that Brian's clothing was coming off. Not being stripped away so much as gradually disappearing, to leave his form naked.

As the couple's momentum increased, the watchers all ducked further until they were crouching on the ground beneath it and Manny's unconscious form was the most upright in the room. Faster and faster the strange dancers spun above their heads, the maelstrom steadily filling the room, blowing loose sheets of paper off tables, turning over chairs. A pane in one of the stained-glass windows cracked then shattered completely. A humming noise that Hannah hadn't noticed until that point grew louder and louder, modulating up and down in something akin to a melody.

The seven people on the ground clung to each other as the wind whipped around them, buffeting them from all sides, and then . . .

It stopped.

Brian, arms and legs outstretched, hung in a fixed star jump, his fingers brushing the vaulted ceiling. He glided slowly to the floor as the smoke serenely returned to Manny, sucked in as if by some invisible force. As Brian's feet touched the floor, his eyes flew open. He stood there, upright, unassisted, all the bruising on his skin gone. His shattered leg was whole once more. His face was open and calm, a blissful smile played upon his thin lips. He was the same but totally different.

He was also bollock naked.

And then Manny collapsed onto the floor.

Preston Still There

This morning a government spokesperson took the unusual step of issuing a statement confirming that the city of Preston still exists. Home to the second-largest bus station in Europe, Preston had previously been in Lancashire and, according to the government, still very much is.

Spokesperson Sally Southwick said, 'Preston is still exactly where it is supposed to be, and there is absolutely no need for anyone to check that. Anything you've heard about massive black holes and immense tentacles is just crazy talk. You're crazy. Stop being crazy.'

We will bring you more on this apparent non-story when we have it.

46

Dr Marsh was apoplectic with rage. 'How on earth could you let this happen?'

'I didn't let anything happen,' protested Doug from his seat at the kitchen table. 'I was sitting there, at the grave, doing what I was supposed to, and then this bloke appears out of nowhere.'

'Oh,' she bellowed sarcastically, 'appeared out of nowhere, did he?'

'He did.'

'OK,' cut in Cillian Blake, 'let's all just calm down.'

'Calm down?' screeched Marsh. 'Calm down? This idiot has ruined everything because he panicked when one guy showed up.'

'It wasn't just one guy,' said Doug. 'There was loads of 'em. They were coming out of everywhere. I nearly ran into a couple more while I was getting away.'

'And where the hell is Kitty?'

'I dunno. He was there, taking care of the guy that attacked me, and then there was a load of screaming and howling and . . .'

'And what?'

'Well,' said Doug, wincing, 'what sounded like a gunshot.'

Marsh screamed and threw out a hand. Doug squealed as the contents of the nearby knife block unsheathed themselves and started advancing towards him through the air.

'Enough,' shouted Blake, loud enough to at least make Marsh turn her attention towards him. Doug remained frozen in position, transfixed by the eleven knives of various sizes that were hovering in the air halfway across the kitchen, thankfully now stationary.

'This is a setback,' said Blake in a calmer tone.

'A setback?' echoed Marsh. 'Are you insane? This is a disaster. We don't have any more subjects. We've lost all the apparatus I gave this buffoon to extract them, and now we'll have even more attention on us than we had after his last screw-up.'

'The kid falling from the sky wasn't my—' Doug yelped as the knives resumed their advance.

'Emma,' pleaded Blake. 'You need to remain calm. Losing our cool here is not going to help.'

The knives stopped again, now only feet away from Doug.

Marsh jabbed a finger in his direction. 'That oaf got Kitty killed.'

'I'm sure he's not dead,' said Blake, before turning to Doug. 'Is he?'

'No, I saw him running off—'

'So why didn't you bring him back with you?' snarled Marsh.

'Because he was going in the wrong direction and I had to get the hell out of there. Like I said, there were people everywhere.'

'Kitty will turn up,' said Blake, 'I'm sure of it. He'll find his way home.'

'He's not been out on his own before,' said Marsh. 'He's a house cat.'

'Right,' said Blake slowly, clearly having the same issue as Doug – namely, thinking of Kitty in the sweet little pet terms that Marsh seemingly did. 'I'm sure he'll be OK. We'll deal with that as soon as we can but, first things first, you said this necro thingy . . .'

'Necromer.'

'Right. You said that it would finally get us over the . . . what do you call it again?'

'The rage problem.'

'Right. It'll solve that. Yes?'

'Potentially,' conceded Marsh, before looking back at Doug. 'But we haven't got any subjects to test it on.'

'Well, then,' Blake continued, 'we're just going to have to rely on your genius, aren't we, darling?'

Marsh muttered darkly to herself.

Blake turned to address Doug. 'Right, first thing in the morning, we're moving on to the next phase in the plan.'

'As in—'

'Yes, that. Problem?'

'No,' said Doug, shaking his head furiously. 'Absolutely no problem at all.'

'Right, then,' said Blake, turning back to Marsh. 'Now, let's all take a deep breath and try to relax.'

Marsh folded her arms. 'I want to have sex.'

'Ehm, maybe we should—'

'Now!' she barked and looked pointedly across at Doug.

'Of course, we just need to—'

She stamped her foot. 'I said now!'

Blake did an excellent job of keeping both his tone and body language neutral. 'Of course, darling.'

Marsh grabbed Blake's jacket lapel and pulled him across the room, shooting Doug a snide look as she passed then disappeared up the stairs with Blake.

Doug sagged with relief, his heart rate finally coming down, only to jump out of his skin with a scream a minute later when all the knives fell clattering to the floor.

47

At least it wasn't raining.

Banecroft eased himself onto the decrepit sun lounger up on the roof of the office. Each time he did so, it protested with a little more creaking vehemence, but yet again, it held. It was damn near the most reliable employee the paper had, and undoubtedly the longest serving. It wasn't warm enough to sit out, but he wasn't sitting out. What he was doing was not being in, which is an entirely different thing. Inside, right now, was filled with people babbling and rushing about while achieving nothing of consequence, save for gradually dispelling the surfeit of adrenalin the events of the previous few hours had left them with.

Brian, miraculously – and there was no hyperbole in the use of that word – was not only alive but also completely unscathed. In fact, he looked healthier than ever, despite being tossed about like an unloved chew toy by a massive feline beast. They'd all witnessed something and Banecroft was too damn tired to speculate on what that might have been.

Grace was oscillating between praying and trying to source appropriate clothing for a ghoul. For his part, Brian was busy happily eating the biscuits people kept giving him. Banecroft was coming to terms with the horrifying realization that the paper's entire staff had been present when whatever had happened happened, and nobody had thought to take a picture. True, he hadn't done so either, but he was an editor. He didn't gather news, he assessed it and determined its newsy value.

This place still had a long way to go.

Nor did they have any pictures of the Greater Manchester Police calling in specialists because a quartet of brass gnomes had apparently dug all the way through a coffin and kept going. Hannah had brought her detective inspector friend up to speed and he'd reported back that they'd found a hole twenty feet deep and growing, not to mention some rather odd artefacts and a copy of *Razzle*. They'd sent a camera down into the hole, which the gnomes had attacked before resuming their excavating duties. Still, it was refreshing to see that kind of work ethic in this day and age, even it was from a bunch of demonic creatures made of brass. If Banecroft had more energy, he'd wonder what would happen to those artefacts, but it probably involved them finding their way into the possession of the Founders. Sturgess might not be in their employ directly, but the entire GMP seemed to be, whether they realized it or not.

He assumed the copy of *Razzle* would inexplicably find its way into some bushes beside a railway track. He had weirdly vivid memories from his childhood of that being the only place pornography could be found. In his case, back in Dublin, it had been nudie playing cards. The seven of diamonds had made quite the impact on him.

Speaking of impact, while *The Stranger Times*'s news-gathering efforts had been piss poor, they had foiled a supernatural grave-robbing operation, so there was that. It was definitely something he could drink to.

It was technically morning – in the sense that it was demonstrably, factually and irrefutably morning – but given that he had been up all night, it was certainly not too early to start drinking. If anything, it was too late, and he had catching up to do. He poured himself a large rum and sat back on the lounger.

'Mr Banecroft.'

'For Christ's sake,' he groaned, rolling his eyes, 'I thought we established you couldn't be here?'

The Pilgrim stepped forward into the morning light, which did him no favours. He still looked like a tumour in fancy dress. 'We are not in a building. We are above one.'

'I thought you were dislikeable before, but now you're a pedant, too. My, my. Normally, I'd set our angel on you, but as it happens, I am in a good mood.'

Besides, they were currently angel-less. They'd had to carry Manny back downstairs to his lair, where he'd made a remark about how nobody should worry, but that he was going to have to sleep for forty-nine hours solid. He did so right before falling into a very deep and peaceful-looking sleep. Banecroft had found himself feeling jealous. He never got to sleep like that any more. Admittedly, forty-nine hours was a weirdly specific length of time but Banecroft was fine with it. They didn't need Manny up and about for printing the next edition until Thursday. As far as he'd been aware, the Rastafarian spent the first half of most weeks in a coma anyway.

'Before we get to the praising and apologizing,' continued

Banecroft, 'can I ask, how does a semi-ghost like yourself still manage to smell musty?'

'What is the phrase you people have about glasshouses?'

'It's "don't go into a hot glasshouse with a semi-ghost corpsicle in a silly hat, the stench will kill you".'

'I cannot describe how pleased I am that our time together will soon be over.'

Banecroft tipped his glass. 'I'll drink to that.'

'Indeed.' The Pilgrim withdrew his pocket watch from his waistcoat. 'By my estimation, it is seventeen or so hours, give or take, until midnight.'

Banecroft paused with his drink in front of his lips, which he then lowered. 'What are you talking about? We foiled the grave-robbing weirdo. Brian nearly died doing so. We found the pattern and put a stop to it. The gnomes will eventually end up in police custody, and a description of the perpetrator has been given to the authorities.'

Ox had been initially reluctant to assist the police with their enquiries, but Banecroft had delivered a pep talk that may or may not have included the threat of termination – of both his employment and existence.

'Admirable,' said the Pilgrim, 'but that was not what you were asked to do.'

Banecroft sat forward, some of the rum spilling unheeded on his trousers. 'Yes, it was. You said fate has put me within the orbit of a greater defilement and I could prove myself worthy by righting an unspeakable wrong. Those were your words. If nothing else, I have a very good memory for words.'

'Yes.' The Pilgrim gave him a smile that would curdle milk. 'But that was not the great defilement. You have not completed your task.'

'Bullshit,' snapped Banecroft. 'You need to stop speaking in riddles.' He sprang to his feet to confront the Pilgrim directly. 'I did what was asked.'

'No, you did what you assumed was asked. As always, your arrogance has been your undoing.'

'So, what is it? Tell me what . . .'

Banecroft realized he was shouting at nothing – the apparition had disappeared.

He turned to see Hannah standing at the door that led out onto the roof. 'Is everything OK?' she asked.

'No,' said Banecroft, knocking back what was left of his rum, 'it most definitely is not.'

48

Throughout history, the dukes of Cheshire had been considered an 'eccentric' bunch. Eccentric in the traditional English sense of the word, meaning someone who has too much money to be considered truly stark-raving mad. As with all the aristocracy, there were the usual issues brought about by swimming in a gene pool that was far too shallow to require a lifeguard: the propensity for weak chins, the odd webbed finger, and the occasional card-carrying psycho who needed to be either locked in an attic or encouraged into politics.

In the case of the Cheshires, though, along with the 'eccentricity' came a hereditary disposition for cunning. They shared certain uncanny abilities, chief among them being an unerring gift to pick the winning side in any war. That, coupled with an eye for commercial opportunities, meant the seat not only survived but also thrived, despite the near ever-present whiff of scandal and smatterings of occasional madness.

Take, for example, the 4th Duke of Cheshire, who not only married his own horse but also shot it when he found it being unfaithful to him with a Shetland pony. He was shrewd enough to realize that if people were going to participate in a hundred-year war, they'd need weapons with which to do so. Lots of weapons. His son, while by no means the inventor of the cannon – that was the Chinese – was behind some exciting innovations in cannon design. That he achieved these advances while firing the weapon at members of his own household staff as they ran naked across the lawns of Cheshire House was tactfully painted out of the rendering of the bigger picture.

And so, on the line of succession went, with subsequent dukes and duchesses of Cheshire adding areas such as slavery, mining, shipping and timeshare sales to the family's traditional warmongering portfolio. They prospered while other aristocratic lines ran out of money, progeny or favour with the powers that be. The Cheshires became one of the invisible hands that steered the British Empire – too important to ignore, too 'eccentric' to bring fully into the light.

In the 1960s, Charles-call-me-Chaz, the 38th Duke of Cheshire, was a self-styled patron of the arts. In other words, he really enjoyed getting high with rock stars and hippies, and was all in favour of free love, provided people paid for everything else. He was a man in search of a purpose in life, and he found it in the idea of cheating death. As seminal moments went, the bass player with a well-known psychedelic rock band leaving behind a copy of Robert C. W. Ettinger's *The Prospect of Immortality* after a three-day party (along with a woman he'd forgotten he was married to) was an absolute corker.

Chaz put the put-out spouse into a taxi, but he held on to the book. Cryonics. The idea of cryogenically freezing yourself until medical science conquered the very idea of death was innovative stuff. The concept caught his imagination and, surprisingly for a man who had previously been renowned for his poor attention span, it didn't let go. Chaz had found his calling. Not only did he want to be brought back to life in the future, but he also wanted to bring some company with him in case, God forbid, future generations turned out to be a bunch of squares. Hence, he built a facility under Cheshire Hall that could cryogenically freeze not only him and his descendants, but also those they saw as the best and brightest of their generations.

Initially, this included friends who signed up voluntarily, but at some point – probably about the time he started dropping acid for breakfast – the duke became convinced that the Ark, as he called it, was destined to repopulate earth after the coming apocalypse, something he thought was going to be brought about by socialism or satanism or possibly one of his ex-wives. It really depended on how long it was after breakfast when you asked.

It was also around this time that his fervour for the project took a darker turn. Charles-call-me-Chaz stopped seeking volunteers and instead became an enthusiastic collector of corpses of the great and good, paying top dollar to anyone who could facilitate a switcheroo. He wasn't even that bothered about how long it took, assuming that being frozen only several months after death just meant a couple of extra wrinkles for all-mighty science to iron out in the future.

The powers that be were aware of his rather unusual proclivity, but seeing as the Cheshires were nice enough to lease the British Army a couple of terribly useful islands at reasonable rates, not to mention the fact that a few royals were literally chilling in Charles-call-me-Chaz's basement, his actions were tactfully ignored. Irony of ironies, Charles passed away in 1978 when, pissed as a newt, he walked out the wrong door of a bunker in the middle of a product display for an arms company in which the family were major shareholders and gave an unwittingly vivid demonstration of an anti-tank mine's ferocity. The incident resulted in his dispersal over a wide area of the Yorkshire Dales. Three fingers, half a kidney and a foot were cryogenically frozen in the Ark, Charles-call-me-Chaz giving medical science one final tricky problem to handle in the future.

The Cheshires had many flaws, but an absence of blind loyalty was not one of them. So it was that Charles-call-me-Chaz's son had carried on his legacy, not only maintaining the Ark, but also adding to its population as he saw fit. This was the eighties, though, so out went the hippies and in came 'strivers' as Charles-call-me-Charlie, son of Charles-call-me-Chaz, had described them. Along with artists that he favoured, quite a few 'self-made men' also joined the Ark. The kind of people who'd taken just a few million quid and turned it into several, often after numerous failed attempts and the occasional assist from jolly nice chaps they'd been to Eton with.

Charlie lived until the ripe old age of seventy-three, before dying in a tragic skiing accident while drunk and screaming racist abuse at a fellow skier he had incorrectly identified as Chinese. His son, Charles-call-me-Chip (American mother) had succeeded him. Sadly, his reign as Duke lasted only a matter of twelve days, as his ill-thought-out decision to hold an unofficial twenty-one-gun salute to his dear old dad on the ski slopes of the

Swiss Alps resulted in an avalanche that killed him and half a dozen other mourners, and ended up necessitating another in a long line of cover-ups.

So it was that the 41st Duke of Cheshire, Charles-call-me-C-Bone (a half-American father and a remarkable lack of self-awareness leading to a rap career that not even money could make successful), had inherited the title at the age of twenty-three. While young, he was not the youngest duke ever – one of his predecessors had been awarded that accolade while still in nappies. (In fact, a second duke had worn nappies too, but that had been more of a lifestyle choice.)

Most of the above information was not known by, or of interest to, Doug. What was of interest was the fact that the new duke was at home in Cheshire Hall with no evidence of security being in place. Doug was parked outside on the large gravel drive in a refrigerated container truck he had rented especially for the occasion. Luckily, he'd done the research ahead of time, so he'd known exactly where to get one and had headed straight here. A Glock pistol lay on the passenger seat beside him. This was the end game. Ideally, he'd have liked to have been better prepared for this moment and staked out the place beforehand, but after last night, the slow and steady approach was no longer an option.

The 40th Duke had been a fan of melodic indie pop, and Nigel Stay of Herschel's Garden had been a somewhat surprising inclusion in the Ark's pantheon of the great and good. Nigel had signed up voluntarily, having decided from a young age that while he wasn't a massive fan of life, he hated the idea of death even more. Instructions had been left in his will and seeing as the turning over of the rights to his music to his sister had been made contingent on her following those instructions to the letter, she'd consented to the idea of her brother's body disappearing quietly while a bag of straw and God knows what else was burned in its place and sprinkled over a nice memorial garden.

The Duke had been trying to get in on the ground floor of Herschel's Garden when he'd made the approach but, even though their star had ascended only to the first floor at the time of Nigel's death, he'd still honoured the agreement. Not every investment paid off, but a man was only as good as his word. He might have been a lunatic, but the 40th Duke of Cheshire had been an honourable one.

Doug had been instructed to get Nigel's body back, and that was exactly what he was going to do. Now that he was here, though, he was losing a little confidence. He didn't like violence, mainly because he'd never been any good at it. Even if the cat had been available, bringing it had not been an option. Kitty didn't do threatening, only killing, and dukes were the kind of thing that people noticed if they got eaten.

Doug kept trying to come up with a pithy opening line, something like 'give me the dead man or you're a dead man', but it all felt rather ridiculous. Still, he was going to do what he had to do. The main trick seemed to be to start off negotiations while holding the gun and at no point in proceedings let the gun go. Everything else would take care of itself. He'd used the electrician qualification he'd gained while in prison to cut the landlines to the Duke's manor and, unbeknownst to him, every house within three miles of it. He'd also bought a mobile-phone signal jammer off the dark web. The supplier had assured him it would block any phone within five hundred metres. He looked at the box on the dashboard and flicked it on, suddenly deeply regretting not having tested it before now.

He pulled the balaclava over his head. It really made his beard itch, but it was, again, a sensible precaution. If this worked, he'd be one step closer to getting back on the road where he belonged. That was all that mattered. No more waking up in his own bed. Knowing instantly where he was.

Deep breath.

Rock 'n' roll.

As he strode across the gravel turning circle, he considered whether he should knock on the door or just try to kick it in. Before he had a chance to come to a decision, a tubby naked man with a haystack of unruly blond hair came stumbling out the front door.

'For fuck's sake, help me, man – she's stopped breathing!'

Under the balaclava, Doug found himself smiling. He might not know violence, but this, this he knew.

49

As she scanned the four screens in front of her, DS Wilkerson felt her head dipping forward and jerked herself awake. She couldn't stomach any more coffee. She'd been mainlining the stuff all night and now had an unpleasant itching sensation at the back of her eyeballs.

She and Sturgess had been at the office, trawling through the CCTV, for hours – or at least they had been until he'd left to deal with what was being referred to as 'the Southern Cemetery fiasco'. The last she'd heard, the cave-diving team that had been summoned were refusing to go down into the hole as they didn't descend into excavations that were still ongoing – especially not ones with angry brass whatever they were down at the bottom, who didn't take kindly to interruptions. Sturgess had mentioned there was talk of trying to find some longer version of the grabby arm from one of those claw game machines they had in arcades or, failing that, a controlled explosion, because nobody wanted to see just how far those little brass dynamos could go if left to their own devices.

In theory, the CCTV trawl should have been relatively straightforward. They had the exact times and dates to within five minutes of when the two subjects had left their respective locations. They'd picked them up almost straight away and, while not perfect by any means, the camera coverage in Manchester City Centre was pretty good. Both women had left their venues clearly distressed and moving fast, which meant they stuck out on the footage too. Elizabeth 'Bea' Yennon could be seen on camera turning the bonnet of a taxi into a rather lovely floral display. It was quite something. More importantly, both women should have been incredibly easy to follow. *Should have been . . .*

In reality, Sturgess and Wilkerson hit the same problem they had many times before. Remarkably, every time they tried to trace an unusual occurrence in the system, they would come up against mysterious glitches. For no good reason, cameras would cut out, footage would go missing or end up inexplicably corrupted. Theoretically, nobody was allowed to interfere with the system, but they all knew there were ways to do it.

Sturgess himself had done precisely that. He'd felt very uncomfortable about it, but she knew he'd been in here, 'accidentally' deleting footage relating to the incident with that girl Stella from Sunday night. Wilkerson made no judgement. The girl had been technically 'helping the police with their enquiries', and protecting a source was a legit reason for messing with the system. He hadn't gone through official channels to do so, though, and she hadn't asked why. Sturgess was as by the book as they came, but the problem was they were ending up in an increasing number of places that didn't appear in the glossary of any policing handbook.

And so it was, with a dreadful sense of inevitability, that

they'd experienced the 'blackhole problem', as Sturgess had dubbed it. They were able to follow the two women to a certain point and then the cameras would suddenly stop working and they'd lose them. This time, it really was cameras not working. They had footage of this Elizabeth 'Bea' Yennon running out of the Maze club looking distressed. They picked her up running across a road, Insta-planting the taxi, and then followed her as she ran for several hundred metres before sprinting down a side street and stopping beside a skip. Then, the static camera whose feed they were watching abruptly and inexplicably ended up pointing towards the night sky. A stationary camera. No hacker in the world could do that. Wilkerson had no idea what could. It made no sense. The camera in question was scheduled to be fixed sometime in the next month, which meant it might happen before Easter. The footage around the woman from the Peacock Lounge, Michelle Creevy, had followed a damn near identical pattern. They had her until they didn't, when another camera inexplicably ended up pointing at the sky. That one wasn't even scheduled to be fixed yet.

And so it was that they'd been forced to get what Sturgess termed 'creative'. In practical terms, that meant looking through all the footage from surrounding cameras for the next couple of hours in the blind hope they might pick up the trail. So far, they were drawing a total blank. Wilkerson was going through the recordings from last Thursday for the second time, in the forlorn hope that she'd missed something.

She spotted the same drunk bloke dressed as Scooby-Doo, who for some unknown reason stopped to pee four times in the space of thirty minutes. The way he moved suggested he was in his early twenties. What young guy had a bladder that weak? The thought had occurred to her that maybe he was doing it 'voluntarily', and she really wished it hadn't. Scooby-Doo had been her favourite cartoon growing up, and she had a sneaky suspicion that this weirdo had now ruined it for her.

This was all starting to feel like a complete dead end as . . .

She immediately hit the button to pause the footage.

She'd missed it the first time because she'd been looking for a woman on her own, not one walking happily with a couple of friends. The girl was walking down Sackville Street with the duo, seemingly in no visible distress. She and another, smaller woman with glasses appeared to be in conversation, and a short man with a long beard was walking slightly ahead. Wilkerson watched the group turn a corner then pulled up the next camera. There they were again. The woman in the middle, who Wilkerson was now certain was Elizabeth 'Bea' Yennon, looked perhaps a little out of it, but then, at that time on a Thursday night/Friday morning, so did quite a few people. Upon closer inspection, it appeared that the smaller woman with glasses was doing all the talking. Wilkerson followed them through two more cameras then watched as Miss Yennon got into the back of a blue Mazda – again, seemingly of her own free will – and the duo took their seats in the front. There would have been plenty of opportunity for her to run, but then that didn't by any means equate to someone being free to do so.

Suddenly wide awake, Wilkerson worked her way back and forward through the recordings, following the trio as far as she could before the cameras eventually lost the car on Oxford Road. Then she ran the number plate. Predictably, it belonged to another make and model of car in the database. It had been either cloned or swiped.

Wilkerson checked the time. It'd be a few hours before the team in charge of the facial-recognition software was in. She looked at the images again. If they got lucky, one of those two people might be in the database, if they'd been arrested since 1984 and their custody picture was on file.

She picked up her phone to ring Sturgess. Time to see if he wanted to add to his ever-growing unpopularity by waking some people up.

50

It was just like old times.

These were the kind of situations where Doug knew he could keep his head while all about him were losing theirs. He'd never been in a 'school' as such, but he'd often marvelled at what they must spend their time teaching students. None of it seemed very useful to him. The grand old Duke of Cheshire, aka the chubby naked blond dude, and whoever his kaftan-clad mate with the classic White-guy blond dreadlocks was, probably had hundreds of thousands of pounds' worth of education between them, and yet neither of them had managed to put the girl in the recovery position. One of them had covered her in a blanket, for Christ's sake. She was overdosing; she didn't need to be tucked in.

Events were unfolding in one of the drawing rooms of Cheshire House. Framed portraits, where highly skilled artists had made valiant attempts at making erstwhile dukes look as if they had chins, hung on the walls, glowering down at them. A roaring fire was burning in the grate. Bob Marley was coming out of hidden speakers, assuring everyone that everything was going to be all right. The comatose girl on the floor provided ample evidence to the contrary.

Doug was now administering CPR, having sent the Duke out to the container truck to retrieve his bag. It was force of habit. He took it everywhere with him because you never knew. He was doing this while still wearing the balaclava, although it was really irritating him now. These things had not been designed with the bearded gentleman in mind. It was probably why so many of those Irish trad bands sang rebel songs. It was where nationalists with big beards ended up because they couldn't get a balaclava that fitted.

As Doug worked, Dreadlocks stood over him, getting in his space.

'What's she taken exactly?'

'Taken?' repeated the guy. 'I don't know anything about any drugs. I mean, I was just . . . I mean, if she did take something, she probably brought it here herself. I don't think you should be doing that—'

'Don't think. Just shut up.'

'Are you insured?'

Doug looked up at him while he performed chest compressions. 'Insured?' He then pulled the balaclava halfway up, bent down and proceeded to give the girl mouth to mouth.

'Whoa, dude – not cool. You do not have her consent.'

While Doug wasn't a violent man, he was unfalteringly practical. Lots of things could go wrong in this situation – the casualty's 'friends' being idiots was one of the biggest. As Dreadlocks reached down to pull Doug away, a well-judged elbow met the guy's previously highly privileged testicles. Some things made all men equal. He crumpled to the floor beside the girl and, in that moment, came the closest he ever would to understanding the suffering expressed in those Bob Marley songs he had recently discovered.

'For future reference,' said Doug, as he checked the girl's pulse to find it steadily improving, 'paramedics don't show up wearing a balaclava, and even if they did, they're not interested in hearing you trying to belatedly establish your legal defence.' Doug looked at the paraphernalia on the rug in front of the fire. 'And get rid of the gear as soon as the shit hits the fan.' He shook his head. 'Amateurs.'

Just then, the Duke came staggering back in with Doug's bag in his hand.

'Oh Jesus, what happened to Ice?'

'Ice?' repeated Doug and nodded at the man lying prone beside him. 'This dozy twat is called Ice? Now that is ironic.'

The Duke spun around, his free hand clutching his blond hair. 'Oh God, oh God, oh God – is he ODing as well?'

'Only on stupidity. Bag.'

Doug snatched his kit out of the kid's hand.

'What are you doing?'

He talked as he worked. 'Now she's got a heartbeat, we're on to the next step. Ever seen *Pulp Fiction*?'

'What?'

'*Pulp Fiction*,' he repeated. 'The film?'

'Ehm . . . no.'

'For God's sake, how have you not seen it? It's a classic.' Doug's hands found everything he needed automatically – it was like riding a bike – and he readied the needle. 'Anyway, old Quentin got a lot of it right, but you don't need adrenalin, you need this – naloxone. And you don't need to go through the sternum – much easier to go through one of the intercostal spaces.' He administered the injection as he spoke. 'What's this girl's name?'

'Ehm . . . Pixie? No, Trixie? I don't . . .'

'Never mind.' The girl's eyes started to flicker open. 'She can tell me herself in a minute. Not that I want to know.' Suddenly remembering himself, Doug looked around, snatched up the gun from the floor beside him where he'd left it and got to his feet.

'Now,' he said, pointing the weapon at the duo on the floor, 'here's what's going to happen next: this idiot is going to drive her to the hospital and, with a little bit of TLC, she's going to be fine. He is still going to be a twat, but there's nothing I can do about that.' He waved the gun between himself and the Duke. 'Then, you and I, fella, are going to have a little chat about a certain dead body. At least we will, as soon as you put some trousers on. I don't know what about this situation has given you an erection, and I don't care to know, but I don't need it winking at me while we talk.'

The vibe with the Duke was considerably different from what Doug had been anticipating. Mind you, a stranger saving some girl you'd brought home from dying on your best rug was a hell of a way for them to ingratiate themselves with you. Doug still had the gun, but it wasn't necessary. He'd also taken off the stupid balaclava, not least because when the Duke had understood why Doug was there, he'd seemed positively happy to help.

Besides, the combination of being filthy rich and still clearly stoned meant that the Duke's desire and ability to remember someone's face would be non-existent.

His lordship popped in the access code and, with a rather theatrical hiss, the steel door in front of them swung open.

'Honestly,' said the Duke, 'I had no idea this thing was even here until I watched the video the lawyers gave me after Pops popped his loafers. Just insane. I mean, I knew there was something down here, but I just assumed it was something normal, like a panic room or a sex dungeon. Would you like a drink?'

The Duke had the peculiar tic of offering someone a drink every ninety seconds. Having turned down the offer five times already by this point, Doug just ignored it.

He hadn't really established an image in his head of what the Ark would look like, but if he had, this wouldn't have matched it. Banks of fluorescent lights flickered on to reveal rows and rows of large fifteen-foot-tall shiny metal vats stretching off as far as the eye could see. It reminded him of nothing so much as a dairy he'd visited once. Touring with Iron Maiden had been a weird experience, not least because the band had an inexplicable fascination with days out that would make for unpopular school trips. In six months, that road crew had found out more about cheese-making, basket-weaving, pottery and nineteenth-century farming methods than any of them had ever wanted to.

'Jesus,' said Doug, taking it all in.

'I know – you should see the electricity bill for this place. I mean, totally mental. Honestly, it could bankrupt me. It's, like, do people even know there's a cost-of-living crisis?'

Doug walked forward slowly. The place was so much bigger than he ever could have imagined.

'There are some guys that come in to maintain the place. Pops and Grandpops sorted the whole thing out. The whole operation sort of takes care of itself. I just need to sign stuff every now and then.' He slouched glumly against one of the vats. 'Cheques, mostly.'

'I thought there'd be, like, individual coffins,' said Doug.

'Yeah, so did I, but the guy says that these vat things – he calls them dewars or something – hold, like, fourteen people each.'

'How do you find who is where?'

'Oh, right,' said the Duke, walking over to a desk near the door, 'there's a computer with a spreadsheet or' – he picked up a large ledger – 'there's this big book thing.'

Doug took the ledger and started flicking through it. 'Holy shit! You've got him . . . and her. And, no way – there's no way that's even . . . He's still alive!'

The Duke looked at where Doug was pointing. 'Oh yeah, that freaked me out, too. Apparently not.'

Doug shook his head in disbelief – all those people he'd dismissed as nutters had been right; Paul McCartney really had died back in the sixties and been replaced by a stand-in. That had to be the most successful tribute act of all time.

'To be honest with you, man,' said the Duke, 'I was thinking of, like, "trimming" some of these back. I mean, aside from anything else, one of the maintenance guys told me that a load of the earlier people haven't even been vitrified, which is where they replace all the water in a body with this kind of anti-freeze stuff, so they've, like, gone bad anyway.'

Doug found the page he was looking for and his heart sank. There was no record for Nigel Stay. 'Wait, hang on a sec. He's not here. How is he not here?'

'Oh, yeah,' said the Duke, looking rather sheepish, 'he might be in the other book.'

'Other book?' echoed Doug. 'Why is there another book?'

Revenge of the Prawns

Experts have long been predicting that, if current consumption rates continue, it is a matter of decades, if not years, before the North Atlantic no longer contains any prawns. However, this dire prediction has taken an unexpected turn following research carried out by the University of Manchester Maritime Investigations Unit. Professor David Draper said, 'While we were monitoring stock levels, we noticed unexpected and remarkable changes in the biological make-up of prawns. Not only are they getting considerably bigger, but some of them have also grown legs, not to mention shockingly strong arms.'

This tallies with reports of alarming incidents off the coast of Maine where several shrimp fishermen – shrimp being the incorrect name North Americans use for prawns – have reported being punched by irate crustaceans, often followed up by a vicious attack upon their tackle. Professor Draper concludes, 'We're still saying that soon there may be no prawns left in the ocean but that's because there's every chance they're coming ashore. We knew there was an extinction level event coming, we just might have got wrong who it is happening to.'

Most experts agree, mankind probably has it coming.

51

Hannah looked at Banecroft across the wasteland of hopes, dreams and takeaway boxes that was his desk. 'I don't understand.'

'Then I've explained it correctly, because I don't understand either.'

'But we stopped the—'

'I know!'

'Does he expect us to—'

'I don't know.'

'Well, this is totally ridiculous. You can't be sent to this hell-like place for not doing something when they haven't told you what you're supposed to do. It's completely unreasonable.'

'Yes,' agreed Banecroft. 'Mark my words, I'm going to write a strongly worded letter to their customer complaints department.'

Hannah chewed on her fingernail for a second as she tried to think. 'OK, so . . . logically, what do we think we have to do?'

'I can only assume that we have to find this fella Ox tussled with at the graveyard. I can't help feeling if we had hired some people who were more tasty in a fight, I'd be having a much better day.'

'Be fair,' said Hannah. 'He said he was winning until he got attacked by some massive homicidal cat.'

'Yes, I'll try to remember that when I'm . . .' Banecroft, as much as it was possible for him to do so, went pale. He looked away for a moment then turned back and returned to being his usual obstinate self. 'Right. Get your detective inspector on the phone. We need to track down this beardy little freak' – he glanced at his watch – 'fast.'

They were interrupted by a loud knock on the door. It opened immediately and Grace barged through. 'I have finally got trousers on Brian.'

'Congratulations,' said Banecroft. 'Great to see we're getting to grips with the really big problems.'

Grace narrowed her eyes. 'What have we discussed regarding your tone, Vincent?'

'I was just . . .' began Banecroft, before trailing off.

'That's better. Now,' she continued, turning to Hannah, 'perhaps you would like to throw some water on your face and maybe fix your hair?'

'What?' said Hannah.

'I appreciate you've spent a large part of the evening in a graveyard, but even so, it's always worth maintaining standards.'

Hannah touched her hair self-consciously. 'What are you on about?'

'You know me, I am not one to judge . . .' Banecroft barked a laugh at this, which earned him some seriously reprimanding side-eye. 'However, I think you might find yourself a more dependable, god-fearing man than some rock star.'

Hannah nodded. She guessed these feelings had been building up within Grace for quite some time, and she'd finally found an opportunity to express them. 'I'm not in any form of relationship with any rock star or . . . Wait, he's not here, is he?'

'No,' Grace said, looking disapproving at the very idea, before her face transformed into a more appreciative smile, 'but that nice, dependable and well-mannered Detective Inspector Sturgess is.'

'Bloody hell, woman,' said Banecroft, 'could you not have led with that? We're all busy people.'

'He's not here to see you, Vincent.'

'Thank you, Grace,' said Hannah. 'I think we'll all have a lot to talk about.'

'He actually wants to talk to Ox,' she said, 'but Ox said he won't talk to him until someone makes him.'

'Jesus,' said Banecroft.

'Vincent!'

Banecroft rolled his eyes. 'He is so obstinately Mancunian it must be physically painful, or it is about to be.' Banecroft threw open the door to the bullpen and roared, 'Ox Chen, with me now!'

Two minutes later, Hannah was standing in reception with Banecroft beside her and Ox behind them, looking a lot like a naughty schoolboy who was being brought to see the head. The remaining members of *The Stranger Times* staff were standing around, mostly trying to look nonchalant or, in the case of Grace, making no effort at all.

Hannah – *thank you, Grace* – was doing her best not to feel self-conscious about how she looked. Heaven save us all from friends who mean well. 'Detective Inspector Sturgess, how can we be of help?'

'Well,' said Sturgess, 'I was coming to update you on the investigation, but I was just hoping to check something with Mr Chen first. I think there might be a link between the incident in the cemetery last night and our investigation into the death of Wayne Grainger and what we are now calling the kidnappings of Elizabeth "Bea" Yennon and Michelle Creevy.' Sturgess glanced around. 'Would you like to have this chat somewhere more private?'

'Anything you want to say to me,' said Banecroft, 'you can say in front of my staff.'

'I have nothing I want to say to you. I was hoping to talk to Mr Chen and Hannah.'

'We all spent the night in a freezing-cold cemetery,' said Stella. 'I reckon we all have a right to know what's going on.'

'Some of us spent two nights,' added Reggie.

'I'm not saying nothing,' said Ox.

Banecroft looked back at him. 'While I applaud the obstinacy, the double negative from a purportedly professional journalist is unforgivable.'

'Right,' said Sturgess, pulling a picture out of the folder he had with him. 'I have a still image from CCTV footage that we think might match the suspect you met yesterday evening.'

He spun it around and held it out in front of Ox. It showed a short man with a long, thick, dark beard. 'Is this the individual you fought with?'

'Might be.'

'Ox!' snapped Hannah.

'Yeah, all right, that's definitely him. Great, now I'm a grass.'

'On a grave robber,' said Reggie. 'Who exactly do you know who is pro grave-robbing?'

'I'm just saying . . .'

'Who is he?' asked Hannah.

'We don't know, but we have footage of him in the company of both women in the' – Sturgess hesitated as he searched for the right words – 'time period they do not remember.'

'You mean when they both thought they were watching *Lawrence of Arabia*?' offered Stella.

Sturgess nodded. 'Yes, then. We also have another woman with them, who we have already identified through facial-recognition software.' Sturgess pulled out another photograph. 'She is one Dr Emma Marsh, although she's technically no longer a doctor.'

Somewhere in the back of Hannah's brain, long-neglected areas of memory fired. Fangirl brain cells, imprinted with every imaginable irrelevant detail of a teenage obsession, started waving their arms about, waiting to be heard.

'She got struck off and sent to prison for some dodgy experiments involving testing on humans,' Sturgess explained, 'but she's disappeared off the radar entirely for the last few years.'

'Oh God, oh God, oh God,' muttered Hannah, because some coincidences were far too big to be coincidences.

'What?' asked Sturgess, giving her a confused look. 'Do you know this woman?'

'No,' said Hannah, 'but I can tell you where she went to school and who with.'

52

Cillian Blake had never seen Doug like this before. If he didn't know better, he'd say he was happy. There was something deeply unnerving about it. The man lived in a permanent state of put-upon misery. That was dependable. You could set your metaphorical watch by it. Him being happy was a worry because you then wondered what could make the most amoral human being on the planet cheerful. It was like seeing a close-up of cancerous cells under a microscope and discovering they'd formed a conga line.

Doug gave what Blake was fairly sure was a smile and held out his hands in a mime of a set of scales. 'It's very much a good news, bad news type deal. Yeah – good news, bad news.'

'What does that mean? Did you get Nigel or not?'

'I absolutely did. Absolutely. Got all the getting that was going.'

'And there were no problems?'

'None. The Duke was actually very helpful. Nice guy. Not the sharpest tool in the box, but then, that's what an education will do to you.'

'So, he gave you Nigel's body?'

'Yeah,' said Doug, 'in a manner of speaking.'

'And what does that mean?'

'In fact,' said Doug, 'he let me take pretty much whatever I wanted. Remember that body problem we had? Not any more. Solved it. Got a whole frozen lorryful. The doc was pleased. Actually pleased.' Doug appeared to be beaming under his mass of beard. There may have even been a twinkly eye in there. 'She is in a very good mood.'

'So, what's the problem?' asked Blake. 'Has Emma not got this necromer thing working?'

'No, she has. It's working great. She's very pleased. She is in a very good mood.'

'Why do you keep saying that?'

'No reason,' said Doug. 'But yeah, she's got a few of the bodies – all them bodies I got for her – and she's got them up and . . . running. Well, shambling, really. Stuff takes a while to defrost, y'see? Stands to reason.'

'And the rage problem?'

'Solved. She's in a good mood. They're in a good mood. Everybody is in a very good mood.'

'So, what's the problem?'

'It's—'

'So help me, Doug, if you say anything else about good news and bad news, I'm going to feed you your own beard.'

'I reckon this is one of those things it's best to see for yourself. Come on back to the lab.'

Cillian Blake followed Doug through to the large concrete barn with a corrugated metal roof that had been converted into a lab. It was where Emma Marsh had been working away trying to make the impossible happen. It represented every last penny he had in the world and now everything they'd done, everything he'd sacrificed, was about to bear fruit. At least, it was supposed to. His heart was thumping in his chest and . . .

He walked through the door and came to an abrupt halt. He had not been expecting this. The loading dock area was busy. It appeared an undead dinner party had broken out there. A throng of people were standing around, chatting. Quite a few of them Cillian Blake recognized.

'What the . . .'

'Yeah,' said Doug. 'It's mental, isn't it?'

'Is that . . . Is that Oliver Reed?'

'Yeah!' beamed Doug. 'Like I said, the Duke let me take pretty much who I fancied. You wouldn't believe who he had. I got Jimi Hendrix, Jim Morrison, Keith Moon – I mean, Keith effing Moon!' Doug was talking excitedly now. 'It was like being a kid in a sweet shop, I can tell you. Then it occurred to me, why not put together the greatest rock supergroup the world has ever seen?'

'Right,' said Blake. 'Not to rain on your parade, but Hendrix is looking a little' – he lowered his voice – 'green.'

'Yeah,' agreed Doug, 'shame, that. Apparently, there's this process where they replace the blood with this anti-freeze stuff, but it's not been done on a lot of the earlier ones. I reckon he'll still be able to play, but I'm not sure anyone would buy tickets to see him in concert. Same for the other two. I almost had Paul McCartney."

'He's not dead.'

'That's what I thought,' said Doug. 'Turns out all those loons who bang on about how he died in the sixties and got replaced with a stand-in are right. Duke wouldn't let me have him, though – said his granddad was a big fan or something. Shame. Also said he didn't have Elvis but that there's a spot reserved for him, which seems very odd, doesn't it?'

'Yes,' said Cillian, starting to wonder if he had in fact fallen asleep after some very strong cheese.

'I took John Entwistle in the end. For the band.'

'The bassist in The Who?'

'Yeah,' said Doug, looking sheepish. 'Well, I thought it was him. Turned out it's some Olympic cyclist who died in his eighties. Don't know what we're going to do with him, to be honest. He's over there talking to Bill Hicks.'

'He looks very fit for his age,' said Blake. 'I mean, apart from the being dead thing.'

'I know. Probably says something about lifestyle, that. Can't play bass, though. I've checked. Still, there's only one Hendrix. I mean, all right, touring might be tricky, but put that trio in the studio and watch the magic happen. Imagine how much new material from them could be worth? Sure, people might get sniffy about the, y'know' – Doug lowered his voice – 'them being dead thing, but worst-case scenario, we pretend they all got together for a jam in the sixties and these are the lost tapes. A bit like the Hitler diaries – only, not fake.'

Cillian Blake kept looking around the room, going from face to face, recognizing more and more of them.

'Is that . . .'

'2Pac and Biggie Smalls, yeah. Getting on like a house on fire. Not my genre but I thought, give it a go. Now they could definitely tour. They're both looking good, despite 2Pac having that many holes in him he'll probably make a whistling noise in a high wind.'

Cillian was still trying to process it all. 'How . . . Why are they moving so oddly?'

'Like I said, they're still defrosting.'

'OK,' said Cillian. 'I might need to sit down. This is all a bit—HOLY SHIT!'

Someone Cillian vaguely recognized as an eighties TV presenter moved, and he spotted a woman sitting awkwardly in a chair at the end of the room.

'Is that . . .'

'Yeah,' confirmed Doug.

'But surely . . . I mean, how would they have got hold of her?'

'No idea,' confessed Doug. 'They had a load of names on that list you wouldn't believe. Those dukes of Cheshire must have had some serious connections.'

Cillian grabbed Doug. 'What about Nigel? Has she brought back Nigel yet?'

'Oh, no. Doc said that's the most important one, so she wanted to test the process thoroughly before doing it, what with the complications and all.'

'Complications?'

'We should go talk to the doc.'

Cillian took one last look at the who's who of the recently undead and headed for the door to the lab proper. Inside, Emma

Marsh was sitting at her desk, using a microphone to chat through a glass partition with what looked like a rotting corpse.

'I am fascinated by your approach to research,' she said.

'Science,' said the corpse, 'is as much art as it is numbers and logic. You must free the mind from the constraints of the known or else we will never find the unknown.'

'That is fascinating,' she replied, before smiling up at Cillian. 'If you will excuse me a moment.'

She took her finger off the intercom button.

'Is that . . .' said Cillian.

'Albert Einstein!'

'Wow. He's . . .'

'Yes,' said Dr Marsh. 'Unfortunately, he died in the fifties, so while they tried to preserve him, they dug him up after a long time and the decomposition was extensive. His arm fell off a few minutes ago.'

'I see,' said Blake slowly, struggling to take it all in. 'He's taking it surprisingly well.'

Dr Marsh held up a wooden staff that was a deep black in colour with extensive gold and red engravings on it. As she moved it, the engravings shimmered in the light. 'Thanks to the necromer, the rage problem is gone. All the subjects maintain a completely even emotional response while under my control. They wake up, realize that they've been dead and just sort of roll with it.'

'Wow.'

'Yes,' she said with a smile. 'I have officially beaten death and I am in an excellent mood.'

She glanced towards Doug, who made a noise that sounded remarkably like a giggle.

'Congratulations. What about Nigel?'

'We have Nigel,' she confirmed.

'Great. Well, can we . . .'

'This,' she said, 'is a bit of a good news, bad news situation.'

'That's what I said,' chirped Doug.

'Why do people keep saying that?' snapped Blake, his voice raised in frustration.

'OK,' said Dr Marsh, 'remain calm. It's just . . . there's been a slight wrinkle in the situation that we did not fully anticipate.'

'What does that mean? I want to see Nigel immediately.'

Dr Marsh looked at Doug then turned to the table beside her. 'OK, I was just trying to warn you, but . . .'

She lifted the sheet.

Blake stood there without speaking for a good thirty seconds. When he finally did, his question was a simple one. 'Where the hell is the rest of him?'

53

DS Wilkerson sat in the back of the minibus, trying and failing to hold her tongue. 'This is bullshit!'

'Yep,' agreed Sturgess.

The staging position for the raid was at the far side of a field near the farm, with the minibus and other vehicles hidden further down the road, well out of sight. The minibus's position also afforded them a view of a large hedge on one side and the side of a police van on the other.

One of life's inalienable truths was that, regardless of how many times the police minibuses were cleaned and with what, there was always an odour in the back of them that nobody could entirely place. The closest description Sturgess had heard was that of pickled onion Monster Munch mixed with turpentine and sweat. He drew in a noseful of it now as the already heavy rain upped its tempo slightly while it hammered down on the metal roof.

It was not the smell that had DS Wilkerson riled up.

'How are you taking this so calmly?' she asked. 'You used to be known for being the bloke who took nothing calmly. You have famously zero chill, as the kids say, but now you're being screwed over and you're sitting here taking it like a wuss?'

Sturgess gave her a look.

'Sorry, that kind of got away from me a bit at the end there.'

'A little,' he agreed. 'I mean, I don't want to come over all "superior officer".'

'That's exactly my point, though, sir.'

As a serial marveller at the ineptitudes of management, Sturgess had to admit that the 'sir' was beautifully judged – on the surface unimpeachably respectful, with a delicious undercurrent of sarcasm.

'DI Clarke doesn't outrank you,' Wilkerson continued, 'but you're letting him swoop in and take all the credit here. We investigated Wayne Grainger when nobody else wanted to, chased Merlins when his almighty taskforce wanted nothing to do with them, found the two women, chased down the CCTV, traced this Emma Marsh nutjob . . .'

Sturgess noted that Wilkerson's summation left out them receiving any help from *The Stranger Times* but he let it pass. Sometimes people needed to vent.

'And then,' she went on, after pausing for breath, 'once we've located their drug factory and whatever else this place is, Clarke gets to come swanning in, knock down a farmhouse door like he's the big bad wolf and claim a success for his bloody stupid taskforce.'

'We are cooperating with our fellow officers to achieve a result,' said Sturgess, without much feeling.

'Bullshit,' said Wilkerson again, with enough feeling for the both of them. 'Did you notice on the ride out here that daft photographer he's got following them around? The guy took pictures of the armed response team, the taskforce detectives, and oh so many of Sam Clarke and his ridiculous new hair plugs. I mean, let's have an investigation into those things. What he didn't take was any pictures of us. We're being written out of this story.'

Sturgess had not failed to notice that. The portly fella with an unnecessary number of cameras had been put in a Kevlar vest, and it was clear from the excited gleam in his eye that all of his *Call of Duty* fever dreams were coming true.

'Do you want to get your picture in the paper?'

'Christ, no,' said Wilkerson. 'But that's not the point.'

Sturgess nodded and gave his beard a quick scratch. 'Andrea, I know Clarke wanted you to join his taskforce. It would've been a major career opportunity, so why didn't you take it?'

She hunched her shoulders up and left a long enough gap that he wondered if she was going to answer at all. 'I don't know. A year ago, I'd have leaped at the chance, even if Clarke is a toad, but, well . . . when I got into this job, that was my dream – kicking down doors, locking up scumbags. All that. Problem is, after a while, you notice you're just doing the same thing next month, and the only people who seem to be benefiting from it are the door-makers. We drag someone else off, so that they can be replaced in turn. And there's no shortage of candidates. Every city in the country has postcodes full of kids who see dealing drugs as their best prospect for the future, because it's all they've known, all we've expected them to know. All we've shown them. That's the real version of that postcode lottery everyone keeps banging on about. We're not digging out the weeds, we're just pruning the garden every now and then.'

'You're from one of those postcodes,' observed Sturgess.

'Yeah, but most people didn't have my gran. I get a bit fed up with people using exceptions like me to prove there's no problem. When I say exception, I don't mean . . . Well, you know what I mean.'

Sturgess nodded.

'Whereas' – she gave him a look – 'no disrespect, but while you're a massive pain in the arse, sir, this week we're looking into a guy who flew for a bit, and then someone who, I dunno, mind-melded somebody so they don't even remember being kidnapped. I've not even mentioned the little brass blokes that are currently being dug out of the Southern Cemetery.'

Last Sturgess had heard, the cemetery fiasco was being handed over to a 'specialist team', with no explanation as to what kind of specialists they were or where they were from. He guessed news of events had attracted the attention of a certain organization and the Greater Manchester Police, or indeed any form of police, now had zero involvement.

'And then,' continued Wilkerson, 'there's people falling through walls and freezing entire gents toilets. I mean, I don't know if we're making a difference, but bloody hell, it's a bit more interesting than kicking in a door that's three doors down from the one you kicked in last year.'

Sturgess nodded. 'I'm not entirely sure the words "no disrespect" atone for as many sins as you think they do, Sergeant.'

Wilkerson grinned back at him. 'Noted, sir.' She leaned forward. 'Can I ask, though – seriously, why did you go to Clarke with this?'

Sturgess shrugged. 'There's every chance the higher-ups would've pushed it Clarke's way anyway. And we needed to get it done fast.'

'Why, though?'

'Because fast is better than slow.' Which was crap, and they both knew it. The actual answer was, Sturgess didn't know. Hannah had made it very clear to him that whatever this was had to be resolved by midnight tonight, and she couldn't say why. She was deadly serious, though, and it seemed an awful lot more pressing than wanting to hit the print deadline for the next edition of *The Stranger Times*.

None of which meant he was any happier about this than Wilkerson was. Seeing as he'd handed Clarke an easy win, it was particularly galling that the bloviating baboon was lording it over Sturgess like he was doing him some kind of favour by taking it. The reason they were sitting in this minibus while the armed response team and a half-dozen detectives from the taskforce were getting into position to raid Cillian Blake's farmhouse, was that it was where they'd been instructed to stay. Clarke had made sure he'd given the orders in front of as many people as possible, too. Sturgess was, well, if not exactly grinning, at least bearing it all, because it was what was needed. He hoped whatever Hannah's reasons were, they were bloody good ones.

The side door of the minibus slid open to reveal DI Clarke and Sergeant Tony Morrison, the head of the GMP armed response unit.

'There you two are,' said Clarke from under his umbrella. 'Snuggling up. People will start to talk.'

'We're where you told us to be,' said Sturgess flatly. 'So, are we ready for the final run-through of the breaching plan?'

'Don't worry your pretty little head, we've already done that.'

'But we haven't discussed the eventualities in the case of unexpected resistance.'

'The infrared shows three individuals in the farmhouse and a fourth in one of the outer buildings,' said Morrison, all military efficiency. Sturgess knew he'd been something unspecified in the armed forces before moving across to the police. 'That lone individual looks like they might be the hostage you specified. Don't worry, my team has been fully briefed.'

'Marcus Divine,' said Sturgess. 'His name is Marcus Divine.'

Morrison nodded. 'How reliable is this intel?'

'Hard to say.'

Morrison nodded again.

'Yeah,' said Clarke with a smirk, 'his psychic is great normally, but it's hard to get good mung beans this time of year.'

Sturgess ignored him and addressed Morrison. 'There's also a possibility you might meet unusual resistance.'

'Oh, for fuck's sake,' said Clarke with a laugh. 'I think Tony's boys can handle it.'

'I appreciate any and all information, Detective Inspector.' The hint of irritation in Morrison's voice surprised them all. 'I'm sending people through a door. My number-one priority is to make sure they walk back out of that door in one piece.' Clarke looked taken aback by the rebuke while Morrison focused intently on Sturgess. 'Anything else you can tell me?'

'Not much.' Sturgess glanced at Wilkerson, thinking back to the CCTV footage of Bea Yennon being led away. 'Watch the woman. Don't allow her to speak to anyone.'

Morrison nodded again. 'Noted.'

'Right,' said Clarke, clearly irritated. 'You two stay here until this is over.'

'What?' said Sturgess. 'Don't be ridiculous. This is my investigation. We'll observe from the command position.'

'Guess again,' said Clarke. 'I'm not having you running about looking for Nargles or whatever crap you're on about this week. This is a bit of actual grown-up policing.'

'I'm a fellow DI,' snapped Sturgess.

'And this is my op,' said Clarke, 'so I have final say. You're staying in your box.'

Before Sturgess could say anything else, Clarke slammed the door closed.

At the sound of a key turning in the lock, Wilkerson pointed a disbelieving finger at the door. 'He's locked that. Are you kidding me? That bald-arsed baby just locked us in this bloody van.'

Sturgess knocked on the window, but all that earned him was a smug wink from Clarke and a wave over his shoulder as he walked away.

Sturgess sat motionless, trying to take a few of those deep breaths he'd heard so much about. 'Well, on the upside,' he said, pointing at the roof where the rain could be heard really pelting it down now, 'at least we're going to stay dry.'

54

Cillian Blake watched as his oldest friend's eyes flickered open.

He gave a broad smile. 'Hi, Nige. Welcome back.'

Nigel Stay blinked a few times while Cillian continued to smile, giving him time to come to. When Nigel spoke, his voice was hoarse. 'Where . . . where am I?'

'You're OK, mate. You're safe.'

'Did . . . did something happen?'

'Yeah. You had a bit of an accident, but everything's OK now.'

'Accident? What kind of—'

'Let's not focus on that now.'

'The last thing I remember—'

'Don't!' snapped Cillian quickly. 'I mean, don't try to remember. Don't worry about it. Just know you're OK now. That's all that matters.'

'I can't. I can't feel my legs!'

'Yeah, it's—'

'Or my arms. Or' – his voice was filled with terror now – 'anything. I can't feel anything.'

Cillian glanced over at Dr Marsh, who was sitting in the corner of the kitchen, holding her newly acquired staff. They'd decided to move in here as it was quieter. The undead dinner party was really coming alive. She made a gesture with her free hand in Nigel's direction and Cillian noticed the muscles in his face relax. He looked back at Nige, trying to keep his eyes locked on his.

'Like I said,' continued Cillian, 'you're OK now.'

'I'm . . . I'm not, though. I . . .' Nigel stopped and looked in Cillian's face. 'What the fuck happened to you? You're so old?'

Cillian pulled back a bit. 'I'm, well, a little.'

'You look wrecked. You're . . . you're ancient.'

'Hardly,' said Cillian, failing not to sound offended. 'I'm a few years older.'

Nigel's eyes widened. 'Have I been in a coma?'

'Sort of.'

'Sort of?'

'The important thing is—'

'Holy shit. You're older. I've been . . . Was I' – his voice lowered to a whisper – 'dead?'

Cillian glanced again at Dr Marsh, who shrugged. He gave Nigel his best smile. 'Kind of.'

'Wow,' said Nige. 'That lunatic duke's thing actually worked?'

'Yes.'

'How did I die?'

'Don't worry about that,' said Cillian smoothly. 'What matters is you're back and everything's going to be OK.'

'WOW!' Nigel's eyeballs scanned the room, trying to take it in. 'I was dead and then . . . I can't— Wait. Why can't I move my head?'

'Don't worry about that either.'

'Screw you. I'll worry about what I want to worry about. And I can't . . . I can't feel my legs, arms, anything, I . . .' His eyes focused sharply on Cillian. 'Am I just a fucking head?'

Cillian was honestly amazed. Nigel was always smart, but he was still stunned that he'd been able to figure it out so quickly.

'You . . .'

'I am, aren't I?'

He was. Cillian was talking to a decapitated head with some type of metallic stopper contraption that lay below its neck. It was resting on a cushion on the kitchen table, and while the good doctor was keeping Nigel calm, Cillian realized that he probably should have sorted out something that could do the same for him.

'You are, but . . .'

'In cryogenics,' said Nigel, his mind suddenly firing, 'there was the school of thought to just freeze the head. Keep the costs down. The logic being that medical science in the future could replace the body.' Nigel's voice was laced with suspicion now. 'Have I got a new body?'

'We're working on that.'

His eyes narrowed. 'You're working on it? What the hell does that mean?'

'I . . .'

'Did you wake me up too early or something?'

'No, I . . .'

'Holy crap. You did, didn't you? What the hell, Killer?'

Cillian's face twitched slightly. In the last year they'd spent together, Nigel had reverted to calling him by his old school nickname. Other people took it as endearing, but Cillian knew the truth. Nigel had realized it bugged him and that's why he did it.

'Look, Nige,' he said, 'just keep calm and let me explain.' He glanced once again at Emma, who rolled her eyes and made another hand gesture. 'OK, like you said, the duke's thing worked but it ran out of money. I've . . . I've spent all I had on keeping you alive, but it's running out, so . . . I had an idea.'

The head of Nigel Stay gave Cillian a very sceptical look. 'Right?'

'We . . . we need to make money and, well, I was thinking, I – we – could release a new album.'

'I see,' said Nigel. 'So, to summarize – you brought my decapitated head back from the dead so that we could record a new album?'

'Well, I—'

'Wow, Killer, did you not see the rather big flaw in that plan? What am I supposed to do? Headbutt a keyboard and hope for the best?'

'No, of course not. Look, I've done so much to get you back. You've got no idea, Nige. Just hear me out. OK?'

Nigel gave him an assessing look. 'OK.'

'You— Before we went into the studio, you recorded a load of stuff, and I thought we could just use that.'

'Ohhhh.' Nigel gave a big grin. A big, worrying grin. 'I get it now. The "secret album" you were so obsessed with,' he said, laughing as he spokc the words 'secret album'.

Cillian could feel the embers of an old resentment inside him being stoked back into life. 'I'm trying to help you.'

'Yeah, you keep saying that, but I think you're forgetting who you're talking to here, Killer. I know you better than anyone. Behind all that smarm and charm, you're the same selfish little shit you've always been. You really think I'm going to believe you've been sacrificing everything you had to keep me alive, and all that other crap you said?'

'I did,' said Cillian, struggling to keep his anger in check. 'You've no idea what I've done. What I had to do.'

'No,' he agreed, 'I don't. But I bet I know why. It'll have only been for your own selfish reasons.' He paused, a smile playing across his lips. 'I've been dead a while . . . How's the solo career going, Killer?'

Cillian guessed he failed miserably to keep the bitterness from his face, given that Nigel now started to roar with laughter. 'Bingo! Oh God, this is so good. It was almost worth dying for.'

'I'm glad you're enjoying yourself, you . . . fucking decapitated head.'

'Well, it sounds like your whole body has been an abject failure without me. And now you've dug me up or whatever because you want that precious secret album you were so obsessed with.'

'Yes,' hissed Cillian. 'And so what if I do? I might have been nothing without you, but you're a decapitated head in a skip without me. Make all the shitty remarks you like, Nige – you're not exactly in the world's strongest negotiating position.'

Cillian reached forward and grabbed Nigel's hair.

'Ouch!'

He lifted up the head and held it in front of him. 'Who do you think is in charge now, Nige? How smug do you feel now? Give me the damn album or else.'

The head of Nigel Stay made a weird snorting noise then gave a hoarse chuckle. 'You enormous baby. Christ, I can't believe you.'

'So, shall I shove your head back in my freezer for another ten years? Give you some time to think about it? Or would you just like to be thrown over the wall at the dog sanctuary down the road? You always did love animals.'

'Look in my eyes, Cillian,' said Nigel. 'This is really important. Calm down and look at me.'

Cillian did as he was asked and the two of them faced each other.

'There was never any album.'

Cillian opened his mouth to speak but said nothing. There was something in the way Nigel said the words. He wasn't bluffing.

With a wide smile, Nigel continued. 'You were so short sighted; you never could see stuff that didn't directly affect you. I wasn't working on music. I was working on an algorithm. A way to encrypt data. Ask Imran if you don't believe me.'

'No, it's . . .'

'Yes,' said Nigel. 'Some of us haven't based our whole lives on just being famous. I wanted to do something different. Something meaningful. Something without you.'

'Oh, piss off,' snapped Cillian. 'Good news on that front. Pretty good odds your mate Imran nicked your idea. He's a bloody billionaire now.'

Cillian had meant his words as a retaliatory body shot, not realizing that it's hard to land one of those on someone without a body.

'Cool!' beamed Nigel. 'It worked? Ah, man, I'm so pleased to find out it really worked.'

Cillian, dazed now, plonked Nigel's head back down on the pillow then stumbled backwards, slumped against the AGA and slid to the floor. 'It was . . . This has all been for nothing?'

He was dimly aware of Emma standing up.

'Oh, hey,' said Nigel, sounding a tad unhinged, 'didn't know we had company. Hello, madam, I . . . Hang on, aren't you that Dr Emma Marsh woman?'

'How do you . . .' started Emma.

'Oh, I know all about you. Killer here told me. We followed your trial closely.'

'Ignore him,' said Cillian, staring down at the floor, tears in his eyes.

'Yeah,' continued Nigel, 'you were the freaky kid in school. He told me how you did all kinds of weird shit. Laughed about it.'

'Silence,' ordered Emma. 'You don't know what you're talking about. We're in love.'

Wallowing in his own despair, some small part of Cillian was still aware that this was dangerous territory.

Nigel roared with laughter. 'Oh, that is good. No offence, love, but you're not his type. He only sleeps with the beautiful people, and only then because he wants to prove he can. Old Killer Blake only ever loved one person, and that's himself.'

'Shut up,' said Cillian.

'Are you really banging her?' asked Nigel. 'How the mighty have fallen.'

Cillian scrambled to his feet, rage suddenly gripping every fibre of his being. 'Shut up, shut up, shut up! You useless tedious little shit. You were nothing without me, don't you get that? Nothing! And I did all of this to get back what you messed up, and for what? We could have been gods, but you had to be an arse about it. I did so much.' He spun around, throwing his hands up in the air before leaning down and placing his forehead against the cold iron surface of the AGA. 'So much money. So much time. So many sacrifices. Christ, I had to let my beautiful body be used by her like some sort of glorified sex toy.' His form shivered visibly. 'I had to degrade myself to . . .'

Cillian's brain only caught up with his mouth when he felt himself being lifted off the ground.

'Wait! I—'

His body flew up and slammed into the ceiling. It felt as if he was being pressed against it by giant hands, but they weren't just holding him. It was like they were trying to push him through it.

As he looked down, Emma Marsh's face appeared beneath him, staring up. A mask of cold rage. 'Excuse me? You had to do what?'

'Sorry,' said Cillian. 'Emma, darling, I . . .' He lost the ability to speak as a dirty tea towel soared up and rammed itself into his mouth.

'You had to' – the words came out laced in venom – 'degrade yourself?'

Cillian looked down into her eyes and felt more fear than he'd ever known in his life. It coursed through his body. He tried to protest but it was impossible to get words out around the foul-tasting cloth shoved into his mouth.

Emma continued to stare up at him with the black staff, its carvings now glowing bright red, held in her right hand while crackles of green energy darted from the fingers of her left.

He was relieved when the back door flew open.

'Holy shit,' exclaimed Doug. He stopped and looked up at Cillian briefly.

'Get out,' hissed Emma.

'We're in trouble.'

'He is.'

'No,' said Doug, 'I mean . . . The alarm I set up outside. It's been triggered.' He held up a tablet device, the screen of which Cillian couldn't see. 'There's cops. Lots of 'em. With guns.'

'What? How?'

'I don't know, but we've got to get out of here. I've whacked on the scrambler, that should mess with their comms.' He stepped forward and reached for her hand. 'Let me get you out of here, Doc.'

Emma turned around and faced the front door. 'No,' she said, slamming the staff into the floor, making a noise that was far too loud to be explained by the physical act of wood hitting wood. 'I have a much better idea.'

55

Banecroft watched the sun setting through the clouds. He'd never been a big sunsets guy, but then he'd never considered that any given one could be his last. As these things went, it was a pretty good one. Nice orange glow, bit of cloud, but just enough to add to the atmosphere without blocking the view. A large bank of ominous dark cloud sat to the north, which he was determinedly trying not to see as some kind of metaphor.

He'd never feared death, not in the conventional sense. He'd received more than his fair share of death threats in his time. Those things were almost always the pathetic eruptions of some tragic fantasist that could be happily ignored. There was even a time when he revelled in keeping score. In pure numerical terms, he imagined he was up there with the big three categories of unforgivable sins: people who pointed out racism was bad, men who missed important penalties in football, and prominent women who dared to say anything. He'd been the editor of a Fleet Street tabloid – rubbing people up the wrong way was in the job description. Death threats had been his five-star reviews. He'd also faced down actual death a few times, particularly recently. While he hadn't run towards danger, he hadn't run away from it either. But no, the more he thought about it, the idea of dying wasn't what bothered him.

What had that Pilgrim arsehat said to him? The greatest mistake the living made was thinking that death was the worst thing that could happen to them. He got that now. Mind you, seeing as the Pilgrim had been nice enough to give him the chilling preview of what waited for him on the other side, that was hardly surprising. There was a cold stone of fear in his belly that he couldn't shift, and he hated that most of all. He'd never been arrogant enough to consider himself a good man, whatever that even was, but he'd like to think that when the opportunity had presented itself, he'd tried to do good. Yes, he'd been wrong and weak when he'd thought there was some chance of bringing Charlotte back to him. He could see that now. It just felt frustrating that there was nothing else that could be taken into account.

Banecroft heard movement behind him. 'You know, I came up here hoping to get some peace and quiet.'

'How's that working out for you?' asked Hannah as she moved forward and perched on one of the bollards that were up on the roof of the Church of Old Souls for no obvious reason.

'Meh.'

Hannah looked out at the skyline. 'It's not a bad-looking city, is it?'

'Oh God,' said Banecroft. 'Please, let's not do this.'

'What?'

'Get all melancholic. If you want to get some early work in on my eulogy, then do it somewhere else.'

'I was talking about Manchester, not you.'

'I know, but you'd probably do some trick they taught you in sixth-form convent-school English where you'd end up comparing me to the city and how we can both be abrasive, but we tell it like it is and yada, yada, yada, please Lord, shoot me now.'

'I would never be that disrespectful to Manchester.'

'I'm glad to hear it.'

'And, by the way, while you're wallowing in your own indignation, I just thought you should know that Sturgess has been on and they're raiding that farm tonight.'

It had been an eventful day. From the moment Hannah had pointed out the connection between the former doctor identified in the CCTV footage, Emma Marsh, and former rock star Cillian Blake, dominos had been falling. While they couldn't locate Dr Marsh, they knew that Blake owned a farm out near Saddleworth, and a fly-by had confirmed that the car from the CCTV footage was parked in the yard there. That had given Sturgess all he needed.

'So,' said Banecroft, 'how does it feel to be personally responsible for getting your former idol locked up?'

'Oh, shut up,' said Hannah. 'We don't actually know he's involved.'

'Don't we?'

'This Dr Marsh woman or somebody else was messing with people's minds, like what happened to those two poor women. Maybe he's been, I don't know, hypnotized.'

'Right,' said Banecroft. 'You should take all this down. Sounds like an excellent starting point for some godawful fan fiction erotica.'

'You're disgusting.'

'I'm not the one digging up bodies. Speaking of which, while this Dr Marsh and whoever else is involved are clearly up to all kinds of weirdness, do you have any clue what it is? Because I still don't.'

'Modern-day *Frankenstein*?' mused Hannah. 'I don't know.'

'They've swiped a lot of bodies. What's she trying to do, build her own football team? Put together a travelling production of *Cats*?'

'Your guess is as good as mine,' said Hannah as she produced a bottle from behind her back. 'Here.'

Banecroft looked at it. 'Why are you giving me a bottle of Glenfiddich whisky?'

'Because I got it as a present ages ago and I hate the stuff. It's been sitting in my desk drawer as I was waiting for you to do something worthy of it so I could get rid of it.'

'And what have I done?'

'Oh, absolutely nothing – rest assured on that front. But, according to you, this might be my last chance to give it to you.'

Banecroft took the bottle and regarded it appreciatively in the fading light. 'You could always have poured it over my grave at the end of the eulogy.'

'Damn it,' she said. 'I wish I'd thought of that.'

She produced a couple of glasses from behind her back. 'You're not getting it all.'

'I thought you hated whisky.'

'I do, but if you drink the entire bottle, you're going to be even more of a grumpy sod in the morning.'

Banecroft spun the lid off with the practised ease of someone who did such a thing often. 'That's assuming I'm here in the morning.'

He started to pour them each a generous measure.

'I still don't get why you wouldn't be. I mean, these whoever-the-hell-they-are people seem very unreasonable.'

'That's the dead for you.'

Hannah looked at her glass, which was now half full. 'You really need to learn how measures work.'

'Never.' Banecroft clonked his glass against hers and knocked his back in one.

Hannah took a sip and coughed. 'Christ,' she spluttered, 'why would anyone do that to themselves twice?'

Banecroft started to pour them both some more. 'Practice makes perfect.'

56

The rain beat down on the world like it was mad at it. In the distance, approaching thunder roared, preceded by a flash of lightning. What light there had been was fading fast, taking most of the visibility with it as heavy black clouds loomed overhead. The news on the drive over had said something about a month's worth of rain falling in a few hours. Tony could well believe it. It was like standing in a carwash. All other sound was drowned out by the angry white noise of vengeful raindrops hammering into the ground around him. Less a pitter-patter and more of a Gatling gun rat-a-tat-tat; the kind of weather that made a mockery of the word 'waterproof'. Tony had never seen anything like it in this country. It was a hair short of an African monsoon, thankfully without the gale force winds.

Jacobs had asked for, and received, permission to ring her brother, to make sure her nan's house wasn't flooding again. Technically, when they were on a raid, everything else should fall by the wayside, but it made sense to make sure your people weren't distracted by things like that, not when it was so crucial for them to have absolute focus. As he was fond of saying, armed response was not a job where you got to have a bad day at work.

Once upon a time, when he'd been a younger man, Tony Morrison's nerves would have been tingling right about now. There was no denying it, at one point he'd lived for this. He'd spent fourteen years being shuttled between war zones, some legal, some less so, all at the pleasure of Her Majesty's government. They'd revelled in being the best. Tip of the spear. The knife in the heart. All that. Then he'd found other stuff to live for and had been glad of it. A wife. Kids. A bloody daft Yorkshire terrier. He'd seen what happened to those who didn't, and it wasn't pretty. So, he'd come home and found a way of using some of his very particular skill set in a way that he could stomach. There was a lot more money to be made as a private contractor, but that came with certain moral compromises he wasn't prepared to make. Some things you learn the hard way and spend the rest of your life trying to make up for.

He laughed when people complained about the hours in this job. His previous position didn't have hours – it had days, weeks, months. That's how long you'd be away from home, and mostly, those waiting wouldn't even get to know where you were never mind when you'd be back. There were reasons those left behind so often got sick of it. As an older man he understood that now. It was the helplessness that wore you down. Being in command, you were treated to a fresh perspective on these things. He didn't get that tingle of excitement any more because it was shouted down by that clenched fist of anxiety in his stomach. Once you'd had to make one of those dreaded phone calls or drop in on a person to break the bad news, it changed you. If it didn't, then you were already broken.

These days, he could set the plan but others carried it out and it was his turn to sit and wait – metaphorically, at least. There was a logic to it, of course, he knew that, but this leading-from-behind approach had never sat right with him. He'd thought about quitting so many times, but then he knew he'd just have that anxiety all the time. It'd be him waiting for the call because the person who was doing his job hadn't done it as well as he could. Maybe it wouldn't come but he wouldn't ever stop waiting for it. It wasn't ego. He knew he was good at this. You couldn't have self-doubt and do the job well. He sometimes wished he wasn't as good as he was. He would walk away happier then and become someone who worried about the weather just because his rose bushes were taking a kicking and not because reduced visibility meant the chances of something going sideways were significantly increased.

He shifted his stance and wiped some of the moisture off his goggles. The rain seemed to be getting heavier, if such a thing was possible. In the five minutes he'd been standing here, the puddles on the ground before him had overflown and formed into a larger pool. Alpha team were an indistinct blur to his left; Bravo to his right not even that. Charlie were out of view behind the lorry, not that he could see more than ten feet in front of his face. Ideally, he'd have preferred to wait for this weather front to pass but they were in position now and past the moment of go/no go. Besides, he preferred going in what scant remaining daylight they had. People got braver in the dark and did stupid things.

They were at a former farm made up of three buildings: a thatch-roofed farmhouse; a large concrete outhouse thirty metres by twenty, which they knew to be made up of several rooms; and a corrugated metal storage shed behind the main house. A large square yard sat to the front, covered in gravel. Recon had determined that entry from behind was out. Officially, it was because of the presence of the cameras, although that hadn't bothered Tony. In his experience, people installed them but rarely, if ever, had someone watching the live feed, something that made the cameras worse than useless. They were nothing more than an expensively acquired false sense of security with the added kicker of them advertising that you had something worth stealing.

No, it was the other stuff that bothered him. Bits of farm machinery were sitting around at the bottom of the slope behind the two outbuildings. Maybe that was all they were, but twice in the last year they'd gone into places only to discover that the targets had improvised some form of booby trap. Wallace had been off work for six weeks and was lucky not to have lost a toe. If Jacobs hadn't spotted the wire stretched between buildings, they could have lost a whole lot more than toes. No, they'd be going in from the front where there was nothing obvious to slow them down. Nine times out of ten, speed and surprise were the only things needed, and people rarely placed booby traps in locations where forgetting to disarm them could take out the Domino's delivery guy.

The yard contained a refrigerated container lorry on the left and three other vehicles – an SUV, a van and a Mazda – on the right. Alpha would be breaching through the front door of the farmhouse and Bravo through the back. Charlie, watching out for unwelcome surprises, would secure the fourth person in the outhouse. All three-person teams.

Tony pressed down on his walkie button. 'Position check?'

He flinched as he got an earful of feedback followed by a squall of static with voices lost within it.

'Alpha team, repeat?'

More static.

Could just be the rain. Could be the shitty equipment they had to make do with. Could be something else.

The fist of anxiety in his stomach tightened further. These weren't normal nerves. By all rights, this job should have been straightforward. Three, possibly four people running a pill mill. The kind of operation that typically wasn't undertaken by young men with automatic weapons, high on their own supply, and a head full of stupid ideas. Those types went more for coke and heroin.

Tony didn't dismiss the weird angle as quickly as that blowhard DI Clarke had. He'd seen some things in his time. Things he couldn't explain. He'd been there in Iraq when they'd been clearing caves. Morrison had put a dozen bullets into something man-sized with wings, which had damn near ripped his arm off before flying away. A woman from an unspecified section of the MoD had dropped in the next morning for a 'little chat' at their advance camp, making clear to him exactly what he hadn't seen. That had bothered him but, as always, he followed orders and kept his mouth shut. What got to him almost as much, what kept him awake at night once the nightmare recollections had roused him, was how practised to the point of seeming downright bored the woman had been. Like this wasn't anything out of her ordinary. It made you think – what the hell else were they covering up? How many other 'little chats' was she having?

Still, today, they had a team of ten to breach a farmhouse and, if he did say so himself, they'd been trained the right way. He'd made damn sure of that. He'd cherished those who knew what they were doing, fixed those who could learn and, finally, after a lot of work, got rid of those that couldn't. You didn't carry passengers or put up with gung-ho liabilities when lives were on the line.

Above his head, thunder roared. He thumbed the radio again. 'Anyone receiving?'

Nothing back but garbled static and snatches of frustrated voices. They'd have to go by timing. He looked at his watch. They could . . .

The shout came from his right. 'Halt! Armed police!'

He couldn't make out who was shouting over the thundering of the deluge, but he saw movement coming around the left side of the farmhouse. Slow.

'Hands in the air!' yelled the voice. 'Hands in the fucking air!'

DI Sam Clarke, with his stupid bloody umbrella, appeared beside Morrison, shouting in his ear. 'Are they giving themselves up?'

'Stay back,' snapped Morrison.

'Hands. Now!' shouted the voice.

'But . . .'

'Live operation,' said Morrison, shoving Clarke backwards. 'Stay back, you twat.'

He didn't make out whatever Clarke said next because he was already hunched down and moving forward, his thick boots splashing through the puddles, Heckler & Koch G36 held firmly in two hands, scanning left to right. Something was wrong. He sensed his team moving around him, knowing without being told that the plan was out the window now. Fanning out to cover all sides, taking up semi-circular positions around the group just as they'd been trained to. Covering the angles, staying well out of each other's line of fire.

The motion-detecting lights at the front of the farmhouse burst into violent life. There were people. Lots of people. Impossible people. In front of the farmhouse. There had been only four heat signatures and the farm was in the middle of the bloody countryside. Where had this lot come from? The bright light behind them made making out faces impossible but the raft of bodies kept shambling forward wordlessly through the teeming rain.

'Get on the ground now!' screamed another voice that he recognized as Jacobs'.

Tony took a couple more steps forward. This was all wrong. This was all very wrong. He focused in on one of the individuals at the front – a man in a suit. He couldn't make out any of the man's facial features but he seemed to be in his fifties, bearded. The man paused, his head tilted at an angle that suggested he couldn't understand what all these people were screaming at him. Then he continued his slow and steady progress forward, like a determined drunk making their way home through the downpour, resigned to the fact that it was now impossible to get any wetter. Maybe they were high? It might explain the behaviour, but not their sudden appearance out of nowhere. If someone had messed this up, heads were going to bloody roll.

Thunder crackled and roared again, ever louder.

Several voices were now screaming instructions at the group, but they continued lumbering forward. Making no effort to comply. They moved at less than walking pace and carried no visible weapons. Come to that, the way they walked was stiff, unnatural. They weren't saying anything either. Just a mass of drenched people. There must be at least thirty of them, many wearing suits or dresses and not an overcoat in sight. It didn't make any sense. Where had they come from? What were they doing?

And then . . . they stopped. All at the same time. In response to no discernible signal. They just stood there in the rain.

Lightning skittered across the sky, offering a moment of illumination. Tony looked into the eyes of the man in the suit and saw . . . saw what? Nothing. An unnatural emptiness.

A group of unarmed civilians surrounded by highly trained armed officers who, by all logical standards, had them bang to rights. Why was it then that every instinct in Tony's head was screaming at him. Instincts. Instincts were what had kept him alive when all the training in the world wouldn't have stopped him coming home in a body bag.

He raised his voice. 'Fall back. Fall—'

Too late.

With a sudden ferocity, the group surged forward.

Someone opened fire on the right side of the semi-circle and several of the rushing figures jerked and fell backwards, but others kept going, overwhelming the team by their sheer number.

To Tony's left, a figure hurled itself at one of his team and dragged them to the ground. A teammate rammed the butt of their gun into the top of the attacker's head, putting them down, before helping their comrade to their feet with one hand and opening fire with their sidearm with the other. A rapid triplet of lightning flashes showed staccato images of one of the assailants spinning around amidst the downpour. The bullet had caught them centre mass but somehow they stayed upright.

To his right, Morrison watched another member of his team – impossible to tell who in the matching tactical gear – expertly hip-tossing an immensely fat bald man, using the momentum of his charge against him. The guy was sent crashing into a large puddle, causing a large spray of water to splash upwards. Hot on his heels, three more of the mob rushed in and dragged the officer to the ground. The attackers weren't trying to get away either. They fell on the officer like a pack of wild animals. Two men and a woman, ferocious in their single-minded assault, relentlessly crashed down on their victim, their limbs flailing.

Morrison ran forward, removing one of the men from his teammate via the judicious application of a kick to the head. Another reared up, blood smeared across his face that didn't look like it was his. Tony punched him hard in the throat, putting him down. The team member pushed off the third attacker – a woman with long raven-black hair plastered to her face – with their legs and, quickly drawing their sidearm, shot her through the chest. The woman fell backwards.

The team member yanked off their mask. It was O'Malley, one of his best.

She tried to stand but her legs gave way. Tony swung his G36 behind him, grabbed the back of her Kevlar vest with his left hand, drew his Glock with his right, and started to drag her backwards.

'Holy shit,' she said, her breath coming in short, tight bursts.

'Focus!' shouted Morrison. 'Focus!'

As he dragged O'Malley back, all around him the chaos of battle raged. It was mostly hand to hand now. Sporadic gunfire mixed in with the screaming and shouting.

'What the fuck!' screamed O'Malley. 'WHAT THE ACTUAL FUCK!'

Morrison stopped when he saw what she was screaming at. The woman she'd just shot in the chest was now standing up as if nothing had happened, blue liquid trickling out of the wound where blood should be, mixing with the rain. The heavy brutal rain.

Another sheet of lightning ripped across the sky and the woman smiled at them with blue-tinted teeth.

'Retreat!' screamed Morrison at the top of his lungs, 'RETREAT!'

57

Doug looked up from his hiding place behind the sofa. He stopped to stare at the hole that had appeared about six inches from his head where a stray bullet had passed through and embedded itself in the wall behind him. A couple of the front windows had shattered and rain was now arcing in through the frames. The air was filled with dust, sofa stuffing and a weird golden glow. The glow was mostly coming from the staff that Dr Marsh held in her hand. There also appeared to be a halo of it around her whole body, like in one of those Ready Brek commercials from the eighties, only she'd achieved hers by summoning an army of dead celebrities to wage bloody war rather than by eating a hearty breakfast.

Doug cautiously moved around the doc, glancing out the window as he went, while being careful to give her plenty of room. 'You OK, Doc? You're lucky you didn't get shot standing th—'

Doug's eyes widened as what looked like a couple of bullets tinkled to the floor in front of Dr Marsh. Ready Brek never had that effect.

'I . . . I think the cops have gone.'

'Yes,' she said, smiling as she turned to look at him, a bright golden luminosity in her eyes. 'My babies did so well.'

'Ehm . . . yep,' said Doug, nodding his head furiously. 'Absolutely, they did. We should probably get out of here before the cops regroup, as I'd imagine you . . . we . . . they . . . A few cops might have been, y'know . . . in the . . . y'know. So we should—'

She interrupted him by grabbing him and kissing him deeply, with quite a bit of pressure and a great deal of tongue. He liked it. It was the first time she had done so. True, they'd had sex earlier that day but there had been no kissing. She'd been too busy screaming abuse at him. She'd jumped him after he'd presented her with a freezer truck full of dead bodies. Not all women want flowers. They'd then made love over the slowly defrosting corpse of, Doug was fairly sure, the guy who used to present *The Sky at Night*. It was comfortably the hottest thing that had ever happened to him.

She released him and pushed him away in one fluid motion. 'You disgust me. You worthless little toerag.'

Doug simply smiled and nodded. Without another word, Dr Emma Marsh, the love of his life, turned and walked back towards the kitchen. Yes, it was a complicated relationship, reasoned Doug, but then weren't they all? They'd got together under stressful circumstances. True. Her ex was still hanging around – literally, in fact – and she had just raised an army of the celebrity undead and attacked a SWAT team. Still, it beat signing up to one of those apps and trying to find a woman who knew who Led Zeppelin were.

Dr Marsh pushed open the door to the kitchen and stopped. 'Where the hell is he?'

Doug peered around her to see the empty space on the kitchen ceiling where Cillian Blake had been. 'Um . . . is it possible, my love, that while you were busy doing the other thing – the . . . whatever holding him slipped?'

'Yeah,' came a voice from the floor. 'He fell down from the ceiling a couple of minutes ago.' Doug looked under the table where he located the head of the formerly late Nigel Stay. 'If you hurry you could—'

They all turned at the sound of crunching tyres outside on the gravel.

'Never mind, that'll be him buggering off,' Nigel continued. 'Typical. He never cleans up his own messes. Speaking of which, any chance you could pick me up, please? I don't know who you've got cleaning your floors, but they are doing a really half-arsed job.'

'Don't worry,' said Dr Marsh, 'I have a very good idea where that snivelling little shit is going.'

'Failing that,' said Doug, 'I should probably mention I put a tracker on his SUV a while ago.'

Emma turned and gave him an appreciative little smile then punched him firmly in the groin. Doug crumpled to the floor.

'That,' she said, 'is for doubting me.'

'Sorry,' he groaned.

She strode off, staff raised. 'Come to me, my babies!'

Doug made eye contact with Nigel.

'Oh, hey, Doug. Didn't know you were here. Long time no see.'

Doug nodded as best he could while he clutched his recently mashed potatoes.

Nigel turned his eyes in the direction of the departed Emma then looked back to Doug. 'If you don't mind me saying, I think you two make a lovely couple.'

Doug winced and gave him a thumbs-up.

58

With one final double-footed kick, Sturgess booted the glass out of the back window of the minibus.

'They're going to dock your pay for that,' said Wilkerson as he assisted her through the gap.

'Undoubtedly.'

It was Wilkerson who had first noticed that their phones were no longer working. They'd waited a good five minutes after hearing all the shooting in the distance before deciding enough was enough. It was now heading towards dark and nobody had been back to the staging area, which was extremely concerning. Over the course of his career, Sturgess had been on plenty of raids, and there'd only been shooting at one of them. A coked-up ex-boxer up in Harpurhey had decided he'd rather go out charging armed police with a machete than go back to prison. The guy had ended up in a wheelchair, spending the rest of his days in a ground-floor cell with an accessible toilet.

Even then, that had been only one short burst of gunfire. Whatever had been going on over that hedge had sounded like a pitched battle. Sturgess and Wilkerson moved up the road until they reached the gate to the field. At that moment, they heard an

SUV tear out of there, heading down the road in the opposite direction.

'How in the . . .' started Wilkerson. 'There was a full squad of armed coppers over there. What the hell happened?'

They found their answer halfway across the field where they met Tony Morrison attempting to carry two wounded colleagues back to the staging area. Wilkerson ran forward, throwing her shoulder under a limping woman Morrison was propping up while trying simultaneously to fireman's lift another.

Morrison collapsed to the ground just as Sturgess reached him.

'What happened?' asked Sturgess, dropping to his knees in the mud as the still-pouring rain beat down around them. Using his phone for light, he checked on the unconscious man. His breathing was steady and, despite there being plenty of blood, the wounds he could see appeared largely superficial.

'I . . . I don't . . .' started Morrison. 'There was a large mob of people.'

'But you said there was—'

'I know what I said!'

As Wilkerson lowered the woman to the ground she saw that she was holding a makeshift bandage to her neck.

'One of the fuckers bit me,' said the woman, her voice laced with anxiety. 'I had to shoot her.'

Wilkerson produced a penknife and neatly snipped the material at the bottom of the officer's trousers.

'Legit shot,' said Morrison.

'Yeah, but . . .'

Wilkerson started to rip the material so that she could get a better look at the woman's calf.

'She got back up,' said the officer. 'She got back—' She let out a yelp of pain.

'Sorry,' said Wilkerson. 'Sorry, sorry, sorry.'

'I don't understand,' said Sturgess.

Morrison looked at his own upper left arm, which was bleeding heavily. 'They weren't . . . They weren't human. They ran at machine-gun fire then got up and ran again.'

'You mean, like . . .'

'Screw it,' said Morrison. 'I'll say the word. Zombies. Yeah. A lot like that. We only made it out because one second they were chasing us, and the next they all just turned around and started walking away calmly. Back. I need to go back and . . .' Morrison heaved himself to his feet and instantly staggered to one side, like a sailor on a boat that'd just been buffeted by a big wave.

Sturgess sprang up and grabbed him just in time to stop him from falling over. He then lowered him back to the ground gently.

'You're not going anywhere,' said Sturgess.

'The rest of my team . . .'

'I'll go. Andrea, get this lot back to the minibus then keep moving until you find somewhere you can get a phone signal to call for help. We—'

They all looked up at the sound of the freezer lorry's engine roaring into life. After a hiss of brakes, it moved off and left the farm, following the SUV.

'I'm going in there,' said Sturgess.

'No,' said Morrison. He tried and failed again to get back on his feet. He gave a frustrated groan then held out his handgun to Sturgess. 'Do you know how to use this?'

As Sturgess reached the side gate that led into the farmyard, the torrential rain finally eased off and faded to a drizzle. The grip of the gun felt slick in his hand. It had been a couple of years since he'd last fired one, and that had been on a range. He scanned the yard for signs of life. Nothing was moving and the motion-sensor lights had clicked off a minute ago.

In the darkness, the only source of light was that which spilled out of the windows of the farmhouse. Sturgess could see the outline of four bodies lying on the ground, but he couldn't tell who, or what, they were. Given that two vehicles had now left, Sturgess was hoping there wasn't anyone else around. He assumed those members of the armed response team who were able to, had pulled back. He had no idea where DI Clarke and his team were. He wouldn't be wildly surprised if they'd got the hell out of there at the first sign of things going pear-shaped. Sam Clarke talked a good game, but he wasn't a man you'd like to spend much time in a foxhole with.

Guns made Sturgess nauseous but if he had to use the weapon Morrison had given him, he would. As quietly as he could, he climbed over the gate, his every muscle tensed. As soon as his feet touched down on the other side, he moved off, crouching low, trying to make himself as small and as fast a moving target as possible.

As the motion-sensitive light clicked on, he froze. Several bodies were lying on the ground around him. One, dressed incongruously in a three-piece suit, was missing a head, with bits of what may once have been the aforementioned body part strewn haphazardly on the ground. Further towards the house lay a figure dressed in the tactical gear of the armed response team. Sturgess didn't need to check if they were alive or dead. The human body was not designed to be twisted in that way.

He flinched as he heard a noise from by the remaining two vehicles. As he started moving across the yard, he began to make out a voice. Gruff. Northern. Recognizable.

'A Jew, a lesbian and a giraffe walk into a pub . . .'

The body of another member of the armed response team lay on the gravel between the car and the van. Sturgess could only see their top half, but it wasn't moving.

The voice was coming from between the two vehicles. Sturgess swung wide, Glock held out in front of him with two hands, finger on the trigger.

'A kangaroo and a nun are in the bath . . .'

Sturgess paused as his brain refused to make sense of what he was seeing. The ARU officer was lying motionless, his intestines visible from a belly wound. There was an awful lot of blood. At the other end of the body, a fat man in a tuxedo, frilly shirt and dickie bow was gnawing on the officer's left boot. A visible wound on the right side of the fat man's head dribbled blue liquid.

Sturgess stood there, transfixed.

The man's teeth ripped at the boot with the ferocity of a rabid dog then, after a few seconds, he stopped. 'There's these two Black fellas and a penguin on an airplane . . .' he began before trailing off to start gnawing on the boot again. Sturgess moved a little closer. He'd almost chewed his way through the boot. At this angle Sturgess could see that the reason the fat man wasn't moving was because he had no legs. Or, rather, he did, but they appeared to be several feet away, twitching every now and then but otherwise not doing anything.

'Stop doing that,' barked Sturgess.

The fat man turned his head and beamed a smile at him through yellow teeth covered in blue liquid. 'Fuckers left me behind. The Pope, the Dalai Lama and Samantha Fox are having dinner . . .'

Then he sank his teeth into the boot again with renewed violence.

Sturgess bent down and, while keeping the gun trained on the man, used his left hand to feel for a pulse on the ARU officer. As he'd feared – nothing.

He stood back up again.

'There's a Spanish fella, a tranny and fourteen ducks on a minibus . . .'

'Shut up,' shouted Sturgess. 'Stop doing that and shut up!'

'You can't say anything any more,' complained the fat man. In an unexpected burst of movement, he used his arms to propel himself towards Sturgess, teeth snapping.

The bullet in the head stopped him dead.

Sturgess moved through the farmhouse quickly and efficiently. There was no sign of anybody. As he exited via the back door, another motion-sensing light clicked on to reveal two buildings. The bigger one lay to his left, its large sliding doors open to show a loading dock, which was empty but with the lights still on. The other building had a corrugated iron door with a chain and padlock on it.

Sturgess hurried across and attempted to peer into the window of the smaller building, but it was too covered in grime to see much of anything. A faint light glowed from inside. It looked like it could be from a candle. He went to the door and jiggled the padlock. Locked.

Sturgess scanned the area again to double check he was still alone then, being careful to angle himself away from the chain, fired at it side-on.

It split on the second shot.

Sturgess yanked the chain away then stood back, gun trained on the door. He'd used three bullets. He was pretty sure a Glock held fifteen rounds. That meant he had twelve left. Or at least, he had twelve minus however many rounds Morrison had used.

He decided not to check. If he didn't know if he was bluffing or not, then neither would whoever was in there. He raised his voice and tried to sound a lot more confident than he felt. 'Armed police. Identify yourself.'

He stopped to listen but couldn't hear anything.

He took a deep breath, leaned forward and pulled the door open before darting to the side for cover.

After a few seconds, when nothing happened, Sturgess risked a quick look around the door.

Then a longer one.

It was clearly a storage shed, with broken furniture and some long-abandoned farm equipment lying around. He noticed a light switch beside the door, so reached in and clicked it on before quickly withdrawing his hand once again.

He took another look.

There was a large, almost throne-like wooden chair at the end of the room, with a stool beside it bearing a guttering candle. Sturgess thought there was a pile of rags on the chair until it lifted its head and looked at him. Even from a distance the man looked emaciated to the point of skeletal.

Sturgess entered the shed. Scanning the space as he advanced, he made his way down the rough aisle in the centre of the detritus, which led to the throne. Closer now, he could see the man was strapped to the chair and there was the unmistakable stench of faeces in the air. The man was so shrivelled and ashen in appearance Sturgess was shocked to realize he was Black. 'Gaunt' didn't do it justice, his skin hung slack around his face. Sturgess disciplined himself to take a final slow look around, to make absolutely sure they were alone.

Satisfied, he shoved the gun into his pocket and went to untie the cords that bound the man to the large wooden chair, but then hesitated. 'Who are you?'

The man blinked slowly as he looked at Sturgess, and he smacked his dry lips as he considered the question. 'Marcus. I'm Marcus Divine.'

'You're OK now, Marcus. You're OK. I'm a friend of your sisters.'

As Sturgess started working on the cords, the man began to make a rasping staccato noise.

'Are you OK, Marcus? Are you . . .'

The man tilted his head and gave Sturgess a weak smile. 'No offence, but my sisters ain't friends with any coppers.'

As the ring of his mobile phone reverberated around the storage shed, Sturgess jumped in shock. He hastily took it out of his pocket.

'Boss,' said Wilkerson, 'you OK? I heard shooting.'

'I'm fine and I've found Marcus Divine.'

'Great. Ambulances are on the way. Phones are working now – obviously.'

'I saw two dead members of the armed response team.'

'We've located most of the rest. Several walking wounded. Clarke and his lot just showed up. No injuries unless you count falling over and getting covered in cow shit.'

Sturgess looked down at Marcus Divine, who was now rubbing at his wrists where the cords had left nasty gashes on the skin.

'So, guv,' asked Wilkerson, 'what was all the shooting? Did you meet resistance?'

'Ehm,' said Sturgess, thinking back to the face of the fat man in the frilly shirt as he'd lurched towards him. 'Long story. I think I just cancelled somebody.'

59

There was no reason for any of them to be here really, reasoned Hannah. She supposed the rest of *The Stranger Times* staff were hanging around the office waiting for news from Sturgess about the raid, but it wasn't like she wouldn't be messaging everybody as soon as she heard. She checked her phone again. Still nothing. Darkness had descended outside save for the occasional early Bonfire Night fireworks that lit up the sky sporadically.

The police were handling everything now, so being in the office was entirely pointless. Still, Reggie was sitting at his desk, reading a book. Ox was sitting opposite, swearing at a game of Solitaire on his PC. Stella was sitting in the corner, ostensibly reading a university textbook, but she seemed to be spending most of her time glancing at her phone.

Grace was giving her reception desk a thorough cleaning it did not need. If they ended up being here all night, there was a good chance she might move on to other areas, and that would cause inevitable friction. She kept threatening to either clean Ox's desk or just take it outside and burn it. She'd have a job finding the actual desk under all the rubbish.

Manny was still fast asleep downstairs and, following his

exertions the night before, they had been informed not to expect to see him for a couple of days. The person he had saved – was person the right word? Yes, decided Hannah, it definitely was. Brian might not be entirely human, but he was still a person – was rolled up in a ball under one of the spare desks, fast asleep, twitching occasionally like a dog chasing cars in his dreams. Banecroft was in his office, at a highly educated guess, drinking.

It was Hallowe'en. Hannah had been so busy with everything that she hadn't stopped to consider that. It was rather depressing that none of them had plans. A nonsense holiday it may be, but still. As the thought struck her that kids would be out trick-or-treating there was a pounding on the door downstairs.

'Is there any chance it's trick-or-treaters?' she asked.

'Round here?' asked Stella. 'Always possible. Could be anything. We had that lad a couple of weeks ago who wanted to know if we could jumpstart the car he'd stolen.'

Grace stuck her head around the door of the bullpen. 'Is anyone expecting anyone?'

Head shakes all round.

'Ohhhh,' said Reggie, 'unless the dashing detective inspector decided to deliver the good news in person?'

They all scrambled to their feet.

'I'm going,' said Hannah.

'And we're following,' said Ox.

There was an undignified rush to the top of the stairs, with Hannah narrowly beating off the competition. She straightened her clothes then wagged a warning finger in the direction of the others. 'Behave!'

It wasn't DI Sturgess.

Hannah opened the door to a rather frazzled Cillian Blake, who was looking around nervously, as if expecting sniper fire at any moment. 'Hannah! Thank God!'

She took a step back. 'Ehm, Cillian – what the hell are you doing here?' She glanced back up the stairs. A great deal of urgent whispering was going on, and she couldn't blame them.

'I'm in so much trouble. You have to help me.'

'Yeah . . . I'm not sure that's the best idea.'

'Please, can I just come in?' His face softened into a picture of lost-puppy perfection. 'Please? I can explain everything.'

Two minutes later, Cillian Blake was sitting in the bullpen with the staff of *The Stranger Times* assembled around him, eyeing him suspiciously. Well, almost all of them. Grace was concerning herself with Brian, who had begun to snarl at Blake as soon as he'd entered the room. She was standing beside him, trying to comfort and distract him with a large bag of Revels. And then there was Banecroft. Hannah had been unsure what to do with Blake until their editor had appeared behind her at the front door and cheerfully invited their guest inside. The fact that Blake had taken this invitation at face value, and alarm bells hadn't started ringing as soon as Banecroft was polite to him, did not speak well of his ability to judge people.

Now that Blake was inside, Banecroft was Banecroft again, only more so. He was leaning on one of the spare desks directly in front of their visitor. Even for him, the degree of belligerence in his stare as he looked down at Blake was really quite something. Blake was a man used to adoring gazes and he was clearly not enjoying the full Vincent Banecroft experience. To be fair, nobody was, including Banecroft.

The tension was becoming unbearable, but Hannah resisted the urge to speak. She could see the others doing the same. This was Banecroft's show and it was up to him what happened next. Hannah appreciated this far more than anyone else in the room because she knew something they didn't. He was hours from midnight and the threatened deadline for being dragged to hell. The key to his survival might be sitting in front of him.

Blake, unable to take the silence any longer, cracked first. 'Look, I don't know what you think you know.'

'I don't think I know anything,' said Banecroft, 'I know I know everything. What I want is to hear your version of events' – he nodded at the phone sitting beside him on the desk – 'before I decide who I'm going to call.'

'There's no need to involve the police.'

Banecroft barked a mirthless laugh. 'Believe me, if what you're scared of is the police, then you really don't know how much trouble you're in. Although the list of charges is extensive: drug-dealing, grave-robbing, kidnapping . . .'

'Murder,' chimed Stella. 'Don't forget poor Wayne Grainger.'

Blake looked at her with wide eyes. 'I had nothing to do with that.'

'Didn't you?' said Banecroft. 'The drugs you supplied certainly did, but I take your point. It's probably only manslaughter.'

'Oh God,' moaned Blake, holding his head in his hands.

'But again, I really wouldn't worry about the law here if I were you.'

Blake leaned back in his chair, tears in his eyes. 'I didn't want to do any of this. It was Emma, Dr Marsh, she' – he jabbed a finger at the side of his own head – 'she did something to my mind. I didn't . . .' He redirected the finger excitedly at Banecroft. 'I didn't have free will.'

'Convenient that. So, why don't you, in your own words, tell us exactly what she was doing.'

'She's . . . This'll sound crazy—'

'Oh,' said Banecroft, 'I think you'd be surprised how far you'd have to go before anyone in this room dismisses what you're going to say as crazy. Try us.'

'She's insane. She . . . she is Wiven. It means she's a witch. Like, a proper witch. She can do magic.'

'Yes, there's a surprising amount of that about.'

'But she's into some really dark stuff. Obsessed with raising the dead. I mean, I hadn't seen her in years and then she appeared in my bedroom one night and brought a badger back to life.'

Despite himself, Ox barked a laugh, which earned him looks of reproach from the rest of the room. 'Don't blame me, he said it,' he protested.

Banecroft returned his attention to Blake. 'A badger?'

'She was showing me what she could do. Reckoned by getting this anima stuff out of certain people, she could use it to bring the dead back to life. But it had to be the right people. She didn't want to take this anima out of the whatchamacallits' – he waved a hand about – 'other magical people, as that'd attract attention.

She used drugs to find ordinary people who had magic in them, because that's a thing, and then she took it out of them.'

'And how,' interrupted Hannah, 'were these drugs able to do that?' She knew the answer, but she wasn't asking the question to find out anything other than whether or not Blake was possibly telling the truth.

'She has this guy, this poor guy locked in a shed out the back, and he was doing something to the pills.'

Marcus Divine. As his sisters had both predicted and feared.

Hannah looked over at Banecroft, but he wasn't taking his eyes off Blake.

'And the digging up of the dead bodies?'

'Tests,' said Blake. 'She has this guy who works for her. Doug. He does all that. And the drugs. He does everything. She was doing these tests, but she couldn't control them – the people she brought back. They all went feral. She was trying to find a way to stop that from happening.'

'And did she?'

'Yes. Just in the last couple of days. She got hold of this magical thing – a necro-something or other – that allows her to do it. I don't know how. Now she has this army of zombies.'

'An army?'

'Doug,' said Blake, licking his lips. 'He— He found these people for her. You see, the dukes of Cheshire, they have a cryogenic place. Totally illegal but they've had it for decades. Doug went there and got a load of frozen dead bodies for her.'

Banecroft nodded. 'Super. And where is this Marsh woman and her zombie army now?'

'She was at the farmhouse.'

'But she's not any more?'

'I doubt it. The police tried to raid the place.'

Banecroft sat forward a little. 'Tried?'

'She . . . I don't know what happened, but she set her zombies on them. There was a load of gunfire outside and . . . while all of that was going on, I slipped away and came straight here.'

'I see,' said Banecroft. 'And what is your part in all of this?'

'I told you,' pleaded Blake, 'I was her slave.'

'Right. And why you?'

Blake's brow wrinkled in confusion. 'I'm sorry?'

'She's a powerful Wiven. She's got this Doug fella digging up bodies and doing the drugs thing. According to you, he did everything, so why did she need you?'

'I . . .' He shrugged. 'Look, she's always been obsessed with me.'

'Excuse me?'

Blake nodded. 'Since we were kids. We were in school together. She's always been infatuated with me. I— We were sort of friends, but she wanted it to be more.'

Banecroft nodded. 'And so she got good at mind control or whatever and thought, I want to raise an army of the dead, but while doing it, I want that guy I fancied from school sitting around as eye candy? And who says the career woman can't have it all?'

Blake folded his arms. 'This isn't a joke. I'm a victim here. My mind has been violated!'

'Yes,' said Banecroft, 'sorry for your trouble. Excuse me while I confer with my assistant editor.' He glanced over at Hannah then straightened up and turned to Brian. 'And you, if he gets out of that chair, you have my permission to put him back in it by any means necessary.'

Hannah didn't know how much of that Brian understood, but he ran his tongue across his wide thin lips and gave Blake a look she really didn't like.

Banecroft moved over to beside the door to his office and waited for Hannah to join him. 'Well?' he asked in a near whisper.

'Well, what?' she replied.

'Do you believe him?'

'I don't know.'

'Isn't . . . wasn't he in a group with some guy who died?'

'I thought that, but Nigel Stay was cremated. They scattered his ashes over a rather lovely Zen garden in Colchester. I've visited it.'

'Hmmmm . . .' mused Banecroft. 'I still don't—'

He looked up as Brian yowled.

'I didn't move,' said Blake quickly.

Brian had started sniffing the air and was running around the room, back and forth, highly agitated.

'What is up with him?' asked Reggie.

'It's not my turn to take him out for a shit,' said Ox.

'Brian,' said Grace, chasing after him. 'Brian – calm down, dear.'

Brian's eyes were so wide now that his pupils and irises were small black pinpricks in a sea of white. He gave a hooting noise and started to jump up and down on the spot, reaching a remarkable height as he did so.

Hannah and Banecroft moved towards him, and Hannah

extended her hands in a calming gesture. 'OK, Brian, it's OK. Just tell us what is wrong.'

Brian started to point furiously at the windows as he continued to jump up and down.

'Outside?' asked Hannah. 'You want to go outside?'

'I knew it,' said Ox. 'I'm not taking him.'

'Shut up,' snapped Hannah. 'There's something outside, isn't there, Brian?'

Confirmation of her guess came in the form of one of the big stained-glass windows shattering as something came hurtling through it.

In a display of a previously untapped sporting ability, Grace put up her hands and caught the object as it flew towards her. She looked at it, realized she was holding a severed human head, screamed as loudly as she could and tossed it in the air.

It landed with a thump in front of her.

'Jesus,' it said. 'Take it easy, would you?'

At which point Grace fainted.

60

The word 'pandemonium' did not do it justice.

Reggie and Stella rushed to Grace to check she was all right. Brian went ballistic trying to get to the head, which required Hannah and Banecroft to stay in front of him, arms outstretched, hopping from side to side, to stop him. Ox, meanwhile, picked up one of the wastepaper bins and shoved it over the head where it lay on the floor. The head for its part didn't take that well, and could be heard shouting and hollering from inside the bin.

After a couple of minutes, Brian calmed down to the level where he was just pacing up and down the far side of the room, sniffing the air and waving his hands about. Grace, having regained consciousness almost instantly, was plonked into a chair while telling anyone who'd listen not to make a fuss and threatening to make everyone a cup of tea.

Banecroft stood over the upturned metal bin in the middle of the floor. 'All right, if we're all as calm as we're likely to get, let's see what this is.'

'Wait,' said Blake, whom Hannah had almost forgotten in the chaos. 'You should know, he's a liar!'

'Excuse me?' said Banecroft.

'Pathological. Cannot trust a word he says.'

'To be clear, you're referring to the head?'

'Yes.'

'The one under the bin?'

Blake gave him a look. 'Is there another?'

'We've all got a head,' corrected Banecroft, 'but seeing as this one just came hurtling through my window and was fielded by my receptionist—'

'Office manager,' corrected Grace, in the surest sign that she really was fully recovered from her shock.

'Office manager,' repeated Banecroft before continuing, 'I'm very interested to know how you've had enough of a prior relationship with it to form an opinion on its moral character?'

'If you must know, I used to be in a band with him.'

'What?' yelled Hannah, considerably more loudly than she'd intended. 'What are you talking about?' She started advancing towards him. 'How is that . . . Nigel Stay is dead. You cremated him. Scattered his ashes. I visited the nice little Zen garden.'

Cillian Blake tried for a whoopsie-type shrug and a sheepish grin that, in the past, had probably got him out of a lot of scrapes. 'I was as surprised as you were.'

'Oh, I don't think you were,' said Banecroft. He pointed down at the bin. 'The head of your ex-bandmate just happened to be at this cryogenic facility?'

Blake's charm was cracking under the weight of his own lies. 'I guess so. Look, I didn't know about any of this. I am a victim here. Why are you all blaming the victim?'

'Right,' said Banecroft, nodding at Blake, 'you shall now only speak when spoken to.' He then turned to Brian, who had stopped pacing and was perched atop one of the desks, watching on. 'And if pretty boy refers to himself as a victim one more time, you have my permission to rip his leg off and beat him to death with it.'

Brian didn't move, but remained staring fixedly at Blake with an unnerving intensity.

'OK,' said Banecroft. 'Well, let's get this reunion tour kicked off, then, shall we?'

He reached down and drew the bin away to reveal a head lying on its side, giving him a very irritated look.

'Finally!' Nigel cried. 'That thing stinks, and oh my God, why are these floorboards so sticky?'

'Sorry,' said Ox, 'I spilt me Vimto. Been meaning to get to that.'

'Disgusting.'

Banecroft ignored the complaints and looked across at Hannah. 'So, is this . . .'

Hannah edged to a better position and tilted her head before nodding. 'Yes, that's him. Nigel. Nigel Stay.' She noticed his eyes turning to look at her. 'Ehm, hello.'

'Hi,' said Nigel, 'always nice to meet a fan. Is there any chance somebody could pick me up off the floor now, please?'

The staff of *The Stranger Times* exchanged glances but nobody moved.

'No?' said Banecroft. 'Sorry, Nigel, nobody wants to pick up your severed head. Don't take it personally.'

'It's not my fault somebody chopped my body off, is it?'

'Fair point,' said Banecroft. He picked up the bin and used it to scoop up Nigel in one fluid motion before dumping him out onto Reggie's desk.

'Oh, good God,' Reggie wailed, 'why did you have to use my desk?'

'It was closest,' said Banecroft, 'and if I'd put it on Ox's, I'd worry it might contract something from the squalor.'

'That's rich coming from you,' said Ox.

'Boys!' snapped Stella. 'Could we maybe get back to why the hell the severed head is here.'

The head in question started to rock itself about on the desk and everyone in the room took a wary step back.

'What's it doing now?' asked Hannah.

Her question was answered when the head managed to pitch itself into an upright position by propping itself against Reggie's monitor.

Banecroft gave an appreciative nod. 'Very clever.'

'Urgh,' said Reggie, squirming and spinning around, 'he's touching the keyboard. I bought it using my own money. It's ergonomic.'

'Hey,' snapped Nigel. 'Do you mind? I might be dead but I still have feelings.'

Reggie settled himself, stung by the rebuke.

'Right,' said Nigel, 'where's that prick?'

'Language,' interjected Grace.

'Killer,' he warbled in a sing-song voice. 'Oh, Killer, where are you?'

The rest of the room looked at Blake, who stayed firmly where he was.

'And wow,' continued Nigel, 'didn't you live up to that

nickname? That's right, I remember now. I remember it all. I totally get how you didn't want to talk about how I died. Overdose? My arse. That night, you came to me. "Oh, we need to reconnect, Nige," you said. "For the good of the band, Nige. Let's come back together, as brothers, Nige." I should have run for the hills when you apologized. You never apologize. I can't believe I fell for your shit one last time. Worse still, I can't believe I was stupid enough to let you prepare the needle.'

Hannah gasped, her hand flying to her mouth. 'NO!'

Blake stood up, his eyes wide. 'That is not true.'

'Ah, there he is,' said Nigel. 'That's my boy. It is true. You little narcissist. What possible reason do I have to lie? You thought with me gone you could have a glittering career, didn't you? Only you needed the secret album for that – isn't that right, *Killer*?'

Hannah looked at Blake as the realization dawned on her. 'That's . . . that's why you brought Nigel back.'

'No,' said Blake. 'No, I . . .'

'Bingo!' shouted Nigel. 'I'd clap, only – no hands.' He barked a laugh that would've sounded unhinged even if it wasn't coming from a severed head. 'You got it in one. Emma and I had a lovely bonding session on the drive over here. She says hi, by the way, but we'll get to that. This whole thing – everything – was one big effort to find out where that album I recorded is hidden. Only' – that laugh again – 'the joke's on him because there is no album. He did all of this for nothing.'

Blake strode forward. 'This is nonsense,' he shouted. 'Who are you going to believe – me or the insane ramblings of the head of a dead guy?'

More glances were exchanged then Hannah raised her hand. 'I vote dead guy.'

One by one, the rest of the room quickly followed suit in casting their votes – even Brian.

'Well,' said Banecroft, 'I don't know how familiar you are with democracy, but that's pretty conclusive. Not that we are actually a democracy. Nobody get any ideas on that front.'

Blake flapped his hands in exasperation. 'You people are ridiculous.' He slumped into a chair, full-on sulk mode engaged.

'Anyway,' said the head of Nigel Stay cheerfully, 'now that we've covered that, on to this evening's entertainment. First things first, I have been asked to inform you that the building is completely surrounded . . .'

They all rushed over to the windows and peered out.

'Holy shit!' exclaimed Ox.

'Mind your lang—' started Grace, but she stopped as she reached the window and blessed herself instead.

Hannah pushed past to look. A line of people was standing in the middle of the street outside, statue still, evenly spaced, all staring up at the window. The line disappeared out of view around both corners, making it look a lot like the building really was surrounded.

'Good God,' said Reggie, sounding horrified. 'They've . . . some of them are missing limbs, and they've got bullet holes in them.'

'Yeah,' said Nigel cheerfully, 'we had a warm-up fixture against the Greater Manchester Police earlier on. We took a few dings, but it was still a conclusive victory.'

'Is that . . .' said Ox. 'Hang on a second, is that . . .'

'Who?' said Nige. 'Jimi Hendrix? 2Pac? Jim Morrison? Sid Vicious? Bill Hicks? It's a veritable who's who out there. The dukes of Cheshire freeze only the crème de la crème, thank you very much.'

'How come,' continued Ox, 'they've all got bodies and you've only got a head?'

Nigel's tone changed to one of bitterness – Ox had clearly struck a sore point. 'Cutbacks, probably,' he said with a sniff. 'Anyway, we should get to the demands.'

At that, the staff turned around as one.

'Demands?' repeated Banecroft.

'Yeah, you know, you're surrounded. They're not out there singing Christmas carols, are they? Oh, I forgot – do check the phones.'

Grace snatched up the handset on Ox's desk. 'It is dead.'

'Yeah, they'll all be.'

Stella held up her mobile. 'I haven't got a signal either.'

'Jammer,' confirmed Nigel. 'Amazing what they can do with technology these days. Now, have I covered everything? Sorry, this is my first siege. Let's see, Cillian Blake is a selfish psycho. Check. You're surrounded. Check. Phones are dead. Check. Anyone leaves . . . Oh, did I mention that if anyone tries to leave they'll be ripped apart?'

'No,' said Stella. 'You forgot that bit.'

'Right, sorry,' said Nigel. 'Yeah, that. I wouldn't test it if I was you. The police didn't fare too well and they had big guns. All you lot have is a plucky can-do spirit.'

'Oh,' said Banecroft with a sideways glance at Stella, 'I think you'll find we've a little more than that.'

'Still, I don't see it,' said Nigel. 'The first match went really badly for the other team, and a lot more of our side have defrosted fully now.'

'Excuse me?' said Reggie.

'Yeah, we were all popsicles this morning. It takes a while for everything to get working but the lads and lasses are warmed up now, no pun intended. No more of that zombie shambling. They had some Olympian cyclist dude leading them in callisthenics in the truck on the way over. One of the weirder things I've seen, to be honest, and we once toured with the Libertines, so that's really saying something.'

Grace sat down heavily in one of the chairs. 'Warmed-up dead people.' She blessed herself and then kept doing it some more.

'All right,' said Banecroft, 'I believe you were working up to your demands?'

'Right,' said Nigel, 'the demands. Very simple, really. You've got fifteen minutes to send Cillian out or else they'll come in and get him.'

'Never!' said Blake, noticeably alone in his reaction.

'And if we do send him out?' asked Reggie.

Nigel smiled. 'I mean, what do you think is going to happen? Massively powerful, ever so slightly crazy jilted lover outside with a smallish army of zombies. I very much doubt she's here for the "it's not you, it's me" conversation. What do you reckon?' He left a pause which nobody filled. 'I'll be honest, I'm a severed head with limited things to look forward to, so I'm guessing this'll be the highlight of my afterlife. The Zombie Allstars out there are in friendly mode at the minute but when she lets 'em go, well, I hear it's quite something. Who doesn't want to see Indira Gandhi opening up a can of whoop-ass?'

'That is certainly an evocative image,' said Banecroft. 'We will talk through our options and let you know.'

'Super,' said Nigel. 'Make it snappy. Fifteen minutes starting . . . Oh, hang on, I forgot the other bit.'

'The other bit?' asked Stella. 'There's more?'

'Yeah. Emma said – and forgive the language here, her words not mine, ladies – you've got to send out the whore, too.'

Grace stood up and pointed at Hannah. 'She is not a whore.'

'Thanks,' said Hannah.

'No,' said Grace, looking mortified, 'I just meant . . . none of us are whores.'

'Okey dokey,' said Nigel. 'Well, I'll leave that for you lot to sort out among yourselves. I'm not one to judge.'

Banecroft stepped forward. 'You can tell her I shall not be sending out any of my staff.'

'Yeah,' chimed Blake.

Banecroft pointed at him without looking. 'You, shut up. We'll give you up in a second, but I am not handing over a member of my staff. If anyone is going to rip them apart with their bare hands, it'll be me.'

'Look,' said Nigel, 'the woman wants what the woman wants. I really don't think she's up for negotiating. Your fifteen minutes starts now.'

Banecroft gave Nigel a long hard look before stepping back and looking over at Brian.

'Brian, dispose of this.'

Brian lolloped across the room and grabbed the head.

'Hey!' said Nigel. 'What are you . . .'

It was impressive. Undeniably impressive. Without much of a wind-up, Brian was able to dropkick Nigel's head out the shattered stained-glass window. He was still rising as he disappeared out of view, and was last seen heading towards the park.

Banecroft nodded. 'I actually only meant drop him out the window, but I suppose that works too. Well done, Brian.' He looked around the room. 'So, does anyone here know how to fight off an army of zombies?'

61

Hannah completed her second circuit of the roof of the Church of Old Souls, as if looking twice was going to improve the situation. The roof consisted of two parts: the flat section with its rusted sun lounger and inexplicable bollards, and then the slanted tiled section, attached to the spire. Between the light pollution bouncing off the clouds overhead, the pools of light thrown by the outside lamps and the arc light that Banecroft had produced from a store cupboard, the main part of the roof was reasonably well illuminated. They'd figured that sitting up here in the dark and hoping nobody checked wasn't much of a plan.

Hannah had even clambered out onto the narrow walkway around the slanted tiled area, which was only a couple of feet wide, to confirm they were indeed totally surrounded. A perfect circle of stationary figures standing around them in absolute silence, all patiently looking up at the building. A large container truck was parked in the car park, which was presumably how they'd got here. Two people, who she was fairly certain were the duo she'd seen on Sturgess's CCTV captures, were standing beside it, the only two people not part of the formation. They were watching them too, while occasionally stopping for bouts of intense and awkward-looking snogging.

She checked her watch – twelve minutes.

Banecroft stood beside her, a pair of binoculars he'd found in his office held up to his eyes, and Chekov, his blunderbuss, propped over his shoulder. He was methodically scanning the ground below.

She'd say this for him, the man was good in a crisis. He'd looked around the office and quickly determined that due to the sheer number of large glass windows, trying to barricade themselves inside the bullpen would be an entirely useless endeavour. Ditto reception, with its multiple points of entry, and his office, which had a wooden door that didn't often close properly. The printing room/Manny's boudoir downstairs was an even worse option, what with all the windows plus its handy ground-floor location easily accessible to zombies of all ages, and hiding in the bathroom and hoping for the best was unlikely. Stella's room in the steeple was briefly considered but rejected, and it was impressive how Stella resisted the urge to point out that if they'd got her the door she'd been asking about for months, maybe her bedroom would've been a more defensible prospect.

The roof. Within ninety seconds, Banecroft had decided on the roof. There was one way onto it from inside, and if the horde had to climb the outside of the building, he reasoned they'd have a decent chance of pushing them back off again. The slanted section would hopefully provide them protection on that side, leaving them with only the other three open sides to defend. How the hell they'd manage that was another question entirely.

That decided, Banecroft had then assigned everyone tasks and asked Hannah to accompany him up here.

'Look,' said Hannah, 'let's think this through.'

'No,' said Banecroft.

'You haven't even heard me out.'

'Were you about to explain how you sacrificing yourself for the greater good would be the sensible choice here?'

'I'm just saying—'

'No,' said Banecroft. 'For all of the obvious reasons.'

'But—'

'Plus, if it makes you feel better, I don't think handing you and pretty boy over to an undead mob is what I need to do to redeem myself in the eyes of you know who.'

'Fair point,' she conceded.

Given the situation and quite how much insanity had been piled on top of her in the course of the last day, Hannah surprised herself by still being able to scream in shock. In her defence, a massive man dressed all in black with a pockmarked face had suddenly appeared in front of her out of nowhere.

'Jesus!'

'Do not blaspheme in front of me, you painted harlot.'

Hannah had had just about enough of this crap. 'I am not a painted harlot nor am I a whore, thank you very much.'

'You go, girl,' said Banecroft. 'Wait, hang on, you can see him?'

'Yes,' said the Pilgrim, 'she can. You were ignoring me, and I do not like being ignored.' He turned to address Hannah. 'You and all modern women are wanton strumpets of unladylike bearing.'

'On behalf of women everywhere and from the bottom of my

wanton strumpet heart,' said Hannah, 'shove it where the sun don't shine.'

'Amen, sister,' said Banecroft, looking at his watch. 'Normally I'd be all up for a bra-burning but we're a little pressed for time. Does this visit have a point?'

'Yes. This,' said the Pilgrim with a wave of his hand, 'is the great abomination.'

'No kidding,' Banecroft responded, then pointed down at the ground. 'Unless I'm very much mistaken, that's zombie Nelson Mandela standing down in our car park, who in about ten minutes, I'm assured, will be turned into a blood-crazed maniac intent on ripping my throat out.'

'Nelson Mandela?' asked Hannah. 'Seriously?'

Banecroft handed her the binoculars. 'Wait until you see who is standing beside him.'

'The time of judgement is at hand,' said the Pilgrim.

'Super,' said Banecroft. 'I don't suppose you can be of any assistance here?'

The Pilgrim gave him a broad smile that was a damning indictment of seventeenth-century dentistry. 'No.'

'Then piss off.'

'Holy shit,' said Hannah, staring into the binoculars, 'is that . . .'

'It is,' confirmed Banecroft.

'Wow, I mean . . .'

They were interrupted by Stella and Ox stumbling out onto the roof. When Hannah drew her eyes away from the binoculars, the Pilgrim was nowhere to be seen.

Ox had been instructed to find anything that could be used as a weapon, and he now held the accumulated items in his hands. Stella had been tasked to find some planks of wood. What she had settled on were the struts from under her IKEA bed.

They tossed their bounty on the ground. 'Right,' said Ox, 'we've got a hammer, a shovel, a baseball bat—'

'How do we have a baseball bat?' asked Hannah.

'I've been kidnapped twice in six months,' said Stella. 'I was going to put nails in it too, but I haven't got round to it.'

'Right,' said Hannah, trying not to sound alarmed. She had been intending to have 'the chat' with Stella at some point about the importance of using protection, but this was very much not what she had had in mind.

Reggie staggered through the door with Manny's limp form draped over his shoulder. He laid him down carefully on the slanted roof then collapsed beside him, gasping for breath.

Grace came out after him, carrying a cross and what Hannah guessed was a large bottle of holy water. 'We have been trying to wake Manny up, but he just will not.'

'Oh,' said Banecroft, sounding dispirited, 'that's . . . inconvenient. We could really use the whole avenging angel thing round about now.'

'Fear not,' intoned Grace. 'Perhaps he will come around in our moment of need. The Lord works in mysterious ways.'

'I hope he works nights.'

Grace ignored him. 'I have also locked and bolted the front door and put several of those boxes from the storeroom in front of it.'

'Good idea,' said Hannah.

'Yes,' agreed Banecroft. 'Paperwork stopping a zombie invasion might be the most British solution to a problem ever conceived.'

'I've got proper good news,' said Ox, pulling a book from his back pocket. 'I found this.'

'A book? How is this good news?'

He waved the paperback about. 'It's not just any book. It's *The Zombie Survival Guide*. It literally was written for this exact situation.'

'Really?' said Banecroft. 'This exact situation?'

'As good as. I borrowed it from Zombie Gary. Been meaning to read it for ages.'

'No time like the present,' said Banecroft. 'And who the hell is Zombie Gary?'

'He,' said Reggie, panting heavily, still spread-eagled on the floor, 'is Ox's mate who really likes zombies. Like . . . *really*.'

'Right,' said Banecroft. 'In hindsight, I probably could have surmised that from the name.'

Hannah went to help Reggie up, but he waved her away, not quite ready to get back on his feet yet.

'All right,' said Ox, scanning the opening pages of the book. 'Let's see, says here "we must separate fact from fiction – the walking dead are neither a work of black magic nor other supernatural forces". Well, that's crap for a start.'

'Anyway,' said Banecroft, 'while I of course encourage your continued efforts to educate yourself, I'm not sure this is going to bear immediate fruit. Where is—'

In answer to the question Banecroft hadn't finished asking, Cillian Blake was pushed through the door, followed closely by Brian.

'Thank God you are OK,' said Grace.

'Yes,' said Blake, 'I am.'

Ox spoke without looking up from the book. 'She was talking to the ghoul, ya knobhead.'

'Language, Ox!'

'Sorry, Grace,' he said, continuing to flick through the pages. 'There's a lot in here about automatic weapons. I reckon it's primarily written for an American market. Ohhhh, does anyone know if these are Romero or Russo zombies?'

'What are you on about?' asked Stella.

'It says here that Romero zombies can be killed by destroying the brains but Russo zombies have to be incinerated.'

'OK,' said Hannah. 'Well, seeing as we don't have any way of doing the second thing, let's hope it's the first thing.'

'Yeah,' said Ox. 'Makes sense.'

'How much time do we have?' asked Grace.

Reggie glanced at his watch as he got back to his feet. 'I make it about six minutes.'

'OK, then,' said Banecroft, clapping his hands together. 'We need to divvy up the weapons.'

Hannah stepped forward and considered the pile. As well as the baseball bat, there was a shovel, a hammer, a screwdriver, a cordless drill and . . .

'A toilet plunger?' said Banecroft. 'Really?'

'Options were limited,' snapped Ox defensively.

'Moving on,' said Banecroft, patting his blunderbuss. 'I shall be using Chekov here.'

'Won't that fire only once?' asked Hannah.

'Yes, but I can always give the old dear a swing about after that.' He bent down, picked up the baseball bat and held it out to Stella.

She pushed it away. 'I've got my thing.'

Banecroft held it out again. 'In case that is playing up.'

'I don't—'

'Please.'

She looked at him then took it begrudgingly as he turned his attention to Hannah. 'Lady's choice?'

'Oh, jeez,' said Hannah, 'this is the world's weirdest game of Cluedo.' She felt sick to her stomach imagining using any of them. 'Fine. I guess I'll take the shovel.'

He handed it to her.

'Excellent choice. Grace?'

She patted her crucifix. 'I will be trusting in the good Lord.'

'But—'

'In the good Lord,' she repeated, in a tone that invited no disagreement.

'As you wish. Ox?'

'Hammer or screwdriver, please,' he said without looking up from the book. 'There's a picture of a helicopter in here. No shit – that'd be handy, all right.'

Banecroft tossed the hammer at Ox's feet.

'Reggie?'

Reggie looked off into the distance and Hannah noticed that

without seeming to have taken them from anywhere, he now held a blade in each hand. He spoke in a soft voice. 'I am fine.'

'In which case,' said Banecroft, picking up the screwdriver and tossing it at Ox's feet, 'you get two.'

'What about me?' said Blake, sounding outraged.

'You get the death you so richly deserve. Or at least whatever is left after Brian picks.' Banecroft stood up. 'Where is he?'

The group, having been focused on the division of the meagre stash of weapons, looked up and, at the same time, collectively noticed Brian crouched at the far end of the roof. They all gave a loud groan of disgust.

'With the sweet Lord as my witness,' said Grace, 'could you not have held that in for a few minutes more, Brian?'

'Well,' said Banecroft, 'I suppose you don't want distractions when you're in the middle of a fight. Still, though, if you could dispose of that when you're done, please, Brian. Health and safety and all that. Don't want anyone stepping in it.'

Brian pulled up his trousers and, without any hint of shame or embarrassment, took a plastic carrier bag out of his pocket. Then, using it as an improvised glove, he calmly picked up what he'd just produced. As he walked towards the others, they all stepped back out of his way. He serenely walked to the edge of the roof and hurled it in the direction of Emma Marsh and her associate.

It was hard to see in the meagre light provided by the street lamps, but judging by the shouts of disgust and angry body language, Brian scored a direct hit.

'I'll say this for you, Brian,' said Banecroft, 'you've got a certain style to you.' He pointed down at the remaining weapons. 'Anything take your fancy?'

Brian studied the pile then looked back at Banecroft, clearly having no idea what he was on about.

'You're right,' said Banecroft. 'Let's let Brian be Brian.'

'In which case,' said Blake, 'I'll take the drill.'

'No,' said Banecroft. 'We're using that to fix those slats over the door.' He looked around. 'Ahhhh. I don't suppose anyone thought to pick up any screws or nails?'

62

Dr Carter looked at the red light above the large blank screen as she spoke. 'We still haven't got all the details, but it appears that this Dr Emma Marsh woman is a powerful Wiven, and she's been extracting anima from these so-called anomalies in order to engage in necromancy.'

'Good god,' said the disembodied voice.

'Yes. The Greater Manchester Police attempted to raid their base of operations earlier today and were attacked by a large number of ambulatory undead, resulting in, we believe, two fatalities. These undead are apparently highly aggressive and seemingly entirely under Dr Marsh's control.'

'This is a nightmare,' said the voice. 'We can't have things like this going on. It'll terrify the plebs.'

'Yes, sire,' said Dr Carter. 'We are unsure as to the exact reason, but this horde, if you will, has currently surrounded the offices of *The Stranger Times* and they look set to attack it.'

'Why?'

Dr Carter resisted the urge to roll her eyes. 'As I said, we currently don't know that. However, I have dispatched teams Annarius, Felstom and Raridi to intervene.'

'Why?' That question came from Tamsin Baladin, who was sitting behind her.

'What?' snapped Dr Carter.

'Why do we need to intervene?'

Dr Carter turned in her chair and gave her a withering look. 'Do you think a zombie horde rampaging through Manchester is a good idea, Ms Baladin?'

Baladin smiled sweetly in return. 'But they're not rampaging through Manchester, though, are they? They're attacking *The Stranger Times*. This woman, Dr Marsh, is a Wiven and not a member of, or associated with, the Founders. Why is it up to us to protect this bloody newspaper? Where is that written?'

Dr Carter pursed her lips. 'Very well. What would you have us do?'

She shrugged. 'Let it play out. *The Stranger Times* has been a growing inconvenience to us for some time. If this woman removes them, all well and good, with no blowback on us from anyone. If they triumph, well, we might get to see this girl in action and determine how big a threat she is.'

Dr Carter narrowed her eyes. 'Haven't you already seen her in action, Tamsin?'

'Yes, but it appears my evidence alone of the threat is not enough. We have our teams on standby, and they can move in and deal with whatever threat remains afterwards.'

'But—'

'Yes,' said the faceless voice, 'I like this plan. I like it a lot. Excellent work, Ms Baladin. Excellent work. Keep me informed as to how this proceeds.'

Dr Carter turned back to the screen, trying to formulate a counter-argument. Before she could muster anything, the red light clicked off. They both sat there in silence for a long moment before Dr Carter heard Tamsin Baladin standing up to leave.

'It's a dog-eat-dog world, Doctor.'

'That it is, Tamsin. That it is.'

63

It was weird, but when it came right down to it, with minutes slipping away, second by second, Hannah couldn't think of a damn thing to say. Apparently, neither could anyone else as they all stood there in silence, looking down at the ring of figures staring up at them, waiting for the signal. The meagre weapons had been divvied up and Banecroft had assigned them positions. Seeing as they couldn't lock the door from this side, four of them were allocated to it, and the remaining three each took a side of the roof in case the attackers were somehow able to climb up. This left Brian in a roving role, given that nobody was entirely confident he would understand or stick to the plan. Ox had been asked to find out if zombies could climb buildings, but the book had been unhelpfully vague. Speaking of which . . .

'I don't suppose anyone here has a flamethrower on them?' asked Ox.

'Sorry,' said Banecroft. 'I left it in my other suit.'

Ox snapped the book shut and tossed it off the side of the roof. 'Guess I'll wait for the movie to come out.'

'All right,' said Stella, sounding like she was giving up on holding something in, 'I'll be the one to ask: if we get bitten, are we going to turn into zombies?'

'Oh, Lord save us,' said Grace, 'is that a thing?'

'Only in the movies,' said Reggie.

'Yeah,' said Ox, 'I reckon we're all right. I mean . . . zombies in films are created by a plague. This isn't that, though – is it? It's magical, so we're OK. Probably. I think.' Then he added, 'I really wish Zombie Gary was here.'

'Yes,' said Reggie, 'ideally instead of me. Having said that, if I do . . . you know, change, I won't hold it against any of you if you kill me.'

'Oh, hell,' said Hannah, 'I don't think I've got it in me to do that to any of you.'

Her concern was met with a general murmur of agreement.

'Don't worry,' said Banecroft. 'I'll do it.'

'Yes,' said Reggie, 'I imagine you would.'

Banecroft jabbed a thumb over his shoulder. 'If anyone wants the toilet plunger, I'll happily do Mr Blake now.'

'Oh, ha ha,' snapped Cillian Blake. 'Very bloody funny.'

'He's not joking,' said Ox.

'Not even a little,' agreed Reggie.

They all fell into silence again and Hannah felt a shiver pass down her spine that had nothing to do with the cold.

'How long now?' asked Ox.

'I make it three minutes,' said Hannah.

The silence returned.

'This,' said Reggie in a quiet voice, 'is oddly reminiscent of the final scene in *Blackadder*, when they're all in the trench, waiting to go over the top into No Man's Land.'

Nobody said anything to this.

'Oh,' said Banecroft, 'I meant to say, I've got good news and bad news. The bad news is that as well as Indira Gandhi being down there, Nelson Mandela's there too.'

The group issued a collective groan.

'There is absolutely no way I am smashing Nelson Mandela in the head with a baseball bat,' said Stella. 'And wow, there's a sentence I really thought I'd never have to say.'

'It isn't Nelson Mandela,' said Banecroft, 'and we all need to stop thinking like that. Those . . . things down there aren't who they used to be. Now they're just corrupted vessels for that crazy woman to channel her rage through. None of what you're about to face is really Mandela, a former Dalai Lama, Betty White—'

'Oh, good God,' said Reggie with feeling, 'please don't tell me that the divine Betty White is down there.'

'No,' said Banecroft. 'Haven't you been listening to anything I just said?'

'Who is Betty White again?' asked Grace.

'The actress who played Rose in *The Golden Girls*,' said Hannah.

'Oh, I really like her.'

'Liked,' said Banecroft. 'Liked. Past tense. She is dead. Whatever is down there is not her, OK?'

A few mumbled assents rose from the group. A moment of silence followed, save for a couple of fireworks exploding in the distant sky and the low rumble of traffic in the background.

'Having said that . . .' began Banecroft, 'it would appear they are joined by Margaret Thatcher.'

'Bagsy doing Thatcher!' shouted Ox excitedly.

'Nobody is bagsying anything,' said Banecroft. 'We will each deal with whatever . . . thing fate puts in front of us. Whoever is confronted with the former prime minister's re-invigorated corpse will do what they have to do, safe in the knowledge that they'll never have to buy a drink in this town again.'

There was another pause in the conversation. 'How long?' asked Ox again.

'About a minute,' said Hannah.

Grace cleared her throat. 'I would like to take this opportunity to say that God loves you all.' She paused, a hitch in her throat. 'And so do I.'

Her words were met with thank-yous and awkward agreements. Hannah patted Grace on the arm.

'Even you, Mr Blake,' Grace added.

This was followed by a gaping absence of any agreement from the rest of the group.

'Thank you,' said Cillian Blake, standing to the side, visibly shaking, drill in one hand, toilet plunger in the other, tears rolling down his cheeks.

God, thought Hannah, he was a really ugly crier.

Suddenly, Stella turned around and grabbed Grace in a bear hug, which Grace reciprocated. After a few seconds, Grace laughed and said, 'Brian had the right idea. I think I should have gone to the ladies' room while I had the chance.'

Stella laughed too. 'We've got about twenty seconds; we could probably make the bathroom if . . .'

Hannah watched Stella as she stood there, her arms still around Grace, with a peculiar look on her face.

'You OK, kiddo?'

Stella stepped back, glanced at her watch, then down at the car park. 'Maybe . . .'

'What?' asked Hannah.

Before Hannah or anyone else could react, Stella darted over to the door and jumped through it, slamming it behind her.

'Stella!' shouted Grace.

Banecroft and Hannah weren't quick enough, and their attempts to pull it back open were in vain.

'Damn it,' said Hannah. 'She's locked it on the other side. STELLA!'

'STELLA!' screamed Banecroft. 'We need to get this door open.'

And then came the terrifying sound from below as thirty-eight vessels for one woman's rage simultaneously screeched their madness at the world and charged.

64

Stella stumbled as she scurried down the rickety steps from the roof, thrown by the unearthly noise that had just erupted outside.

They were coming.

Damn it. Why had she not thought of this sooner? Why hadn't any of them?

As she reached the bottom of the stairs to the roof, which took her into reception, she could hear the thunder of bodies being thrown against the doors downstairs, and the tinkle of breaking glass coming from several directions.

No time to think about any of that. She had to act.

She sprinted down the staircase to the ground floor, skipping the dodgy step fourth from the top out of sheer instinct. The front doors were visibly shaking under a sustained assault and as she reached the bottom, she heard the sound of splintering wood. A flailing arm appeared through a gap in the door.

Terror clawed at her, and she could feel the thing rising inside her. That terrifying, sickly sensation.

'C'mon, you stupid thing. Time to own you.'

Stella ran down the hall and into the bathroom, slamming the door closed behind her.

★

'What the hell does she think she's doing?' bellowed Banecroft over the din from below.

'I have the same information you do,' said Hannah.

'I mean, I'm worried about her, but also, she and Brian were my only realistic hopes for us surviving this.'

'Thanks for the pep talk, boss.'

★

Stella stood in the bathroom and tried to find the exact spot on the floor. They hadn't actually removed it; they'd just closed it up. It was still here if she could just find it.

She hefted the baseball bat above her head and brought it crashing down on the tiles.

The reverberations of the blow rattled through her entire body and caused the baseball bat to fly out of her hands, ricocheting back up and hitting her full in the face.

Stella held her hands to her nose as blood began to spurt from it.

She looked up as something slammed against the door.

'It's occupied!' she roared.

★

'They're coming up the stairs!' screamed Blake.

'No kidding,' shouted Banecroft.

'That's not our only problem,' added Ox, from his position on the ledge.

'Are they climbing up?' asked Hannah, her hands sweaty as she gripped the shovel and watched the door in anticipation.

'Worse.'

'What do you mean—'

Hannah stopped as a male zombie wearing a shell suit and drenched in gold jewellery floated up past the lip of the roof. His long white hair trailed behind him as his teeth snapped and his hands scrabbled to reach Ox.

'Jesus!' screamed Hannah.

'You've got to be kidding me,' shouted Ox. He dodged nimbly out of the reach of the zombie's grasping hands as he approached the edge of the roof and slammed a well-aimed blow into the side of the creature's head with the hammer. 'Fix that, knobhead,' he yelled as the zombie fell soundlessly back down to the ground below.

He turned back to Hannah. 'God, that felt good!'

★

It happened fast.

The bathroom door gave way and three zombies, literally falling over each other to get to her, came tumbling through. Without thinking, Stella pushed her hands forward and a blast of blue energy came flowing out, hitting the first one centre mass and sending all three of them hurtling backwards, along with half of the wall.

Her broken nose temporarily forgotten, she looked out into the hall. Quite a few bodies were there, still moving, gathering themselves up. She guessed the majority of the invaders had rushed upstairs to where most of their targets were.

She found herself laughing, the taste of blood warm in her mouth as it flowed freely from her ruined nose. 'OK, if I'm going to own it, let's own it.'

She turned her attention back to the floor. Drawing in a deep breath and summoning every ounce of concentration she could, she imagined pushing at the floor.

A slim shaft of blue light emanated from her hands. It cracked one solitary tile.

She looked at her hands and then down at the floor. 'You have got to be kidding me.'

★

Hannah closed her eyes and swung. She then opened them, genuinely shocked to discover that her blow had indeed made contact with the head of the large fat zombie in a three-piece suit that had floated up on the right-hand side of the roof. He stood there, dazed, looking at her as if he didn't know why she would have done such a thing. Some weird instinct in her felt the momentary urge to apologize. Then the man's face transformed into a snarl and he lunged at her.

Hannah pulled back and was about to swing again when Brian hurtled in and drop-kicked the massive man backwards, sending him tumbling off the roof.

Before Hannah could do anything else, Brian was gone, throwing himself at another zombie that was standing over the still-slumbering form of Manny. The Rastafarian looked incongruously peaceful among the mayhem. He also didn't look as if he was about to sprout a vengeful angelic cloud anytime soon, which remained unfortunate.

★

Stella stood in the bathroom, clenching her fists. 'Come on, goddamn it! Come on. One chance. We've got one chance.'

She looked down the hall to where a couple of the formerly dazed zombies were now back on their feet and stumbling around.

Stella turned her attention to the floor and then to her hands.

'Screw it,' she said, aiming her left hand at the floor and her right hand down the hall towards the zombies.

'Hey, you stupid undead idiots, come get me! C'mon! Come rip me to pieces, you dead has-beens.'

This attracted precisely the kind of attention she had been hoping for, and considerably more besides. A guy bejewelled in gold and sporting a white blood-spattered fur coat roared at her and charged, with a small woman in a nun's habit following close behind.

As the two figures sprang down the hall towards her, Stella felt it rise inside her again.

'Ohhhh, shiiii . . .'

★

Hannah headed over to the door to the roof, which was now rattling under the force of bodies being thrown against it from the inside. It was reasonably sturdy, as far as these things went, but it was not designed to withstand a sustained assault. She and it had that in common.

Grace stood staring at it, her trembling hands clutching the wooden crucifix to her chest.

Hannah looked down and noticed Blake cowering behind the upturned metal sun lounger. She dragged it away from him. 'Get up, you pathetic shit. God, I cannot believe I ever fancied you.'

★

It had worked, in a manner of speaking. Stella had managed to thingy the zombies while simultaneously blowing a hole in the floor of the bathroom, where a trapdoor had previously been. All that was good. The only bad part was, it turns out that if you eviscerate the floor you're standing on, you'll end up having a rather painful landing.

She added a bruised backside to the things she didn't have time to think about right now and looked around. The basement's lights weren't on, so the only illumination was that which spilled in from the rather sizeable hole she'd just created in the ceiling. She attempted to orientate herself. As she took a step towards where she thought the main doors that led outside were, something caught beneath her foot and she almost went back on her arse. She bent down and picked up the baseball bat.

★

Doug, with nothing else to do, sat on the ground beside his beloved Emma and watched in awed fascination. She stood there, staff in one hand, her other hand stretched outwards, her face a picture of concentration as her gold-tinged eyes blazed behind her glasses. Her free hand was working up and down as she grabbed individual zombies and sent them skyward towards the roof. She had brought up the first few gently, but now she was tossing them up there, hurling them with wild abandon and landing them wherever. Some missed, but most made it, judging by the ever more frantic mêlée he could see on the roof.

She was incredible. Utterly incredible.

He found himself wondering what their kids would be like.

★

As the door finally splintered, Hannah and Grace, holding the sun lounger in front of them, charged at the mass of zombies as they spilled through, sending most of them tumbling back down the stairs again.

They pulled back and attempted the same trick once more, but Hannah was blindsided by something sliding down the slanted roof and barrelling into her. She lost her grip on the sun lounger as she was sent sprawling onto the ground. A heavy body fell on top of her, knocking the air from her lungs.

As she twisted herself around, the first thing she saw was the teeth, snapping and snarling at her, inches from her face. Summoning every ounce of desperate strength she had left, Hannah shoved at the top of the woman's chest, buying herself a little bit of literal breathing room.

It was then that she recognized the face. Blue liquid was

dribbling from several orifices and the eyes were glowing red, but the face was still unmistakable, even for someone Hannah's age.

Thatcher's head pinwheeled around, and her teeth caught Hannah's forearm and bit down. Hannah screamed in pain, losing her grip, and then the blood-stained teeth filled her vision as the creature roared in triumph. Blows rained down and all Hannah could do was hold up her hands and try to deflect as many of them as she could. The back of her head slammed against the roof and Hannah saw stars in front of her eyes.

And then . . .

A blessed moment of relief flooded through her as the weight was somehow lifted off her.

She pulled her hands away in time to see Brian holding Thatcher above his head as he staggered to the side of the building and, with one massive effort, hurled her off into the night.

Before he could turn around, three zombies tackled him to the ground.

★

Stella opened the coal chute doors that led to the basement as quietly as she could. Looking across the car park, she realized she needn't have worried. Emma Marsh was entirely engrossed in the battle above, as was the little guy with the beard sitting cross-legged on the ground beside her. Stella crouched down and darted to the left, working her way around the car park, putting the freezer truck between her and them.

★

Hannah staggered to her feet.

Zombies were everywhere now.

Reggie was a blur of motion to her left, his knives darting left and right as he attempted to fight off two zombies at the same time. They were leaking the blue liquid from several spots, but seemed otherwise unaffected. Ox and Banecroft were standing back to back, waving their respective weapons around desperately, trying to keep several zombies at bay simultaneously.

Grace. Where was Grace? Hannah turned around to see her colleague lying on the ground, blood pouring from a wound on her forehead, with a zombie standing over her.

Hannah rushed forward and slammed into Grace's assailant, catching it off guard and pushing it all the way to the edge. It fell off, and she nearly followed it as she stumbled, landing on her knees and grabbing the ledge just in time to stop herself from pitching forward and over the side.

She spun around, expecting another attack to come instantly. At the door, yet more zombies were streaming through.

★

Stella's hands were sweaty as she held the bat and took in the sight of Emma Marsh's exposed back. She had one shot at this. One shot.

From behind the container truck to where the duo was situated was about twenty feet. She tried to summon her thing, but nothing happened. If there was one thing worse than a curse, it was an unreliable curse. She was going to have to do this old school. She'd never physically attacked someone before – at least, not as far as she could remember. She didn't know if she had it in her.

The image of Grace, Hannah, Ox, Reggie, and even Banecroft standing on that roof came back to her. She looked up, but all she could see were thrashing limbs.

This was it. Stella ran full pelt with the bat held over her head. Her sole focus was Emma Marsh standing before her, arms raised.

Anger surged through Stella as she realized Marsh was laughing. *Laugh this off, you bitch.*

Stella hadn't intended to scream. The urge to do so came from somewhere other than her brain.

She was running as hard as she could as Emma Marsh started to turn.

She wasn't going to make it.

She wasn't going to . . .

Her foot caught something and she stumbled forward, losing her footing as something hot flew over her head.

With a last surge as her legs went from beneath her completely, Stella pitched her hands upward.

With a resounding whack, the baseball bat made contact with something.

★

Hannah, with no weapon, little strength and even less hope left, charged at the zombies, a despairing scream in her throat.

She watched numbly as they all looked at her, a peculiar expression on their faces, then simultaneously dropped to the ground. So surprised was Hannah that she kept running past the fallen foes. Reggie tackled her to the ground before she ran herself clean off the other side of the roof.

They both looked around.

'What happened?' asked Hannah.

'I think . . .' panted Reggie. 'I think we won.'

'We did? How did we win?'

Banecroft stood up, his face covered in blue liquid. 'Is everyone all right?'

His enquiry was met with an assortment of mumbles and groans. He scanned the rooftop before walking across to where Grace was sitting on the ground, clutching her cross to her chest. 'Are you all right, Grace?'

She assured him she was fine before asking, 'Brian, where is poor Brian?'

A pile of bodies beside the door moved and Brian emerged from beneath them, covered in blue liquid and green blood. His left ear was hanging off but he had what was probably a smile on his face.

'Holy shit,' said Ox, lying on the ground with a lifeless zombie on top of him, a screwdriver sticking out of its earhole. 'Brian is a total badass.'

Brian turned his head, looked down at the car park and then, in one fluid motion, dropped off the roof.

'Scratch that,' said Ox. 'He's Batman!'

★

Stella, panting for breath, looked across at the unconscious form of Emma Marsh lying prostrate on the ground beside her, the black staff no longer glowing as it lay across her body.

'And that,' said Stella, 'is how we do that.'

She was halfway to standing up when what felt like a ton of bricks landed on her. By the time she knew where she was, the guy with the massive bushy beard had her pinned down and his hands were wrapped firmly around her throat.

'You killed her, you monster,' he wailed. 'She was the love of my life and . . .'

The man's romantic ode was interrupted as he was lifted off her just as suddenly as he had hit her. Gasping for breath, Stella watched as Brian, gripping the back of Beardy's T-shirt in one hand and the arse of his trousers in the other, hammered the man's head into the side of the lorry several times, before dropping him on the floor in a crumpled heap.

Unable to speak, Stella gave Brian a cheesy thumbs-up. She was as surprised as anyone when he returned the gesture.

65

The next couple of hours passed in a confused blur. Paramedics showed up and strongly suggested that Banecroft go to the hospital to get checked out and have his injuries dealt with properly. Banecroft had rejected the suggestion equally strongly. While he had nothing against hospitals, he imagined A & E on Hallowe'en would be a never-ending display of idiocy, and he greatly doubted his ability to get out of there without attempting to inflict physical harm on somebody – not that he had the energy to do it.

Besides, their offices were full of all manner of people he didn't know. People in uniforms he didn't recognize. He was going to observe everything they did and make damn sure they took nothing they weren't supposed to. He watched as they started loading bodies into body bags and carted them away with an alarming degree of efficiency. It occurred to him that this may not have been the first time they'd done this.

A fight had nearly broken out when one of the bodies they attempted to take was Manny's. After a paramedic verified Manny was in fact alive, the men in weird suits left him be. John Mór showed up with an odd-looking woman wearing a woolly hat and an unnecessarily cheery disposition, who put something on

Brian's wounds that stank out the whole office. Nobody said anything because, from what little they'd said to each other, it appeared Brian had saved everyone else's life at least once. Banecroft reckoned he owed him three. It'd be a while before anyone complained too loudly about when and where he took a dump.

Banecroft was sitting on the sofa in reception because he was too exhausted to move. As far as he could tell, the others were gathered mostly in the bullpen. He'd gone looking for Stella as soon as it had all finished and had found her being walked back in by Brian. Her nose had been bleeding and her clothing was ripped, but she seemed otherwise largely uninjured. She'd nodded at him, mentioned she'd blown up the bathroom and disappeared off into her room. Teenagers.

Injury-wise, overall, they had come out remarkably well, considering. Grace had a nasty cut on her forehead; Hannah had a large chunk taken out of her arm. The two of them were on their way to A & E, as was Stella, once Grace had dragged her back out of her room. They had pretty much all been bitten, but Hannah's wound was considerably worse and required stitches. It appeared that Ox's theory that these zombies weren't the kind that recruited through the medium of biting had been correct. Quite aside from anything else, zombies didn't complain about sprained ankles as loudly as Ox did. Reggie disappeared somewhere and reappeared wearing a clean suit, so Banecroft assumed whatever injuries he had sustained weren't too serious either.

As for Cillian Blake, Banecroft neither knew nor cared. Sturgess, who had shown up with the rest of the circus, said he was in police custody and on his way to hospital. Banecroft had also asked about Emma Marsh and her little furry friend but, while Sturgess didn't care to admit it, it was obvious he didn't know. Banecroft guessed people like her didn't go to ordinary courts or ordinary jails. He'd mull that one over at some other time when he wasn't so exhausted.

He looked down at his wrist. His watch was gone. It must have come off during the mêlée.

'What time is it?' he asked of no one in particular.

One of the paramedics who was in the process of packing up, an unnaturally friendly Scouse lad, piped up with, 'Five to midnight, fella. Happy Hallowe'en.'

Banecroft nodded and heaved himself off the sofa. On weary legs, he trundled down the stairs then, before he stepped through what remained of the church's front door, he glanced down the hall. It appeared his junior reporter hadn't been joking about the bathroom. That was a tomorrow problem.

He never normally went outside for a smoke, but this was a special occasion. He walked away from the doors and plopped himself down on the wall and leaned back against the metal fencing. He'd looked out the window earlier and seen men in nondescript uniforms removing a zombie that had been impaled on the spikes. The refrigerated truck was gone too. This lot really didn't mess around. He pulled out his cigarettes and lighter and lit one in a practised motion. It was as he was taking his first deep drag that he heard the voice he had been waiting for.

'I have been instructed to inform you, Mr Banecroft, that you have been given a temporary reprieve.'

Banecroft blew a smoke ring into the cool night air and looked up at the Pilgrim. His face was not a party at the best of times, but he looked gratifyingly pissed off.

'Temporary?' Banecroft echoed. 'You can blow that right out of your arse.'

'Always with the vulgarity.'

'My debt isn't paid,' he said, 'but it was never to you and the league of shadows, or whoever the hell you are. It was, and is, to Simon. How I repay it is by keeping his friends alive and doing the job he believed in so passionately. And that is what I'm going to do. By the way,' he continued, standing up and stretching out his back, 'I've been meaning to say' – he took a couple of steps forward until he was inches from the Pilgrim's face – 'you should really consider a moisturizing regime.'

Banecroft felt the foul waft of the Pilgrim's breath on his face as he spoke. 'Always so tedious.'

Banecroft nodded, smiled and turned around. 'One more thing . . .'

He knew the odds were against him, but he felt on a cosmic level that it was worth trying. Like the universe owed him this. Not normally a man of violence, he spun around and his right fist made a full flush contact with the Pilgrim's jaw. He felt the weird sensation of hitting something that both was and wasn't there, and the Pilgrim once again split into myriad versions of himself in numerous colours all out of alignment with each other. They gradually reformed into the figure of a large man tumbling to the ground and whose silly hat went flying to reveal a gratifyingly large bald patch.

'And that,' said Banecroft, 'makes us even on the sucker-punches.'

The Pilgrim sat on the ground before him and rubbed his chin with his hand.

'Don't let the door hit you in the semi-ethereal arse on the way out.'

Banecroft turned and walked away, his smile falling from his face a little as he realized the Scouse paramedic was standing in the doorway, watching him and having no doubt seen him throwing a roundhouse punch at the air.

Banecroft nodded at him.

'I tell you what – the midges around here are awful annoying.'

EPILOGUE 1

As unassailable truths go, one of the biggies is surely that life finds a way. Sometimes, even through death.

She did not know who she was, what she was or why she was, but she knew she was and that was enough. Some spark of what had brought her back to life had somehow remained when it had been blown out in others. She did not question it. All she knew was that she must get herself away as fast as possible, and that was what she did.

★

He had hidden himself away in the daylight and licked his wounds. Waited. Then, when night had fallen, he had begun walking, staying away from the bright lights. The people. He didn't like the people. Previously, he had enjoyed the people greatly, but then they had attacked him. He only enjoyed them fighting back when he could bat their efforts away. One of them had leaped at him, though, clawing and fighting, and then another had shot him, leaving a wound in his right thigh. He wanted his mummy. How could he find his mummy?

★

'Right,' said Zeke, the sort of talking bulldog, 'that's it. I've had enough. This is officially an intervention.'

Cogs looked up from his plate of baked beans. 'What are you talking about?'

'I'll tell you what I'm talking about. I don't want to be here. It's rubbish.'

Cogs waved his fork at the abandoned dock off the Bridgewater Canal where the *Nail in the Wall* was now moored. 'What are you on about? It's perfect here. Listen to all that peace and quiet.'

'Exactly. It's boring as all hell. Nothing happens. We are out of the way. We're eating dinner at two in the morning because you can't sleep.'

'No. It was just raining earlier, and you know I like to eat outside.'

'Whatever,' said Zeke. 'Look at us. We're just two old farts sitting on a riverboat all day long doing nothing.'

'Oi,' said Cogs, 'less of the old fart, thank you very much.'

'Which brings me to my next point. Now we've moved, nobody can find us.'

'That's exactly the point of us moving,' protested Cogs.

'Yeah, but it also means nobody comes seeking your truth-telling services and we don't get no tributes. You've eaten nothing but baked beans and potato waffles for two days and I'm reduced to eating' – Zeke stuck his tongue out and made a retching noise – 'dog food. And, speaking as your bunkmate, that cabin is way too small to be trapped in it with your arse, if you're going to insist on this diet.'

Cogs shook his head. 'Do you know what your problem is? You've gone soft!'

'Soft?' echoed Zeke. 'I'm going to go soft in the head. We get to see hardly anything here.'

'That's not true,' said Cogs.

'Joggers and cyclists don't count.'

Cogs pointed his fork at Zeke. 'You shouted at the bloke on the bike yesterday and he cycled straight into the water. That was pretty funny.'

'I know,' said Zeke, 'but it's not the same. I need people. I need excitement.'

'Them apartments over there are full of people.'

'Great, we get to look in and see them watching TV.'

'We saw them boobs yesterday. Nice pair of boobs.'

'They belonged to a fella.'

'Still counts,' said Cogs. 'The thing is, there's plenty of excitement here. You just need to know where to look.'

'Like where?'

Cogs nodded in the direction of the pedestrian pathway on the far bank. 'Look at this. Here's a woman walking up the pathway on her own. What's going on there?'

Zeke sniffed the air. 'She smells funny.'

Cogs looked the other way. 'And . . .' He stood up and moved to the bow of the boat, ducking down. 'What the hell is that?' he hissed excitedly.

Zeke joined him. 'It's a cat.'

'It's massive. Size of a bloody elephant.'

'It is a very big cat, all right,' confirmed Zeke.

The thing was limping along.

They looked back in the other direction.

'This is going to sound mad,' Zeke said, nodding his head in the direction of the woman, 'but does she look familiar to you?'

'She's . . . No. That's not possible,' said Cogs. 'She's dead.'

Zeke smelled the air again. 'She definitely is, but that doesn't mean it isn't her. Trust the nose.'

The two figures had seen each other now. They both stopped.

'Holy moly,' said Cogs.

They both started walking towards each other again.

'The lady is not for turning.'

'Look at that body language,' said Zeke excitedly. 'There's going to be a ding dong!'

'Who you got?' asked Cogs.

Zeke's tail thumped against the deck as he looked back and forth between the two figures approaching each other. 'Hard to say. As a committed socialist and dog, it's really difficult for me to pick a side here.'

Cogs looked up as the sound of whirring helicopter blades suddenly filled the air. The chopper appeared over the apartment block, flying low, its blindingly bright searchlight illuminating the duo on the far bank. Both creatures came to a halt and hissed up at it.

Then, suddenly, men in uniforms were everywhere and a speedboat came zooming up the canal, causing the *Nail in the Wall* to rock from side to side in its obnoxious wake.

Nets. Darts. Cages. It was all over remarkably fast.

As the circus pulled out of town, Cogs sat back on the deck. 'All right, fine. We'll go back.'

EPILOGUE 2

This was Emma Marsh's worst nightmare.

Manacles were wrapped around her wrists, and they were not the ordinary type. They somehow felt cold and at the same time burned her skin. She reached within herself and found nothing. These were Maradan manacles, and they were doing their job depressingly well, robbing her of her abilities entirely.

Outside of that, she was strapped inside what felt a lot like a glass coffin, packed in so tightly that she could not move beyond wiggling her fingers. All she could see was the occasional balaclava-clad storm trooper walking in front of her, none of them even looking in her direction. The glorified muzzle on her mouth prevented her from speaking, and even if she could, the total absence of any sound leaking into the box meant that nobody could hear her. The occasional swaying motion was the only indication that she was in a moving vehicle.

These things in themselves were bad, but what they represented was so much worse. The Founders did not have prisons, they had 'facilities', and they answered only to themselves. There would be no trial, no sentencing, and definitely no appeal. People who earned their displeasure simply disappeared and were either dead or buried in a hole so deep as to be essentially the same thing.

A terrible empty feeling sat inside her where her power had once resided. For a while there, she had been a god. A true god. Granting life and death. And what's more, she had known, however briefly, what it was like to be truly loved. She didn't have long to consider her misfortune when it happened.

With a violent jerk the vehicle started to somersault sickeningly around her. Thanks to her glass coffin, she was held firmly in place as the world flipped on its axis. It was like being trapped in a washing machine on spin cycle. A storm trooper slammed against the glass in front of her, leaving a bloody smear. Everything was a blur of violent revolving movement and she felt as if she was about to throw up in her muzzle.

Eventually, after several queasy rotations, the world finally stopped spinning. Emma's neck hurt, her head was throbbing, and her stomach was still very much on the fence as to how it felt about everything. She was dimly aware of flashes of light outside the glass – gunfire and other things. The world shook once again. At some point, she must have passed out.

As she came to, she heard a pop, as the seal surrounding her glass coffin was broken. The sounds of groaning, distant sporadic gunfire and an alarm's plaintive wail trickled in, along with the strong stench of smoke and cordite. Two figures in red masks pulled away the back door of the vehicle, it having evidently been taken off by some form of explosive charge. What the hell was this?

Then a third figure appeared between them. A man. He was wearing a cape, for God's sake. Who the hell wore a cape? His skin was also a milky colour she'd never seen before and he had prominent canine teeth. Still, there was something about him that looked oddly familiar.

'Dr Marsh,' he said, 'apologies for the rude introduction, but I assure you it was necessary. I do hope you're all right?'

She tried to speak but couldn't. The man gave the masked individual to his right an irritated look. When that didn't achieve the desired result, he pointed at Emma. 'The gag.'

'Sorry, sir,' said the masked man as he reached forward and pressed something on the side of Emma's face.

She spat out the now-released muzzle and coughed several times. 'Wh . . . what is going on?' she asked when she eventually recovered the power of speech.

'Simply put,' said the man in charge, 'the Founders are intending to punish you for your uncompromising and brilliant research to advance the causes of both science and magic.' He placed a long-nailed hand on his chest. 'Forgive me, I am quite the fan boy.'

'You . . . you're V Tepes the Third.'

He laughed and gave a bow. 'Guilty as charged. I am your awestruck benefactor. If you come with me now, I will assist you however I can in continuing your work.'

Something in Emma's brain clicked. 'Wait, I know who you are. You're Alan Baladin.'

Anger flashed across his face. 'I no longer go by that name,' he snapped, before recovering. 'You may call me Mr White.' He bowed again. 'Charmed to make your acquaintance.' He tilted his head as someone out of view said something to him that

Emma could not make out. 'It appears we must be going. So, Doctor, what is it to be? Life in a cage or working for me and getting everything your heart desires?'

'Everything?' she asked.

He smiled again. 'Within reason.'

'I want my Dougie-wougie!'

Mr White narrowed his eyes and looked off to the side. 'What the fuck is a Dougie-wougie?'

FREE GOODIES

Hi,

C. K./Caimh here – thanks for reading *Relight My Fire*. Would you like to watch an exclusive video, where I discuss the inspiration for the book, the real locations featured in it, and where I risk getting sued by the worst hotel in Manchester? Then scan the QR code below with your phone right now, or visit TheStrangerTimes.com/BackForGood.

And if you'd like to receive some exclusive *Stranger Times* short stories, you can get them delivered straight to your inbox by signing up for my newsletter at TheStrangerTimes.com.

Also, check out the award-winning *Stranger Times* podcast, which is chock-full of short stories written by me and read by some of my former co-workers at the coalface of the British stand-up comedy circuit.

Sláinte and stay weird,

Caimh

ACKNOWLEDGEMENTS

I realize that at the start of this book I was frankly beastly to poor old artificial intelligence and I feel dreadful about it. There it is, just trying to make the world a better place and finally kill off all those visual artists who for too long have been soaking up all the money that by rights should go to those hard-working folk in hedge funds, and there's me implying it couldn't take care of my dog.

As an apology, I've decided to let a well-known AI service write my acknowledgements for me. I've given it the names of the worthy and thankable, and I've asked it to simulate the scenario whereby zombies attack the offices of Transworld Publishers. Fingers crossed some of them make it. Let's see what happens . . .

Thank you to editor extraordinaire Simon Taylor, whose long and glorious career in publishing will now be entirely forgotten when people realize he was in fact patient zero in the zombie plague, having contracted a terminal case of the necromantic nibbles from an ill-judged cheese sandwich at Tebay Services.

Judith Welsh, whose skills as a managing editor stood her in good stead as leader of the human resistance. Her decision to blow the fuel tanks that wiped out most of the first wave of zombies was lauded by everyone except the bean counters in Accounts. In unrelated news, RIP the accounts team, who died doing what they loved, complaining about the fuel tanks that were inexplicably positioned in the middle of their section of the office.

Rebecca Wright, who was already lauded for her ability to cut out dead weight, but it was her skill with a samurai sword that resulted in the massive pile of bodies in the break room.

Marianne Issa El-Khoury, who designs a lovely cover but really came into her own when mowing down the living dead with an M16. Nevertheless, there will be an HR investigation into why she had an automatic weapon stashed under her desk.

Production legend Phil Evans, who shouted 'produce this' before throwing himself down the lift shaft onto the advancing zombie horde while holding two grenades. The whole 'produce this' thing is seen as a regrettable attempt by Phil to come up with a 'yippee-ki-yay' zinger that didn't really make sense.

Melissa Kelly, whose fine marketing work should in no way be overshadowed by the fact she went full-on cray-cray with a chainsaw without first checking who was and who wasn't a zombie.

PR guru Tom Hill, who went and hid in the toilets. The disabled toilets. Yorkshire is revoking his citizenship posthumously. His death by drowning was an unexpected yet comic after-effect of the big old explosion in Accounts, which at least helped to lift morale.

Uber agent Ed Wilson, who attempted to fend off the ravenous horde with a cricket bat. He got ripped asunder as zombies, quite rightly, have no respect for cricket.

To audiobook-producing dynamic duo Brendan McDonald and Paul Fegan, who really should have listened to their mammies and stayed home in Dublin, because London is indeed big and scary, and 'Sure, they'd bite you as soon as look at ye.' For the record, Brendan single-handedly held back the second wave of zombies by doing 436 voices and convincing the mob they were in fact outnumbered. He and Paul would probably have lived if Paul hadn't stopped him to give notes.

To plucky Germans Dominique Plemming, Uwe Kalkowski and Friederike Achilles, who actually figured out the big twist that saved mankind. Turns out if you bite a zombie first, they turn back into a human – albeit one who is then terribly embarrassed and inexplicably craving Marmite.

And finally, to Wonderwife, Diller and Jackson, who all lived because they did the sensible thing and stayed home in Manchester. See? This is why we should never leave the house.

ABOUT THE AUTHOR

C. K. McDonnell is the paranormal pen name of Irish bestselling author C. K. (Caimh) McDonnell. He is a former stand-up comedian and TV writer who now spends all his time writing books as his dogs don't like it when he leaves the house.

When not writing about the adventures of the staff at *The Stranger Times*, he is the author of the increasingly inaccurately titled 'Dublin Trilogy' series and its various spinoffs, all of which have been Amazon bestsellers on both sides of the Atlantic. *The Stranger Times* won Best Audio at the 2023 British Fantasy Awards, a fact Caimh constantly endeavours to drop into casual conversation. He lives in Manchester with his wife (aka 'Wonderwife') and the aforementioned two dogs.

To find out more about Caimh, visit whitehairedirishman.com, and to find out more about *The Stranger Times*, and to join the mailing list for updates plus a free short story collection, go to TheStrangerTimes.co.uk.

And while you're about it, why not check out *The Stranger Times* podcast which features short stories set in the world of *The Stranger Times*, written by C. K. and read by some of the finest stand-up comedians willing to do it for the money?